# The Masterpiece

Also by Anna Enquist

*The Secret*
*The Injury*
*The Ice Carriers*

Anna Enquist

# THE MASTERPIECE

TRANSLATED BY
Jeannette K. Ringold

*The* Toby Press

First English edition published in Great Britain 1999

*The* Toby Press *LLC*
www.tobypress.com

Originally published in Dutch as *Het meesterstuk*
Copyright © Uitgerverij de Arbeiderspers, 1994

The right of Anna Enquist to be identified as the author of this work
has been asserted by her in accordance with the
Copyright, Designs *&* Patents Act 1988

Translation copyright © Jeannette K. Ringold 1999

Publication has been made possible with the financial support of the
Foundation for the Production and Translation of Dutch Literature.

ISBN 1 902881 05 2, *hardcover*
ISBN 1 902881 21 4, *paperback*

A CIP catalogue record for this title
is available from the British Library

Typeset in Garamond by Jerusalem Typesetting

Printed and bound in the United States by
Thomson-Shore Inc., Michigan

# Contents

# Part I
## *Leporello:*
## *"Notte e giorno faticar"*

*Chapter one*

# Helpfulness

The goldfish have eaten their young. During the warm, windstill summer they were spawning for days on end. The small one with the black spots on his face tirelessly chased the large sluggish one and drove her crazy pushing against her swollen rump, until she released her eggs between the water plants. Squirting, he dashed over them, a detached coupling in which many elements of the act are present but have become meaningless rituals, work to be carried out as part of reproduction as soon as the water temperature rises and the wind dies down.

Does the black one ever think: Oh delightful fat and sluggish one with your chubby sides, you are the love of my life, I want you, I want you? He wants eggs; he wants to propagate so that the fertilized eggs, like miniature beads, can stick to the water plants in the small domain of oak staves that is their world.

Lisa squats down next to the barrel and watches. Within the small globules, cell division is taking place at a furious pace, until the small fish are strong enough to extricate themselves from the tough membrane. Dozens at a time float through the warm water.

The small fish are not cared for by the parents, who are no longer a couple. They themselves continuously slurp water filled with invisible food and eat the element in which they live, just as they did in the egg. If they have the bad luck to stray into their parents' territory, the parents shape their mouths into a pinkie-size funnel through which dead flies, birch seeds, small fishes are swallowed up. Nonchalantly the sluggish one spits out the birch seeds.

I should have protected them, Lisa thinks. Last week it was still teeming with small fish, transparent animals half an inch long with a front and back and a dark core in their bodies. And now all is quiet. Damn, if I'd only put them in the salad bowl, fed them, raised them safely.

The truth is that she doesn't feel like it. The truth is that this woman, who has learned with difficulty to accept life as it is, finds that it goes against the grain to make allowances for her goldfish. In the morning before the start of her workday, and in the evening when she is off again, she always sits by the barrel for a short while to observe the cruel universe with fascination. Sometimes she wanted to give the fish a sporting chance (but whom do you help, and why?), for example by using an axe to cut a crack in the ice during hard frost, but just as often she let the ice have its way, and in the spring the discoloured bodies floated motionless on the water surface. One time a bright orange fish was completely embedded in the ice like a touristy glass paperweight, broke loose in the spring, moved his tail slowly and uncomfortably, and shook his gills. You see, Lisa then thought, surviving in the ice is possible after all.

Lisa is a psychiatrist. She lives about six miles outside the city, in a village taken over by commuters. Mornings she has her practice at home, afternoons she works in the psychiatry clinic at the university. She gives lectures to residents, she teaches the nursing staff, she does a modest amount of patient care. Her house is an old mansion, square, symmetrically constructed on both sides of the grey-blue front door. Behind the house, an orchard (apples, plums) extends to the river.

At the left front is the doctor's practice area: Lisa's office with large windows in two walls. A modest waiting-room has been set up underneath the stairs, behind a screen. It's rare that anyone sits there because Lisa leaves fifteen minutes between her appointments, and the patients from the city usually remain in their cars parked along the road until it's their time.

A free hour because of a sick patient—biking! No wind, Indian summer, no parking aggravation at the clinic. Along the river where fishermen sit concealed under their green umbrellas, through the city park, and through the busy shopping street to the clinic. Lisa is wearing expensive jeans and an even more expensive creamy white sweater. At the last moment she changed her running shoes for blue boots. She is a good-looking woman and remains so with the passing years. She dresses well but inconspicuously.

Lisa is forty-five and still menstruates about three times a year.

The telephone rings as she is packing her briefcase. "Hannaston?"

Lisa has been experimenting with several ways of answering the telephone. Without thinking she always used to say her first name followed by different last names (Blech, Bleeker, again Blech, Hannaston). Since her fortieth birthday, she feels that it should be different, but how? A man can use his own and even his friends' last name without making a boorish impression. Not so a woman. She thinks that announcing herself as "Mrs. Hannaston" is sappy, "Doctor Hannaston" sounds affected, "Hello" by itself is impolite. She says her last name in a questioning, almost apologetic tone.

"Lisa, it's Johan. I'm glad to catch you, shouldn't you be curing nutcases?"

"I'm just about to leave."

On the bulletin board above the telephone hangs an invitation to the opening of Johan's exhibition: Johan Steenkamer, paintings, etchings and watercolours, reception on Sunday from four to six in the Municipal Museum. Dark suit. Dark suit? Yes, dark suit. Sponsors: Government Fund for Visual Arts, Postal Services, Nicolaas Bijl Lumber Company.

A half-profile photo of Johan: a pointed nose, an unnaturally closed mouth, eyes of someone who is engrossed in himself at the moment of the shot. Shoulders in a dark suit which looks good on him.

"Listen, afterwards we're going out for dinner with the family. Alma wants it. It certainly is modern, but it should be acceptable."

The family, that is to say Johan's mother Alma herself, the instigator; brother Oscar; sons Paul and Peter. Is Johan's girlfriend Zina the modern element?

"Is Ellen coming too?"

"Alma has called her. She said yes."

That ought to be possible, the mother of his sons at the same table with the new woman.

"I'd like to come, Johan," says Lisa. She doesn't want to leave her friend alone in this situation and is also fascinated by the complicated family relationships.

"And Lawrence, I'd like him to be there too. Is he back yet?"

"He just left, he won't be here until the end of next week, when the children have to go back to school."

"That really isn't acceptable. I'd like to have everyone there. What's he doing in England? Does he have a commission or something?"

"No, not yet. Maybe he'll draw up extension plans for his father. It's just an ordinary family visit. The grandchildren visiting grandma and grandpa. I've got to go, Johan, thanks for the invitation."

They say goodbye. Johan still sounds rather angry.

When you are bicycling, you can really think. When you are walking, thinking soon turns into dreaming and letting your imagination go, but the minimum of alertness required by bicycling makes for an appropriate attention to reality. Action. Lisa has taken Lawrence's bike, risking a stiff butt after an hour's ride, but with the advantage of gears. She gets up momentum, zooms over the grey asphalt between the large trees, and shifts to the lowest gear. The road bends to the river: hogweed gone to seed, grebes tired of playing on the water.

To think that they are friends, Johan and Lawrence. What do

they talk about? Paintings? The future of rural architecture? Certainly not about parents, not about family visits.

Lawrence is from York. His parents own a large hotel on the eastern coast of England. Giant windows overlook the sea; the rooms that the British always need for different functions in their recreation buildings (Lounge, Dining Room, Tea Room, Morning Room) are as large as soccer fields. The decline of the economy decimated the number of guests. Those who kept coming were rich and elderly and did so out of habit. There is an "Emergency Room" sign on a door in one of the long, hospital-like halls. Behind it a stretcher is kept hidden in a narrow, deep cupboard. During a stay with her parents-in-law, Lisa once witnessed an elderly guest collapse after dinner (purple, foaming at the mouth, Yorkshire pudding) and being wheeled at breakneck speed to the back exit by the cook and the receptionist. The ambulance hurriedly ordered by Lawrence's mother was waiting unobtrusively. In the Dining Room it took a while before the mood was back to normal.

Advertisements in America only yielded more old people who, moreover, wanted to drink gin in the Morning Room. Closure threatened. For a short while Lawrence's mother considered making it into a real home for the aged but dreaded repetitions of the stretcher scene.

Grandpa England, as Lisa's children Kay and Ashley call him, took the plunge and made numerous agreements with companies that wanted to offer their employees vacations or a quiet weekend. At sharply reduced prices, large groups of people now fill the rooms. They play miniature golf (constructed in the hotel grounds) and take walks along the coastal path.

Sometimes there are conferences and working weekends during which the Morning Room functions as a meeting room. The addition of a covered swimming-pool with sauna and exercise room is being considered. Lawrence will advise his parents about this. The stretcher is still there.

A hotel child. Sleeping in an unoccupied room at the end of a hall.

Mother behind the bar, father in the small office with the bookkeeping or behind the reception desk with the keys on large, wooden balls with "Sea View" on them. Hearing the Guest, who determines the rhythm of life in the hotel and who is the measure of all things, called a nag or a stingy bitch by your parents during the quick and early dinner in the kitchen.

Lawrence went to London and studied architecture (lines, weights, materials, everything that can be calculated) at the school of art. There he met Johan who was painting for a year on a meagre scholarship. After that year, Lawrence went to Holland with his friend Johan and stayed.

"Did you run away from your parents," Lisa asked, "could you not stand their demands and expectations, were you so furious that a whole sea had to be between you?"

"Certainly not. It was windy. Always stormy."

"And here? Half of the year your ears are blown from your head, the trees grow bent, and the wind doesn't even die down at night! And the flooding?"

"Even the wind is cosy here. It's flat; you have an overview. There you stand on the cliffs, at the mercy of storms. The water pounds constantly against the land and devours it until the whole hotel goes crashing down into the sea. I was scared stiff of that as a child. It will certainly happen."

Absolutely true. But absolute nonsense, she thinks: he doesn't hate his parents but runs away from the wind.

Lisa has no parents. Her father died in the war. Not a hero but instead a scared young man who, after curfew, walked into a canal in the dark city and drowned because he didn't dare to scream. Her mother, who masked courage and a sense of reality by being permanently aggrieved and wronged, died in hellish pain from a cancer that was discovered too late. Four years ago. Lisa, an only child, would visit her. I supported my mother in so far as it was possible, she thinks. Not much was possible, and what was possible was done with great difficulty. Lisa did not deceive herself that her extremely busy working week and the needs of her children prevented a greater involvement with her dying mother. In contrast to Lawrence, she is able to recognize her own motives. She can look inside herself and see a determined child who fights for her own interest, an egotist with a bad character. The reflection turns to the mirror, the child merges with the mother's expectations.

Lisa won't drown in the murky waters of childhood. Because she allowed herself to hold her head above water, to turn from her mother as soon as she felt the pull of the past, it was possible for her towards the end of the terrible illness to press the grey bird's head to her breast, to close her arms around the painracked body, and to cry in regret over the lonely and spoiled life of this woman. During the hired nurse's weekend off, Lisa washed her mother's body. The buttocks hung down like small wrinkled bags. Carefully she dabbed the large scars on the place where the breasts had been.

Where I used to drink has disappeared, burned in the hospital oven. I must have done all right in those arms like sticks and at those inadequate breasts, otherwise I wouldn't be here. But the evidence is gone; I cannot return to that source. Grey pubic hair on the genitals where I came out. I look at it, I see it.

Her inability to talk about herself makes her into someone who is a good listener. Contemporaries pour out their hearts to her and tell her their secrets. Lisa listens, recaps, asks a thoughtful question. She helps, and receives gratitude and acceptance in return. She expands her role as helper into the physical arena and during her vacations she works in the local hospital. There, too, the roles are clearly defined; she doesn't need to divulge anything about herself. There, fatherly doctors walk around who do not suspect that at night their pupil crawls onto their laps and hides in their arms.

Lisa has retained her curiosity, and that will eventually lead her out of the quagmire. Trembling with fear as to what she will encounter and poorly armed against what she will discover, she nevertheless wants to know.

Some time it will go wrong; that is unavoidable. On a rainy winter morning during her fourth year of medical school, her glance crosses that of her pathology teacher. She doesn't look away.

For a long, a timeless moment their eyes remain locked together. The word last spoken reverberates in the air: *mitralis-stenosis*. The long pause lends weight to this concept; the students bend over their lecture notes, write it down in capitals, underline it. Lisa sits up straight and looks into the eyes of the forty-five-year-old man. She gives him a look in which all her longing, all her passion is exposed without defence. For the first time in her life, she opens up.

Gerard Bleeker (married, mortgage, sailboat) is hoarse when he continues. His knees feel light and unreliable. After the faculty cocktail party, between the smelly coats in the cloakroom, half-drunk, kiss the friendly secretary who shows her ass so faithfully when she gathers his files. After the last lecture, drink a glass of acidic wine in the neighbourhood café with the only intriguing student in this year's class, a good conversation, a hand on a knee—he knows those things, he can brake in time because he doesn't want to continue that ride.

Lisa's surrender awakens adolescent dreams in him and for a while drives him crazy. He loses his grip on reality, he forgets the existence of others in his life, he denies the impossible position in which he has landed. For half a year they share a blissful lunacy. As soon as it's spring, Gerard fixes up his boat and makes it into their house, their nest. In order not to arouse suspicion in the home port, they arrange meetings in faraway places. Lisa makes complicated trips to Medemblik, to Hindelopen. They make love on the bottom of the boat, rocked by the water. On the river bank they lie in the grass, naked in the burning sun, and they have sex until the sun goes down, they have sex with total concentration without noticing the ships sailing past ("good for you! go for it!") and the cows that have approached out of curiosity. In the evening they eat greasy fish in the harbour café before falling asleep satiated in each other's arms, under the mainsail.

The summer vacation is a disaster. For three weeks Gerard sits on an Alp with his wife and takes melancholy, lonely walks. Despairing, Lisa sits in her room and catches up on her neglected examination material, meanwhile writing long letters to her lover's post office box.

He is not the first one for her. He is the first one with whom she does it because of an irrepressible urge and with total commitment. Feeling his sex deep inside her is her absolute, only goal in life. She has slept with friendly fellow students, to be polite after an intimate conversation; she has had sex with a pilot she picked up in a cafe, out of curiosity. She has done it with a just-graduated lawyer on the night before his final departure for the Antilles, to teach him.

They have the good fortune of a mild autumn in dunes and in parks, but in November when the boat is being overhauled and the wife becomes suspicious, it leads to a crisis. Gerard moves into an apartment in a new housing development; out of guilt he lets his wife have the house and generous alimony. Between the bare walls of the anonymous rooms he feels a new freedom. He sleeps with Lisa on a mattress on the floor. They marry in the spring, after Lisa's final exams.

How much chance is there for such a passion to change into a normal human relationship? Gerard is not the father who can nourish and satisfy Lisa's yearning. Lisa is not the panacea for transience with which Gerard can redeem the sorrow over the failed first half of his life. Life resumes. Lisa comes home excited after her internship. Gerard's job is as much of a dead-end as before. Suddenly there does appear to be a twenty-year difference between them. When with boundless energy she wants to make love to him night after night, he is tired and worries about not getting enough sleep. During the weekends when Lisa is reading and looking up in her reference books the illnesses that she encounters on the wards, he misses the boat he has sold. Because of the alimony, there is no money to buy a new one.

Then comes the moment when there seem to be fascinating female students in Gerard's audience again. Lisa is deeply hurt. Inside her something is broken that cannot be repaired, even when Gerard cries in her arms, even when he promises absolute faithfulness until death and thereafter. Lisa is frightened by the coldness and the disappointment that she feels; she doesn't want it to be true and does her best to get over it. It gives her headaches and inexplicable attacks of depression.

She throws herself into her work and does brilliantly in the medical finals. She receives offers for training in three different specialties. She chooses psychiatry. She chooses herself, although she doesn't know that yet.

Gerard wants a child. He has failed as father of his wife and clings to dreams of real fatherhood with which, in addition, he would tie down his wife who is quietly slipping away, would force her to bend over something that his seed had brought forth, would entice her to admit that they again shared something. Lisa is aghast.

"I just can't."

"Don't you trust me?"

No, thinks Lisa, I don't trust you, that's true. I'd be crazy to tie my future to a man of fifty, well, almost fifty. But that's not it, it's worse.

"I can't be a mother. I simply can't."

But I can be a woman, I learned that with you, from you. Making love in the sea; sand and salt in your pussy. Without underwear to the hospital dance, intensely satisfied with my body, thank you, thank you. But a child that's growing inside me? That I will push out and to whom I have to give the illusion that the world is a nice place? How will something good come from that? I would poison my baby before its birth; I would kill my child before it came alive.

Gerard rants and raves. Lisa cries over her decision but it's her decision: never.

By the time she starts her psychiatric training, Lisa has left Gerard. Lisa Blech, a single woman, a well-off student living in an apartment in the city. A nasty depression pushes her into analysis; the curiosity which has never left her becomes her real rescue. She may retain the desire for a father but, angry and lying desperately to her analyst, she has to give up the prospect of fulfilling that longing.

Through her friend Ellen she meets Lawrence, with whom she establishes a pleasant, loving relationship. Calmly they respect each other's native language, each other's profession, each other's thoughts. Their relationship tends towards coolness but is based on a solid bond between two people who can each be themselves and don't ask too much of each other.

Lisa becomes a mother as a matter of course. And a good one, to her own surprise and joy. They buy the house on the river. One day Lisa is bicycling along by the water, one child in front and one at the back, smelling the hay scent of her son's hair, feeling her daughter's arms around her waist, and they sing aloud the song of the three drummers who came from the east, rarum, rarum. This is it, Lisa thinks, this is the life I have wanted. Tears run down her cheeks as she sings.

*

"Everything is transient—Giesendam" it says on the freighter gliding past. In a cage on the deck a boy rides back and forth on a plastic tractor. He's lucky, thinks Lisa. The boat creates diagonal waves that crash slowly against the bank and make the long grasses that hang into the river move in a jumbled way. The river is a model of gentleness. It pushes the strangest boarders gently to the sea, it wets everything that wants to grow in it, and its capacity for poisonous junk has no limits.

Lisa heads into town. Shopping street; across the tram tracks; left; right; sharp turn around the parked cars; through the archway without getting off; into the bike stall of the clinic where one-toothed Bertus is waiting for bikes. She swings her right leg over the top tube and saddle and unfastens her bag from the seat rack. Bertus appears like a ghost.

"Nice bike, doctor, must be your husband's!" He shuffles to the back with her bicycle, between two rows of wooden racks. Lisa sees nothing because her eyes are still adjusted to the outside light. She smells all the more: oil, iron, heavy tobacco, old man. From his office she hears the radio, two voices in thirds: "Roses, rum bonbons, and red wine…"

Lisa runs up the steps, pushes open the black glass door. Her heels clatter rhythmically on the marble floor of the hall, tempting her to do an extra lap. In the back of the hall a double staircase leads upstairs where on the left and the right there are locked units behind closed doors.

Downstairs, the administration offices are on the left, and to the right is the small neglected auditorium that serves as church on Sundays and as classroom during the week. When Lisa opens the door, she is as always struck unpleasantly by the stained glass in the high window of the back wall of the lecture hall: Jesus, outlined by wide string liquorice. He looks dazed and clumsily carries a sheep in front of his stomach. Its long legs hang straight down.

Lisa sits down behind the altar, her back to the depiction of the shepherd. Sunlight makes blue and yellow spots on her lecture notes. The psychiatric residents enter in small groups. It's their weekly afternoon for lectures: sixteen people, among whom are four women, one black, and possibly two homosexuals. All are around thirty years old, exhausted by their busy schedule in various regional training clinics, confused by the ambiguity of their situation. In the hospitals where they are employed, they have responsibility for their patients. They are confronted by violent suicides, vehement aggression, and social circumstances that render them powerless. During their supervisory sessions and courses these people have to behave like students, are tested, and are taught. Dissatisfaction at being asked too much surfaces during the lecture afternoons: they gripe, badmouth, gossip, and above all complain. The instructor is wise not to become a target, and not to choose sides if at all possible.

The hospital residents enter last: a sturdy lesbian who covers her insecurity with a lot of dynamism and with whom Lisa has the greatest difficulty in supervision; a thin, fairly young man with a nice face of whom Lisa is fond.

Lisa is a hawker in the market place. She displays her wares, clearly visible; she talks about them and plays to her audience. Everyone is interested in him or herself, provided that the insight doesn't hit unexpectedly close to home: certainly people who have chosen this profession and who are all in training therapy. It's delicate going; if it hits her students too close to the bone, they will be obstructive and complain, and Lisa can't stand that. Narcissism, which is on today's programme, is a sensitive subject. She looks around the circle: that one and that one, and perhaps her? There is a silence that she lets develop to its maximum.

She opens her mouth, and the sentences automatically follow the thoughts she develops. Thinking is ahead by a fraction. On her paper she has only the main points.

"Always searching for self-assurance, the hunger for admiration is a bottomless pit."

The young man with the nice face hardens his expression.

"Partners, friends, are used as need-satisfying objects, machines to satisfy the hunger for love. If they fall short, the narcissistic personality flies into a primitive rage. That is the 'narcissistic rage'."

The young man has bent his face over his notebook. Lisa switches to the healthy aspects of narcissism, she talks about the necessity for self-love, she refines the concept, she brings in genetic connections and manages to make eye-contact with her offended student. And for extra effect: fear of bonding, the incapacity to really trust someone because of the early hurt. And the narcissist's charm: when they need you to boost their self-esteem, you can have a fantastic evening. And a feeling of relief that you're not tied to such a person.

I'm talking about Johan, Lisa realizes suddenly, and for a moment is silent from shock.

"How is narcissism related to the Oedipus complex?" asks a stern blond man in a corduroy jacket.

Oh Jesus, him again. Lisa is caught unawares, she must regain control. What do I know, Oedipus complex, narcissism, what's it about? What are we doing here anyway? What does that man want?

The thought of Johan helps put her back on track.

"Anyone who dares to compete with his father in a healthy manner and can attract his mother already has a solid base of self-respect and is no longer a bottomless pit. The real narcissist has been so severely short-changed and wounded, perhaps even traumatized in an earlier phase, that he can never settle the Oedipus subject in a well-balanced manner. He desperately needs his father to fill that pit and at the same time is unmanageably furious about being short-changed."

How strange that I speak so calmly about something so terrible. Johan as a four-year-old boy, who didn't understand that his father was gone and would never return. Who every day made a drawing for his father which Alma then used for lighting the fire in the evening.

Now the sturdy lesbian revolts: obscure bullshit and astrological nonsense; what's the good of it, what proof is there that people are like that?

"None," says Lisa. "Not much at any rate. It's a theory that was thought up, which is amusing to reflect on. We have only percep-tions and thoughts. The fact that we classify them under the headings 'libido' or 'conscience' is a trick. You can also take another theory and fit people's thoughts into another construct. That was done for centuries. Then your patients were possessed by the devil. That's how people looked at it then, and that was also possible."

So there, that struck home. The robust young woman is bewil-dered, the stern blond guy has burst out laughing, the rest of the class looks bewildered. The good shepherd, who has not yet let the sheep drop, looks down on the class. A good moment to conclude.

In the smoking area near the coffee machine, Lisa encounters Daniel, the head of the clinic. His red hair sticks out on all sides. Actually he's someone for garden overalls and a beard. Fortunately he wears normal people's clothes. He smokes a big cigar with which he gesticu-lates vehemently as soon as he catches sight of Lisa. A terrorist with a bomb, an activist with a banner on the barricades. Daniel suffers from enthusiasm and naïveté. He is a driven planner and did group therapy before anyone had heard of it. His last project was making depressed patients run; screaming, his hairy legs in sneakers without socks, he cheered on a group of grey men on a playing field.

"And it helps! It helps!"

"Everything helps, Daniel. Do you remember that factory in

America where they did experiments with working conditions? Whatever they did, bright light in the work place or total darkness, pleasant temperature or icy cold, the production kept increasing."

"That must be a statistical error."

"Those workers started enjoying themselves because there was a bunch of interested men constantly hanging around them. As soon as the experiment stopped, production fell back."

"What do you mean?"

"That I might also forget about being depressed if a screaming fanatic were running around me."

"Oh. I've thought of something new: everything must change."

Lisa starts laughing, and Daniel joins in. They are sitting on sad wicker chairs and are drinking bitter instant coffee from plastic cups in a building filled with people in extreme distress. Everything must change. People like Daniel become ingenious out of powerlessness.

"Time, Lisa, think of *Time*!"

Surreptitiously Lisa looks at the watch in the open side-pocket of her bag, as if her colleague were urging her to pay attention to her schedule. But this visionary has other intentions. Like a prophet, he points with his cigar to the big clock above the coffee machine. Three-thirty.

"Everyone is squeezed into an identical corset of minutes and hours. Try and imagine what that means! Young or old, small or large, with fast or slow metabolism, with quick or sluggish pulse, in the summer, in the winter, during work or on vacation: always that same speed of the hands of the clock. It'd drive you crazy, don't you think?"

Daniel has jumped up and paces up and down the worn linoleum. All is transient, Lisa thinks, Giesendam. The river. Push time aside. No more war.

Daniel continues holding forth. He's enthusiastic. His cigar has gone out, but within him smoulders a fire.

"The boredom! The limitation! If your own rhythm is faster than the damn clock and you always have to wait, always have to restrain yourself high blood pressure, colleague, strokes!"

Lisa sees before her a wild horse that, snorting, lets itself be bridled. Perhaps a safe feeling?

"When you run behind the clock, you're always short of time, everything races, and you drag behind, always too late for an overview and understanding, helpless. And what do you get? A depression, Madam, probably a major depression. I'm going to figure it out, the plans are ready!"

Daniel will lock his patients in soundproof rooms without daylight. No contact with the outside world because if a victim calls home, he should not get a yawning partner on the telephone and not hear the television news in the background.

"Day and night there should be a student working in the office. That student should have training in even-temperedness. Bring coffee, meals, or whatever, as soon as somone asks for it.

"Finally the patient can live according to his or her own rhythm. A situation free from time will cure him, Lisa, a situation free from time!"

And he's right, in a way. Time is a tyrant who with his knife draws grooves in my face, who will take from me all that is dear to me: my ability to look, to think, to walk. He pulls my children away from me. He destroys my friends. He will kill me.

"If there is no time at all, can people handle that?"

"You think too much about what people feel. Consider the mechanism. The machine has become unbalanced, that has nothing to do with sadness or protest. The gear doesn't fit in the chain. In my subterranean timeless vaults the machine is oiled and adjusted. You'll see! Hey, don't you know Steenkamer, that painter?"

Lisa wants to leave; she has to go to her department and then has a supervisory session.

"He was married to my friend. They've been divorced for years, but I'm in touch with him once in a while. Why do you ask?"

"I was wondering whether that man is right in the head. This morning there was a big article in the paper against figurative painting, that it was an admission of weakness, and so forth. Even though he himself makes beautiful paintings that really do have a subject! That series of etchings about time; that's how I got onto this. Beautiful, superb! And then to disparage your own work with such a piece. How is it possible?"

"I think that you're mistaken."

Lisa sighs and gets up.

"He has an older brother, Oscar, who is an art historian. He works at the National Museum and sometimes writes for the papers. So it must have been him. Do you still have the paper?"

Daniel digs in his canvas bag and finds the crumpled art supplement. Under the full page article it says: O. Steenkamer.

It took years before Lisa found out that Johan had a brother. This man, who loves to speak so entertainingly about himself and all that is his, kept silent about his own brother. She understood why when she first saw them together during a dinner at Alma's. Six people at the oval table in the dark old-ladies' room. Alma lofty and straight at the head, already with a cane next to her chair, at her right Johan with Ellen next to him, at her left, Oscar and Lawrence next to him. Lisa sits across from Alma. Where are the children? Probably at home with the regular baby-sitter. The food is disgusting: soup from a can, burned but still uncooked rolled meat with pulverized potatoes and frozen peas; they didn't get to dessert. Alma considers it a point of honour that she can't cook, and in preparing and serving meals she is slow and absent-minded. When you finally sit down, an hour later than expected, someone always has to get up to get the salt, some knives, or a serving spoon. The kitchen is a smoky chaos. For small children it's a disaster: wait a long time and then get nothing. The fight began about the children: couldn't Johan take Ellen to Brussels for a few days, to an exhibition, and leave the children at Alma's?

"It doesn't suit me well at all, Johan. In that week I'm planning to go to Bergen for three days, my annual visit to Aunt Janna as you know—no, unfortunately it would be quite awkward."

"Well, couldn't you just cancel it? I'd like Ellen to come along, and the children like to be here. You can feed them at McDonald's if you don't want to cook. And it's during the week; they're at school—just a matter of taking them and picking them up."

Ellen intervenes: "I don't think that we can ask that of Alma, four times a day back and forth to school. No, if it isn't possible, I'll just stay home."

Johan explodes: "We're asking nothing. Keep out of it! Dammit, can't I ask my mother something without everyone meddling?"

Strategically placed, Lisa sees to her surprise that Alma feels in her element. She flushes and watches with lively interest how her younger son snaps at his wife.

"Janna would be disappointed, Johan. And I myself also appreciate good planning. I raised you and Oscar all by myself; it was my sole responsibility, as you know." Alma pauses. "Now that you're grown up I want to take it easy. I've done enough running and slaving. I'm crazy about the children, but it's too much for me. On Fridays Oscar always comes for dinner. You should have some consideration for my age, really!"

"Oscar, Oscar, what does he have to do with it? So he doesn't come for once, is that so bad? Why does Oscar always come first? You're never willing to do anything for me! Every Friday you sit together scheming and gossiping, the lame and the blind."

"Enough, Johan!"

Alma roars, but with satisfaction, Lisa notices. Johan has jumped up, his napkin lies on the floor, he paces back and forth in the small space between his chair and the door. Now a sound comes out of Oscar, like out of a waterpipe that hasn't been used for a long time. Until now he has been sitting at the table looking rather pale and weak, his thick spectacles bent over his plate. He looks up at his brother. His mouth trembles.

"It's pretty cheap to make fun of someone's physical infirmity. For the rest, I don't understand why you are bothered by my get-togethers with Mother. You have your family, you are married, and you have your art. You have everything, and then you also want to stir up trouble in our lives. I'd like to say: leave us alone."

Oscar is shaking. He looks at his hands and places them on

either side of his plate. Ellen tries to catch Johan's attention; if he would just sit down again the situation might still be saved; the fire might be doused by Lisa and Lawrence who stand ready like firefighters with shovels to throw dirt on it. But Johan cannot be controlled. He gets caught up in a furious speech. Oscar and Alma conspire against him, Oscar begrudges him the light of day (poor blind wretch, Lisa thinks) and is jealous of his talent.

"And whining. And nitpicking in your laboratory. And you not daring to touch a brush yourself. A Ph.D.! And in what, in what? How many hairs were in Frans Hals' paintbrush! The doctor has taken biopsies of the paint layer; placing art under your microscope is all you know. Attempt nothing and yet know everything better. Damn you, to hell with your paint samples, with your Friday yammering over your glass of port. I'm leaving!"

It's a great performance. Johan exits with an elegant swing of the door which makes the tablecloth billow. His high black boots, which Ellen polished this afternoon, sound resolutely through the hall. At the table there is silence until after the bang of the front door.

Is Lisa imagining it, or did Alma slump? Oscar places his hand on hers, she shakes it off impatiently. Finally she addresses her audience.

"Please excuse us, we have temperament in our family. The boys were always so difficult with each other, so much envy, so little fun. I'm glad, Ellen, that it's so different with Peter and Paul. I've done my best, but as I said, I was all alone. I think it's best now to break off dinner. I need to retire. Oscar, could you stay for a moment?"

Alma rises like a queen of the night; slim and stately, she leans on her cane. Lisa and Lawrence say goodbye hurriedly (can you in all conscience say thank you for such a meal?) and ride home with Ellen to where Johan is already drinking whiskey.

Did the four of them then eat sandwiches with smoked salmon and talk until late into the night? Johan, glad to be out of his mother's clutches and relieved by his outburst of anger, wasn't bothered by anything.

At that time their conversations concerned their own lives, their work, their plans. The trembling brother with his thick spectacles had no part in it.

*   *   *

Towards six o'clock Lisa bicycles through the city that is coming alive. The paving stones and the houses radiate heat that no wind blows away. People sit in outdoor cafés and have pulled chairs onto the sidewalk, with all their might holding on to the summer for a while longer. There are yellow leaves on the trees, but people are still drinking beer in the street.

The restaurant where Lisa is supposed to meet Ellen has a terrace on the water. After Lisa has locked the bike to the bridge railing, she walks straight through the noisy restaurant to the outside terrace. The water smells of water. Amazing how difficult it is to describe a scent. There's a hint of iron but also a smell of wild roses—or is that only because the nostrils are opened wide, as you do when you sniff a flower? Lisa hangs over the railing and inhales, feels the coolness that comes off the water against her flushed face and is happy. She looks forward to eating and to seeing Ellen. She chooses a table in the corner, right next to the water, and orders a bottle of white wine from the suddenly-appearing waiter, a student with a large white apron and a skinny ass in jeans who addresses her ironically as "Ma'am".

A summer wine, greenish and dry. The young man places the frosted bottle in a cooler and nods shyly at her when she raises her glass.

He thinks that I'm a lonely woman who is going to get drunk because I'm sitting here with my bag on the other chair. Does he feel sorry for me? He probably doesn't care; what should a boy like that think about women over forty? Nothing, or vague thoughts of mother.

Lisa watches the people who are coming onto the terrace. Married couples, tourists, a group of well-dressed men with attaché cases, a family with lively children.

I have a sham independence. What's it like to be always alone?

This, the way it is now, is wonderful. Alone in the house, not disturbed or annoyed by noises from others, following my own daily schedule, no cooking, alone in bed so that I can smoke and read as long as I want.

She fears that her contented solitude is due to a trick, that the safety of the family to which she belongs and the certainty of those bonds make it possible for her to enjoy the freedom fully. Her shoulders shaking involuntarily, she remembers how intensely miserable she felt after her divorce, how convinced she was that she could not be alone.

But I was alone, I managed. I forced myself to sit at home alone during the evening and not phone anyone. I wove engagements into the weekend and made plans for my days off. But I had my analysis, there was always an ear, always someone who was interested in what I thought. Jesus, I sure have doubts.

More wine. Think about it. What is bothering me? The airport, only a few days ago. Parting from Lawrence, in his arms for a moment with the children shouting around them.

"Will you call when you arrive? Don't fall off the cliffs, say hello to grandpa and grandma. Don't work yourself to death, let your mother do something with the children for once, and look up some of your own friends, won't you?"

Kay and Ashley, excited, each with a backpack filled with treasures for the trip: "Mummy, don't forget the fish. We're going to play golf with grandpa! We're going now, are we going to the aeroplane?"

She kisses her children. She sees what is dearest to her disappear behind the check-in counter; they turn around, wave once more, and then quickly run to the stores, to the moving sidewalk in the large departure concourse.

The floor now moves under Lisa, everything turns black before her eyes, but she recovers quickly. It's also true that she walks at a spirited pace to the parking lot and with dash drives her car through the traffic. Nice. Alone. At her own speed.

Ellen is truly alone. Ten years ago she was divorced from Johan, and since then she has lived in an apartment in the centre of town, no garden, but a roof terrace instead. First the twins still lived with her; Peter and Paul were sixteen and both had to repeat a year. At nineteen they left home. Ellen left their room the way it was; the boys come back often. Is Lisa jealous of her friend? Envious admiration is what she feels. And curiosity: how does Ellen manage?

Meanwhile, the platform has become crowded. An already half-intoxicated party comes sailing up in a boat, they moor next to the eating guests and, shrieking with laughter, are helped ashore by the student waiter. Lisa watches and therefore doesn't see Ellen until she takes the bag from the chair.

Meeting her close friend, under any circumstances whatever, always gives a basic feeling of reassurance: all is well; this will continue forever; hush. They stand up and look at each other, one blonde and one grey. Ellen turned totally grey in the year of her divorce. It looks fabulous on her.

"Sorry I'm late. I couldn't get away. Have you waited long?"

"Two glasses. It was nice, lots to see and pleasantly seated."

Idle talk, nonsense. This is what I love. Kissing. You look good. Wonderful that it's evening. Are you as hungry as I am?

Ellen is wearing a beautiful linen jacket, "It wrinkles incredibly, but they say that's as it should be. Very expensive, fits really well, is always right."

She has placed Lisa's bag on the floor, her own next to it. The waiter comes with the menu. Lisa pours the wine, across the terrace comes a whiff of grilled shrimp, the sun has disappeared behind the houses.

"Have you heard anything from Lawrence? Is it nice, by yourself for a bit?"

"I think so, until now. I was just thinking of you, before you came, how you like being alone, always."

Ellen drinks, lights a cigarette, looks at her friend searchingly, and reflects.

"It's OK. It took some getting used to. At home there were

always so terribly many of us, always a godawful ruckus, always screaming, and eating from pans as large as baby baths. The years with Johan weren't exactly quiet, but I didn't know what I was missing. I never experienced a situation in which no one is screaming at you and always distracting you from your activities. I've discovered that I like it. Nowadays I'm very good at sitting. Just sitting on the roof, doing nothing. I don't know how it would be if I didn't have a nice job. It's a blessing that I got my degree. I was still working on it when the boys left; that made a difference."

Lisa admires Ellen who started studying sociology later in life and, one of the few of her graduating class, has a job. She got her degree in The Care of the Helpless, a Comparative Study of the Municipal Services for the Aged, for the Homeless, and for the Mentally Handicapped. She sent her substantial thesis, written in everyday language, to the mayor himself. The next week she had a position with the Municipal Policy Section for Welfare Services. It sounds vague, but it's fascinating. Ellen allocates the budget, she has an important voice in planning new services, and she monitors the use of the money that has been provided. Visits to centres for the homeless, conferences with homecare staff for the aged, hilarious afternoons in the residence for the mentally handicapped. To top it all, she herself doesn't have to drudge and toil: she says how it should be, and others do it. If all goes well.

Smoked halibut salad with pine nuts and curly red lettuce. Drops of water bead the butter; the bread is perfect.

After the halibut there is a cigarette break, legs stretched, view over the water in which the streetlights, just turned on, glimmer.

"And your love life?" asks Lisa. "Are you still seeing him?"

Ellen sings in a choir, a good choir that last winter gave a concert in the Grote Kerk, together with a paid orchestra. They gave an impressive performance of Brahms' *German Requiem:* a pure, touching soprano sang the consolation aria, and the bass soloist was absolutely overwhelming. He had a voice that for both Ellen and Lisa went straight to their guts, and the text did the rest.

> *"Herr, lehre doch mich dass*      *"Lord, make me to know*
> *ein Ende mit mir haben muss,*      *mine end, and the measure*
> *dass mein Leben ein Ziel hat,*      *of my days, what it is;*
> *und Ich davon muss,*      *that I may know how frail I am."*
> *und Ich davon muss."*

The stout, thickset man who sang these words seemed to understand what he was singing. Lisa sat crying unashamedly. Ellen fell in love instantly.

"Nevertheless it sounds wrong in German," says Lisa who has the theme of transience in her mind, "you think of a goal, but that's not it, it means an end, that it's finished."

"A hand's breath of days," says Ellen. "God, that really grabbed me. But it also helped, because of that text I thought: Do it! Soon I'll be dead, or he will. That same night we were in bed together. Do you know that I felt remorse towards Johan, even after all these years?"

Grilled salmon with rock samphire and small potatoes. Another bottle of wine. Soft music over the water.

Ellen's sweet singer is married and lives in an ebb and flow of discord and reconciliation with his wife. He also has children, fortunately grownup.

"Do you know that he sang in the opera for which Johan did the scenery at the time? Johan knew him long before I had anything to do with him."

The waiter comes to ask if everything is satisfactory; the boating party gets back on board, casts off, and slowly sails away from the terrace, carrying off the party noises.

"And if he weren't married, would you live with him? Is it terrible that he has someone else, that he always goes off?"

"Recently he lived with me for a whole month. A quarrel at home. Frankly, I found it so-so. Of course it was wonderful on Sunday morning, enjoying a cup of coffee in bed and the whole day ahead of you. But the shit, Lisa, the shit! About his marriage, his career, fatherhood. Before you know it you're supporting and soothing again.

When we both have our own lives it seems as though there is more equality. Does marriage make a man revert to childhood?"

"The same for women. You become dependent, you leave things. Lawrence does my car. And the rubbish."

"I was ironing shirts again. And he was just sitting around dejected, his beautiful head of hair in his hands, lamenting his failed marriage. I got angry, I didn't feel like putting up with it. It was a wonderful feeling that I could kick him out with his shirts and his singing exercises. I immediately regretted it, and the following weekend I went to one of his concerts and then things were as before. Only on the weekend, if it's possible, and otherwise preferably not. His work rhythm also drove me crazy, deep in the night he'd come home, excited after a concert; a prick in your back when you're sound asleep is very nice the first two times, but after that it's annoying. Isn't that awful?"

"Yes," Lisa says, "how dare you!"

Blackberry, raspberry, or lemon sorbet? Or a pear tart, no, rather dark chocolate with cherries marinated in liqueur and slightly bitter chocolate curls on top. The rest of the wine and then coffee. Ellen goes to the bathroom; Lisa smokes.

"Johan called this morning, about Sunday. The dinner."

"Yes, Alma is thinking big. She wants to glory in her son's success. And Johan likes to see all his women around him in admiration. We're going to eat really well this time, she said that she has hired 'The Lost Carp'. Seventy-five years old and a will like a buzz saw. She can hardly move with that worn hip, but she goes everywhere. I get along with her better since the divorce; I've always had the feeling that she resented me because I was involved with her son. Or maybe I've become more easy-going, that could be it. The way she manages to set her two sons against each other, how she tugs at Johan and then repels him—I couldn't bear to watch that before, but now it doesn't bother me so much."

"What I used to find so fascinating, even during that terrible dinner with Oscar, was her pleasure in these witch's tricks. And she's no victim. She presents herself that way, always stressing that she was alone, bitching about Charles walking out on her, but she radiates such pleasure as the dangerous heroine; I've always been susceptible to that."

Ellen doesn't see it that way. For almost forty years Alma has had a make-believe relationship with the man who left her, a relationship that exists purely in her head, for she never again had contact with the father of her sons. He left for America, left behind his paintings and his family, and began anew, as an opera director. From the papers, from the *Friends of the Opera* newsletter, Alma knows that he remarried three times; she sees his wives' faces on the photos. For Alma there is no distance, she rails about Charles' shameful flight as if it happened last month; she has made it impossible for her children to speak or even think about their father.

"Do you know that she really has a very nice relationship with Paul and Peter?" Ellen asks. "Even when they were small there were special things she thought up and did with them. Going to the movies on Wednesday afternoons, to curious small museums about which she told marvellous stories. The boys still visit her often. Not a trace of the tricks she always pulls with Oscar and Johan."

Lisa muses: how would it be with such an old body? Does she still masturbate sometimes? She certainly is beautifully straight and not fat. Still, your hips crawl up to your armpits when you get old; when will that happen with us? A body like a loaf of bread without a waist. Pain in your joints. Sleeplessness. *Dass Ich davon muss.* Jesus. At that age it's almost finished.

"Alma gets her energy from that. And Johan's exhibition agitates her. It's as if Charles lives again; Johan has the success that Charles never had with his painting. Sunday's get-together is going to be explosive. There's going to be a thunderstorm."

Ellen shivers in her linen jacket. A chill creeps up from the water. Lisa has drunk so much that she feels no cold. She looks at the floating, almost transparent blanket of mist above the still water surface.

"Come and sleep over, Lisa, then we can keep talking. Tomorrow morning early you can bike home, then you'll be wide awake."

Slowly the two women bike along the canal. At home Ellen fixes a bed for Lisa on the big leather sofa. A little whiskey, a last cigarette, lights out, doors to the roof terrace wide open. They sit across from each other, against the arms of the sofa, legs pulled up.

When Lisa finally wants to go to sleep, she thinks of the newspaper article that she got from Daniel, the sterile attempt at fratricide. Ellen hasn't seen it but is not surprised; Johan's success makes Oscar well-nigh suffocate with envy. Once Lisa saw Oscar walking around the red-light district: "It was raining, he wore an oilskin coat and those rubber galoshes over his regular shoes. I greeted him but he didn't recognize me. Because of his fogged glasses, I thought at the time. But perhaps he was slightly out of it and was going to give vent to his pent-up lust? Away from office life, so to speak."

"He's not a man for women," Ellen comments. "I've never felt any attraction to him although I do like him. He paid a lot of attention to me, even if it was only to bug Johan. In fact, I've always considered him as asexual.

"Such a contrast with Johan, who makes erotic contact with every single woman. I've never felt so much a woman as I have with him. And that's not finished. That still makes me afraid."

Ellen is almost whispering now; she's speaking more to herself than to Lisa.

"Last week he was here again; once in a while he looks me up to discuss matters about the boys. Sometimes he's sweet, asks if I need money. But there's also the old Johan, totally rude: how are my singing lessons, can the fat pig get it up, that sort of remark.

"He came to talk about the exhibition. A TV crew will come, all the interviews, all the journalists, his whole life summarized in a room with canvases and people, that sort of thing.

"Then he told me that he's written to his father. Through the Opera he figured out who his agent is in Los Angeles; Johan called there. They didn't want to give out Charles' private address, but he could write to the office, they'd make sure that Charles would receive the letter. Johan was furious. He waited for months. This happened in January. But when the invitations were printed, he mailed one with a note.

"He sat here in the room and talked about it so quietly. That he had finally approached his father. That he longed to see him. Despite everything.

"I just snapped. Suddenly I loved him as much as when I met him. Here, on this sofa, we did it. It took me days to escape his spell."

## Chapter two

# Mother and Sons

At seven o'clock, just before the digital alarm will sound its discreet beep, Johan pushes in the button. He always wakes just before it, out of habit. Or does the clock make a soft preliminary sound, a deep breath before the scream that never comes?

Johan turns onto his back, hands behind his head; he works his feet from under the duvet. He wiggles his toes. To his right lie the immense mounds of Zina, a mountain ridge with her large bottom as summit and slopes on all sides. She lies curled up and is totally covered except for a wisp of red hair.

Through the tall, curtainless window morning light streams into the bedroom. At this early hour the sky is pale but cloudless. A glorious day. Johan feels that he is eagerly anticipating something, but what? A birthday feeling from when he was very young, that something wonderful is going to happen, something that he has looked forward to. A short wait and then he slides into his everyday life: this afternoon the carpenters from the museum are coming to crate up his paintings.

He throws off the duvet, tenses his buttocks, quickly pushes the stomach with the swollen member up into the air: he is ready! Out of bed, to the window, yes, no clouds, grand green countryside, hurrah, sing out, out, the golden oriole.

The bathroom is square and tiled in black. The large mirror on the wall across from the door is never steamed up because of an ingenious placement of heating elements.

Johan looks at himself height slightly above average, posture straight, build more athletic than leptosome. Do the buttocks hang down? A little. Chest hair black as yet, too much grey to weed out. No fat.

A step closer. The head. Part the hair with two fingers to inspect the scalp: dandruff. Critical observation of the facial features: has been worse. Fortunately not puffy and doughy, although he should watch it. No drinking for two days. The wrinkles can be called lines, a face marked by life, not by old age. Johan drinks a large glass of water from the tap, brushes his teeth to freshen his nasty morning mouth.

Above the sink a second mirror. Bring the face closer to it. Strong lights, never but never glasses.

Starting next week that face will be in all the papers. What expression to wear?

Make faces as before. Exercises in expression, this time with a serious undertone. Stern; supercilious; mild; absent-minded; slightly surprised; bored. Serious is best, although he does have to remember to keep his lips together so he won't look unintentionally stupid. Slightly tighten the small cheek muscles at the top to hide the bags under the eyes. Better not, it makes the eyes smaller, flatter. Try and get a few nights' good sleep.

This is the painter. This will be the breakthrough.

Johan nods at himself and recognizes Alma's posture: the same haughty neck, head straight on the shoulders. Suddenly he wonders where the rest comes from; he looks at his face in a different way, with restless eyes.

Do I look like my father? Am I walking around with a face that I consider mine but that is his? Does he have such full lips? Alma has a thin stripe, Oscar too. The heavy eyebrows? The indeterminate eye colour? Alma has blue eyes. In mine there's some brown. But isn't brown dominant? Then he must have brown eyes. The sharp nose is Alma's, I recognize that.

Johan tries to remember Charles' face but swims around in a void. From photos that he must have seen in newspapers and magazines, all he remembers is a vague fright, the desire to turn the page quickly. Charles has changed his name in America, at the agency they didn't know whom Johan meant when, curtly, in a voice pitched slightly too high, he asked for Charles Steenkamer. His father has become "Mr Stone"; he even threw away the name and nonchalantly left it in the old country.

Take a leak in the black toilet, spatter on the seat. The smell of concentrated morning urine strikes him unpleasantly, what a stench, an old-man stink, an olfactory message from hell.

Get dressed: yesterday's briefs, old sweatpants, T-shirt, running shoes. Johan is going for a run, at the kitchen door he stretches his calf muscles to the utmost, first right, then left. With small, loose steps he trots around the outside of the house, over the lawn which immediately gets his feet wet, past the high studio, out through the gate. A bit further down, a path between the houses leads to the woods that lie behind the houses. For years Johan has been taking the same route, in all weather except for snow. He doesn't run because all men his age run, or at least have the notion that they should. Except for the shoes that almost run themselves, he has no expensive running outfit. Also he doesn't run in the early evening hours, when the woods are swarming with sweaty people. He chooses a time and a route that offer him the most solitude. Because he doesn't want to be lumped with the flushed-red, panting men and the wiry, too-old men with overtrained faces. Certainly, every reference to middle age or worse should be avoided. But the real reason for Johan's running circuit lies in his need to start the day in a ritual manner. He marks the beginning of the day with his whole body and makes it into a secret exercise of his power.

Power over time, over the boundless, unstructured days. He sets the hours as he pleases: seven o'clock, running; eight o'clock, shower and breakfast; nine o'clock, fiddling around in the studio, administration, preparation; ten o'clock, begin. Always. With a cold, miserable, drunk, without sleep: always.

Power over space. Every morning Johan conquers the land. Like an animal that marks its territory, Johan runs around his own property, in a wide circle. He appropriates the woods, the field; he inspects the waterways: the water course, the wide canal; on the way back he impresses his footprints into the small dikes of the old polder, and finally he touches the asphalt of the road that winds through the residential neighbourhood.

The deepest satisfaction is in the power over the body. Johan compels his forty-seven-year-old tendons and muscles to obedience, he thinks up a rhythm for his feet that they simply have to carry out, thousands of times he forces his knees to catch his weight in turn. Along the canal, on the flat part, he increases the pace. Blood pounds in his head, sweat pours down his shoulders and back. It is of utmost importance that respiration remain controlled. There is to be no panting here. When everything turns black before Johan's eyes, when his lungs scream and whine for more air, then the point is to continue running. Sometimes he's lucky and, at the moment of almost giving up, a new dreamlike episode begins in which the body doesn't transmit any signals of pain and fatigue but only information about direction and weight distribution. This is how it should be: a smoothly running machine, undisturbed by feeling and desire.

The state of blissful anaesthesia is not always reached, alas. But running is always done.

Also, not all parts of the body are compliant to the same extent. Teeth are treacherous and make themselves felt more through the pumping of blood than when at rest. Teeth are Johan's weak point. This man, who is so eager to sink his teeth into the day and who like a predator feels dependent on the soundness of his teeth, has bad teeth.

With Oscar in the dentist's waiting room. The wooden bench chafes against Johan's bare legs. Johan feels no fear, he has a stomach ache and looks continuously at the heavy door, waits for the loud buzzer and breathes rapidly.

"Os, I'm dizzy! Will you go first?"

Oscar never has cavities. He doesn't eat sweets and at the age of twelve is already a compulsive brusher. Oscar dares to look at the instruments that lie displayed on the small glass table next to the dentist's chair. Oscar dares to talk to the dentist and asks questions about the various tongs, drill frequencies, and dentures.

"Yes, I'll go first. Anyway, he always works on you for a long time. If you cry, he pricks your throat with a needle, you know that, don't you? And you must not move. That makes the drill slip, then your tongue is torn and you suffocate in your own blood. There's lots of blood in your tongue. A tongue can't heal because you can't stick a band-aid on it. And if your tongue is torn you can never talk again. Or eat. If you move you die, that's for sure."

The buzzer rings through the room and Oscar disappears. Johan sits on the bench like a small statue. Nothing hangs on the walls; the window is covered with venetian blinds. Emptiness.

When he is grown up, Johan goes to his own dentist, a contemporary with whom he confers about the state of affairs, the prognosis, and the strategy to follow. In an expensive and painful series of treatments, his decrepit teeth are restored without losing any. After that, all goes well for years.

Around Johan's fortieth birthday, when his gums start receding, the necks of the teeth start showing. A horse's mouth in the mirror. On both sides of the upper jaw Johan appears to have large gaps between the teeth and the unwilling tissue that surrounds them. Raspberry seeds are lodged there and lead to severe inflammations. Johan doesn't acknowledge it. With swollen cheeks he stands painting; he swallows handsful of painkillers but cannot suppress the stabbing pains. The dentist shakes his head and refers him to a specialist.

A swarm of periodontists and oral surgeons bends over Johan's wide open mouth. Stretched out, his feet slightly elevated, on the high torture table. Bright light from lamps with grids in front of them. There will be an operation, the gums will have to be cut away so that the dangerous small caves will be able to offer access to toothpicks and brushes in a nightly cleaning ritual. Johan is covered with green sheets, sharp clamps are put between his jaws, nauseating liquid anaesthesia is injected. (If you cry, they'll prick the back of your throat.)

The surgeons dance around in sneakers, they don't worry about the person under the lamps but converse excitedly with each other about the interesting findings they're making in the moist, pink hollow.

"Jesus, that pocket is an inch!"

"Strange that the infections are so localized. Two bacterial pockets?"

"You can't do anything more with this, it's a lost cause."

"The teeth have become mobile, do you feel that?"

"There is considerable bone damage. Let's put things in order and maybe later an implant, but in what? You might first have to implant a bone fragment. But will it take at that age?"

"Extract. A bridge. Perhaps anchor it to the cuspid because the molars around it are not reliable. Have you got your boat in the water yet?"

"No, dammit, I was on duty this weekend."

\*

Johan goes outside, into the restorative sunlight. Rubbery blobs are stuck over the stitches by way of band-aids. He is wounded and is determined never again to return here. Rather permanent pain than this humiliation that renders him powerless. At the Dental Drugstore he purchases a complete set of cleaning instruments with which he tries to keep the gaps and traps between his teeth free from bacteria. Twice a year, conspicuously often in tandem with disappointments in work or love life, his upper jaw becomes inflamed, first on the left, then on the right. The dentist sprays the bifurcations clean, mumbling that it can't go on like this.

His eyes half shut, Johan runs over the small dikes of the polders. Does he feel the pounding in his jaws? Bite carefully. It's OK. No compression pain. Sprint, get a good pace, homeward.

Zina has made coffee and sits at the big table in the kitchen polishing her nails, the tip of her tongue against her upper lip. She is wearing Johan's dark green bathrobe which goes well with her hennaed hair. Johan stands behind her, blows across her round shoulder on the shiny nails and rubs his sweaty face in her neck that smells of sleep and old perfume. Zina has no wrinkles or creases anywhere, she is lined from the inside out with a uniform layer of fat that makes her skin shine and stretch. Despite being overweight she has a quick and lively way of moving. She jumps up, arms waving in the air, she rubs against Johan with her fat bottom and, laughing, pours him coffee. Barefoot he sits at the table, buttering his bread. Eat first and then clean the teeth.

"Did you boil eggs?"

From a knitted oven mitt Zina pulls two eggs; they lie warm in her hand.

"What are you doing today, are you staying here, have you actually moved in with me?"

Johan likes it that she's there, that she warms his bed, tidies his kitchen, folds his laundry. The fact that she has a friend always gives him a light, a good feeling of conquest. It suits him fine. He doesn't want a deeper bond but from time to time he likes to dominate, to look at Zina across a full room during a party, raise his eyebrows, questioning, and know that she'll come, that she'll leave Mats alone this night in order to crawl under the covers with him.

Also, he wants to be able to tell her to leave when he finds her stay in his house is too long. What is most difficult to abide is her loyalty to Mats. When Zina comes home from her adventures there are scenes, Mats runs through the room, a tall converted attic which is so large that it's windy, and calls her a whore, a pleasure-seeking sow without a conscience. She has to tell: how often, how long, how? They both get pleasure from it, Zina again experiences her nights of love with Johan, and Mats, in his jealousy gets dished up a lively erotic film in which his admired teacher plays a major part. Afterwards there is consolation, caressing and rest in Zina's sturdy arms.

Johan knows all this but never thinks about it. He can, however, become excessively angry about the fact that Mats with his absurd forged silver objects takes up a permanent exhibition space in Zina's gallery while seldom any of them sell.

"What do you care?" says Zina, "I sell plenty of other things, and it's good for Mats. Why do you get excited about it, isn't it my business?"

No, she's not staying today, the administration of the gallery needs to be done and the mailing for the next exhibition is going out this afternoon. But she'll come back tonight, if Johan wants it. She's a free agent; Mats has gone to Africa where he is going to study primitive forging techniques. That will inspire him, and what results from it will be exhibited by Zina in her modest art shop.

"And what kind of folk will you get then? Multicultural social workers, home-weaving frumps with questions like can it be done in an enamelling oven, holistic boys who want to become one with the world—use your brains, there is no money in it at all."

"I don't know. Perhaps Mats will be discovered. I have many friends in arts and crafts circles. He really makes beautiful things, sometimes. Let me be, my shop is going well. I sold a lot of these cleaved stone objects."

Johan sniffs. Granite cunts that people use as letter holders. Proud that they have Art in their homes. It costs, but you've *got* something.

"I'm going to Alma to pick up her painting. This afternoon I'll come back, then people from the museum are coming to pick up the masterpiece and some other things. Then they can take along Alma's *Postman* at the same time. Do you want to ride along later?"

After tooth cleaning, there's shaving, with a blade. Take a crap. Under the triple jets of water. Shampoo hair. Let the water beat against your eyelids. Feel good and strong: a conqueror. As though showing the paintings means the *coup de grâce* for everyone who has ever misjudged or crossed him. Now they'll see who he is: Steenkamer, Johan, painter. Will his father walk into the place, recognized by no one, seriously examine the four walls, turn to the artist, my son, my son, finally?

And Johan, will he then say haughtily: what do you mean, I don't know you? Or will he, with pent-up tears, embrace his reclaimed father, finally?

With both arms, clenching his fists, he makes a victory sign to the shower walls and gets dressed. Silent cheering.

Alma lives in the southern quarter of the city where there is still space for parking cars. After the boys' departure, she left the house in which they grew up as it was, but now hardly uses the upper floor where their rooms were. Sometimes she drags herself up the stairs to take a bath in the old-fashioned bathroom. Usually she washes herself in the shower that Johan had installed for her on the ground floor. She sleeps downstairs in a minuscule room with barred windows that face the street. During the day she putters around in the large living room which is very empty for someone her age. To be able to move around with her cane or walker, she had Oscar take all the excess chairs upstairs. In contrast, the garden, visible through the dirty garden doors, is crammed full with overgrown bushes and showy acanthus. It is clear that here lives a woman who knows what she wants and pays no attention to things that don't interest her.

She sits at the table in a straight-backed chair and waits for her younger son. During the first years after Charles' disappearance she watched with dismay as Johan's talent flowered. When the child indicated that he wanted to become a painter and nothing else (at fifteen or sixteen?), she told him that his father had started as a painter.

*39*

"And then, did he stay a painter? What does he do now? Where does he live? Is he still alive?"

Forbidden questions, never asked, stirred up by the emotions of the moment. Alma's mouth becomes a line that lets nothing pass.

She turned her sails into the wind and, after the first shock, enjoyed her child's gifts. He could have all the materials he asked for, and from adolescence on she focused her attention on what he produced. When Johan no longer liked that, she paid an instructor at the academy to give her son private lessons and she pulled back her own involvement, although she remained interested. She forced him to finish high school before going to the art academy. He obeyed.

To the best of his knowledge Johan never connected painting with the image of a father. When after four whiskeys Alma once confided to Ellen that she couldn't bear to look at the drawings the four-year-old child made for his recently vanished father, and that she threw them into the fire, Johan could recall neither the incident nor the feelings that would have been appropriate to it.

Certainly Johan has always felt that he touched his mother intensely with his talent, but he never understood why. Through her involvement he became her very special knight; together they shared a world of understanding because of his talent.

Questions about his father occurred to him at regular intervals during his development as a result of what he read or experienced, but Johan let these questions be silenced within him when Alma didn't want to answer them. They have a pact to ignore Charles completely; upholding the treaty was the only way to survive. But does the treaty square with the truth? Johan never agonized over it, all the more because the imaginary rivalry between himself and his absent father was amply overshadowed by the bitter daily war with Oscar.

Although Johan as youngest, smallest, most innocent was clearly the victim in this desperate battle, he never really believed in his role as victim, as if being Alma's favourite were a protective armour. Alma divides and conquers. From the beginning she dashed to pieces the bridges between her children. They won't join to turn against her but will try to massacre each other: Johan because he can't bear competition, Oscar out of the dismay caused by the arrival of the little brother who destroyed his whole world and all his security. From her front row seat at the edge of the battlefield, Alma incites and seduces.

She is waiting for her son. On the table lies a newspaper. Behind her straight back hangs the painting that Johan is coming to pick up, because he has set aside a place for it on the side wall of the large exhibition gallery. Johan painted it for her, a present for her sixtieth birthday.

The painting, mounted in a simple black frame, is called: *The Postman.* It depicts a man in a postman's uniform from the sixties. He carries a heavy mailbag on a strap over his left shoulder. In his right hand he holds a letter which he practically hands to the viewer. On his head the postman wears not a uniform cap but an old-fashioned fireman's helmet. The face under it is serious and radiates a calm emotion that contrasts with the scenes in the background. The postman stands in a field. Behind him the forest is burning and on the horizon can be seen a city in flames. Yellow and red tongues of fire blaze out of windows, even the church tower is burning. Still the postman is quietly offering his letter. The left hand with broad, wrinkled fingers lies on the mailbag. With intense compassion the postman presents his letter. On the envelope, slightly larger than a normal envelope, the name of the addressee can be read upside-down: Alma Hobbema.

The address is illegible because the postman's thumb lies over it. From the corner where the stamp is glued, a small pale flame rises straight up and turns into a plume of smoke. The stamp itself is so scorched that it cannot be identified, only the serrated edge at the bottom is still visible.

"Better open the window, it stinks in here like a home for the aged, it's glorious weather outside, do you have coffee?"

Johan has entered energetically and opens the garden doors.

A sickly sweet summer smell wafts into the room. He can have sour-tasting coffee from a thermos. Sitting at the table across from Alma he looks at his painting. Beautiful colour contrasts, impeccable technique, fine threatening atmosphere. Satisfied, Johan is satisfied. He stretches his legs, puts his hands behind his neck, and squeezes his eyes shut.

"I have reserved the side room of 'The Lost Carp' for around seven o'clock on Sunday night," says Alma. "I had to leave open the number of people, eight or ten, I didn't know. They'll arrange a fixed dinner for us; that way you don't have all that business with menus and everyone wanting something else."

"What will they make? Not crab cocktail or that sort of inane stuff?"

"They have a very civilized kitchen, Johan. We'll have the carp in a distinctive sauce as main course. Their speciality. I've been to speak to the chef. The first course will be a pastry with chanterelles, garnished with summer vegetables. In between, a clear soup, a game bouillon. Soup is essential, I think. For dessert we'll have a profiterole tart. They make that themselves. The chef is a patisserie virtuoso, they always have beautiful tarts when I have tea there with Janna."

Johan snorts.

"It's a bit like a Christmas present menu. Everything is wrapped inside something else. Seems dangerous! And what's the situation with the wines? Of course you know nothing about that; do they have a pretty good cellar these days?"

"I'll leave that to you. Can't you drive by there on your way? Then you'll see for yourself. I'd like to know ahead of time, I want to make a menu for everyone, a souvenir."

"A light red with the mushrooms; yes, I should consult with that magic chef of yours. Pouilly-Fumé with the carp, that's definite. A lively wine, yet expensive. Very good. With the profiteroles a Moscato d'Asti. Nice. Have you got money, Alma; can you pay for all that? I'll pay for the wine.

"Absolutely out of the question. I'm inviting you and your family, or what passes for it, out to dinner. You may help me with advice about wines, but I'm paying. That's an old lady's privilege."

"And your way of controlling things, of arranging the seating and running the show."

"Exactly. I don't tolerate interference. You direct in the museum and I at the table."

She looks terrible, his mother. A vest with stains over a brown dress; the grey hair sloppily coiled at her neck with ingrained gestures from very long ago. Johan sees her standing in front of the mirror with hairpins between the compressed lips and her hands behind her head. Why can women do that, braid their hair without looking, tie their apron strings in a bow on their back? She looked like a snake with a split tongue; an absent look in her eyes, just like the girl tuning the lute in the painting by Vermeer. He thought that she stuck the pins straight through her head, that it was that way with mothers, that's why they were always in pain; they nailed their hair to their scalp. The worst was the hat, when Alma went to a reception. The blue-grey suit would be brushed, the silk blouse ironed (brown, tentshaped scorch mark on the back because the bell rang and the iron remained standing on the delicate silk: doesn't matter, no one will see it, I'll keep the jacket on—but I know it, thinks the little boy, my mother is marked by fire), and as apotheosis The Hat would be taken from the shelf, placed on Alma's head and anchored with a four-inch iron pin with an oval pearl on one end and a sharp point on the other. Revulsion, living room horror, women s secret.

"Do you have something with you to wrap *The Postman?* You can take the red blanket, I've put it ready for you. Are you going directly to the museum?"

"No, I'm taking him home. That way they can wrap him together with the other pieces. They do that in a kind of wooden envelope, with soft, protective stuff in between. First class. Today they're picking up everything, the loan pieces and whatever is still standing in the studio. The small gallery has already been installed, with prints and watercolours. The frame-maker has been working on that, everything has been newly framed in the same way. Tomorrow we do the large gallery, I want to be there myself."

Johan gets up to walk to *The Postman*. He lifts the painting down carefully and places it on the floor with the picture facing the wall, away from foot traffic. When he walks back behind Alma, his eye falls on the newspaper that she has put on the table and in which he recognizes his name.

"What do we have here? What's that? Oscar?! Why didn't you say anything? Is that today's paper?"

"Yesterday's, Johan. Oscar came to give it to me. I'm surprised that you didn't see it, don't you have a clipping service? Don't you get the morning paper yourself?"

"I've stopped that a long time ago. All that droning at the start of the day makes me ill. Don't have time for it either. Besides it's an absolutely awful paper, it always has bitter and fashionable reviews. I cancelled it years ago, their jealous and malicious chatter made me sick. They always know best, and never find anything beautiful or good—they've invented God's own art code right there. No, I don't want anything to do with it. Why does Oscar write for that shitty paper? Has the National Museum been approved by the editorial board? That would surprise me. Let me have it?"

Alma hands him the paper. She makes herself comfortable and examines her son attentively. His arms almost completely extended, Johan raises the paper in the air; his eyes race over the lines. Slowly the colour disappears from his face and his cheeks tighten.

My child is an old man, thinks Alma. He needs reading glasses, his face is ravaged, that glorious baby face has become a grey rag. Now he receives a blow, I see him reel. He cannot stand adversity, he needs more spring but he's losing elasticity. That's what time does with my wunderkind.

Johan laps up his brother's words. A solidly founded plea for sober, truly contemporary painting. Continuation along the daring line of letting go of the old structures, the line of study of isolated elements: material, light, colour, form. The art of painting should take music as an example: a contemporary composer who uses Mozart's idiom is unthinkable. Kitsch. Leaning back into Vermeer's chair. Crying boy with Tear On Cheek. Crawling before the sponsor. Obeying the public. Genuflection before stupidity.

In his article Oscar mentions many examples but not his brother's name. He does mention the Municipal Museum which is devoting its most important autumn exhibition to a figurative painter.

"Johan," Alma says with a piercing voice, from another world, "I've just remembered that Oscar is coming to have dinner tonight, it's Friday. Would you please go to the bakery and get two Napoleons, I don't have a dessert and Oscar is so fond of having several courses. Where is my wallet?"

Napoleons! Oscar! How does that woman's head work anyway? Renting a whole restaurant for me, spending thousands of guilders for a banquet in honour of one son and meanwhile stir up the other one in order to put that success into perspective! Johan is struck dumb. He looks from Alma to the newspaper, back and forth, helplessly back and forth.

"Look, you've got to look at it this way," says his mother. "Oscar is an academic, that's what he studied for, that's his job. He was always counting and stacking and matching things. Do you remember that giant box of coloured pencils you got at Christmas?"

Oh yes, Johan remembers, it was the fulfilment of his heart's desire. It lay in the window of an art supply store: the box with one hundred coloured pencils in two rows. Every afternoon after school Johan spent fifteen minutes in front of the shop window, sighing, longing, fantasizing. He got an erection from excitement when he saw the flat box lying under the Christmas tree, the impossibly expensive, superb pencils that Alma couldn't afford?

But it *was* true, he got them—who from, Mummy, who from? Mister Caran D'ache, Alma said. It says so on the box. I thought: Mister Caran D'ache is my father. Dammit. Underhand tricks. Secrecy. Fucking bitch.

"Evenings on end you would draw with the pencils," Alma continues. "When you were done, Oscar put them back in the box, arranged by colour. You left everything lying on the table, every which way, you never put anything back. But Oscar could. Sometimes he was busy with it for an hour if, at the end, he found one more pencil on the floor that had to go in between. He'd then move forty pencils in order to get one in the right place. Yes, Oscar lives for scholarship. He has an overview and opinions. He gives those in the paper when he is asked to do so. That's how it goes. You shouldn't lose your temper over it."

"And you, and you," Johan stutters, "you can go to hell with your Napoleons and your scholarship. Stumble to the bakery yourself to get that stale stuff. Count me out. And if Oscar, that traitor, comes to the dinner on Sunday, I'll leave at once. You can choose: him or me."

Now Alma is scared. Her dinner must not be jeopardized, that's going too far.

"Don't be so touchy. I'll speak with your brother, it's surely not meant against you, he can explain, he must, maybe he'll offer you his excuses, would you like that?"

"I don't want to sit at the table with him. Period. Not now and not Sunday."

Johan stand up and wraps *The Postman* in the red blanket. At the door he turns around. Furious.

"I have a surprise for you. A guest you can seat at the table instead of that fraud. I've written to my father. I've invited Charles, you hear, Charles, Charles?!"

Johan stalks off, the door bangs shut. He places *The Postman* carefully on the back seat of his car and calmly drives down the street.

The woman remains behind at the table. Her breathing is shallow. She has pain in her left chest and her upper left arm.

Relax and think. Remain seated like this. I want to lie down, I want to go to my room, that's better. Get up carefully, lean on the table. Catch my breath. Cane on the right. To the door between table and cane. How *can* he do something like that? Sit on the small stool next to the door. Open the door. Hold the left arm in front of the body. After all I've done for him. Get up, cross the hall. He couldn't have thought up a worse affront. Bedroom door. The bed. What I feel in my gut, in my stomach. That's fear. I have to lie down. Lie down for a while, for an hour. Then call Oscar, or Ellen. Lie down, think a moment. I'm afraid, no, furious. Upset. I've got to keep my thoughts together. With the boys to Xanten, why do I think of that? Forty years ago, they should see a Roman settlement. So I thought. Afterwards into town, coffee with pastry in one of those disgusting German cafés. Just walk into the church. So I thought. Impeccably restored. Bulletin boards with photos taken right after the bombardment: a damaged cage without a roof. The boys played catch in the garden, Johan wailing because Oscar was hitting him too hard. At the entrance to the church three crosses made of grey stone, it looked like concrete. Those hanging on them had their bones broken, destroyed. Bone splinters sticking out. I vomited behind the rose bushes. My arm hurts. I called the boys, told a story, talking softly when we walked past the crosses so that they looked at my face and not up. They hung up high, the tortured men. I was so afraid, so afraid. I don't dare to lie down. Remain seated, it will be all right soon.

She lifts her right arm and takes the pins from her hair one by one. Places them on the table next to her bed, next to Johan's invitation. The thin hair veils the woman like a mourning cloak. She opens her mouth to cry from fright or pain, but there is no sound.

Lie down, I must lie down. Legs up, head down, on the pillow. Not daring to. What am I fighting against? I am a torn kite with a broken back which is tumbling into the abyss. The thread is broken. The black abyss. Charles. Johan mentioned his name. After all these years. It can't be. I'm a tainted bride. I'm sick with fear.

Driving through the sunny city, Johan is feeling in high spirits. The fact that he can throw Alma into confusion makes him feel cheerful. He reads his name on billboards in the big shopping street and glances at the shopwindows. Here is the most elegant pastry shop in town. So distinguished that the name is only shown in very small letters on the black façade: Maison Davina. A dark woman in a summer coat comes out of the store and walks to a large Volvo parked in front of the door. She places the black box with the gold imprint on the back seat and drives off quickly, right in front of Johan. On an impulse, he shoots into the empty parking space.

The store is dark and silent. A young man in a morning-coat stands on a platform at the back and watches. Behind the counter, a display case mounted in shiny black granite, stands a young woman dressed in a white blouse and a black skirt. Spotless. Not a pastry to be seen in the whole store. There are a few boxes with plain chocolates, there is a bowl with sculpted pieces of marzipan, and there are small pots of chocolate sprinkles. The prices are exorbitant; for a moment Johan thinks that they are indicated in French francs out of pure snobbery, but they most certainly are Dutch guilders.

Questioning, the girl looks at him.

"Cake," says Johan, "apple cake?"

"No, we're sorry, that is not possible."

Why does the staff in better patisserie shops often have a slight German accent? It gives Johan confidence in the quality of the pastry, he thinks that pastry-making is an art-form in Germany.

The young woman doesn't trust him with her pastries. A cake has to be ordered, demands discussion and attention. To buy a cake just like that, on impulse, is like a spontaneous brothel visit. Johan starts to sweat.

"Do you deliver? In the city?"

"Throughout the whole country, sir. We have our own delivery service."

"Could you deliver a cake for me this afternoon?"

The girl glances at the platform. The morning-coat opens a book and studies it. Yes, he nods.

Johan gives Alma's name and address.

"What time did you have in mind?"

"Four o'clock."

"And which cake may we deliver for you?"

No idea. The girl will reject all suggestions. Can't they think of something themselves? Then Johan notices that under the glass of the display case there lies a grey stone dusted with powder, a fossilized log cake.

"This one," he says without flinching.

The girl starts a discourse about the contents and preparation method of the stone. She stops when the morning-coat coughs discreetly.

"And whom shall we note as sender?"

"Steenkamer," says Johan.

On a card with the gilded company name the girl writes: Mr Steenkamer. "One hundred twenty-five guilders please. That includes delivery. Thank you."

Light as a feather and whistling, Johan leaves the store. Across the street, Lisa bicycles past.

On the terrace they drink sparkling water. Lisa takes coffee with it. No eating, that distracts in the middle of the day. Johan looks at Lisa. She is wearing a long skirt with her creamy white sweater over it. She can do that with her figure. Shiny, just shaven legs, bare feet in nice leather shoes. High heels. The tanned neck is borderline: sinewy but no loose skin. Beautiful brown wrists. Very nice, actually. How would it be to stick your hands under the waistband into that skirt and knead that muscular bicycling ass? Very nice, certainly. It has never happened, although he feels that his way of looking isn't wasted on Lisa. I know so little about her. How does she live when Lawrence is gone? Does she have someone else? Does she still see her ex and do it with him, in honour of the past?

How easy it is with a familiar body and familiar gestures, as it was recently with Ellen, as if it were those days again. Johan feels that making love to your ex doesn't actually count.

He is so immersed in what he sees that Lisa's stories don't

register. He sees her gesture with her beautiful hands, her lips moving, the eyes becoming larger and smaller. She talks. He hears about Lawrence, about the children when he comes back to the surface.

"...they walked a part of the coastal path, with a real backpack and an overnight stay. High above the sea, at the edge of the cliffs. The week before someone had fallen over them. Yes, you never know, he may have jumped. That abyss lures and entices. But it had been exciting, they all screamed at the same time on the telephone. Lawrence said that nowadays works of art are displayed on the path; can you imagine! Metal objects that make noise in the wind, as though the sea doesn't create enough of a racket. And ugly to boot, he said."

"Yes, don't you think it's odd," says Johan. "All these local artsy-craftsy folk who make pots and carve drinking bowls out of root wood; it's good for nothing and it leads to nothing. They should just be sent into the coal mines. The muddle-heads who 'work with metal' first."

Intolerant but fun to listen to, thinks Lisa. Merciless out of vanity but also out of his craftsmanship. Lisa can understand that quite well, although she doesn't dare to be so outspoken.

"How are the preparations going?"

Johan reports. *The Postman is* visible through the car windows, at least its red blanket. Jesus—Alma, Charles, Oscar!

"Why does he write something like that, especially now, do you understand why? After all, you're the psychiatrist. He wants to break me, mow me down. And in that newspaper he has succeeded; they won't give me a rave review. He has always pestered me and put me down horribly, as long as I can remember. I used to look up to him, of course, because he knew so much. And I was scared of his stories. When we were very young we slept in the same room, and when Alma had gone downstairs, he would whisper about the most awful things, monsters under the bed, vampires through the crack of the window—then I would lie awake for hours, stiff with fear. Later I had the big room. That must have been when Charles left. Funny actually, that Oscar didn't get it. Alma started sleeping downstairs, and

I got a large drawing table in my own room. Would it have belonged to Charles? I've never dared to ask that."

"Have you ever seen any of his work, didn't he paint before he went to America?"

"I don't know, Lisa. I believe that I've never thought about it much, everything happened as usual, things went as they did. It wasn't until recently that I've started wondering, I've even approached him, Charles; I've sent him an invitation to the preview!"

"Do you think he'll come?"

"No, that seems unlikely." Surprised, Johan looks up. "Damn, a boat. Now I remember again. The large bedroom, later my room, used to be Charles' work room. His paintings were standing there. He couldn't have done many, he was twenty-seven when he took off, and at that time, of course, it was practically impossible to get materials. But I still remember a night, or an evening, when he took Os and me to that room, it was solemn. And he showed us his paintings. Four, I think. Perhaps because there are four walls? I still remember one, with a boat on it, a big, black boat. And at the bottom left, four people with very scary, sad faces. A threatening, gigantic boat with yellow portholes, like eyes. But it's quite possible that this is a kind of memory after the fact, because I know that he left on a boat."

"Did Alma tell you that?"

"Papa has gone away on a boat and is never coming back. We are now going to live without him. Immediately got rid of all his things: paintings, the big bed, his clothes, everything. That drawing table, I'm not sure about that. What did she do with the paintings? No idea.

"Later I heard from Aunt Janna how it happened, that Charles had a commission for opera scenery and that he fell for the soprano. That woman took him with her, from one day to the next. Never let us hear anything from him again, as far as I know. You couldn't discuss it with Alma."

"She must have communicated with him about legal matters: division of property, guardianship, that sort of thing?"

"I don't know. You couldn't ask anything. If you did, she simply gave no answer. Oscar accepted it sooner than I did. He became a kind of substitute husband for Alma, and he still is. He does her chores, he eats with her, and he even did his laundry in her machine until a short time ago. No, Oscar is out for my destruction rather than his father's, I think."

Lisa feels pity for the oppressed son. So faithful in trying his best to be a good man for his mother and then, year in year out, right up to the present, he has to watch how Alma's eyes begin to sparkle as soon as Johan comes in sight, Johan who breaks all the laws and still is the darling, time and again.

"And then he becomes an art historian!" she says. "Always busy studying and documenting the kind of men who have caused him the most suffering. No wonder he lashes out in the paper."

Johan sniffs scornfully.

"He knows a lot about technique. There's no one with whom I can discuss technical matters as well as with Oscar. But we fight easily, just as we used to do. I'm going home, Lisa, I want to be on time when the packers come. Great that you're joining us for dinner on Sunday. Is Ellen dreading it?"

What can I say, Lisa thinks, what will you understand if I say something? You and your father are the seducers, and whoever is seduced will pay for it for years. What is it with women? That you feel weak in your knees with such a man, that everything that you know is of importance to you, is good for you, suddenly loses its meaning when he appeals to you. That he needs you at that moment, that he has to be saved and never again be hurt, and that you can do that? And that you want him, that you want to press his dark head against your naked belly, and more, and further, at that moment, at that very moment.

\* \* \*

After sitting motionless on her bed for an hour, Alma picked up the telephone and called the National Museum. Oscar was at his desk and sounded slightly irritated by the unexpected call.

"Oscar, I'd like you to come a little earlier today. Something has happened. Don't ask me what. I can't tell you on the telephone."

"What, what's going on Mother? Is something wrong with you, are you sick, have you fallen? I'm coming immediately."

The irritation has disappeared. Oscar is worried; he can tell from her voice that she is confused.

"No, I'm not ill. The telephone operator is listening in, Oscar, that always happens in organizations where there is not enough to do. I would appreciate it if you'd come an hour earlier; I want to discuss something with you. You don't have to race out of your office this very minute."

Because Oscar's goal in life consists of keeping Alma on her feet and on an even keel, he can no longer concentrate on his work after the telephone call. His mother has a heart attack. She's lying on the floor with broken legs. The house is on fire. There is flooding. She has been robbed. She is dying. He packs his briefcase: a thick report from the board of directors, a file about an investigation by the principal restorer, his reading glasses, the big bunch of keys that gives access to the museum and to the departments that are under Oscar's management.

Sweating, he walks to the house of his mother who is barely surprised to see him so soon. She has somewhat recovered from the morning storms; the pain in her arm and her chest has subsided, but she still lacks sufficient strength in her arms to put up her hair. Dresses, skirts, jackets are draped over all the chairs. Oscar removes a silver-blue iridescent silk dress from his usual seat. He has arrived just in time, for before Alma has a chance to sit down, the bell rings and the delivery man from Maison Davina is at the door. Puzzled, Alma enters the room, cane on the right, pastry box on the left.

The old woman with the loose hair and the bespectacled man with the bird-like neck bend in surprise over the shiny object that is standing in the centre of the stained tablecloth. Alma flips open the lid. There lies the fossilized log cake with a small card on its bark: "sent at the request of Mr Steenkamer".

Quick intake of breath from shock. Then a deep sigh. Alma

sits down. Confused, Oscar remains standing, picks up the card and brings it close to his glasses; it's as though he doesn't understand what it says.

"Mother, what's this about? I don't understand."

"I think, my boy, that this has something to do with the subject that I wanted to discuss with you. You should know that Charles is in the city. Your father. Johan came to tell me this morning. And I think that he sent me a token as a kind of preparation for getting acquainted, for seeing each other again."

Oscar is baffled. Steenkamer? Steenkamer! Of course his father's name is Steenkamer, at least it used to be. His mother sits sighing like a young girl, and staring with glazed eyes at the stone in the lovely box. This has to stop. This is not allowed.

"Mother, you're mistaken," Oscar says hoarsely. "I ordered this cake during my lunch break, as a festive dessert for tonight. I had it delivered because I didn't want to carry it around with me in this heat."

"You're lying, you'd never buy such an expensive cake. You're lying, Oscar, you're lying!"

"Not true, yes true. It's a festive weekend, an important weekend with the opening of Johan's exhibition. Given its importance for the family, I thought that an expensive cake would be in order."

Oscar's voice becomes softer. He sinks down on his chair and takes off his glasses. Powerless, he wipes the lenses with a handkerchief. Lost. This move has failed. What now? Distract her. Make it clear to her that she's been deluded, that Charles doesn't exist, anyway isn't in the city, anyhow has no interest in Alma. But how?

Alma fingers the fabric of the blue dress. "I thought I'd wear this one on Sunday. With the blue shoes. It's really awful that I have to walk with that cane, will he find that embarrassing?"

Simply tell her: you're an old witch with dirty hair, your skin hangs in folds in your neck, you're a shapeless bag of bones, and long white hairs are growing on your chin?

This is much worse than the boundless admiring bullshit about Johan. He's used to that, he knows how to handle it in his own way.

A game of being hit and, after careful consideration, hitting back deliberately. When Johan was with Ellen, it was easier; Alma paid less attention to her darling. Oscar knows that his mother couldn't tolerate Johan being wrapped up in his family. Well, wrapped up? In the art world stories made the rounds about Johan as a skirt-chaser. More than once Oscar witnessed Johan assaulting a student or a model while Ellen sat at home with the children.

For Oscar, the divorce was a direct threat. Ellen hadn't moved yet when Alma threw herself on Johan as per usual. Oscar could only look on. The divorce made him sad, not only because of the machinations of power and the changing family kaleidoscope, but also because he is fond of Ellen. She is perhaps the only woman with whom he feels at ease, insofar as he is capable of that. She doesn't think anything is weird, she wants nothing from him, and she has no hidden agenda. He was sorry to see her so upset and sad.

His anger over the increasing brilliance of Johan's star is of a different order. With stomach cramps Oscar learned of the Municipal Museum's intention to organize a special exhibition of Johan's work. On Friday evenings he couldn't eat from misery when he heard Alma yapping about her son's talents. It nauseated Oscar and he regularly retreated into the renovated bathroom where he hung over the toilet and had dry heaves next to his mother's bath slippers. During the weekend he recovered somewhat and devised plans. With grim satisfaction he wrote his newspaper article, which he cleverly brought to the attention of the art editor, taking advantage of a feud between the Municipal and the National Museum. Feuds in the art world, that's meat and drink for the morning papers, and guess what, they bit immediately.

But now I'm undone, thinks Oscar; this euphoria is too much for me. She never showed any interest in Charles, she repudiated him completely, we were not allowed to mention his name, there were no longer any photos of him in the house. All he has to do is send a cake and she loses her hold on reality. This can't be. Or maybe it can? Who had this pastry delivered?

"Alma, don't you know that Charles hasn't had the name

Steenkamer for a long time? He's married to an American woman. He has children. He's called Charles Stone. He has forgotten us, Alma. He is oblivious to us."

Alma looks askance at him, from underneath her disquieting loose hair. Oscar shivers; it's all so creepy and different than usual. She wants to wear the blue dress, she wants to make herself beautiful for her lost prince!

"Things can change, Oscar. In your world there's no room for that, you live with dry scholarship. More is possible than you think."

She looks at the stone, as if it were the proof of her nonsensical words.

Oscar becomes cold in the overheated room. Has she deceived him all these years, did she continue to long for Charles, was Charles there anyway? What should he believe, how can he bring the changed world back in line, what can he build on?

"How about going to the kitchen now, Oscar, to make a cup of tea?"

Oh yes, four o'clock, tea, tea that's standard. Oscar gets up, with new hope.

"And take along that cake, you can cut a small piece of it for us. We have to test it, right?"

Alma giggles and pushes the box across the table to Oscar. He sees that the card is gone, where? Probably into her bra, into her secret pink harness, against her heart.

Slowly he raises his hand to the grey fossil, lifts it, carries it from the room.

"Meanwhile I'll tidy up around here, it looks like a market stall with all those dresses, clean up, put everything back in place."

Alma's voice disappears behind two doors, Oscar sinks down on a kitchen chair. His hands hang between his knees. Time-out.

As an adult in the kitchen of one's childhood, you are a stranger in familiar territory. You know the way. At least think you know in which drawer the bread knife, in which cupboard the pepper, and on which shelves the mugs are concealed. But the beacons have been moved, and on the way to the colander you encounter a stack of unfamiliar plates. In the cupboard under the sink, where the enamel dishwashing basin with its sudsmaker and its wooden-handled brush used to stand (you had to be brave to take out the basin because the sink cupboard had a direct connection with the city sewers, you could smell it; if you kicked hard against the basin, the sewer animals were warned and they stayed at a distance for a while, a short while), a small waste bucket is now mounted whose jaw is opened automatically when the cupboard is unlatched. Although Oscar putters around in Alma's kitchen every week and therefore is aware of all the gradually introduced renovations, today he is struck by a sharp memory of the kitchen of days gone by. The greenish linoleum, laid down in pieces so that the tile pattern just failed to match (in front of the sink it was worn, and you saw the planks stick out from under it; at night the animals came to eat from it) has been replaced by a dark grey synthetic floor covering with slip protection. The sink now has a double basin and turns seamlessly into the synthetic countertop where the pastry box is now standing. Granite, a cold rock-hard stone. A shallow, wide wash basin with black and white tiles. At the drain (air grate for the sewer animals, you could sometimes hear them breathe if you held your ear there) three tiles had loosened. For a long time they were kept on a small plate near the window before they disappeared—when? why? The space opened up became a haven for macaroni and tea leaves, to be scooped out with a teaspoon by the person washing dishes. Aunt Janna's fish platter still stands on its old spot in the dish cupboard: a composition of a stone head, tail, and scales where the fish to be eaten was carefully nestled in a final mating.

Oscar looks behind the earthenware mugs for the wide teacups from when he was young, for the dark green ivy pattern on the creamy white ribbed background. Yes! Top shelf. At the back.

He steps down from the chair with two cups in his hands.

Hiding places. What else has she hidden? For thirty-five years he has missed those cups, considered them lost; in a moment of confusion, of lack of self-control, he climbed on a chair and found them. He feels the familiar house around him turn into a deceptive hiding place filled with threatening treasures.

She can count on me, Oscar thinks. I'm totally predictable. I don't look for secret drawers, I leave the attic alone, and don't climb on a chair to look on top of a cupboard.

Set down the cups. Smell my fingers: a greasy, stale smell. But I've done it, today! I can do it! Like Captain Cook from the boys' book, who had the gift of knowing where land was, he could tell from the waves and smell it in the wind—in the same way I smell the hidden love letters, the mouldered shirts, everything of her lover that the faithless witch saved. Turn it over, I'm going to turn the whole house upside down!

The teakettle. Carefully rinse the teapot with hot water. Quickly back on the heat, to let the scale boil out of the water. Three spoonfuls of Lapsang in the pot. Sniff. Smoky plantation. Ships filled with spices. Brew it. Hear the tone of the teakettle rise. Everything under control. The captain clasps the helm and trims his sails. Forward!

Cake out of the box, on the cutting board. Without thinking, take the large meat cleaver out of the drawer. The intruder lies with its head on the chopping block, numbed with fear, a paralysed victim. Oscar stares at the log and out of the corner of his eyes sees the afternoon sun flicker on the steel blade. His head becomes light and carefree. Almost despite himself he rams the knife through the cake, jumping up when the chopping block is hit. Zap! Raise the knife. Zap! Jump. Zap. And again. Zap! Zap!

"Son, where are you? Hurry up!"

Bewildered, Oscar looks at the knife in his hands, at the mutilated log, at the small cloud of steam that rises from the spout of the teapot. Pieces of bark are stuck against the wall, a dark cherry lies in the sink, and on Oscar's glasses there are spatters of chocolate cream. Also on his shirt, he notices when he has wiped his glasses clean with a dish towel. Put away the knife. Button the jacket. Take two pieces of cake from the bloody carcass and put them on two glass plates. Model them into shape. Use the index finger to press the cherry back in. Smell: luxury, pleasure, debauched sweetness. Small spoons. The serving tray. Sail through the hall fully loaded, tack into the room, set the load on the landing quay.

"Just what's with things here at home? Where is the stuff?"

Oscar's voice is louder than usual, he speaks through his fear, like an intrepid sailor.

"Things, what things? This is your own home, you've grown up here, you know everything here."

"Papa's things."

Alma leans back, the teacup in her hand. With raised eyebrows she has observed the cups and the ruinous lumps of the cake. The chocolate spatters on Oscar's pants and the excited colour of his face also haven't escaped her notice.

"When Charles left us," says Alma in a low calm voice, "I removed all his possessions as soon as possible. He knew that he wouldn't return and he didn't care for the stuff that he had left behind. I could do with it as I saw fit. When you were in school during the day, Aunt Janna came to help me clear out. I sold the big bed, as well as the portable easel and all the painting stuff to an auction house. And his chair. Janna packed the clothes and took them to the Salvation Army. Also the shoes and the coats. Everything is gone; there is no longer any tramp walking around in your father's boots. Gone, finished. Ask Aunt Janna if you don't believe it!"

Oscar leaves his tea untouched and looks intently at his mother's face.

"And the drawing table, the one that Johan could have in the big room?"

"Yes, you're right, that did belong to Charles. It was brand new; he had just purchased it to use for drawing that scenery. So I felt that that didn't count, it was not a contaminated object that he had used for years. And it worked out well for Johan, so I left it."

"You see, you're lying to me. You withhold things; if I ask you nothing, you tell me nothing, and no one, never. Where are his letters? Someone who's twenty-five must have papers, old report cards, diaries, whatever, a sketchbook? Photos!"

"Burned, Oscar. In the heater. It was a chilly, wet summer. In the evening I would light the heater when you slept, and bit by bit I burned all of Charles' records. You remember, we didn't have central heating then, only a coal heater in the room."

Oscar thinks of the heater with its shiny maw and the fire behind the small mica panes. In the evening, before going to bed, Johan and he stood in front of it to get warm. In their pajamas. The heat scorched against your buttocks until you could no longer stand it, even less when you faced it. A large leather chair stood by the heater, with wide stuffed armrests on which they sat, he and his little brother, their bare feet in—in what? between what?

Between their father's thighs! under the book from which he was reading to them. Carefully, in order not to touch the disgusting bare skin of Johan's fat little feet, carefully move the toes in that wonderful secret space; a smell of tobacco; a feeling of ecstatic tension. Afterwards between the icy cold sheets, the door open a crack because Johan was scared in the dark. Listen, listen intently to what? To the hated breathing from the toddler's crib? No, the feeling is filled with expectation, happy. Four plucked notes, from high to low: a, d, g, c. Then fuller, bowed two by two. The lower note floats up and down until the two notes played together suddenly glow. And then: The Song. Johan has fallen asleep. Father plays only for me, the most beautiful and saddest song in the world. For me, because I hear it, I hear the notes rise and fall back down, so sad that it makes you cry; I wait for the end, until the very last piece when the song finally goes up and stays there.

"The viola! Where did the viola go? You didn't throw it into the heater? Or did you? Where is Papa's viola?"

Oscar has jumped up and gestures wildly at his mother, the words stream out of his mouth, she is a fraud, a sneaky, underhanded witch, he doesn't believe her stories at all, she has to shut up and he's going to look for himself, he wants to see himself what of his father's has been secretly saved in this house. Blindly he storms up the stairs, tears in his eyes, but he can climb these stairs in the dark. Upstairs the floor covering is the same as before: matting which immediately dampens the angry footsteps.

The contradictory motives cause him utmost confusion: he wants to throw overboard every sign of life of his father, out of the reach of the faithless mother, he wants to erase Charles from the house so that Alma will never again think of him. But, staggering on the staircase to the attic, doesn't he also want to find the viola in the musty attic, press the instrument against his heart and swim home with it like a drowning man with a lifebuoy?

Behind him he hears Alma labouring up the stairs; the cane clatters against the wall. She shouts, she screams at him, Oscar, her son who suddenly is as out of control as a jib on a broken stay.

With his aching head he pushes open the attic hatch. It falls down with a bang. Dust clouds rise. Alma shakes the ladder: "Leave that! Come down!" With her cane she pokes against his buttocks; the lower part of his body is in a chaotic situation. The upper part, however, enjoys total quiet: when his eyes have become used to the faint light, Oscar sees straight floor boards as far as the eye can see. An empty floor, covered with a delicate layer of dust.

## Chapter three

# Escape Routes

The land still holds on to the summer. The water lies unruffled between the grassy banks, the night's coolness is given up uncomplainingly within half an hour, as soon as the sun has cleared away the mist. All the green is dark and the spring colour gradations, yellowish, silver-grey, and light green, have already disappeared in the lush trees. The opened leaves are satisfied with dew and don't think yet of parching, pulling back saps, falling off.

On the ground there also reigns tranquil wealth: bulging clumps of grass with long, fat blades; large, hairy leaves on the creeping plants under which zucchini and orange pumpkins are hiding; the lettuce has burst out of the heads and has bolted.

From the bedroom window Lisa looks across the orchard at the river where a grebe glides by, as still as a paper boat, and to the steaming meadow behind it. For fifteen minutes she sits lost in incoherent morning thoughts, her elbows on the window sill. The long free day that lies ahead of her gives her a languid and timeless feeling. No pressure to get dressed, no make-up, no schedule! The house behind her is emphatically and wonderfully empty.

She goes downstairs in her long bathrobe. Barefoot she walks in the damp grass under the trees to the river, back along the exuberant and neglected vegetable garden, to the terrace where the weeds grow uncontrolled between the tiles. Bent over the barrel, she sees the large sluggish one swim, tail barely moving, at the bottom. She places a chair among the hollyhocks and looks at the fig tree with many trunks. Dozens of figs this year, as if the river were the Mediterranean. Lisa picks one, the tree lets go with difficulty. Sweet. Vacation smell.

Sit with coffee and read yesterday's paper. It's not yet warm or cold, the temperature is exactly that of the body. Peace and quiet, peace and quiet, quiet.

Lisa has made the front of the house as inaccessible as possible: closed the curtains and locked the gate. In an hour, the streams of people will start coming; the villagers will do their errands and, hungry for conversation, will lean on their shovels in their front yards. From the city, groups of men will come on racing bikes, with shiny black pants covering their rears and helmets on their heads. They let out warning shouts as they whizz at top speed through the village street, narrowly missing the stately couple bicycling along with their shopping bags hanging from the handlebars, indecently close to the ladies walking in their plaid culottes. Smell of sweat, body heat perceptible against the ladies' arms, three yards further down a theatrical blob of spit on the shoulder of the road. Then the smooth water surface will also be broken by the fleet of motor boats, by the impatient sailors who have to wait for the lock for their passage to the lake, by the rowers with their backs to where they're going and don't care where they go.

Lisa sits safely in her garden. She doesn't dare to disconnect the phone: the children might call, and that's going too far. She doesn't want to isolate herself, but she also wants to be able to say no. Asocial, she thinks. Am I afraid of people? I always say that it's because of my work, all week long I listen to people, I have to put myself in their place, think with them or ahead of them, shape a conversation, always consider what effect my words will have, constantly be available.

Nonsense, baloney. It's true of course, but you could just as well use the opposite reasoning in which the patients helpfully bring all sorts of interesting material to challenge Lisa's ingenuity.

When she walks through the village, she closes her face as soon as someone seems to show signs of wanting to talk with her. Being forced to be in a small space with another person costs her no effort when it concerns a patient but exhausts her completely when it's someone in a lift, someone waiting with her at a bakery counter or a less desired person in her own living room. To have to sit at a table with people who are not her intimate friends is the very worst. To be forced to listen to eating noises—slurping, smacking, chewing, swallowing. She can stand that only by stepping outside herself and by making herself as inaccessible as the front of her house. The vehemence of this aversion makes her afraid, but that's how it is: Lisa has to flee everything connected with biting, crushing and guzzling.

At nine-thirty, as early as decently possible, Ellen calls. Lisa's revulsion doesn't extend to her. Even living in the same house with Ellen is imaginable and would only cause minimal difficulty, Lisa thinks. Less difficult than living with a man.

Ellen sounds restless. It's as if the excitement of city life surges through the telephone into the quiet kitchen.

"Do you have plans for today, are you doing anything?"

"Absolutely nothing. I'd like to get out, shall we go for a walk?"

Ellen and Lisa are hikers. They walk long distances, sometimes days on end in foreign countries, they carry their clothes in a backpack and stay overnight in country inns. Throughout the year, regardless of the season, they regularly free up a day to walk at a tremendous pace out of the city to a bus stop or a train station twenty-five or so miles away.

"I can't really, today," says Ellen. "I want to be back in the afternoon, there's still so much to do for tomorrow. I'm restless. But a walk around the lake this morning, that's possible."

"Come out here, then we'll see."

Ellen has tied her hiking boots on the back of her bike. Lisa is already wearing hers. They are beautifully constructed of good leather, to be folded and laced in such a way that no water penetrates, on a sole with three layers. The tread holds on rock, on slopes covered with fine pine needles, and in shallow rivers. Walking in these shoes is a joy: each step taken gives lots of confidence for the next, the feet feel treated right and wouldn't dream of developing blisters. Just putting on this hiking equipment causes a discreet inner joy.

Lisa locks up. She puts two small buckets in her backpack; along the small lake grow blackberries that she wants to pick.

Silently they walk out of the village and don't start talking until there is grass under their feet.

"I think that Alma is becoming soft in the head," says Ellen. "It's not that she's growing demented or anything, but the tension is becoming too much; she's acting strangely. Ever since she's found out that Johan has written to Charles, she really believes that he's coming. For forty years she's lived without that man, and you know what she does? She fixes herself up, she dolls herself up, she carries on like a lovesick fifteen-year-old."

"How do you know that, have you spoken to her?"

"She called yesterday. Totally out of sorts. Johan had walked out angrily, they'd had a fight about that article by Oscar, she mentioned in passing that he didn't want to be at her dinner, but those were all unimportant details. She talked exclusively about Charles. That he was in the city and wanted to see her. She rattled in a high voice, she wasn't herself. It frightened me. Lots of stories about what she should wear, what would I suggest, whether I had still time to buy something new with her. And the cane, what to do with the cane. She can't take a step without it! What he would think if he saw that she couldn't walk well, perhaps she could sit on a chair during the entire reception. It kept going through her head. That he would of course have to join them at dinner; she would immediately call 'The Lost Carp'; should he sit next to her or not—she couldn't stop."

"Jesus, Ellen. Seventy-five years old. That means you always have to watch out. There should be an age limit; after that you don't care how you look, then you're no longer susceptible to signals from males. It should actually stop with fertility. That way you have half of your life really for yourself."

"The hairdresser! She wanted to go to my hairdresser! Even though she has always refused; she felt her neighbourhood hairdresser was good enough. Do you remember that I wanted to offer her a total make-over when she turned seventy? Nonsense, she said. I should give the money to saving the whales! Now it has to be done right then and there, that's why she actually called me."

"Oh well, her hair does look like compressed hay," Lisa says reflecting. "Going to a good hair artist couldn't do any harm. In this case. Could he still fit her in, your hair prince?"

"Not really, but he'll squeeze her into his schedule this afternoon. He must have heard in my voice how much it bothered me, the dear. The boys are meeting her afterwards. I've got a feeling that she has to be taken care of and watched by the family."

"It's still your family, isn't it?"

"Yes, it's stayed that way. She's my children's grandmother, Oscar is their uncle. Yes. In the evening she called me again. Had quarrelled with Oscar who had also left the house in anger! He couldn't stand the idea that she was in touch with Charles again, Alma told me. Are you actually in touch with him, I asked, for I really wanted to know what was true in all those stories. Yes, she said, that afternoon Charles had sent her a package from Maison Davina with a beautiful cake inside it. That's what caused Oscar's anger. He hadn't even tasted it, she said. She sounded as if it gave her pleasure, as if her lovers were fighting over her. I hope that she doesn't have a heart attack."

"And Johan, have you spoken to him? I ran into him yesterday, we had a drink; he'd come from Alma. I didn't have the impression that he was angry or would make trouble at her dinner. We talked about Charles, about Johan's memories of him. He told me about the attempts to contact him, but he was rather relaxed. Johan is often relaxed after he's raised hell, isn't he?"

Ellen laughs.

"I'm still glad that I no longer have to experience those mood changes from up close. And I don't think that he's going to disrupt the situation this time. He has more important considerations right now; compared to those, family frictions pale into insignificance. He's going to be on TV, in the papers, suddenly he's a leading painter, that's what counts for him.

"I haven't seen him since last week. I've got to keep some distance, it makes you waver. And I don't want that. I was so happy with my peace and quiet."

"Was there anything between you and your old boss?" Lisa asks, curiously. "That lumber king who was so sweet to you?"

"He liked me, and I was flattered that he liked me. Johan was such a prick at the time; I was very susceptible to someone who thought of me, who was polite and nice. But physically nothing ever happened. We did try once, but it became ridiculous. With your bare bottom on a desk, in a deserted office. And he with his nice grey slacks round his ankles, we both burst out laughing. That's definitely a sign that there's no question of real passion. We were serious enough to have to try. Later on we had to laugh about it, but we gave up on office sex. So there wasn't any wavering."

They walk. Across wetlands, between reeds and over high wooden bridges with chicken ladders. People sit eating on spread-out blankets, sit reading on folding chairs they've brought with them, and sit fishing from piers. Children are swimming, pushing one another into the water from rubber tyres, wild-looking men are busy with surf boards, the middle of the water is crawling with sailboats.

No one is walking. The path widens into a strip of meadow between two bodies of water. It is bordered by tall blackberry bushes. The branches are heavy with black fruit.

"Shall we?" asks Lisa. "You do get totally scratched and bloody; they have such mean thorns."

The most beautiful blackberries lie in the grass, on the lowest branches. They kneel, bend aside the grasses, carefully lift the branches and take off the blackberries which are so ripe that they fall into their hands. Gather. Think only of this branch, then that one. Then the next bush. Ellen feels herself calm down, Lisa no longer thinks. There is only the sun which warms their backs, the buckets which gradually get filled, the sweet scent of blackberries, the black spots shimmering before their eyes.

Then homeward, with blue mouths and scratched arms. Sweaty. Hot. The harvest on the garden table. Satisfied, with a cigarette. Shoes off.

"I'll make jam for you this afternoon," says Lisa. "I'll bring it to you next week. After everything."

"Good. Nice. Wonderful."

Both think of tomorrow. Not quite yet. Sit together in the garden like this, without a family, no obligations, no work. In the back of their thoughts they're already going through their wardrobes. Do I wear stockings, do I still have a pair of pantyhose so late in the summer; they look for a parking place, think of what time, how long, who will be there, what will actually hang there, how to keep the drifting family members in line.

"Swim?"

In the back of the orchard, out of sight of possible neighbours, they step out of their clothes and lower themselves into the brown river water. The bottom is soft, their feet quickly stir through the mud. The cool water removes the burning of the horseflies, the skin pulls tight and lets go of the blood and blackberry stains. With eyes closed, float on your back in the river, water in your hair, in your ears. Being sucked along gently by the slow current, turn over, sluggishly swim to the side, left cheek in the water, right cheek, left, right; and then let yourself be carried along again by the water, without intervening, without fear.

Lisa takes the large pan for making jam from the top shelf of the kitchen cupboard. She weighs the blackberries in the light plastic containers and lets them drop into the pan. Fire underneath, lid on top. The berries are so ripe that no water needs to be added. After five minutes Lisa lifts the lid and reveals a gruesome sight: dozens of small worms or maggots, or whatever they're called, crawling up from their comfortable berries, fighting to survive as the heat increases. They sit against the lid that Lisa rinses under the faucet, they shrivel against the hot sides of the pan (wipe off with a piece of paper; squash to death in the garbage can) and they raise themselves up, waving back and forth with the small black dot which Lisa assumes is the head, finding no place to stick to, waiting helplessly until Lisa rescues them from the heat with a spoon. Not to put them back in the blackberry bushes in the garden but to wash them mercilessly down the drain.

Keep cooking until the sturdy berries are reduced to black skins, floating in a sea of blood. Whichever berry is unwilling to let go of its shape is squashed against the side with a spoon. That works. Trails of blood trickle down. The sugar stands ready. Unbelievable how it stinks when you really smell it. The fruit juice in the pan gets large portions of sugar forced down its throat. After every sugar bombardment Lisa stirs the pot forcefully until the scratching sound stops, indicating that the syrup has absorbed the sugar. Then the next scoop. And the next one.

Slowly a miracle takes place. The syrup becomes tractable, lets the spoon roam around in it more easily and becomes more pliant. The steam rising from the pan is fragrant and makes the tooth-enamel crack. The miracle is in the change of colour. When all the sugar is absorbed, the mixture looks like a red-hot incandescent sea, clear and sparkling, where there first was ooze and darkness.

Lisa measures the level of the liquid. She makes a pencil mark on the spoon. She has to reduce the moisture by a third in order to obtain the proper consistency after cooling.

Tame, dominate, subdue. Leave the flame on high.

Meanwhile Lisa washes the glass jars and places them in hot water.

Again the pan becomes the scene for a cruel spectacle. The thick layer of peaceful fruit pulp at the surface starts to move; the circle of gas flames becomes visible in the pattern of bubbles and bulges in the blackberry soup. When the tension increases, they burst one by one and like small volcanoes let go of their lava. The movement becomes more violent and the hills higher. The mountains become one, form a massif against the side of the pan; the lava collects in the middle. Two mountain chains turn against each other, push each other over, fight for domination until one loses and slides under the other like a tectonic plate. The volcanic activity is so fierce that the hot liquid rises and rises in the pan; with bursting air bubbles, with bright red geyser jets the berries carry out their last offensive. If Lisa doesn't intervene now by turning down the source of fire and by mixing air through the boiling liquid, if she remains standing like this with the spoon idle in her right hand, the gas knob immobile under her left hand, if she can't keep her eyes off the aggressive red crucible—then it will all boil over and make sticky purplish red stains on the stove and the floor.

It's her choice: be absorbed in the fight or calm the struggle.

While the jam simmers quietly, Lisa sterilizes the jars and places them in a row. The drops which after stirring remain hanging on the wooden spoon become gradually thicker and fall less easily. From time to time a cloud of pink foam floats in the middle of the pan, and Lisa scoops it off so the glittering red remains intact.

Suddenly the colour deepens, the red darkens as a sign that the right consistency has been reached. The heat can be turned off, the jars can now be filled. When the last bubbles have simmered down, Lisa stirs a spoonful of sodium benzoate through the mass of fruit. It stinks for a short while. It is beautiful and deeply satisfying to have nature stand intact on the kitchen shelves, but it leads to intense disappointment when a green-white layer of mould becomes visible upon opening a jar of jam. The conqueror takes care that the conquered doesn't turn against him when he has retreated. If he is clever, he leaves behind a surveillance garrison.

Slowly she pours the hot jam into the jars. Lid on top, turn over quickly, set them aside on a tray covered with a wet rag. Subdued, imprisoned, and shamefaced, the blackberries stand blushing. Lisa has won.

*   *   *

Alma has started a fight whose magnitude she cannot possibly calculate. In the heat of the day she sits on a wicker chair in front of the open garden doors. She is dressed in a pink slip. Purple veins crawl up against her white legs like a vine in winter; her feet are overgrown with lumps, yellowish calluses and calcified nails. Leaning on her cane, she looks down, at this mess that only now strikes her as disturbing because it never bothers her.

A pedicure appointment is no longer possible, and she herself cannot do anything to fix things up. There is nothing to be done but to wrap everything tightly in heavy stockings. Alma has a small bench on which she can rest her feet while pulling up her stockings. She fastens the stockings with garters, easier to pull on than pantyhose although less comfortable to wear. All her life Alma has felt the metal hook of a garter belt in her back.

She looks around the room. She's made a mess of it with all those dresses she has thrown down. One by one she brings them back to the closet. Except for the blue silk which she puts on a hanger in front.

I can't go to the hairdresser in my slip. If I put on the blue dress it might get dirty. I sweat. Small hairs may get on the collar. Traces of hair dye. It's good I thought of it.

Alma takes a cotton summer dress out of the closet, blue with white flowers. She takes it to the bed and dresses herself while seated. Every manoeuvre that requires moving or taking along an object demands careful consideration ahead of time. She cannot do without her cane, even for standing she needs a support. Because of heightened concentration everything runs like clockwork, but any reflection is impossible.

A taxi. I have to order a taxi. The number of the taxi stand has

been solicitously written down next to the phone by Oscar. At three
o'clock someone will come, certainly ma'am, you can be sure!

Alma puts several hundred guilder bills into her handbag; she
has no idea how much she'll have to pay the hairdresser and no idea
what else she'll do. Everything has become so different. When she
becomes aware of her body for a moment, she notices a nagging pain
in her hip joint and a tired feeling in her back. The pain in her left
arm is gone; the arm does feel strangely tired as if it isn't really a part
of her. She still can't put up her hair.

Soon it will have to be undone anyway. I'll leave it like this.

Looking in the bathroom mirror she no longer is so sure of it.
The wreath of loose hair gives an unhealthy air to her pale face with
the bony nose; she looks sickly and frankly unpleasant. A headscarf,
a shawl over it.

Have I eaten anything today? I have to drink something with
this heat.

Alma stumbles to the kitchen which is an immense chaos.
On the counter lie the remnants of the stone cake. On the stove are
pans with yesterday's food, the evening meal for Oscar that was never
consumed. Dirty plates, cups with leftover coffee in them, a sickly
smell of dirty dishes.

She drinks a glass of water and closes the kitchen door. One
has to set priorities. With the handbag on her lap and the cane next
to her, she sits down on the chair next to the front door. She sighs.
She dries her face with the white handkerchief. Tears? Yes, tears.

What am I doing, what's happening all of a sudden? I was
going after something, but why? And I can't even run anymore. The
boys. I'm meeting the boys!

The thought reassures Alma. Her grandchildren are picking
her up at the new hairdresser. A vague feeling that everything is all
right if the family knows about it comes over her. Breathing quietly
she waits for the taxi. She has the house key in her hand; she will
lock the door before she steps into the car. Key and handbag on the
left, cane on the right, feet on the floor.

Without hesitating, Alma enters the hair salon and stands in a bright reception area with display windows. There is a counter behind which a woman sits telephoning. Her head is shaven, light blond tufts stick out in all directions. The woman looks in Alma's direction but keeps talking on the telephone. In front of the display window there is a small table with chairs. Another customer is sitting there, a woman of Ellen's age. A staircase goes up to the actual hairdressers' area where mirrors stand scattered with tall chairs in front of them. In between them, young men in black move back and forth, dancing. Desperate pounding music reverberates through the whole store.

Now Alma is seized by an impulse to turn on her heels. But the taxi has already gone. What could she do on the street, and she has an appointment here; she'll embarrass Ellen if she doesn't keep it.

It's even warmer here than outside, if that's possible. A smell of shampoo lingers which is not unpleasant in itself; however, it has an undertone of wet hair. Queasy. Can't stand any longer. Sit at the table? But then will have to get up when punkhead has time. Better wait a bit. Please, look at me!

Punkhead puts down the phone, leafs in a large appointment book, finally turns her face with a glistening crimson mouth to Alma with a questioning expression.

"My daughter-in-law has made an appointment for me. At four o'clock."

The woman looks surprised, almost disparaging. It's not yet three thirty. She seems to think that people who admit that they have time to spare don't count. She has no eyebrows, otherwise she would have raised them.

"Your name?"

Hobbema is nowhere in the large appointment book. Sweat prickles Alma's back. And pain. If she could only sit down.

"Who made the appointment?"

"My daughter-in-law, Ellen Visser. Yesterday."

The telephone rings again. She picks it up.

"Hair Technique, good after*noon?*"

"Two weeks. Yes, very busy."

"Tuesday at one-thirty. With Olav. In three weeks then. Your phone number?"

Punkhead writes in the appointment book and resumes her conversation with Alma.

"What did you say?"

Alma repeats, hopes, waits anxiously.

"Oh yes, he has fitted you in. An exception. Edwin will do you. You may wait here. He's still busy. Would you like tea?"

Alma lowers herself into a chair near the shop window. On the street people walk by; if there were no window in between, you could touch them. They are wearing shorts and sleeveless T-shirts. On a terrace across the street, people are drinking beer under awnings, their legs lazily stretched out in front of them.

Alma thankfully receives her tea. She doesn't dare to ask for sugar. The thought of sweetness suddenly makes her hungry; she must have forgotten to eat today. Nothing to be done about it.

A young man comes down the stairs and shakes the hand of the waiting client. He is wearing a ballet leotards with a black tunic. The armholes are so big that you can see his bare chest. On his feet he has high black laced boots that look like Ellen's hiking boots. The young man has long, unwashed hair that falls sloppily around his shoulders. He takes the woman upstairs; their heads close, they confer about the hairdo to be created.

Strange that they advertise their trade so poorly, thinks Alma. All the people who work here have hairdos that are a disgrace. A girl in a black bathing-suit is sweeping the floor. One half of her head has been shaven. On the other half, her hair is stuck to her cheek like a raven's wing.

"Is Edwin in yet?" Punkhead calls out to the upstairs in general, through the music. No, Edwin isn't there yet. Alma leans back; the back of the chair is too low. A blond man in jeans comes down, holding a credit card. His face looks familiar to Alma, from the television? From the papers? His hair looks like it's dripping with grease;

it hangs over his forehead stuck together in strings. At the back it's shaven very high up; the transition from tanned skin to fresh pallor can be seen clearly.

"It turned out great," says Punkhead.

While the man is paying his bill, a husky black man enters the shop in a hurry; he's wearing smoothly flowing, wide harem pants which are tied at the ankles. Bare black feet in sandals, a sleeveless sweater from which extend two sturdy upper arms. Punkhead whispers to him and together they look in Alma's direction. The black man nods. He goes up to Alma and extends his hand.

"Edwin. Would you come with me?"

Alma smells a strong odour of gin. Oh God, what is going to happen to me? How do I get away from here? If I'd only stayed home!

To her surprise, Edwin helps her up the stairs solicitously, at an unhurried pace. He leads her to a chair near a window.

"We're first going to decide what should be done. Please sit down."

The chair is made of canvas and is high. The chair into which Edwin lifts her looks like a children's high chair. She finds no hold for her feet, her legs dangle helplessly, Edwin has placed the cane against the wall.

Now Alma looks into the mirror. She sees Edwin's head, bald on all sides, but with a sturdy little hair mat on top. He looks at her in the mirror. Then she looks at herself also. Shocked. Blushes with shame. A neglected old woman. Unkempt. A pathetic old witch. Tears well up in her eyes. This undertaking is hopeless, this isn't good, she must get out of here.

Edwin has taken a comb from the wide folds of his pants. Not very clean, Alma notices, but protesting is the last thing she wants to do. No sound would come if she tried to talk.

The black hands lift the dirty grey hair from her shoulders, move it, up, down, with a twist to the back.

"Putting it up must have become troublesome? Do you want to keep it long?"

No, Alma shakes in the mirror, distraught.

"You know, if I were you, I would have it short. Nice, now that it's so warm. And it looks so much sweeter when it falls around your face."

He models the worn hair around her cheeks. He sees something that I don't see, thinks Alma, he sees a sweet grandmother who can no longer get her hands to her neck. "We should really colour it white. Silver white. It would look lovely on you. But the colouring studio is already closed for the day, so that's not longer possible. I can cut it short, slightly rounded so that it falls against your cheeks. Yes?"

Alma nods, struck dumb.

First Edwin wants to wash her hair and helps her out of the high chair. At the back of the room is a wash basin; Alma has to sit down in front of it, it's quite a fuss, and stumbling around with the cane, with towels and the adjustable chair until she is seated just right.

Head back, the neck hurts; Edwin makes calming noises and fiddles with a tap outside her field of vision. He's testing the water temperature! Alma surrenders.

Defenceless, her pounding old-woman's throat lies exposed, she no longer wants to flee; what must happen will take place without interference from her.

The man washes the woman's hair. The warm stream, the first massage with fragrant soap. The scalp is touched lightly, almost playfully the fingertips go over the temples, down against the back of the head. Goosebumps.

"Cold?"

Alma shakes her head no. The water is exactly right. Rinse. Still more shampoo. Vigorous movements, the soap is rubbed in firmly but carefully. Both temples at once; Alma closes her eyes. Oh.

Clumps of foam on her forehead. The solicitous hand wipes them off. Shivers of pleasure when the fingers press deep into her neck. No more thoughts.

"Let it penetrate for a while. That's good for the hair."

Edwin moves away. Alma, motionless, listens to the distant

clatter of his sandals, to the passionate music (a high voice cries out about love), and to the scraps of conversation that rise all around.

"The photographer wanted it exactly the other way. Not right, I thought."

"A few reddish tufts, but no more, above all not too many."

"Golf is no longer acceptable, I think. Croquet perhaps, in the garden at home. But golf absolutely not."

The sandals approach. Stale cigarette smoke mixed with something spicy. Hash? Rinse out. The large hand as a protective shell against her forehead so that the soap doesn't get into her eyes. The hair squeaks when the foam is gone. Dry off. Sit upright. Slightly dizzy. Edwin drapes the towel around her head like a turban. Move to the canvas chair. Mirror.

A white face with a trembling chin. The cheeks hang in creases at both sides of the nose. The mouth is a straight, pale line. Under the corners of the mouth those treacherous spots of very old, very fragile skin. The look in the eyes comes from far away.

Disillusionment when the turban comes off. Through the wet hair the scalp can be seen. The head itself seems so small, so vulnerable as if I'm becoming continually smaller and will shrink until I disappear, thinks Alma.

Edwin is busy with the dirty comb and large scissors. He is sitting on a bike saddle mounted on a pole with castors; he pedals around Alma on his sandals, taking a snip here and there with his silver tools. In the mirror Alma sees the street; people who get into their cars on the wrong side and drive away like the British. With endless patience Edwin cuts her hair, layer after layer, continually checking the symmetry of the composition by using both hands to bring the ends of her hair simultaneously to her chin. He lifts a strand of hair between his fingers and cuts the ends of the hairs with the points of the scissors. This is how he goes round, and round, and round. On the floor lie grey black wisps. He has wrapped Alma in a black cape, under it her hands lie in her lap.

He combs her hair from her forehead to the back and lets a part fall. After three quarters of an hour, he picks up the hairdryer that is lying next to the mirror on the floor. All that time Edwin and Alma have not spoken.

With the hairdryer he blows life into the old woman. The hair colours to a lighter grey, waves away from the head, surrounds the face.

The eyes begin to shine, the lips shape into a smile. When Edwin takes off the cape with a sweeping gesture, Alma gets up out of the chair without help. Taking no chances, Edwin hands her the cane. In her free hand Alma gets a mirror; she turns around and sees her back. A beautiful back: the hair, freed from weight, dances against her summer dress. It shines, it curves in smoothly and easily. She shakes her head and the hair moves with her.

Edwin sweeps the old hair together with the broom; then he escorts Alma downstairs.

"Ninety-two fifty," says Punkhead.

Alma gives her one hundred guilders and turns to Edwin into whose hand she also puts a bill of one hundred guilders. He looks dumbfounded. Without being able to utter a word, Alma steps outside.

Meanwhile Peter and Paul have sat down on the terrace across the street and are watching the door of the hairdresser's. When Alma appears, Paul crosses the street to get her. She sits down between her grandchildren. Countless young men take care of me, she thinks, of different races, with different hair colours, with or without recompense. Tomorrow I'll see my husband, whom I loved, who painted me. It is an eternal shame that the large portrait has been lost. I've always been surrounded by painters. Always the stink of thinners, always stains that didn't come out in the laundry.

"Your hair turned out beautifully, Grandma. Do you want to eat something? What would you like to drink?"

The boys, Johan's boys, on a Saturday afternoon in town with Grandma. Like the old days. Special tiny pancakes in the large stand on the market, pastries in the tearoom, later, hamburgers at McDonald's. And now the roles are reversed. The weekend has started, the wave breaks on its way to the beach, whoever wants to come along has to float along.

"Beer," says Alma. "It foams so beautifully, and the water beads up on the glasses because of temperature variations. Look, next to us, how beautiful. And let me have a croquette with it. I'm hungry. Two croquettes, with mustard."

Without batting an eye, the two boys fulfil her wishes.

"They're hot, Grandma, shall I cut them open for you so they can cool off?"

Steam bursts from the warm croquettes, the cold beer glass is indeed exquisitely frosted, and the cold beer is a refreshment, a reward, a promise.

Between themselves the boys talk about amazing fish catches, about fishing poles, about imitation insects to fool pikes. During their vacation they caught salmon in the north of Scandinavia and look back on it with nostalgia.

They're always together, thinks Alma. For twenty-five years they've slept in one room, experienced the same things, never alone. Peter says what Paul thinks. In conversation with others they are always disappointed that the person they're speaking to cannot read their thoughts and needs so much explanation. When they're together again, it's a relief. Paul is slightly smaller than Peter. Peter has a scar on his cheek where one time the hook of a casting rod got caught. For the rest they are the same. The feeling that I've known all my life, being alone with yourself, they don't know what that is. Are the two of them alone together? Or are they never alone, is there no alone when you lie in the cradle with your mirror image?

Maybe they have quite different feelings from ordinary people. At any rate they don't know the explosive irritability that was always present between Johan and Oscar. Then I never sat so relaxed, listening to the peaceful rippling of the conversation, setting aside all alertness. A trip to the city was an ordeal during which all parties kept a very close watch on one another; it could end in a scuffle at any moment. Who was allowed to sit next to the window in the tram, the other looking away, surly-faced. Who got the larger pastry in the lunchroom of the department store. Kicking each other's shins under the table. Comparing birthday presents, bedtimes, privileges.

Still there was something to it, that fight for your own territory, the never-ceasing fight for your rights. It was fascinating. It was creepy when it was missing for once, on a free Wednesday afternoon, during a vacation, at a rare Christmas celebration that satisfied both children. A person who fights and is jealous, that person is alive.

"Are you feeling all right, Grandma?"

No, suddenly Alma feels far from all right. The beer feels cold in her stomach, the greasy croquette has made her nauseated, and she feels a terrible headache spreading up from her shoulders.

"Everything is so different. I never go to the hairdresser. He was so nice, such a nice young man. Now I'm suddenly quite tired."

Peter goes to get the car and Paul pays the bill. Alma remains sitting in her chair. Across the street, the hairdresser's shop is closing. Punkhead and Edwin leave the store together. Alma touches her new hair. It's still there.

*

The boys go inside with her. Paul takes a look at the kitchen and starts stacking dishes and throwing away the leftovers of the cake. In the living room Paul misses *The Postman.*

"Johan has picked him up; tomorrow he'll hang with the other paintings. You'll be there at the start, too, won't you?"

"We've been sent for. Are we supposed to come and pick you up?"

"Ellen is going to come by, you can make your own way."

I wish they'd leave, thinks Alma. From the kitchen there is the clatter of cutlery and plates, afterwards the roar of the dishwasher, a present from Oscar.

When they've left I'll go to the toilet. Take off my stockings. To bed. Go away, do go!

The boys stand in the living room, hesitating. Clouds have appeared outside. It's hot and muggy, the air is damp, there is no wind.

*81*

Alma kisses her grandchildren and pushes them to the door; thanks for bringing me home, for the croquettes. The boys always walk and stand close to each other without bumping into each other or being in each other's way. Like a four-legged animal they leave the house.

This is alone, Alma thinks. This, the way it is now, is alone. It's terrible, but I can no longer be otherwise. Another person's touch makes me sick. The hands of that black man made me beside myself, I couldn't bear it. If only the wind would blow so you could feel it.

In the bathroom, Alma bathes her face with cold water. Sitting on the toilet she wriggles out of her stockings and reaches behind her back to loosen the garter belt. She takes off her dress and in her pink slip walks into the garden where she sits down between the high acanthus.

\*   \*   \*

"Oscar? It's Ellen, am I interrupting you?"

"No, no." Oscar gets palpitations, clammy sweat, trembling hands.

"I thought I'd call to check how you're doing. Was it awful yesterday?"

Oscar sits down to calm his breathing. Was it awful, she asks. Yes, it was awful.

"Alma isn't herself, Ellen. I'm worried about her."

He tells about the dramatic visit to his mother and the mysterious appearance of the cake.

"She was in a state of euphoria. I didn't know what to do. I said: he has never thought of you again, the cake is from me."

"Did that help?"

"It made no difference what I said. She didn't hear me. I smashed that wretched cake to pieces in the kitchen, Ellen. That's how angry I was. And I was in the attic."

"In the attic?"

"I no longer believed anything. That she'd never again been in touch with Charles, that she had kept nothing of his, suddenly I no longer believed it. I went looking; I wanted to look everywhere. It was because she acted so strangely, she acted as if she's having an affair with him. And who sent that cake?"

Ellen is quiet for a moment.

"Ellen? What do you think? Was it Charles? Someone must have done it, and it wasn't me!"

"You know, Oscar, it could be Johan. Maybe he sent her the cake, out of spite because she's always going on at him about Charles' painting skills, or because he was angry at her. Or just because, on an impulse, to do something nice—after all, his name is Steenkamer!"

That reduced Oscar to silence. The puzzle is solved but there is no relief. Now it's about Charles and Johan again, and he sits barking harmlessly behind Alma's chair like an old lapdog.

"Yes, that could be. Johan. Of course." Oscar's voice sounds flat. A great weariness comes over him, holding the telephone next to his ear is almost too much for him. Ellen is talking, her voice comes from very far. She is talking about tomorrow, that she will pick up Alma, he doesn't have to do it; if he will please come to the dinner anyway; if he actually found anything in that attic?

"It was completely empty. There was nothing. There were shelves with nothing on them."

"What had you expected?"

"People save things, don't they? She's seventy-five years old and has always lived in the same house; then you must have junk, stuff from the past that you don't want to get rid of, things that you keep because you might need them again some time, who knows, whatever—but there was nothing. I was looking for things belonging to Charles, of course, sketchbooks, perhaps letters, his viola. I looked like a fool on that ladder with my head in that empty attic. I ran away. I was so furious, I didn't even stay for dinner."

"You have to relax. Put on some beautiful music, take off your shoes. It's Saturday, you have the day off. Tomorrow will be bad enough. Is it warm in your place as well?"

"Oppressive. I'm going to open the windows, 'Sweet of you to call, Ellen.'"

Oscar's energy returns when he again sees himself standing on the stairs to the attic, capable of unexpected heroic deeds. He gets up from the grey office chair next to the telephone table in the hall and goes into the living room. The orderliness in the room makes him content. On the giant grey table lie neatly stacked papers and magazines, several stacks in front of each of the three chairs. There is one spot for the administration, one for office chores, and one for keeping his music catalogue up to date. Oscar never has to tidy up because it's always neat. He eats in his kitchen and looks at television in his bedroom. His bookcase is also in the bedroom, that way he's not so lonely at night. Near the table in the living room are two easy chairs next to a stereo set. Against the wall are the records and CDs; on narrow shelves underneath the sills of the tall windows he keeps the cassettes.

As a concession to the weather, Oscar removes his shoes and places them on the shoe shelf in the hall. The top button of his shirt may be unbuttoned, the necktie off, subject to being put away in the bedroom closet, just like the jacket.

Messy, all those different sound-recording mediums, and ever more equipment to play them. Whenever he walks into the room, the music area with its variously shaped objects bothers him. Acquiring, buying all that gear has repeatedly caused him dizziness in cluttered, inconveniently arranged music warehouses. Sweating while going through stacks of CD boxes one by one, as other buyers rush you, grab things out of your hands, and push against you with their bodies. He doesn't even dare to ask if he may hear a piece; he buys at the suggestions from music magazines and the newspaper.

There should be a central sound registry where all kinds of music and all performances were perfectly recorded. You would then be able to subscribe to it, for jazz, or choral singing, or several categories at once. Of course it would be more expensive then. The subscriber would receive a monthly paper with the newest acquisitions and of course the catalogue of his preferred areas when he starts his subscription. All advertising becomes superfluous. Cursing while searching through crackling radio stations will be a thing of the past.

Through the telephone (access number, catalogue number of the work you want to hear) you indicate your wish; the sound comes almost immediately via the speaker which is attached to the system. No more confusion, no more missing something, never again be rendered speechless by contacts with rushed salespeople. The arrangement of the catalogue demands more study, but he'll work that out.

The large record companies will be against it, that's for sure. This plan means their demise because musicians will be under direct contract with the Central Archive. Oscar sighs. No music now, work has to be done, catch up on time wasted yesterday.

He takes the management report out of his briefcase and places it on the table, in front of the chair intended for business concerning the museum. Socks off also? No, better not. A glass of water. Windows open, light grey shade down. Glasses off, reading glasses on.

The report is written in the director's woolly, nearly impenetrable style. The subject of the document is the demarcation between the collections of the Municipal and the National Museums.

Since the Municipal Museum's establishment in the fifties, there has been an ongoing battle between the brazen newcomer and the experienced veteran which until then had had hegemony over paintings. The Municipal Museum did not have an old collection but acquired new works and became "modern". Old art was the domain of the rival who was, however, unwilling to resign himself to this and continued making acquisitions. The result: inflated prices, two hot-headed directors against one another at auctions, painters who played one museum off against the other and, after some time, cabinet-level intervention.

The director was always in a foul mood when he came from the monthly working group meeting on Wednesday afternoon. His collection was eroded, that windbag from the Municipal with his rolled-up jacket sleeves was attacking his integrity; he would rather blow up the entire collection of paintings than hand over even one canvas to that good-for-nothing.

"As for restoration, they can't do that at all, Steenkamer, they simply have no feeling for history. Everything is now, immediate. They never think that it's decaying before their eyes if you don't intervene. Intervene expertly! Expertly!"

Now the report is ready. They haven't come to a agreement, but there is hope. Oscar is leafing through it. The director of the Municipal Museum wants to merge; he's got big ideas. All plastic arts under one management, preferably under one roof, prestigious new construction, ultimately under one director, he himself.

A bit too ambitiously stated, Oscar thinks. It would have been wiser for him to have held his tongue about the division of director's functions, it harms his position. The working group members agree that the stopgap measure is not pretty and has caused absurd splitting of oeuvres. Sometimes there are misunderstandings, not every painter dates his work equally carefully; there was a case of fraud with purposely incorrect dating so that the artist in question could see all his work gathered in the Municipal Museum (the casually fashionable Municipal Museum director looked innocently into space when that point was being discussed); management, artists and the public all are dissatisfied. The government official suggests making a division on grounds of artistic criteria: modern art here, old art there. A permanent commission would have to be appointed to decide what is modern.

Oscar yields to inner jeering. Everything is modern. And nothing. Take Johan, who would have to house his old, abstract work in the Municipal and his later figurative work which has made him famous in the National! Absurd. Unworkable.

Actually the suggestion of Oscar's own director is the most sensible: take the age of the painters and not that of the paintings as criterion. Whoever was born before 1950 belongs in the National, irrespective of the character of his work. The young painters come under the Municipal, the National is not concerned with them.

Good, thinks Oscar. A delimited collection which will gradually be completed. Then the emphasis will be on conservation, expanding the scope of the collection, placement policy. The hare-brained hotheads with their megalomaniac projects, carried out with poor quality materials, can be placed with the windbag. Very good, and very well presented too. But Municipal doesn't buy it and threatens to leave. The division has to be made at the turn of the century. Not later. Implicitly the Municipal therefore agrees that the principle is acceptable; there still has to be a struggle about the year. Oscar knows for sure that his director can't stand to have all that trash of the painters who are now forty or fifty years old all over the museum. They'll settle on 1925, probably. Then Johan will definitely belong to the Municipal, and Charles to the National.

Charles! Charles' paintings! Is it possible that they're in the National? 1950. Made well before that time. The Municipal didn't even exist.

Oscar feels as though he's going to faint; his idea has totally taken him by surprise. The museum that he knows, where he feels safe, that is his own trusted domain, contains a bomb. Or possibly contains one; it is after all by no means certain that Charles' work is in the storage rooms, by no means. Even rather unlikely, for how would it have landed there? And how could it have been hidden from Oscar's observation for all these years?

First my mother deceives me and now this, everything has become different. They keep things hidden from me, they tell me nothing because I'm unimportant, I don't count. Dammit. In my own museum. That's impossible.

Yesterday's agitation flares again and takes possession of Oscar. The file lies opened on the table, the chair in front of it stands crooked, and Oscar paces up and down the room, mumbling.

"Searched, searched for things belonging to Papa. And now right under my nose! And no one ever said anything? I have to go there. I have to know it now.

He stuffs the bunch of keys in his pocket, puts on his shoes, and races down the stairs. When he closes the front door behind him the muggy, clammy heat descends on him. Hurriedly, in shirt sleeves, he goes to the museum.

The stores are almost closing, but the street is still filled with people. They're restless, they still have to buy something fast, they're in a hurry, they're in a bad mood because the sun has disappeared, they bump against Oscar without apologizing. With screeching brakes a convertible stops for him as he crosses, fucking blind bastard, idiot, looking for a fight, screams the driver. To deaf ears. Oscar has deactivated one sense after the other and notices nothing.

At the museum entrance the last visitors are being led outside where buses are waiting for them. Oscar hurries up the stairs, the doorman looks surprised. Oscar is completely drenched in sweat, his shirt sticks to his shoulders. Left jacket at home. Stupid. That's not done.

"I'm just going to my office. I've left something. Have to check on something. I have the keys with me."

Oscar shows the heavy bunch of keys. Why explain everything, is it any of their business? I'm a child that has to give a justification. As if I'm going to do forbidden things, as if I'm not allowed to be here!

This phrasing is in keeping with what Oscar feels: illegal presence, reprehensible motives. I'm supposed to be at home with my reports. They have a right to be present, the coat-takers, the ticket-sellers, and the attendants. Not me.

"The office is working today!" the guard says appreciatively. "Mrs Bellefroid is still here, too; she's been typing all afternoon."

For a moment Oscar is scared: will Keetje Bellefroid throw a monkeywrench in the works, make it impossible to carry out his plan? Does he dare to go and look in the registration system if she's there?

Most certainly he dares to do that. The possibility of finding something as the result of his search for Charles, of counteracting some of the terrible hurt and frustration in Alma's attic, gives him wings and heroic courage. It's actually a nice idea; Keetje can perhaps help him, and the fact that she's there legitimizes his own presence somewhat in his mind.

She's frightened stiff when he walks in with his pale bird's head in which the eyes flame darkly from behind the thick glasses. With the bunch of keys raised in his fist, he stands in front of her desk as if a giant has flung him down right there.

"Oops, you gave me a fright, Mr Steenkamer; I didn't know that you were going to come. Do stay for a moment, shall I make you a cup of tea? Everything seems to be taking extra time: a new report for the extra meeting on Monday, the working group with the Municipal you know, you've seen the file, that's what it's about, we are going to submit a proposal, well, we, that's to say the director. He would like to have it this evening, it's much more work than I thought but I'm just talking, do sit down, you don't look exactly great!"

Keetje Bellefroid is an elderly lady, plump and pleasant. For Oscar her words are a tepid, relaxing shower. He sits down across from her while she boils water in the electric kettle. Tea with a lot of sugar. Oscar stirs absent-mindedly.

"You know, Keetje, I'm not coming for that. But it's nice that you're here now, so I can ask you something. Do you know the painter Steenkamer?"

"You mean your brother? The one who's having the big exhibition in the Municipal? Of course I'm going there, next week on my day off, I certainly know him, Steenkamer. But you don't look much like him, I think, I wouldn't say that he was your brother."

"He's not the one I mean, Keetje. My father was a painter too. His name was Charles. Well, that's still his name, but he no longer paints. He lives in America. He left when we were very young. I've actually never seen work by him. I can vaguely remember that there was something, a few paintings, but I have no idea what's happened to them. This afternoon, suddenly, I realized that I've never looked here. But there's probably nothing, otherwise I'd know it."

"Well, Mr. Steenkamer, that isn't certain. How old is your father?"

"Born in 1920, Keetje."

"Now, you see! You aren't that far yet with your catalogue. You've never seen data from that time. Shall I take a look for you?"

Keetje is totally ready for this romantic task: pathetic, lonely Steenkamer is looking for his father. On his Saturday afternoon off.

"Steenkamer, 1920," mumbles Keetje as she walks to the room

where the old files are kept. She has bare legs of whitish flesh and sandals because of the heat, white summer shoes with a low heel, above them a loose flowered dress. Oscar watches her with a certain pleasure.

"Well this is strange," says Keetje as she scurries back to the office, "there is a card in the Steenkamer file: 'see Bramelaar bequest' it says, nothing else, yes, it says four pieces, up here."

Bramelaar, Bramelaar—that name sounds familiar to Oscar. He closes his eyes to help his memory, Bramelaar—it doesn't work.

"I could look at the correspondence, in the old archive? I'll be gone a little while, it's a bit of a walk."

The offices lie at the back of the building, on the second floor is the board of directors and membership, on the third, where Oscar and Keetje are now, is the administration, and on the fourth is the research department. That's also Oscar's work area. The archives are kept on the fifth floor, underneath the immense attic which is the storage depot.

Oscar waits and drinks his tea. He tries not to think. If she finds something will it be good or terrible? And who was Bramelaar?

*

"Leo Bramelaar Sr. and Jr. violin makers," announces the letterhead. Keetje hands him the letter from the yellowed file folder. It was typed on an old machine and signed by hand by Junior, in 1949.

The viola, remembers Oscar. Papa plays on a Bramelaar which Mr Bramelaar built for him. A shiny, flawless instrument with golden red varnish, it smelled special, of oil, a new smell but still like furniture wax, distinguished. In the letter Junior outlines the situation succinctly: when Steenkamer left, he brought the viola and four paintings to Bramelaar. Bramelaar bought back the viola and later put it up for sale; the paintings remained in the workshop, for it was unclear whether they had been given outright or given in safekeeping. Senior passed away, Junior wants to renovate the shop. What to do with the works of art? Mrs Steenkamer-Hobbema, approached three times in writing, didn't respond. (The stove, thinks Oscar, unopened into the fire, out of anger!) In his will, Senior seemed to have determined that the paintings could be given as a gift to the National Museum if the family was not interested. This is why Bramelaar Jr. now donates four real Steenkamers to the museum. Bramelaar bequest.

Oscar feels himself becoming faint. Have I eaten today, so dizzy suddenly. Yes, went shopping this morning; bananas, milk, it was so busy in the supermarket, eggs. In the kitchen emptied a jar of applesauce, standing next to the refrigerator. Mr Bramelaar wore a large leather apron; a head with curls sticking out like corkscrews, a large head. In the workshop lay a violin which was completely bare, no varnish on it yet and no strings. There were sick violins and a cello without a neck. Papa played on the new viola that Mr Bramelaar had made for him. On the floor lay wood flakes and in the back there was a dark room in which small boards had been stacked in a special way in square towers. When Mr Bramelaar tapped against such a piece of wood, with the knuckle of his index finger, a tone would come out even before you played. Before it was a violin the wood already knew what it would become. Papa. The paintings. This means they're there. Four. In the storage depot in the attic. Never exhibited, says Keetje.

"Then we should go and look right away, Mr. Steenkamer. To make sure. Or do you want to go by yourself? Is it indiscreet? You have a key to the upstairs, don't you?"

The whole undertaking is indiscreet, thinks Oscar, it's a desecration, a transgression which should never take place. Let her come along, I can't do it alone. I also can't look at those pieces of paper any more, I've lost my bearings, I'm shaken, so much is happening.

"I would appreciate it if you'd accompany me, Keetje," Oscar says solemnly. "It is a special occasion, it has affected me somewhat, and it's easy to get lost in that attic."

"Come on," says Keetje Bellefroid. Resolutely she strides to the lift. Oscar follows with the bunch of keys.

In the museum attic it smells of dust. Keetje flicks on lights, but the lamps don't give much light. Behind the attic window the sky has become dark. The paintings are stored against wooden frames that you can pull out of a row; about six can hang on each frame. On the sides of the frames are numbers and letters. Keetje has a piece of paper in her hand and walks through the space between the racks. She knows where she has to go. Coughing from the dust, Oscar walks behind her, afraid to lose sight of her. At the end of a sort of passage, she is pulling at a frame, he helps her, it works, the rack, hung with four Steenkamers, rolls into the aisle.

Four paintings, three small ones and one large one, an upright rectangle. The smaller ones are square. Oscar recognizes Mr Bramelaar in the work-shop. He looks up from a violin on which he's working, as for a photographer.

A group of people with suitcases and bags; with sad faces they hold one another. In the background lies a black boat. The third painting is without people; there is an apple tree with a tawny, weather-beaten trunk. The bark is grey and fibrous, but in the crown there is nothing but life, cheerful green leaves and hundreds of small, yellow apples. Oscar can't take his eyes away from it, so strange is that image of an ancient body that with its remaining strength, denying time, carries a load of smooth, unwrinkled apples as if nothing is wrong.

Look, Oscar exhorts himself, stand in front of it and look, you've wanted this yourself, this is what you were looking for.

From the tender darkness of the rack, young Alma looks directly at him. She is wearing a jacket of black velvet with long sleeves and carries something in her arms that is lost in the dark lower half of the painting. She looks so serious that Oscar and Keetje hold their breath. Unremitting, the pouring rain rumbles on the roof; unavoidable, the gaze from the woman's face wreathed by springy blond hair.

Part 11
Elvira: *"ma tradita e abbandonata provo ancor per lui pietà"*

*Chapter four*

# Stab of Mortality

J ohan and Ellen's house stands like a run-down ship above the city's water. Everything that they and the children eat has been dragged up the steep stairs to their domain on the third and fourth floors. Mostly by Ellen. In the large living room, stacks of clutter that seem to be a part of the place accumulate, year in year out, as in a neglected garden.

Cleaning up means rearranging, placing new clutter on top of the old, leaving as little space as possible. The twins' soccer scrapbooks, Johan's magazines with photos or with reports of exhibition openings, and boxes of toys form the substratum on which newspapers and journals rain down weekly: periodicals with advertisements for middle management jobs for Ellen, rock magazines for Paul and Peter, comics for Sara. Johan keeps his art journals and one or two catalogues elsewhere.

Lately Johan himself is often elsewhere as well, and doesn't come for dinner or comes too late. He gives courses at the Fine Arts Academy where his objective and professional attitude makes him a prized teacher. He is one of the few painters of his generation who is able to live from his work: he has a proper feeling of its importance and knows how to approach the right people in the right way without compromising himself or acting contrary to his principles. By and large he works on commission; he gives form and colour to industrial halls and stations. Recently he started designing the décor and scenery for a contemporary opera. This is why he walks around in the theatre in his very expensive brand-name shoes. For him it's a new world, where director and composer show a work that will last but a few hours while his own mountains and foreshortened benches will remain in storage for years. And then there are the singers, male and female. Fascinated, he observes how they handle their bodies, their intertwined instruments. He feels how the rehearsal hall takes on the physical atmosphere of a sauna. Johan feels at home in the realm of the body.

He won't follow in his father's footsteps; he sits in the back and watches. In flashes he thinks of Charles: that's how it went, he stood up and touched those sturdy thighs, took hold of these stomachs, moved those arms, and finally became director.

Next to Johan sit Mats and Zina, students from his senior class at the Academy. They assist him. In dirty jeans they mix the paint for his strange landscapes; at the end of the work day Zina changes clothes and becomes nothing but sturdy body in soft, shiny clothes. She is fat and moves easily, she wears high heels.

After work Johan makes love with her, groaning and grunting between and over the abundant flesh. Zina renders him seigneurial rights because she belongs to Mats. The forced relationship with his admired professor creates powerless anger but also a deep satisfaction for Mats, who draws her out and, sighing, accepts the situation. He too knows Johan's attraction; when Johan stands near him during the lesson, he feels both their skins and can scarcely pay attention. The triangle remains.

When Ellen comes home this February afternoon, she finds her children in front of the television. Schoolbags and dirty plates are standing on the wooden floor. The boys have their homework on their laps;

looking pale, Sara slouches on the couch. Fortunately they don't have a cat, because the stench of a cat box would push this scene just over the edge of grubby neglect.

"What are we eating Mum. Hamburgers? Pizza? Garbage?" ask the boys.

"I think that there's nothing," says Ellen, "I'm going shopping tomorrow." Pancakes? She can already see the blue smoke hanging. In that case rather the can opener: beans, applesauce, smoked sausages.

"Is Daddy coming home?" says Sara.

"I don't know, he didn't say. We'll just start eating, we'll see."

Herringbone blazer off, old sweater on. Apron. Catch stockings on splinters. Sara, you want to help? No, too tired, rather lie down.

The children are never hungry because they eat all day. The kitchen countertop is filled with mugs of chocolate, plates with egg stains, dried-out sandwiches. Ellen puts things in order, washes dishes, clears up, sets the table and gets dinner ready in ten minutes.

Halfway through the meal he enters, the father, the man. He serves himself from the pan on the table, lukewarm beans with onion and sausage. When are you going to do some real cooking again?

This is our family, thinks Ellen, when are you going to start really being part of it again? Am I part of it myself? I've taken refuge in fatigue and overwork. Because he does it with Zina and smells of her pussy when he steps into bed. Why don't I kick him out of the house?

Peter places his mythology book on the table to show a dreadful painting: Goya's Kronos who is eating a child with sensual enjoyment.

"Now that's eating," says Johan, "too bad that you're too thin, Sara."

Frightened, the girl looks at the picture and then at her father's face.

"Lisa's fish eat their children because they forget that they're their children. Aha, there swims food, they think, but they're their babies!"

Paul asks about the opera and Johan tells how they worked on the stage for the first time today, that the director moved walls and stones because otherwise the singers can't walk freely.

"You have to be there, you have to say if that's allowed, so you're the boss, Daddy."

"Sara, you're a dummy. The conductor, he's the one who is the real boss. May we come, Dad?"

Yes, in a week it will be that time. Then we'll walk into the auditorium behind Johan, thinks Ellen. Then he'll say: for once wear something pretty, nice shoes and a sexy skirt. Buy something for once. Why, why? Why can I no longer stand it?

Ellen can't bear it that Johan has girlfriends. And that he looks for affirmation everywhere, even the children have to reassure him that he is important, everyone has to have an opinion of him, otherwise he doesn't exist. The fact that others exist, on their own, apart from him, doesn't occur to him.

Tomorrow I have important interviews, Ellen thinks; I have to select someone with whom I'll collaborate closely; and Johan doesn't understand why someone wants to work at such a shitty organization. To be totally disregarded, nothing means anything if it doesn't reflect on him.

She sees herself tired, thin, crushed.

In the small girl's room it strikes Ellen how pale and listless Sara is. As long as she can go to school tomorrow, I can't take time off, not tomorrow.

"Do you have any pain, darling, do you have a fever?"

The smooth forehead doesn't feel hot; the child sighs when she glides into bed next to Gijs, the flannel goldfish with the mysterious smile. Read aloud. Ellen sits on the bed, her back against the wall, the child between her knees, leaning against her. Nothing smells as earthy as children's hair. The slightly grubby sheets form a snug tent over their legs, the book rests on Sara's knees. Ellen reads about the captain who had to sail the seven seas, his hands were bolted to the rudder and he kept shouting: save me, save me; the courageous little girl fed him pancakes. Sleeping wasn't possible, and rescue was unlikely, for who would want to assume that fate?

Ellen falls silent. They sit together quietly, the mother and the child, high up in the house that looks like a ship.

Something of that still mood is within Ellen when she opens the kitchen windows wide the next morning. It's an in-between season that the Germans would call *"Vorfrühling"*: no bud has opened yet, the branches are as naked and black against the grey sky as in the past months, yet it is clear that it won't really freeze again.

Yesterday's gym clothes still lie stinking in Sara's backpack. Ellen puts a plastic bag with sandwiches in their place. Sara had to be woken up this morning; looking pale, she was sleeping on her back and breathed lightly. Now she slumps at the table with Gijs in her arm and doesn't eat.

"Shall I take you today, you want to ride with me?"

The child nods. The boys have already left on their bicycles, laden with books and food they cross the city at tremendous speed. Ellen puts the leftovers of their giant breakfasts on the kitchen countertop. What a blessing that no one here has been brought up in the English manner and wants smoked fish and potatoes in the morning. She herself takes coffee. Her leather bag stands at the door; for today's task she has dressed in a grey silk blouse with a black skirt and intact stockings, has made up her eyes with mascara and silver eye-shadow, brushed the herringbone jacket and hung it out. When inner order is lacking, it's important to take care of the outside as well as possible in the hope that the confused body will find support in it, that the legs know what walking is as soon as the shoe surrounds the foot, that the back will straighten under the soft silk. This is how she does it, the thirty-five-year-old woman.

She combs the dull hair with her fingers. Johan would like her to colour it; he cannot stand decline. He himself looks as if time has no hold on him. Although he sleeps little and irregularly and now and then drinks a lot, it never shows. His hair is dark, his shoulders supple, and his ass is that of a boy. A strong inner resistance against mortality takes care that his skin is taut. The people he meets in the theatre don't believe that he's the father of fifteen-year-old twins. He withdraws more and more from that role and has difficulty recognizing his children in the growing boys' bodies with giant feet.

Driftwood, thinks Ellen—we've been washed ashore, and the waves that brought us here, beautiful, happy and strong waves full of passion, have long ago been drawn back into the sea and can no longer be heard. Sparkling, the foam bubbles burst around us and we lie lost, loose from one another in the sand. Jesus, it's time, stop thinking about that.

Bag along, backpack along, coat on, shoes tied, shopping bag from the hook, keys in the hand, leave Gijs at home, down the stairs, oh, note for Johan on table about when back, button Sara's coat, down the staircase, down the staircase, out the door, outside. The car is close by. Sara is leaning against the shiny fender when Ellen unlocks the doors. She slips inside and sprawls in the leather seat, backpack between her thin girl's legs. The silver Saab starts moving and glides like a fish into the morning traffic.

"We're a fish, Sara, they also swim all together in the same direction."

"And the bicycles, they're the water fleas. We'll eat them soon. Mum, are there people who eat their babies?"

Oh yes, thinks Ellen, people who suck their children empty and throw them away. Suddenly she sees before her the kitchen where she sat with her just-born twins: one screaming on the table and one at her breast. How large the refrigerator door appeared behind the child that had turned red, how frightened she was at the idea of getting up and placing the baby in the freezing cold, closing the door, then listening to the screaming cease from between the milk cartons and the tomatoes.

"The wild men eat Captain Cook in Paul's book. He showed it to me."

Ellen says that Cook's name worked against him. And that animals and people are less inclined to eat their young as they care more and longer for them.

Then we're all right, observes Sara.

The school is adjacent to a small park. Ellen places a hand on her daughter's thin neck and opens the door. She sees the child walk slowly under the bare trees, the backpack hanging over one shoulder. Sara turns around and walking backwards she waves at her mother in the silver-grey car.

*       *

The business where Ellen works coordinates wood trading in Europe. She started in the typing pool and then for years managed the office of the executive secretary. The company grew; the director needed someone to work fulltime; the number of employees increased, and Ellen became a manager in the personnel department. Her salary is too low because she never had the required education. She works four days a week and has Fridays off for errands and laundry. The manager's name is Nicolaas Bijl. He wants her to study sociology and to specialize in business organization. He will give her part-time leave and will finance her studies, just as he also offered her the Saab. ("Has to be driven till it falls apart. It's no good to me.")

Ellen hesitates. At home she's another person than with Nicolaas Bijl. When she drives towards him, her spine straightens and she notices that her rearview mirror is too low. How can she go to evening courses, prepare examinations and projects amidst the children, under Johan's disapproving eyes? If I really wanted to, I'd do it, she thinks. Then I wouldn't be so sensitive to his disparaging looks and would stack my reference books up in the living room. No problem.

But it most certainly is a problem for the time being. She doesn't dare yet because after difficult school years she doesn't trust her mind. She feels that Bijl overestimates her because of her efficient behaviour at work, something which for her is more connected with running a household than with setting up research. However, the plans remain in her mind, and every summer she requests the university catalogue.

\*

Wood. You can't tell from the building, which is made entirely of steel and synthetic materials. Bijl doesn't want to offend the person offering Bosnian pines with a tabletop made of natural Norwegian birch. Ellen thinks that the absence of wood facilitates the concentration on pure trade. Mess and fuss are kept outside. Shivering, she sees on a computer screen the shipping of large quantities of wood from Helsinki to Antwerp in November (foghorn, blizzard). Thank goodness that no one has actually to be there.

The people who come to speak about the transactions don't remind you of wood in any way. There never enters a group of massive he-men, singing raucously, kicking against the plastic baseboards with their big shoes, carrying with them a smell of moss and rotting foliage in their corduroy pants, swinging axe and saw. Ellen generally has to be satisfied with attaché cases, trendy jackets, discreet scents, as she converses cheerfully and watchfully at the conference table of reinforced frosted glass.

On the wall of the conference room hangs a black and white photo, six feet wide, of a Swedish birch grove, a thin cloud of fragile trunks. Bijl started the photo collection, Ellen has expanded it. The oldest parts of the collection are about wood in its original state: a flowering chestnut in a British parkland, a solitary German oak with leafless twisted branches. Ellen went further and acquired a Scandinavian whitebeam hit by lightning and a fossilized Arctic palm tree. A jaunty Christmas tree salesman from Rotterdam, with spruces like dark birds that alighted at his feet, hangs in the downstairs hall. In his office Bijl has a gigantic felled beech tree with the woodcutters standing proudly around it. For the conqueror's pose the forester has to lift his leg slightly too high to be able to place his foot even on a side branch, and he looks faintly uncomfortable.

The use of wood is the next step: a South German violin maker poses proudly in front of the crosswise stacked, wedge-shaped pieces of maple that make up his capital.

A marine archaeologist is working on the restoration of an eighteenth-century sailing vessel; a sculptor cuts a chess set out of juniper branches.

Afforestation and seed trade are part of the new business line and are expressed in much enlarged images of a pear core and a little, newly germinated spruce. The black and white principle is retained adamantly, even when people turn up with beautiful colour photos.

Staff members choose the photos that hang in their field of vision; they are supposed to have a quarterly exchange among themselves which doesn't actually take place because people become quickly and fiercely attached to a scene they themselves have chosen. The only photo that Ellen has never been able to give to anyone is a picture of a coffin in natural planed oak. It now hangs in the supply room with the notepads and the pencils.

Ellen throws open the door of her room. Photos of the children on the wall, no woods. One day she'll hang the ultimate forest fire on the wall. Bijl comes and stands in her doorway while she is taking the interview papers from her bag. He is a giant in a light grey suit. His hair is cut short and is plastered against his head.

"So, my girl. We're going to select a capable assistant for you. You'll train him and then you'll continue your studies. Listen to Nicolaas."

Ellen laughs. He creates around her an atmosphere in which she flourishes, without suspicion and without guilt; a father who checks the swing and the garden gate: here you are safe.

"Listen to Ellen! We're not going to sit at that giant glass table but in your office."

Bijl walks back with her, they arrange and rearrange chairs and coffee cups until they've found a good set-up. Taking care of something together, striving for something without a struggle, respecting each other's wishes and idiosyncrasies, why is that never possible with Johan?

It's a thought that blows away fast; worry and doubt don't fit in this work climate. Here she is considered cautious at the most but never indecisive.

Friendly and concentrated she guides the conversation, letting the chair of the Work Council have the floor in time, leaving room for Nicolaas' spontaneous eruptions.

("Wood!! What is your relationship to wood?! What is your first wood memory?")

Afterwards the three of them go out to eat a sandwich.

Back in the office, towards two o'clock, she finds a note next to her telephone: "School has called, Sara ill, call back, urgent!" The operator has written down the school's number, and that's good because in the calendar of the current year Ellen has not copied the less commonly used telephone numbers.

Trembling she stands in front of her desk, angry because of the disruption to her work time, feeling guilty because she lets others take care of her child, worried when she thinks of Sara's white little face.

Standing up she calls the school, as if she has to make clear to herself that she isn't just hanging around here but is doing her heavy work, at a jog, panting. Via a parent volunteer who had stayed behind ("Are you a parent? I don't know if you can interrupt now. It's class-time.") and the concierge who starts holding forth about his mobile home and his dogs, she is put through to Sara's teacher, stern Mara. This vegetarian feminist dresses in grey cloth and wide trousers, she knows no make-up, no bras, no mercy. Certainly not for women who close their eyes and exhale slowly when, with naked shoulder blades, they stand leaning against a man's chest. She leads the class without humour but with much grim justice. Her life truths (never go outside without your laces tied; even without a clock be on time for everything; skin colour and country of origin are irrelevant) are mercilessly etched into the ten-year-old heads. What Mara says is baggage for later. In her class no one has to feel like a fool. But there is seldom laughter. When on her tenth birthday Sara treated the class to chocolate éclairs, sometimes called "black kisses", she received a lecture on discrimination and sexism. Ellen was furious when she heard the story at Sara's birthday dinner. Because things are never ever good, because such a woman can by definition never be satisfied as long as there is injustice anywhere. If the child had brought decorated carrots, it would have been considered as a repression of the lesbian part of the nation, or as blind love for the royal house of Orange.

Ellen remains at a distance, she tries to keep good and open relations with those who take care of her children and therefore settles for things which she would otherwise not accept. She lets the children pull their own chestnuts out of the fire, sometimes urges them to protest, to follow their own intuition.

Grumpy and curt, but with a sincerely worried ring in her abrasive voice, Mara addresses her:

"We couldn't reach you. Your husband wasn't home either. Fortunately Nadja from the kindergarten still remembered where you work. But you weren't there either."

Ellen senses the reproach and suppresses her fiercely flaring exasperation. If I'd been sitting at home she would have been angry that I was doing nothing while she is working herself to death with the children. The woman has a job herself, doesn't she? Am I responsible for Johan's being reachable? Why doesn't she call the theatre, it's in the paper every day that he's working there. Tell me what's wrong with my daughter, I'll take on all the guilt, I'm standing ready to do penance, head bowed but straining at the bit.

Sara has been taken to hospital.

In class she turned white and whiter, she didn't participate in the singing and slowly slipped to the floor during the group discussion. She lay on a stretcher in the office of the school principal; Stanley, a big black man from Surinam who was a nurse before going into teaching, saw that she became bluer and seemed to hear little of what he said to her. At his urging they called: home, in vain; the lumber company office, in vain; the general practitioner in attendance who, without seeing the patient, immediately called the ambulance when he heard that the child was unconscious.

Sara has been taken to hospital.

Stanley abandoned his class and sat next to Sara's head in the ambulance, her small backpack with her sandwiches on his lap. He called her "my pet", held her cold hand, but she didn't notice. He took along the paltry data of the last checkup by the school doctor (Sara Steenkamer, weight 34 kilo, foot position neg.). Ellen understands Mara's words and feels nothing.

Sara has been taken to hospital!

\* \* \*

On her way to Southern Hospital Ellen is disoriented. Not as regards the direction but in time—the large signs along the beltway indicate the exit to the hospital clearly and in plenty of time. It is as though the partitions in her head between the various compartments of her life have been rammed together. At around three in the afternoon she is supposed to feel uncomplicated, safe in the work area of Bijl's garden. Her main feeling is exasperation. She feels annoyed, the backpack with domestic duties and conflicts has landed back on her shoulders too early.

Where to? Neurology? Internal medicine? First aid? Children's section, of course. The indescribable fear that is linked to the specialties seems to be wiped out by the addition of "children". *There* nothing is wrong, there it's supposed to be pleasant. Now park, way too far from the entrance. Against the cold wind to the big revolving door which moves excruciatingly slowly. Past the doorman, the doorkeeper team, six of them are drinking coffee and chatting with visitors, caps on the desk, jackets over the chairs. Information signs, stand still, think. Top floor. Arrow to lifts. Lifts. I have to go to the lifts. It looks like a Mediterranean square here, people sit at small tables with glasses and ashtrays in front of them, a buzz of conversations. So much white: doctors' coats, legs in plaster casts, sheets on the beds that have been pushed up. Restless children who clamber on the sculptures, a mother calling out harshly. Children's section, I have to go to the children's section.

In front of the lift doors stands a group of people: patients in bathrobes, visitors with full plastic bags and whole flower arrangements, a janitor with a kind of ice-cream cart filled with cleaning equipment, doctors with their coats hanging open. When a lift stops, people crowd in good-naturedly. Ellen recoils at the small crowded room although a friendly dark woman makes space for her. Two people in wheelchairs come from the next lift. Skilfully they make the turn to the lobby, shout to each other and laugh. Ellen steps into the lift, a room with closed walls and a panel with buttons as the only exit. She pushes the top button and stands in the back against the wall. People who come in also push their button, prepare to wait patiently. All know the rules. A woman comes in with two children who silently hold onto her by the hem of her coat. Two residents with tired faces talk about a weekend sailing trip as they stand leaning against the wall. A lab technician gets in next to Ellen. She has a stack of records in her arms. On the top is a board with a yellow paper clipped to it. Patient Sneefhart. Doctor Baudoin. A list of lab results. If you could concentrate, you would be able to take in Sneefhart's condition and prognosis. There are no secrets. In the outpatient clinic where Ellen sometimes went for Paul and Peter's hay fever, the most intimate patient data were revealed on a kind of television screen to all interested parties. Loudly they discussed kinship ("Is that also the biological father?") and present and past venereal diseases. There are no secrets. Except for the secret. Does Sneefhart know his own diagnosis? Will Baudoin hand him the yellow paper and patiently explain the meaning of numbers and symbols to him? Racks with files stand in the hall, for inspection by the passer-by. Will they tell you what's wrong with Sara? They? Suddenly Ellen notices that her legs are trembling as if she's going into battle.

The lift stops. When the doors slide open there stands a high bed that seems even higher because of the IV stand mounted on it.

The nurses stand on either side like helmsman and sailor. The passenger lies with his head to the side. A tube comes out of his mouth. His hands are tied to the nickel bed rails.

All the people quickly leave the lift. Patients have priority, provided they're in bed. Ellen shuffles out behind the others. Immunology, it says on the wall facing the lift, fifth floor.

Her throat feels thick and her eyes are stinging. This isn't good at all. This is a sort of hell where you're mistreated and misled and from where you never, never leave. Isn't there a staircase? Mastering the stairs with buckling knees might bring about some self-motivation, a flickering illusion of power. Ellen looks behind the doors of the fifth floor, haematology. No staircase. The glass stairwell at the end of a hall is locked. A nurse wearing a mask points with her bare arm to the group of people in front of the lift. *That's* your place. Blindly, Ellen plunges into the next lift, in between a Surinam family with bags of dirty laundry, with half a roti on paper plates. It smells of the market, of a fair. There is no happy-go-lucky music, only the sound of jaws chewing gum, a coughing man, the noisily chewing roti eaters.

When she opens her eyes, Ellen is again standing in the main lobby with the small tables. A quarter past three on the large clock without numbers above the exit. She suppresses the impulse to run out of the hospital and sits down on a bench on the side of the lobby. It says "Quiet Centre" on a white arrow.

Slowly the panic sinks from her head, shoulders, stomach and knees and gives way to intense anxiety. Now Ellen wants to know where her child is. She takes an lift and goes up to the top floor without stopping once.

Sara lies in a small examining room. There are no windows. Glaring light from a ceiling fluorescent fixture. The bed is jammed between an examining table with white paper on it and a small writing table along a wall with a sink and a closet above it. There is a chair between the table and the sink. A young girl with a book on her lap is sitting there.

Ellen squeezes in between the examining table and the bed. Her daughter lies propped up on the pillows. Out of the wall behind her comes a tube that whooshes oxygen into her nose. When Ellen puts her hand on the cold cheek, Sara looks at her and smiles.

"Stanley brought me. In the ambulance. He went along. And the backpack, he thought of it. I fell, I kept being so sleepy. Mara said go and lie down."

Be still, save your words. Everything will be all right now. Or will it now really go wrong? What's going on? What are we doing here?

The young woman is a nurse. Children are afraid of white coats, that's why she's wearing jeans and sneakers, and a checked shirt. The doctor who examined Sara, Baudoin, will come in a moment. He has been warned. He knows that the mother has arrived. You may stay here, he'll come as soon as he's ready.

"Baudoin?"

Do I know that name? A quick search through her memory is different from the usual. Ellen doesn't get farther than a vague feeling of recognition.

"Cardiology," says the young woman. "Consulting paediatric cardiologist. You're lucky. He's here only on Mondays and Thursdays. Unless for urgent cases, of course."

Now Sneefhart comes floating up and causes strangling fear because in her lift fantasy that yellow-papered patient came to a bad end.

Sara seems to have gone to sleep. Ellen sits down in the hall and waits.

"Shrivelled heart valves?"

Not understanding, Ellen repeats the strange words. Her children's insides are supple, with smooth organs, nerves elastic like new rubber bands—nothing in there is stunted, blocked, stiffened.

Baudoin asks whether it runs in the family, perhaps on the father's side?

He is a short, husky man with a friendly face behind thick glasses. When he looks at his papers, he puts down the heavy glasses;

he puts them on again to look at Ellen. This doctor is wearing a white coat. Short sleeves, bare, hairy arms, broad hands with carrot-like fingers, and clean, straight-cut nails.

Black, slightly greasy hair hangs over his collar. When he bends over Sara's case report, the brown scalp is visible through the thinning hair.

With supreme concentration Ellen registers the slightest details of the appearance of this man who has the key to her daughter's insides. Short black hairs on the back of the fingers. Yellow callus on the outside tip of the left pinkie. Grey and black chest hair that crawls up from a grubby T-shirt. Full cheeks with fine red blood vessel lines above the shaven part. Pay attention to what he says, pay attention.

It's about blood flow, litres per minute, the morass of capillaries, pump and valves, valves. Tube linings.

It's a waterworks specialist who's sitting before me. But he's wearing a white coat, a stethoscope sticks out of his breast pocket. I eat the bread of charity here, my child has broken down, pay attention, pay attention, listen!

No heart conditions in the family. But how unbearably her heart suffered when she fell in love with Johan, a devouring and crazy-making love that caused her poor heart to race and be exhausted and break. But that isn't meant here. The twins, asked about by Baudoin, are in perfect health except for their hay fever. Was Sara ill when she was little, a high fever that was not caused by a childhood illness?

Every paediatrician overestimates the mental apparatus of the mother. With his questions he awakens memories of wakeful nights, the agitating warmth of a feverish child's body, the smell of pressed oranges and cough syrup. Ellen doesn't know.

The telephone buzzes piercingly through their conversation, Baudoin barks into the receiver.

He'll examine Sara tomorrow. Photos and measurements will show why she holds her oxygen supply at such an inadequate level. He speaks about operating, about heart valves made of synthetic material by human hands. In children's sizes?

They stand up. Ellen is surprised that he's a head shorter than she. He extends his hand to her and kindly sends her to the head nurse; after all she has to call her husband, undisturbed from the office, discuss what Sara needs from home; he will inform the family doctor himself, don't worry too much Mrs Visser, I'll see you tomorrow.

Later that day, still connected to the oxygen-feeding tube, Sara lies in a bed by the window in a large ward. The bed next to her is empty. Across from her, also at a window, lies a fat girl with a bald head. She is being read to by her mother who looks exactly like her but who sits up straight and has tight brown curls. But the first thing Ellen sees is the black boy in the bed next to the door. At the foot of the bed a high scaffold has been erected over which runs an iron wire with weights on it. The wire ends in a brace which clamps around a steel pin. The steel pin has been driven through the skin, flesh and bones of the boy's dark thigh. He lies reading. He reads Donald Duck.

Ellen has to throw up. She tastes this afternoon's pickled salmon. Controls herself. No thinking now. She pulls a stool from under Sara's bed and looks at her daughter. The rotund woman from across the way is watching her, Ellen can hear it from the pace of her reading, from the hesitations. She turns her back to the bald child and looks straight at Sara.

"You have to stay here for a few days; they're going to see what's wrong with you."

"How will they look?" asks Sara. "Are they going to open me?"

Ellen tells about the photos, the EKG-machine, about blowing into balloons and blood pricks. Not about anaesthesia, operating tables, waferthin, transparent hand-made heart valves.

"Will I be back before Daddy's opera? And I haven't finished my maths homework for Mara. Do I have to sleep here? Alone?"

She has to. The head nurse, a hurried woman with a tired drab face above her half-buttoned sweater, has told Ellen that parents may nowadays stay at night with their hospitalized child. But that gives more work than it saves, she sighed. If the child is very small, very confused, or if it can't speak any language spoken by the staff, and if a child is very scared of a big operation, then it's allowed. But normal healthy children who are in the hospital, without language problems and without fear, they have to do without parents overnight. The grey sparrow had suggested that Ellen sleep at home for the time being. If Sara is frightened and cannot be soothed, or if something happens (what?), Ellen will be called and a bed can be pushed alongside. There's enough room on the ward, for the time being.

Ellen sees herself lie sweating on a stretcher next to Sara, within six feet of the bald child and the rotund mother, with the threat of the steel traction construction in her left field of vision. Oh Jesus. And if it comes to an operation on Monday, then we'll see again. Thus the sparrow. Now Ellen is going home. ("Do I have to eat here, Mummy?"); tonight she's coming back with the toothbrush, the strawberry pajamas, and *The Little Captain*.

"And I want Gijs, you have to bring him."

Ellen calls Johan in the theatre, and she gets him on the line immediately because of her flat and abrupt tone. He sounds annoyed and unbelieving, as if a child of his should be immune to illness and flaws. He's coming home, now, in fifteen minutes, and will bring along Chinese takeout because the shopping didn't get done.

She calls Bijl to give him a report. To say that she doesn't know if she can be there on Monday. "The new employee can come immediately," says Nicolaas. "You can teach him the ropes by telephone if that's necessary. Take care that you eat something, a child in the hospital costs two kilos per week."

Ellen thinks how wonderful it would be to cry helplessly next to a Bijl-like father who says to her: be still, be still, everything will be all right and you can't do anything about it, it's not your fault. However, her eyes are dry; she marks Bijl off her list and dials the next number. Lisa. Lisa is still busy with an end-of-the-afternoon patient, Lawrence listens to Ellen's story, sympathizes, will pass it on, they'll be in touch, take care, greetings to Johan, am curious about the opera next week. Kay and Ashley are talking in the background, there are television sounds. Dead tired, Ellen puts down the receiver. And where on earth are her own children?

Rhythmic thumping from upstairs answers her question as soon as she walks into the hall. In the bedroom Ellen changes into her weekend clothes: jeans, a sweater over an old T-shirt. Then she goes to the boys' room where Paul lies on his bed with headphones on and Peter sits at his desk in front of a booming radio. When Paul takes the set off his ears upon Ellen's entrance, the music from it is identical to that of the radio, with only a measure's difference. Ellen is no longer surprised at such things; at the most she registers it as an illustration of how they, her sons, are from one accidentally-split egg-cell.

Her pregnancy was that of a giant's embryo, so it seemed. Ellen had such an enormously swollen stomach that ultimately she could no longer feel her body as hers. Delivery came as a liberation; in a true deliverance she would be returned to herself. And to Johan who at night was pining away at her back and encountered her stomach no matter from which side he approached his wife. She would again be able to breathe deeply, to lie on her stomach, walk nimbly up a staircase. The double cradle was standing ready, the extra packs of nappies were stacked under it.

It became a lengthy torture; finally the gynaecologist used the scissors in her ravaged bottom and pulled Peter out with the vacuum pump. Ellen, hoarse from screaming, no longer uttered a word out of sheer terror. Paul followed without difficulty, the way later on he also imitated his brother in everything as a matter-of-course.

She lay on the delivery table, a blood-smeared baby in each arm. Peter had a large, swollen contusion on his little head. Johan and the doctor were both looking at her. They ram you with their hungry pricks, from the front, from the back, until you swell up and are stirred up inside, and then they kick the child out of your stomach so that you no longer have anything. She was shaken, she had been scared to pieces by the ease with which the strange man cut into flesh that he himself didn't know. At such a time you think that sort of thing, not well-considered, not fair. For a moment she felt abandoned by everything and everyone, lying on her back there with the two big and the two little men.

The rough scar bothered her for months. Taking a crap with difficulty and pain, fucking with gritted teeth, lifting the children with fully tightened sphincter. She concentrated all her energy on the twins and beyond that could stand no comment or touch. Johan swallowed his rage, his disappointment at the loss of his nimble love partner, his growing jealousy of the two screaming little boys. The days in his studio became gradually longer, he would put off the time when he had to enter the gradually dirtier house that stank of sour milk until he could fall into bed drunk next to his exhausted wife without turning on the light. If Ellen had had the energy to pay attention and had been interested in Johan's activities, she would have known that he had started fooling around with his models during that period.

But Ellen paid no attention and noticed nothing. During the scarce moments that the twins were sleeping, simultaneously satisfied, she sat exhausted on the couch and felt an intense anxiety. These feelings were no more than a vague notion of a basic lack: the most important thing, that which should bind them inextricably, drove them apart. Johan ran away in panic from the children who united in them his sharp nose and Ellen's slender build.

Ellen faced things alone and managed by living only partially. What was hidden in the hastily walled-off areas of her head could not be uttered. The dream about the unstoppably rolling ball of disaster that would crush her was the only message she sent herself from that desolate area.

The twins didn't force her into extreme involvement the way an only child might. The little boys were often sufficient to each other and demanded from her only feeding and care. When she became more conscious later on, it was too late and she could no longer enter the circle of secret communication around the two children.

Sitting on Paul's bed, she tells them what has happened. The boys are frightened, Paul throws an arm around her. They are more frightened by Ellen's tense face than by the hospital story. A boy of fifteen who has just started enjoying his big body (tennis, shaving twice a week, the wonder of masturbation, time and again) inevitably cannot imagine anything but a pimple on the side of his nose when considering physical suffering. Something wrong with the heart is for old people; they never wondered why blood throbs in their temples and their groins.

They hear Johan come home and go downstairs. He places plastic containers with bahmi and satay on the table; again Ellen can barely suppress her queasiness.

Johan scowls. They eat. They talk about practical things: the name of the doctor, who will bring the stuff later (Johan), what he will take along (Gijs), in which room Sara is (with the bald child, with the chained child) what time is visiting hour (later, right now), whether the boys will go along (yes).

Then they're all gone, Peter swinging the plastic bag with Sara's pajamas and toilet kit, Paul with Gijs Goldfish under his arm. Ellen sits at the table with the half-empty containers of greasy food. She puts the forks and spoons in the sink and wraps everything else on the table in the dirty tablecloth, a wedding present from Alma. She pushes the tightly folded bundle in its entirety into the garbage can. On the clean table she pulls the telephone towards her; she continues with her list.

Mara's telephone is picked up by a man, the last thing Ellen would expect. Mara herself audibly sucks the soybean fibres from her teeth but sounds simply nice. The class will write letters and make drawings. Ellen gives her the room number, thanks for the caring attention, for Stanley's sweet care. Cross through Mara.

Smoke, make coffee. Telephone: Lisa.

"I'm coming over. Lawrence is home; he can put the children to bed. See you in a short while."

Women's friendship is my salvation, Ellen has often thought. The walks and discussions with Lisa saved her during the years after Peter and Paul's birth. You don't have to explain anything to a woman friend. You don't have to watch if you're taking too much time in telling your story. You don't have to see to it that you mix a certain amount of admiration for the other in every statement about yourself. You don't have to undertake anything. You don't have to be witty. Nothing is required from you. The only relationship that comes even close is the relationship with a daughter, but there you miss the connection of similar experience—and perhaps also the element of choice.

Ellen and Lisa haven't chosen each other, they think. They stumbled across each other and don't exactly know anymore when and in what circumstances. Both come across numerous women every year, so there most certainly was choosing. Without many words, as a matter of course.

This is how they sit together at the empty table.

"I flung Alma's tablecloth into the garbage can. It got to be too much."

"Have you called her yet?"

"Johan can do it when he returns."

They giggle like girls.

"It's possible," says Lisa, "a heart-valve defect as the result of an early childhood infection. Wait and see what they'll to do tomorrow. Whom did you talk to? It could also be an allergic reaction, or something in the respiratory system that's going round now. It's rather aggressive to start right away about new valves. Does he love cutting? Did he need to score?"

"A nice man. And human too, for a doctor. Only one telephone interruption. And he said something about take it easy, and that I could call. No, nice. Certainly has the hots for those valves, but rather as a beneficial invention, it seemed. His name is Baudoin. Rather hairy and with coke-bottle glasses. He plays the cello, I think."

Lisa knows him vaguely, from the time she was an intern in the paediatrics department. He is indeed a musician. His small patients love him, and he's a conscientious doctor.

"His wife died last year. Cancer. A rapid melanoma for which nothing could be done. Terrible."

Ellen thinks of the dirty collar, the grubby clothes under the white coat. She sucks in all this information about her child's guardian as though she can influence Sara's fate by identifying completely with the doctor. About the possible diagnosis she doesn't want to hear much, about its presenter, everything, everything.

Lisa takes Ellen's hand. They sit sighing and cursing together when the others come home.

Conversations, interrupting one another about Sara, about the ward, then also about Johan's opera and the upcoming opening night. Alma is called, Peter and Paul go upstairs, Johan opens a bottle, Ellen goes to kiss her boys goodnight because it's such a strange evening. They've gone to bed far too early. They barely react to her questions but burst out in unintelligible grunting as soon as she's in the hall.

Sara's bedroom door is standing open. When Ellen looks in, sees the duvet thrown back, the stack of comics on the floor, the red tights over the chair, she feels the inner shades crash down. Self-controlled she closes the door and walks downstairs.

That weekend Ellen tastes the dregs of hospital hell that make you powerless.

Friday afternoon, visiting hour: in the spot for Sara's bed is a large empty space surrounded by flowers from Lisa on the night stand and postcards from classmates taped above the disappeared head of the bed.

Sara has been taken away for examination, says Sparrow. Will Baudoin still come by this afternoon, report anything? Sparrow doesn't know, it could be, but perhaps not.

"He's on call this weekend, you'll surely see him Saturday or Sunday."

Wait. Go to the store on the square downstairs. Everyone is walking around with identical yellow bouquets. What am I doing here?

Go upstairs. Wait. Hang around in front of the department

desk. Baudoin's name hangs on the bulletin board. His schedule behind it is printed slightly too small to read. Almost six o'clock. I have to go home. I have to see Sara. Why does it take so long? They're looking at me as if they're thinking: leave, woman. They're surely thinking it as well. All this is not real. Why don't I wake up. Cigarette in the smoking room at the end of the long hall. Filled ashtrays with old butts. Do they let it get dirty on purpose to discourage smokers? Even the windows are filthy, there's a brownish deposit on them.

Sara's bed is pushed out of the lift. Cigarette out, bag over the shoulder, into the ward. A nurse reconnects the oxygen tube. Sara looks bluish and tired. She has a large band-aid on the inside of her elbow and pieces of gauze on her pale fingertips.

"How was it?"

"Not bad."

"Hungry?"

"No."

"Do you want anything?"

"Don't know."

A tray arrives with food. Bread slices wrapped in cellophane, butter in plastic, cheese in a bag with a hidden closure. Sara doesn't want to eat or drink.

Ellen consults Sparrow in her office. Pen in hand marking long lists.

"We're waiting and seeing for the moment, Mrs Visser. Right now she's tired from the examinations. Tonight we'll let her drink something and go to sleep early. Tomorrow we'll see again. You would do well to get some sleep yourself."

Sleep? Petrified, Ellen lies in bed next to snoring Johan. What if she called Baudoin now? Cooked for him in his lonely house? Crying, the fat doctor crawls into her arms, she caresses his thinning hair very carefully. I'll do everything to save your child, he says, if you come to live here and keep up the place; the vacuum cleaner is there, behind the curtain.

I must have slept a little after all.

Saturday is completely devoted to family visits. When Ellen comes into the ward, a large Surinam woman is sitting next to the bed of Marlon, the chained child. Open bags stand at her feet; two small sisters with dozens of braids and pink summer dresses over wool sweaters sit, their arms crossed, looking at their big brother.

Marlon's mother has rented a television set for her son. It is mounted on a stand at the foot of the bed, next to the instrument of torture. It's on. Loud.

She has brought barras bread along for him and home-made porn, Surinam chicken, in a small container. Marlon is nonchalantly eating the food.

"Where is Pa?"

"He doesn't say where he is. He goes with his friends and lets me go with the bus. He doesn't say if he's coming, he gives me no money for a taxi. That Pa of yours he'll see, for sure, he sure will see!"

Ellen feels for the boy. Aside from the terrible pain that he must have, there is also the humiliation of no longer being able to do anything yourself. Marlon pees in a urinal that he cannot get himself. Taking a crap is pure agony. Then the curtain around his bed is closed and he is very carefully placed on the bedpan by two nurses while he clings to the halter above his bed. Because he cannot turn himself, it is a feat to wash his ass. A thirteen-year-old boy who is washed by an eighteen-year-old nurse's aide? Not good, Ellen thinks.

Grandmothers enter, as well as cheerful neighbours. It's a party around Marlon's bed, the mother beams, the sisters warn everyone not to bump against the weights.

Eating, chattering, laughing; it looks like the Surinam Kwakoe festival. Ellen pays attention. She even listens to the television sounds. She lets her eyes and ears be filled with everything except Sara.

The bald girl's father comes. For weeks his wife and his daughter have been living in the hospital. He comes with clean laundry and with a life-size baby doll that looks creepily like the bald child.

Next to each other the hairless heads lie on the pillow; it's almost impossible to tell them apart. The father is a neat-looking man in a shirt and tie. He wears slacks with sharp creases and a jacket with a strange piece of belt in the back, secured with buttons. The man gives the impression that he's made entirely of plastic and smells of nothing. He is nice, he kisses his rotund wife and strokes the daughter over her smooth head.

"Hi Winnie's father," says Marlon, "I got a TV!"

Winnie's father shakes the hands of Marlon and his mother. Then he comes to make Ellen's acquaintance. Sara is too drowsy to shake his hand. It looks like a youth hostel here, thinks Ellen, we're all crazy, out of our minds, and no one does anything about it. People who introduce themselves to each other, have a chat, eat, and laugh at the television. But a hose sticks out of the wall, a pin is stuck through a living leg, and an eye protrudes from a girl's face.

With red eyes and stripes of mascara over her cheeks, Winnie's mother sits in the smoking room. She sits straight up in a chair, feet next to each other. She holds her big handbag on her round, fleshy knees. When Ellen sits down across from her, she starts speaking rapidly in a toneless voice. The eye nerve in Winnie's right eye was not connected properly. She's never been able to see well with that eye. The left eye seemed to get gradually larger. Because of excessive use she thought at first, and it also moved, and the other, the dead eye, did not. But it was a growth the doctor said. She was almost three years old at the time, and when she walked on the street, she'd walk crookedly, diagonally. She also fell often; at home that was a problem because Conrad, my husband, is so neat. And always bruises, sometimes I was afraid that they'd think that we beat her. They irradiated the tumour, she lay tied up and alone in the radiation room and no one was allowed to be with her. Her hair fell out, she doesn't mind but I do, she had brown curly hair. I found the curls on her pillow, every morning. If only they make her eye better I thought, I'll buy her a wig, it doesn't matter.

It didn't work. The tumour keeps growing. Her eye socket is full. Monday they're going to take it out. The eye also. That's how it is. Then she will no longer see anything at all. You can't explain that to a three-year-old child. They decided it this week. The doctor told us, we had to come together. Conrad cried. Now she can still see us. The day after tomorrow, no longer. You can't imagine what it's like. Even the doctor thought it was awful.

Ellen imagines it quite well. Destroying what is whole is her private nightmare. The baby in the refrigerator. Not let the wasp fly out of the window but press it in half. The worst, the most elusive part is the desire. No one tells her that she must freeze her child, she thinks it up herself and therefore she also wants to, somewhere in the back of her head. How can that be? She put the meat knife and the serrated bread knife in the back of the drawer, out of fear that the children would be able to get to them. Of course not, they were much too small for that. Out of another fear.

Indulging in fantasies at home, in your own kitchen, with your children healthy and happy with you is one thing. Indulging in fantasies in this horror film in which every white coat holds a scalpel behind his back, and where in peace and quiet a plan is formulated to tear out a good eye and throw it in the garbage, that's quite something else.

Smashing a smooth intact sachertorte, straight through the innocent glaze with a garden trowel is one thing. Resolutely sawing off a living leg, thinking of where to place the saw, how much pressure to exert, putting yourself in place, in place! That's something else.

Sara is bothered by the noise.

"Can the television be turned off, Mummy?"

Every time when she's just fallen asleep, she wakes up with a start from the roaring laugh of Marlon's neighbour, from Winnie who knocks a glass off the nightstand, from people calling out as they enter the ward.

Sparrow comes to take a look. Sara may move to a single room which became empty this morning. Baudoin has been called. He'll come by later. Sara isn't drinking enough. Sparrow folds down the sheet, pulls up the pajama top and with two fingers pushes against the skin of Sara's stomach.

"Creases. You see? She isn't getting enough fluid."

My daughter takes in the elements insufficiently, thinks Ellen when Sparrow has tripped away. Air and water are injected into her with force. They come with fire when she is chilled. What is the fourth element? My memory isn't working, I can't think of it.

It's pitch dark outside when Baudoin finally enters the single room where Sara now lies. Ellen remembers her dream about the vacuum-cleaner and smiles. The doctor smiles back. He stands still for a moment, his hands behind his back. They look at the sleeping child. A nurse comes in with an IV stand. She hangs two transparent plastic bags on it. A tube comes from each bag. The tubes come together in a Y-shaped piece.

Baudoin pricks into a vein in Sara's forearm. The drip is connected to the plastic tube which goes through a kind of computer station before it gets to the Y. Red numbers light up on a black screen; are the drops being counted? The apparatus starts beeping, always three beeps followed by a small drum roll. The rhythm is just too slow to make a song from.

"We're giving her fluid, she needs that. And at the same time something to pep up the heart."

The bright light is turned off when they leave. Ellen sits next to the bed and is holding Sara's right hand. The left one is tied to the bed rail. The child is sleeping. Ellen listens to the drip. It is Saturday evening, it's eleven o'clock. It's time to leave.

The next morning Sara is less blue. She has eaten half a cup of yogurt, with one hand. She is listening to the radio through a shell on her ear: spiritual songs sung by the staff choir in the lobby downstairs.

Under the grey cloud cover, the polderland lies stretched out to the horizon. There used to be water here, waves that carried boats or devoured them, that pushed pieces of wreckage onto the beach and sometimes entered the land. A wild intractable sea was slowly restricted: the dike which twists crookedly through the land has calmed the water surface. Sucked empty and dried out, the lake that was created in this way showed its bottom, capitulating. Whatever grew in the water died. Now grass is allowed to grow in the ditches that are perpendicular to each other, in which the water still glimmers as before. A polder is a pressed together, seething implosion of anger, a dangerous landscape.

"Lift up your head, O ye gates... and the King of glory shall come in!"

Sara lets Ellen listen with her. They laugh when Baudoin enters at this text. The King of glory is wearing loose-fitting jeans and wrong-looking shoes with buckles. The white coat is buttoned.

Ellen cannot connect the doctor coming so early on a Sunday morning in any way with the condition of her child. No, he's overly conscientious; he has nothing to do at home; he flees the rooms filled with painful memories of his dead wife; he has fallen for Ellen and takes every opportunity to be with this fascinating mother.

He takes her outside. In a dead-end part of the hall a white painted wooden bench stands in front of a window. On it they sit next to each other, the mother with her head filled with messy, distraught, desperate love, the doctor with a carefully thought-out plan.

Tomorrow morning, early, he wants to operate on Sara. He is going to give her the newest artificial valves, the nicest he can find. She'll be able to get along with those for about four years, depending on her rate of growth. When she is fourteen, heart and blood vessels will also be wider and larger; then new valves will have to be put in.

Give me a new heart, thinks Ellen. Did the choir sing when she walked through the lobby on her way to the lift this morning? Tomorrow morning an eye will be taken from Winnie, something will be added to Sara. I have to listen to what he's saying.

"With broken valves the pump leaks, you know, just like in the polder outside. The operation as such is complicated, but we have a lot of experience with it, even in children. The channel, the rate of flow of the fluid, sogginess, dryness, irrigation—it's a fascinating area."

Must be a sailor. Or the son of a dike warden. Two swans fly up from a ditch and wing up majestically on their broad wings. My legs carry me wherever I want to go, even when I'm tired, even when my feet smart in shoes that are too narrow. My daughter is ten years old. It's Sunday morning. Her heart valves are shrivelled and I didn't know it.

Together they go to Sara. Baudoin explains to her what is the matter with her heart, why she is tired and often dizzy, and how he is going to repair the broken organ. That the nurse is going to shave her tonight.

"Like Winnie? Will I be bald?"

Her chest, under her arms. Very small hairs grow there, and they have to go. When you operate, everything has to be very clean. Then they'll roll her to the operating room and a doctor will make her go to sleep. That's easy to do through the little hole in her arm, she won't need to get another shot.

Sara will also see him, but he'll be wearing a bathing cap, a green one. And a piece of cloth in front of his mouth so that his bacteria won't go to her. When she's asleep he'll make the new valves.

Ellen understands this language. An icy panic now grows within her. This is serious.

"Okay," says Sara. "It's fine with me."

During the visiting hour (Lisa, Johan with the boys, Grandma Alma) she sleeps. When the people have gone, the IV drip sound structure (pr, pr, pr, prrrrt) starts up again. The oxygen tube blows a basso continuo.

Tonight I'm staying. I'll never abandon you. We should never have come here. I'll stay till we can leave. Do you remember how we once got lost while we were picking berries? I knew that the lake lay down below, had seen it when we climbed the mountain. We left the bucket of berries behind, we clambered straight through the forest over dead spruce trees and smooth stones until we came to the path around the lake that we knew, that was our own familiar path.

The smoking room. A cigarette. And another. Marlon's big cousins sit smoking hand-rolled cigarettes and are playing cards. Winnie's father nods pleasantly at Ellen. At four o'clock they all depart and leave Ellen alone in the smoke. She looks at the people industriously walking back and forth in the long hall; opens the door to thin out the smoke and to listen. Visitors say goodbye, wave in the doorways. Nursing staff walk around with chamber-pots and IV bags.

The nurse who wore a checked blouse the first day is now wearing a uniform. She walks down the hall and opens the door to every room to see if quiet has returned.

She goes inside a door in the middle of the hall. She comes out again quickly and calls out in a clearly audible and controlled voice, first to the right and then to the left: "Assistance please!"

That clearly is a watchword, thinks Ellen. The nurses in the hall set the objects they're carrying at that moment down on the floor. One quickly walks to the desk and telephones. Two male nurses come riding up with a small cart with hoses on it. Four of them go into the door above which a red light starts blinking.

Ellen stretches, her hands above her head. Just say goodbye to Sara and then home to eat (Alma, Chinese again) and pick up stuff for tonight. Slowly she walks through the deserted hall, past the blinking light, into the ward. Marlon with his leg in the air, Winnie with her mother. A new child in Sara's place.

Again into the hall. From the flashing-light room the small cart is pushed back out. The nurse with the checked blouse has tears in her eyes. Why do all these people's arms hang down like that? They draw back against the wall to let Ellen through. The room is brightly lit. The room is deathly quiet. The numbers on the IV are extinguished. The oxygen tube is silent. In the bed lies a ten-year-old girl who is not breathing.

## Chapter five

# Merciful Frost

Ellen has read somewhere that true despair never lasts more than two days, because a human being starts eating after that. Despair is not what she feels during the first months after the death of the child. She is out of joint. Just as the earth's crust is not supposed to crack in order to absorb a mountain range, so children are not supposed to die before their parents.

There has been an earthquake, a flood, an all-consuming hurricane that dragged along, destroyed everything and flung it back down in strange places. But when she opens her cupboard doors, her clothes hang there as always. The staircase has twenty-nine steps, then and now; the view from the kitchen window has remained exactly the same.

Ellen is not desperate, not melancholy, not rebellious, not at the end of her wits. She feels absolutely nothing except the structure of her body. She has become a wood-like structure, a building with old rafters and beams that make a wheezing sound when they rub against each other. Her sense of her body has been reduced to her joints which she always feels. Bending the knees, the position of the elbow and the neck rotation, those are the data that Ellen receives in the shaken headquarters of her brains. No messages about the skin because she doesn't feel the scratch made on her arm by an iron wire sticking out from Peter's bicycle. She is not warm, not cold. No messages about the internal organs, she's not hungry and she doesn't realize that she has to pee until she's sitting on the toilet.

The position of her body is the only thing of which she's conscious, to the smallest details: by a stabbing pain in her scalp the hair-roots tell her minute by minute at what angle her hairs are anchored in her head. Maintaining her respiration is a task which takes up all her energy. In, with a slight expansion of the chest, barely raise the shoulders; out, when something drops in the direction of the stomach, something that has to be restrained; wait a moment, in again, out again, wait a moment, in again.

She eats when she sits at a dining table and someone places a plate in front of her. Absently, a few bites without paying attention to food combinations and without tasting anything: spaghetti without sauce, a slice of bread without butter. She sleeps because at night she stretches her body out on a mattress and unfolds all her joints. After a few hours she wakes up stiff; when it's light she gets up. The body doesn't like being stretched out.

Nothing is heard from the soft body parts, certainly not if they're without bones. They are gradually disappearing: Ellen has never had much of a stomach, but now a negative stomach comes into being, her skin hangs like a slack sail between her pelvic bones. Her buttocks shrink and her breasts become slack.

Once in a while thoughts concerning bits of information about the process of mourning circulate in the stuffy silence of the skull. Sitting motionless on the sofa (knees and elbows at right angles, toes bent, fists clenched) she looked in her inner landscape for signs of rage or guilt, meanwhile paying attention to the rhythm of her breath. Should never have let her go to school; never knew that she'd had an illness; must have been too preoccupied with being unhappy about Johan; neglected; what an egotistical mother; I came first; I shouldn't have stayed in that smoking room; at her bed, of course? Then I would have seen it, then it wouldn't have happened?

She pushes the air out of her lungs and sucks in new air. She should be angry, furious.

At that fucking bitch Mara? She was aware too late that something was really wrong, she exhausted Sara with maths assignments and intimidated her about being childish, about complaining.

But Mara's white face evokes a vague sort of connection, no annoyance, no fire. She imagines how she could have a go at Baudoin, knock the glasses from his face, stick the scalpel into his throat, kick him in the stomach; with iron fists she would break him because he let her child slip away. Out, wait, in. It's a silent cartoon in her head, the helpless doctor with the furious woman who pursues him between the filing cabinets, chases him around his desk.

Ellen moves her feet. Liquid runs from her eyes. She blows her nose in a handkerchief that she always carries with her now. Suicide is not a serious option, Ellen doesn't consider it, it isn't up for discussion. Breathing is up for discussion. And the position of the back. Her carefully guarded breath is sourish and spoiled, her urine smells of acetone.

The only feeling that Ellen is aware of is that of irritation when her concentration is interrupted. Loud noises in the house: the front door slams, there is a pounding crescendo on the staircase, the door is thrown open and bangs against the wall, "Mum, Mum," shouts Peter, a painting in the doorframe. She thinks: leave me in peace. When Paul asks what he should cook, she closes her eyes. He distracts her; he should stop that.

The worst is Johan. He comes close with a body that emanates warmth; he folds hot arms around her and presses her head against his shoulder. He wants her to caress him, to hold him. He crawls against her in bed; he bombards her with his thermal emanation. Howling he cries; he strikes his pillow with his fists and groans. Then Ellen has great difficulty in paying attention to her shoulders, how they lie straight against the sheet, parallel to the knees. Suck air in, press it out, not too far, wait a moment, let him stop with that hot tossing and turning, breathe in, go away, go away, and out, evenly, calm, calm, cool.

"You're confused," he says to her, "you have to take pills to really sleep well, this can't go on any longer."

No longer wanting to listen to this, Ellen takes the medicines that are offered; however, she is not visited by liberating sleep but by alarming sounds that cannot exist. A silent telephone next to the bed rings, the closed door bangs open, absent people call out her name loudly and urgently. Sitting up in bed, Ellen fights against falling asleep; she waits till the pill has worn off.

The household is taken over by the twins. They go shopping and together they wander along the racks in the supermarket looking for products that they know. Ellen can't give them advice; she is mute when it comes to eating. In the evening Peter sets the table, four plates, while Peter fries eggs and serves unwashed lettuce without dressing. Lisa comes a few times and shows the boys how to fry sausages and chops: butter in the pan, turn the meat from time to time, lower the flame, meanwhile start the potatoes. There is no more toilet paper, so Peter puts the napkin holder on the bathroom floor. Johan stays away ever longer and more often; he is in the studio; he's working. He eats out because he doesn't know what to do with himself at home.

Family life disintegrates. The twins skip school; in view of the recent loss, the school does nothing so Ellen and Johan don't know about it. Alma does know; Peter and Paul are with her during the day. They drink hot chocolate and eat fried cheese sandwiches. For hours on end they play monopoly with their grandmother. Sometimes they talk about Sara. From the library Alma has borrowed a medical encyclopaedia for the layman in which she looks up heart diseases. She reads to the boys: no incantations or lamentations but facts. She bears the loss of her only female descendant stoically and slightly embittered, but she bears something; there is a loss, something has happened that can be discussed and about which questions can be asked. This relieves the boys; in the encyclopaedia they look up valve defects and heredity, they are shocked but also satisfied when Alma has one of Sara's drawings, goldfish in a transparent pond with water plants, framed and hangs it on the wall. Alma doesn't cry and doesn't let them cry either, but by opening her house without restrictions during school time, she makes it clear to her grandchildren that something serious is going on and should be allowed to.

Ellen's wood-like emotional paralysis set in immediately after Sara's death and protected her during the week of organizational rigmarole that followed. She was present during the funeral, she heard Sara's class sing a song, Lisa tell a story, Johan say a word of thanks. She looked at the small coffin. She held Peter and Paul's hands, or they held hers. She wore a black dress that was chosen by Lisa. It was spring, the trees at the graveyard had just turned green. Morning, it was in the morning, and very many people walked behind them. They brought the coffin to a special area of the churchyard, a children's area with small memorial stones and less space between them than for the adults. "Our Ray of Sunshine", Ellen read on a stone, and "Evertje". They lowered Sara into the earth and everyone placed flowers next to that offensive hole. His shoulders shaking, Johan was at her side, supported by Lawrence. At least a hundred people came to shake her hand, to kiss her. She saw their mouths move. Baudoin was there, and Mara, and Stanley. They all spoke to Ellen who understood nothing. Nicolaas Bijl, with red eyes, embraced her. That made her dizzy.

Afterwards there was food at Lisa and Lawrence's. The orchard was full of people. The boys went around with glasses and coffee cups. Lisa had ordered sandwiches, people were hungry. Ellen looked across everything at the treetops with their new leaves. The springtime sun was pleasant, but higher up clouds raced against the sky. This is, she thought, this is. Lisa took her upstairs and put her on a bed. Later Johan came to pick her up, led her to the car, drove home. Ellen bent her joints in the prescribed directions and thought of breathing. It was Thursday.

Ellen can remember nothing of the Sunday night before. Were they at Lisa's with the whole family? On Monday morning Ellen lived for a few hours. Johan and the boys were still asleep, at Lisa's. Ellen asked Lawrence to drive her home. Like a chauffeur he remains sitting in the car when she enters the house.

A glass of water from the tap. A plastic bag from the drawer. In Sara's room Ellen sits down on the bed and reflects. The strawberry underwear, undershirt, and panties with a favourite pattern. The fish sweater which Alma bought for Sara last year. The new jeans, with a real brand name. Socks? Warm socks without a heel that always fit. They are worn but don't have holes yet. The nice sneakers.

Ellen selects the clothes from the cupboard, the sneakers are under the bed, the socks on the pile of clean laundry. The fish sweater is on the couch in the living room. She folds everything and puts it in the plastic bag. On top she places a small box of paints that Johan gave Sara for her eighth birthday and a bear that the boys bought for her when she turned one.

I'm going to bury my daughter, thinks Ellen. It feels as if both her hands have been chopped off, a pain that cannot be described, mixed with horror about bone splinters in the blood, with the realization of being forever irreparably mutilated and never again, never again being able to hold something.

Panting, Ellen sinks down against the door post and remains lying down, clasping the plastic bag against her. She hears herself making a strange sound, a kind of roar. She feels her own nails in her cheeks.

Lawrence calls through the mailbox, is she coming, is everything all right, can he do anything? She drags herself up, holds her face under the kitchen tap, walks down the stairs and sits down in the car with the bag on her lap.

Lawrence drops her off at the hospital. He kisses her, tells her to take care and drives off. She waves after him with her free hand. Rituals, old habits with which to encircle this new, this absurd, unreality.

In the children's department everything is different. That's because of the light; it's early in the morning and the sun makes light in places where Ellen hasn't seen it yet. There are no visitors around; only people who have to be there professionally walk though the lobby and stand in front of the desk. A janitor is busy mopping the floor with a machine and an older lady makes her rounds with a coffee cart.

In the smoking room at the end of the hall Ellen sees the heads of Winnie's parents. She looks away quickly. Jealous of parents whose child is being blinded at this moment—this feeling is so confusing that she can't deal with it. She wouldn't be able to empathize with them and she wouldn't be able to bear their compassion.

"Mrs Visser, it's good that you're here. Please come with me to the office."

Head nurse Sparrow shakes her hand, goes ahead of her, closes the door. The small office has no windows; the only window there is has a view of the desk behind which sit two nurses who are going over a list together. They have pens in their hands and a stack of case reports is lying between them. They're bent over them together, they see to it that the children are operated on time and get back to bed so that they get better and can go back home.

"Would you like coffee, Mrs Visser?" asks nurse Sparrow, holding up the thermos. Ellen straightens her back. She has placed the plastic bag at her feet and accepts a mug of coffee.

"You may smoke here, if you wish; it doesn't bother me."

Sparrow pushes an ashtray across the desk to Ellen and looks at her. Her face is tired and serious.

No speech now, thinks Ellen, no sympathy and no department apologies.

Nurse Sparrow knows better. She limits herself to the concrete things that have to be done. She gives Ellen a light. She closes the lace curtain of the window facing the information desk.

"The nurse is washing your daughter. She'll be busy for a little while and will come to get you when she's ready. She'll return things to you that are still here."

Toothbrush, thinks Ellen, pajamas, cards, drawings. The remains. The proof that she was here. Lay out, they call it, lay out the body. Percussionists lay out their sticks on the trap table, the princess takes off her fur stole and lays it out before going on the dance floor, the nurse with the checked blouse and the frightened face is laying out my child.

There are papers to sign, there are administrative details to finish. Nurse Sparrow does this calmly and clearly, she speaks in a quiet voice. Ellen listens, does what is asked, drinks her coffee, and smokes. There is a knock at the door; Ellen says goodbye to Sparrow and goes down the lobby with the nurse who has come to get her. What was her name again, forgotten, how stupid. Ellen looks sideways at the name tag that the nurse has pinned on her shoulder strap: Paula. Nurse Paula reports that she has washed Sara, Sara is in the bathroom, that's where we're going now, here it is, we're going in here, have you brought the clothes with you?

A door opens, Ellen sees a folding screen. The nurse goes ahead of her, around the screen into the brightly lit bathroom. There is a bath tub along the wall, there's an exercise bike, a hair drying hood, a walker, a bundle of IV stands. There is a stretcher with a sheet over it.

"Here is Sara, Mrs Visser."

Searchingly, the nurse looks at Ellen. Ellen nods.

Take the sheet and carefully lift it up, fold it back, take it off. See the naked child. See the child. See the dead child. Look at the dead child yourself, at the dead child. A cut on the knee from last week's gym class. Foot soles with a callus. Sara has a pad between her legs and under her buttocks. Her eyelids are held closed by white tape: a clown's face with pale lips. Under her chin the nurse has pressed a thick rolled up towel so that the mouth stays closed. Ellen puts her hand on Sara's hair which still feels the same; on Sara's forehead, it is cool but not cold. It does feel un-alive, without hidden movement, not yet a thing but on its way to it.

Nurse Paula puts on a big plastic apron, and gloves. She asks if Ellen also wants gloves but Ellen doesn't want them.

"Then you'll have to wash your hands carefully afterwards," says Paula. "Now we're going to dress Sara, we'll manage with the two of us."

She continues talking while Ellen unpacks the plastic bag and lays the clothes ready on a narrow table next to the stretcher.

"Start with the panties, if we both take a foot, stick them through, then I'll just lift the legs and you can push the panties up, like that. If you hold on to her, I'll take care that the diaper fits in nicely, yes, now we'll put her down again, go on."

Ellen holds her cold child in her arms when Paula pulls the pants over the buttocks. She thinks intensely about the difference: yesterday warm, today cold. Yesterday Sara joined in the embrace, today she doesn't give. Yesterday pink, today yellow. Ellen thinks that the very possibility of the existence of these differences is the worst thing ever. Having to experience these differences, having a memory and powers of observation, having to apply these to the varying conditions of your own child—that is worse than anything you can imagine. My hands, my memory, my eyes subject me to this. I observe. I'm still here and I have to perceive and remember.

"With the undershirt we first do the arms, yes both arms at once, and then I lift her head and put the shirt over it; now you can pull it down over the back."

"That's how I did it when she was a baby, in one movement over her head, that wasn't so scary and you already had the arms through the sleeves. Now the socks I suppose?"

They're the boys' old socks. Sara liked to wear them. They pull them up high over the thin shins. Now the jeans. The material is stiff; they have to tug and pull to get them to sit right.

"It seems disrespectful," says Paula, "but it's important that she have the right clothes on, that's why we do it like this. The sweater is the most awkward."

She stretches the neck opening as wide as possible. First the sleeves over the straight arms that can no longer bend. They don't manage to get the head through the collar. Paula grabs a pair of scissors.

"I'm going to snip the back of the collar, then it'll go on easier. It's too bad, but you won't see it."

Now they're able to slide the sweater over Sara's head and pull it down. Paula rolls Sara to Ellen and sticks a band-aid over the notch. Ellen doesn't believe what is happening, but it's happening. The sneakers. Tying the laces.

"Do you want to comb her hair? We'll leave the stickers over her eyes for now. Do you have a comb? The toilet kit is over there."

Ellen takes her own comb out of her handbag and combs her daughter's hair. She then takes off the small gold chain that she always wears and fastens it around Sara's neck. She places Gijs Goldfish in one arm and the bear in the other. The box of paints next to her.

Paula packs Sara's left-over belongings in the plastic bag

"Will you pull back the sheet when you're done? I'll now leave you alone for a moment, I'll see you in the hall."

The fluorescent bulb is radiating heat so intensely that it buzzes and vibrates. The child is at peace, dressed in her favourite clothes, accompanied by her dearest things. A wave of fury rises in Ellen who stands next to her: that *her* eyes have to remain open, that *her* memory will from now on have to accommodate that which she has experienced the past half hour, that *her* legs will soon carry her out of the hospital, that she exists and the child no longer.

She waits. The rage ebbs away. She kisses the child, fixes the small chain, strokes the hair. She doesn't dare to speak now that she's alone. She looks around in the absurd room, smiles, takes the sheet and places it over Sara's legs. She hums a song, a lullaby, a children's song, but she doesn't sing aloud, not with words.

"Sara, I'm leaving the light on."

She pulls the sheet over the stretcher and quietly leaves the bathroom.

\*   \*   \*

Ellen is unaware that spring continues and changes to a warm summer. Daffodils push up from the earth, and the banks of the river are dotted with the yellow stars of buttercups. House windows are opened, music sounds in the street, people wash their cars, prune their hedges and stand talking with each other. When it rains, it's a caress for the land, mild and soft. The city flaunts its secret smell of wet asphalt at the end of the afternoon, dust thickens, skin shines, bike tires whoosh. Johan comes home whistling.

There is a letter from the principal of the high school, addressed to "the parents of Peter and Paul Steenkamer".

"In this unusual manner," the principal writes, "I wish to prepare you for the fact that both of your sons will have to repeat a class this year. Undoubtedly this is linked to the sad family circumstances and not to a possible intellectual inadequacy of the boys who, after all, showed themselves as interested and hard-working students before the death of their sister."

The principal assumes that with the restoration of pychological balance the original motivation will also return, and that in this way there will be an end to the long string of truant hours, "unauthorized absences, that we, despite all our respect and understanding, cannot tolerate, of course, but about which we have not wanted to bother you until now. I trust that you will discuss these matters with your sons and will, on my part, take care that Peter and Paul will again be placed in the third year at the beginning of the new school year. Sincerely."

"Goddamit," says Johan.

He flings the letter on the table and looks at Ellen.

"Did you know about this? That they're never in school? Now they'll have to repeat a grade, that's a failure, that's not necessary at all, they're not stupid! That asshole says it himself! It's your fault, you should have watched it, Ellen. You just sit here doing nothing, you can't even keep tabs on your own children. Playing hooky! Does that make any sense, don't I work also?! And what do they actually do, do they smoke dope in a 'coffeeshop' or what? Well?"

"Yes," Ellen says slowly, "I do know about it. I think that it's probably my fault, I haven't focused on them. I haven't paid attention."

"Then do something about it! I've had it, the way things are around here. It's a mess, no one is ever at home and you all have such long faces."

He pulls a straight face. Sits down at the table. Sweeps newspapers and mail aside.

"They've been at Alma's, they're not doing drugs. They don't even smoke as far as I know."

"But you don't know much. At Alma's! Why, for God's sake?"

"I don't know, company I think. Someone who acts normal, who is there. They played games, Paul said."

"Games, yes. And now they have to repeat a grade. My children have to repeat a grade! I'm going to give that principal a piece of my mind, you know. With some tutoring they'll catch up and then they can just go on to the fourth year. Absolutely no exception, absolutely no special circumstances. They'll pass, just like every normal child. What's that slimeball thinking, patronizing us with his obliging attitude, his sad family situation. Ugh!"

"I actually think that it's all right, Johan, the way he wants to arrange it. It's not so bad for them to repeat a year, it does take a while before things return to normal. Meanwhile won't it be nice for them that the expectations at school won't be as high? I'll have a talk with them, tell them that they should go to school again and I'll make an appointment with the principal to discuss matters."

"Do you know that I'm getting sick of that indulgent carrying-on? Take time, cope, discuss. It makes me want to puke! It has to change, there's no longer anything wrong, there is no reason whatsoever to hang around the house. Not for them and not for you. It's enough, enough. And I also want you to clean Sara's room."

Johan is shocked by what he's just said and is quiet for a moment before lashing out again at full strength: "I can't stand it when you shuffle around the house like you're half dead. You have to start cooking again, put on make-up, wear something nice and go to the hairdresser, whatever. It's been long enough. It's got to be over, and if you can't manage that, you can just go. You can just go away. I've had it up to here with your sorrow, it has to stop!"

Actually it has barely started, thinks Ellen. Sorrow. He's right, I'm going to clean up the room, put Sara's stuff in boxes, strip the bed.

Slowly Ellen begins to move. Lisa helps her with Sara's room and there, on the narrow bed, in her friend's arms, Ellen has her first real cry. Johan is standing in the doorway and looks straight into Lisa's face, a horror-stricken face with eyes wide open. Lisa has her arms around Ellen who lies with her head in Lisa's lap.

Without saying anything, Johan goes downstairs. The front door bangs shut.

It's summer, it's vacation. Ellen goes with the twins to the island of Terschelling for a week. Johan stays home, he wants to work. The boys run over the wide beach and swim in the waves. Ellen sits on the terrace of the rented house and lets herself be burned by the sun. She cries and the sun makes her tears evaporate. She feels her skin sting; at night her burned skin is on fire and tells her that she's alive. On the last day of their stay a strong east wind rises up. Ellen bicycles across the island to the eastern point where there lies a house that's called Finisterra. With the greatest effort she bicycles into the storm, she clutches the handlebars and yard by yard she conquers the shell-covered path. The wind blows the tears from her eyes into white crusts on her face. I'm back, Ellen thinks, I have legs again, I have a voice. I have a loss. I have had a daughter. On the way back she lets herself be pushed by the wind. She's hungry. They eat pizzas in the village.

When they return to the city, the boys start to work at a supermarket. They fill bags and sweep the floor. Ellen does her shopping there to see them and to know what they're talking about at dinner.

"The manager, you know, the one with the cowboy hair, he lives for the store!"

"He's already there at seven in the morning! And taking a vacation bothers him, so he comes anyway!"

"Filling the soups is the worst, so many kinds that all look alike, shit, today I just did whatever."

"He said that we're one big family and that at lunch we may choose a microwave meal, but not the most expensive."

"Only the house brand. Incredibly great stuff. Dig in. Awesome!"

Sometimes Johan comes to eat at home. He has set up a bed in his studio to which he returns as soon as Ellen's face looks as though she's about to burst out in tears. He refuses to talk with her about anything other than the household or his work. These discussions are very short.

"The Municipal Museum has bought a painting."

"Nice for you."

"There's going to be an article about me in the *Museum journal.*"

"How lovely."

"Jesus."

Silence.

Ellen calls Nicolaas Bijl. He called her regularly during the past months, but put off by her infinite apathy, he stopped. He continues paying her salary although Ellen asked him to give her unpaid leave.

"You're out on sick leave, my child. And you'll stay that way."

He's elated that she calls. Of course she can come to work again, he'd like nothing better, immediately.

"What if you start with an odd job that's not pressing. And not too many hours, but every day. You have to rearrange the photos; your last year's order has arrived. We left everything for you. Beautiful pictures, very lovely."

Every day Ellen goes to the office for a few hours. Then she sits in her room on the floor with the photos around her. She leans against the wall and cries. After an hour Bijl comes in and takes her in his arms.

"Come, child, it's all right."

Fumbling he gives her his handkerchief. Every day. Then Ellen gets up and they go to have a cup of coffee. The photos are of tools that are used in connection with wood: a crosscut saw, iron climbing shoes, a beautiful 'small violin-builders' gouge, an axe. During the last hour Ellen collects data from a file of correspondence for an article that Bijl wants to write.

"Now go home, my child, come back again tomorrow."

"I don't want to hear about it anymore," says Johan. "Go and complain to Lisa, or to whoever, get a therapist, as long as you stop going on about it to me. For me it's finished, do you understand that?"

Does he mean our marriage, thinks Ellen, why am I not frightened? Don't I mind it if he leaves me? If only the summer were past, if the wind would blow. I'm out of my mind. Nothing matters to me anymore.

Johan has continued speaking: "I'm successful, finally I'm selling something and they're writing about me. I'm going to count, I'm getting commissions. You should think about that and not only about what has happened. Life goes on."

How can he say such a thing? He's always right. His life has continued. He has been shaken, he's had sorrow but it's gone; he does something with it which causes him not to notice it anymore. He becomes furious when others remind him of it. He's tanned, he looks good. He's bought a new jacket. What is he painting, I haven't been in his studio for months, what is he working on so passionately?

"Johan, what are you making?"

"A pietà. I think. I can't say anything about it and I can't show it to you. In addition I have to make a fresco for the post office, that's what I'm working on. Take care of yourself, I'll manage."

The nights he sleeps at home are dreadful. After Ellen has gone to bed, Johan drinks whiskey until he has enough courage to lie with her. He fucks her unresisting body. When she feels something she starts crying. It's unbearable for both parties. Gradually it occurs less often.

He has a girlfriend, thinks Ellen. That's why he takes care of himself and goes running every day. Do I mind?

\*

"Do you mind if it's true?" asks Lisa.

"Yes, of course, dammit. It's no way to act, don't you think? Actually I don't give a damn. It makes it easier for me now. He can demand so terribly much attention, Johan, he sucks it out of you. That's less now. No, I don't mind too much. But what does that mean; isn't that terrible?"

They hike. A trek that lasts the whole day, over dikes and meadows. Through polders, through shallow ditches. There is a strong wind which hampers the conversation. Ellen walks behind Lisa, keeping pace with difficulty. It isn't until the past weeks that she has noticed how totally exhausted she is, an intense fatigue that she remembers from the period right after giving birth.

"You have to walk through it," says Lisa. "Shall we do the water route on Sunday? Can you stand it?"

Yes, actually it's nice. The wind roars around her head, her legs grind away at the land, and she thinks only of walking, only of following Lisa's back. In the shelter of a row of trees they stride along next to each other.

There is movement in the ditch along which they're walking. Large fish come to the surface, one, three, twenty. They circle around each other, suddenly there are signs of a fight, splashing water, the slap of a tail. Dozens of giant carp thrashing in a small space; the rest of the ditch is still.

"There must be a drainage here," says Lisa. "Potatoes, old milk, whatever the farmer's wife wants to get rid of. Or warm water, a tropical fish paradise in the polder. And if Johan were to leave, if you could just stay in the house with the children?"

At the end of the ditch they climb up a dike behind which there lies a wide body of water. The cold wind and the sun give a feeling of being pickled, soaked in lye. They laugh. But still...

The lake has become an estuary. The path runs against the stream, a village lies in the distance.

"Perhaps we'll be able to buy some kind of a snack there," Lisa hopes. "Don't you think that there are a lot of anglers today?"

The closer they get to the village, the higher the concentration of anglers. In the end they sit elbow to elbow. Every fisherman has one green umbrella, under which he sits as if under a tent awning, but several fishing rods. Mostly one in the hand and one at the foot, two floats in the water. They sit on a kind of sewing-box in the shape of a square stool. It has small drawers where hooks, floats, worms, and other necessities can be stored. The black tips of the fishing rods lie across the towing path where Ellen and Lisa walk, jump, are doing a hurdle race. Some fishermen look up annoyed, certainly when Ellen hits a fishing rod with her shoe. Sidestepping to the shoulder is bothersome; it's occupied by the cheering and supply teams; the fishermen's wives sit there in camping chairs and on beer crates, with bags of rolls, boiled eggs, and thermos jugs filled with coffee between their legs. They look disapprovingly at their walking sisters. Here and there a fisherman's child sits next to the father at the water's edge and is allowed to hold the large hand-net in which a fish sometimes hangs. When a fisherman stands up because he has a nibble, the accompanying woman behind him also rises and shouts: yes, hurrah, hurrah, go for it, go, hurrah!

On a side road stands a camper with banners above it: Big championship competition! Anglers Organization "Never Enough!" Teach Your Child to Fish!

Out of the forty anglers there are at most two women: one old lady wearing a sou'wester sits in the central group where it's busiest. She has a nice whispering exchange with her two male neighbours. When they've almost walked past the long row, Lisa and Ellen see another woman sitting at the end, a short way from the others. She is young and has short hair around a dissatisfied face. Her hand-net is still empty. She's talking to no one.

"Never enough," says Lisa.

When they leave the village, the river makes a turn and the wind hits them straight in the face. The sun has gone down and no longer gives warmth. The farms and houses that they pass have in their gardens old fruit trees with angular branches on which the pears are still hanging while the leaves are already turning, already coming off, already going along with the wind. All that decoration has to go, thinks Ellen, all those flowers and fruits, all that coloured foliage. Away with it. Once autumn has settled in, the land becomes distinct; it is no longer veiled. In the city it's better, too, with a real difference between inside and outside. It takes an effort to leave the house, you notice it.

The wind has died down now that evening is coming; the muscles are warmed up and limbered up, effortlessly Ellen lifts her feet over the road, without exertion she floats forward, and for an instant she sees herself walking on high heels through a conference room (hair put up, a nice suit) with a smooth briefcase in her hand and a clear-cut sense of well-being within.

At November's end winter sets in, a severe season that doesn't know how to yield. The heater, which is roaring day and night, cannot drive out the cold in the hall, and when the windows in the large room are opened for airing, it takes more than an hour before it's at all warm again. In the morning the windscreens are ice-covered and have to be scraped clean. It's a blessing when the engine starts.

There is no snow, the land lies unprotected under the biting wind; frost is lodged in all surfaces. Outside the city the fields and meadows are frozen deep down into the ground. The grooves made by tractors and carts in the mud of autumn have congealed into rock-hard farming witnesses. The trees stand and endure the cold. They have thrown off their foliage and have stopped their streams of sap. They concentrate on the farthest points of their root systems, deep underground in the cold earth. Canals, water courses and ponds lie under a thick layer of ice that postpones all rotting and disintegration. In the city, garbage bags and half-filled boxes of French fries, dog turds, and hamburgers are preserved. In the black ice of the pond stilled fish are caught, lifeless reeds are held up straight, and birds become icebound in thin ice.

Peter and Paul skate to school via the waterways. During the weekends they and their classmates make long trips from which they return glowing, with frost in their hair and frozen sweat in their sweaters. Skates, gloves, and pots of skate grease lie on the floor in their room for weeks on end.

Johan doesn't skate but paints instead. Because it's impossible to warm the tall studio he dresses in a mountain-climbing outfit that holds body heat. He's not bothered by the cold, he has lots of body heat: ambition burns, passion blazes, and revenge smoulders. Ellen doesn't skate either, although it's her passion. She still doesn't feel comfortable with easy locomotion, she's not in the mood for gliding; she looks instead for resistance, for the difficulty it costs to get into the car and get it started, for the nagging feeling in the knees when the foot continually comes down on ground which doesn't give. She makes use not of the winter but of the resistance to it. This helps her to feel her own resistance. She has been compliant long enough.

During this period, the members of the disintegrating family (frost arrests rotting and veils weak structure) think little of the narrow grave and as little as possible of what is taking place under the surface. Embarrassed, Paul admits to Ellen that he thinks it's sad for Sara: "As if she's cold, she isn't home. But that's not possible, is it? Stupid, isn't it?"

Johan has not brought up again his plan to design a memorial stone. Ellen waits. A stone might now crack open from freezing, or if erected during the frost, might settle again in the spring. When it was summer, Ellen was at the grave to put plants in the ground: blueberries, wild strawberries, and mallow. She had brought along a plastic watering can, a trowel, and gloves. A kindly supervisor walked her to the grave; Ellen hadn't managed to find it by herself, for half an hour she roamed through the quiet paths and looked at the great variety of grave designs; her agitation grew when she couldn't locate the children's area and finally she walked back to the administration office, laden with her plants and her paraphernalia. It's nearby, it's easy to find, next to Ray of Sunshine and Evertje.

Ellen feels exposed. Nearby people are working like she is, they've set a low cardboard box with African marigolds on the path and, squatting down, are planting them on a grave. Ellen doesn't dare to look at the dates on the stone. They're two slightly older people, a husband and wife. They give Ellen a friendly nod. Ellen puts on her inaccessible hiking face and unpacks the plants. Here planting must be done, thinking about rate of growth and ultimate size of the plants, here there must be no speaking with the buried daughter, no thinking about the present state of the jeans and sneakers, no thinking, no, no.

It's also better not to walk on the grave so that the foot sinks suddenly into the soft earth up to the ankle and the heart leaps in the throat, blood drains from the head, terrifying dizziness forces sitting down, on what? On the broad border along Evertje's grave. Just for a moment.

Ellen gets water from a central pressure pump, she sniffs it: it's river water. She waters the plants liberally, without thinking about the course of the water.

The planting is caught in the frost. Later, if spring ever comes, she will have to consider how many plants have survived and if they've been able to keep a germ of life. Now there's nothing to do.

Christmas, in God's name, what to do about Christmas? That's three whole days when everything is dead and quiet, when you have to sit indoors and devote yourself to cheerfulness, no matter how uncheerful you're feeling. No work, no school, no shops. What did we do last year? Sara received the fish sweater from Alma. The children staged a quiz show; Sara was the assistant and was wiggling her bottom while walking in Ellen's high heels. Johan roared with laughter. They drank champagne. It was cheerful.

This should be avoided, these memories have to keep a low profile. A house on an island? Skiing? Something altogether different?

She consults Johan.

"I'm going to Paris. I won't be here."

"Oh?"

"I'm going with Mats and Zina. Perhaps a few other students

as well. A kind of school trip, we're going to visit museums, look at things. And I want to buy some materials."

"To Paris?"

Paul and Peter are surprised.

"Are we going along? Are you going together? We are going along, aren't we? And what about Grandma?"

"Johan is going by himself. With his students. We're not going along."

Paul looks at his mother.

"Is that horrible, Mum? Are you having a fight?"

Now, thinks Ellen, it would be good if I had an opinion, if I had some thoughts on the subjects. What do I think?

"No, we're not having a fight. Johan would like to go to Paris. And I actually think it's pleasant to be home with you."

Coward, coward, coward. What I say to the children is all right as far as it goes, but I should let Johan have it. That he can't come back home if he doesn't show up, that he can stay and screw his students in that hotel room till he's blue in the face, that I've had it, that I don't want to anymore. No more.

Ellen doesn't let him have it. Coolly she looks at Johan when he steps into his car to pick up Zina. In his new coat. Slash the tyres? Sugar in the petrol tank? Oh, never mind. In the kitchen he had looked helplessly at Ellen. The suitcase stood ready next to the stairs. She saw he was already thinking of something else in the back of his mind.

"Ellen, I can't. Be here now, I mean."

You mean that you can't resist losing yourself in a new love, you mean that you're in love, that you're going to cheat on me, and in Paris no less! You mean that you do everything in exchange for admiration. That's what Ellen thinks. But saying it is something else.

"No. I see that."

"When I'm back, we'll have to talk."

"Yes."

"I don't know what to say."

"Just go."

Like an arrow he darts to the stairs, grabs his suitcase, and rushes down, liberated.

On Christmas Eve, Ellen looks at a detective film on television with the children. They eat hamburgers and chips with coke; later Ellen makes hot chocolate. The next day is the Christmas dinner with presents. In the afternoon Alma comes in a taxi. She plays Monopoly with the boys while Ellen is in the kitchen. She has taken note of the fact that Johan has gone on a trip, but for Ellen she brought a gorgeous bouquet of roses. They're glowing in a corner of the room, deep red.

Oscar reacted nervously when Ellen called to invite him.

"I think I have something else, another engagement, it won't work out.

"Johan isn't here, he's in Paris."

She suspects that Johan's presence might be a hindrance, but her tactical approach turns out all wrong.

"That I should therefore come especially you mean? How awful, how awkward."

"No, I don't mean that at all, Oscar. If you have something else or if you don't feel like it, then don't come. You don't have to. I just thought that you'd like it, that's why."

"I enjoy seeing you, I'd like that. Can't we arrange something else, the day after, the second day of Christmas?"

What could he be doing, thinks Ellen, Gay Christmas? Christmas-a-thome for singles? Treat yourself to a day without family stress? Whatever it is, he doesn't want to talk about it.

"Good, it's National Walking Day, I don't care too much for it. Do you?"

"No, I'll come in the afternoon and we'll stay inside. I'll bring something beautiful to listen to. I hate walking in parks. Also it's much too cold; my glasses can't stand it and my ears go to shreds if I don't wear a hat. I'm sorry about the Christmas dinner, Ellen. Especially now, you know, after, I mean last year everything was so different, it's difficult. I thought you'd perhaps go away, with the family. In order not to be at home now."

"Yes. I don't know. The boys think it's fine to stay at home. Alma is coming, we're going to play games."

"And you?"

"I've bought a plum pudding. I'm going to flambé it festively. I'll serve you the left-overs when you come."

"And your friends," says Alma, "why aren't they here? They celebrate Christmas, don't they?"

"They're in England, with Lawrence's parents. A real English Christmas for the children. Lisa called this morning, it's freezing in the hotel and the whole country stinks of carbon monoxide fumes. They're baking cookies all day long to stay warm."

They'll be back on New Year's Eve, but Ellen doesn't say that. She's going to make salad and sauté the potatoes. The steaks can be done later. Pommes parisiennes. Jesus. What do I think? He's a shit, he humiliates me, I'm leaving when he returns. But it's actually all right like this. Nice to be alone with the children. Not bothered by his lousy moods. Not freeze when I hear the front door open. Think only of myself. To get through the day without Sara. That card from Mara on Sara's birthday; those are horrible days, just like now. It's better not to have children. It's better to be dead. Later at the table it'll be all right again. Concentrate on the steak, on the boys' plans, on Alma's heating problems. Speak. Pay attention. Participate. But it's a conversation in a foreign language. Participate and know that it's not my language, that I'm not naturally the way I feel within: washed out. Scorched earth. Deserted battlefield.

Pathos. I've got to stop this. It's just as if I can't live yet, everything that's beautiful makes me cry, I can't stand it. As if it's a sin now that she's no longer there. Beautiful skies, trees, music. No enjoyment, otherwise I abandon her. If I leave the battlefield, I lose my daughter forever. The potatoes are going too fast. Saved just in time. Alma is sweet to the boys. Both her sons are alive. But they're not there, they've skipped out, they run after their own passions. Oscar is disturbed, I never noticed that he has friends, he goes on vacation by himself. If he goes at all.

The steaks. Hopefully Alma will get through them with her old teeth. They're from a good butcher.

*When I'm as old as Alma is now, I'll still have a dead daughter.*

The thought hits Ellen like a bolt of lightning, she has to sit down on the kitchen chair. What has happened will never pass. The way it is now, it's not waiting for healing but a new point of departure. She has become another person, someone who perhaps will be as old as Alma one day, someone with a gruesome scar. Hoping for recovery makes no sense at all and leads nowhere. Admitting that the situation has changed gives an unprecedented feeling of relief, hilarious, irreverent, hooray, I've become an invalid!

The knives glide smoothly through the meat, the sauce turns out well, the Parisian potatoes are all eaten. Then the light is turned off. Peter holds the tablespoon of cognac above the gas flame, Paul is ready with the matches, and Ellen with the steaming purple-black plum pudding. The fireworks are lit; flushed and laughing, the three of them parade into the dark room. The blue flames dance over the black mountain. That we also have to eat this, unbelievable, thinks Ellen. Blow out. Light candles. Forgot the cream, quickly to the refrigerator. This is nice, this is not wonderful but memorable.

This year there is no Christmas tree. Johan acted as if there were no Christmas, the children didn't ask for a tree, and Ellen didn't want to think about it. In the English store where she bought the plum pudding, she purchased a plastic miniature tree at the last minute. It has batteries, you can turn it on and then the candles start burning, a Christmas song rings out, and the tree itself rotates slowly. This wonder stands on the table between the dishes and the serving plates. From time to time someone turns it on and sprays a dash of Christmas ambiance through the room.

For lack of a tree, the presents were placed near the large vase with Alma's roses. There is a big package that Paul had to get out of the taxi for Alma. It's for Ellen. It's a CD-player.

Why is she so sweet to me? Something that I want so much; I was too lazy to buy it for myself. How does she know that I care so much about music?

Johan thought it was nonsense, after all they had the record player, moreover he never listened to that racket, and expensive also, these things. And then buy everything once again, no way, modern nonsense, a clever trick of the manufacturers to make money, he wasn't going to let himself be taken in by that.

All true, but I'd still like one, Ellen had thought, at the time, before, then. The boys shout with joy. Ellen blushes with embarrassment and emotion over such a beautiful present. She kisses her mother-in-law, the old woman who has thought of things with which she could please her son's wife and has chosen something that is totally perfect.

She wants to thank me because I'm going to give her son back to her, flashes through Ellen. I'm relinquishing her son, she may have him again, she'll never again be bothered by me and for that she rewards me. What a mean thought, how could I think of it? She thought that I was going through a difficult time and she wants to console me, isn't that possible as well?

Sitting erect, the old woman looks at the excited goings-on. Peter is connecting the machine, Paul is reading aloud from the manual. Alma's eyes shine. Ellen smiles at her. Both are true, she knows that she wants to console me, she doesn't know yet that she wants to thank me for returning her darling. Both are true. Ellen turns on the Christmas tree. It's a party.

The next day Peter and Paul go skating in the watery winter sun. Ellen receives her brother-in-law who stumbles up the long staircase in his rubber overshoes, showing a bent head covered by a leather cap with lined earflaps. His glasses are fogged up, in disarray he stands in the hall—coat, scarf, gloves, where to, how meanwhile to hold the package that is clasped in his hand, to kiss Ellen?

She peels him down to his neat white shirt, his shiny suit. She doesn't ask what he did yesterday but settles him on the sofa, across from the roses, next to the new music set.

"Beautiful isn't it? I knew; I went with Alma to buy it. I've brought CDs along for you, where are they? I was holding them when I came in, and now?" Ellen hands him the plastic bag. Such a dishevelled bird's head he has, such a thin neck, such a helpless blind look. They drink tea and Oscar eats with relish a portion of cold plum pudding. His eyes are poor, without his glasses he sees blurred spots, and his movements would fit those of a blind man's cane, that's how little confidence he has in his visual capacity. On the terrain of his deficiency, which must obviously have been a handicap in a painter's family, he has overcome his weakness and still struggles daily. He has become someone who contemplates art, someone who works by the grace of looking, but it's a second choice, forced by the milieu in which he was brought up.

Ellen looks at his ears: large, beautifully shaped outer ears which still look slightly red from the cold. The earlobes stand loose from the neck and have the right degree of fleshiness. How was it, an ear-child with eye-parents?

"It always took a minute before I realized what they were talking about. Johan was much quicker than me, even though he was three years younger. They found my noises a nuisance. I sang in bed, I made up songs for myself with different sounds. Then Johan would start screaming, he couldn't sleep because of it. OSSer, he called me Osser. Shut up, he'd say. I would then pester him by telling him scary stories in the dark with creepy songs. Then he'd cry and Alma would come upstairs to bawl me out. I was the oldest, I should know better. I imitated the snake that was under his bed, he wouldn't get me because I could play the flute and with it you could charm dangerous snakes, I'd hiss louder and louder until Johan pissed in his bed out of fear. No, shut up, Osser!"

Oscar chuckles. It's a sweet memory.

"And the flute," asks Ellen, "did you go on with it?"

"I wanted to play the violin. Papa had a viola and that was the most beautiful thing I knew. When he practised in the evening, I lay in bed listening. Once they played Mozart quintets with two violas. Beautiful, beautiful. Alma didn't like it much; I think they usually practised somewhere else. Then Charles would leave with the viola under his arm and I wanted to come along. I think that I was a musical child, I repeated what he played. He gave me a recorder, I was about four years old. I discovered by myself how to play it. That wood, that oiled wood of the recorder, I thought it was so beautiful and it smelled so nice. Charles said that I was too small for a viola. I would get a violin when I could read and write and go to elementary school. But by that time he had other things on his mind."

"And Alma, couldn't she send you to violin lessons?"

While she's asking it, Ellen already knows: no. Alma was happy to be freed from the string sounds, she could no longer stand hearing a violin. If Oscar were to ask for it, it would be as if he were asking for his vanished father, and that must not, that could not happen. But Johan, didn't he also remain loyal to his father with his drawing talent?

"Yes," says Oscar, "somehow that was possible. I still remember how she looked at Johan when he was painting. She put his drawings up on the wall and showed them to people who came to visit. I always felt alienated from painting, but I saw everything. I stood there and looked. And I thought about it: why he and not I? Why did everyone stand cheering in admiration before Johan's drawings, Alma in the lead, and why did no one listen to my songs on the flute? I had received a book with fingerings and notes from Aunt Janna. I learned to play all sorts of melodies, undoubtedly disgusting Dutch folksongs. In the back of the book was real music, what I thought was real then. A sarabande by Handel, a courante by Chédeville, so sad, so beautiful. But I didn't have much success with it in the living room."

Sad, thinks Ellen. Was Alma a real bitch of a mother who

favoured her youngest and stimulated him in all possible ways while she mercilessly snuffed out the creative impulses of the older one? That's how it looks, that's how it seems, but was it like that?

"Charles left before I got the violin. He took us upstairs one evening, he held Johan's hand, I walked behind. In the big bedroom he showed us his paintings, actually it was very strange, why would he do that? Johan was quiet, he stood looking intently at each painting for a long time. I looked at Papa. I felt uncomfortable, as if something bad were going to happen. And that was so, of course. I don't remember at all anymore what these paintings looked like. Too bad. I always think that there was a violin, a painting of a violin, but I don't remember anymore."

He's been unable to shake it, thinks Ellen. He has remained gripped by jealousy, he didn't let them go to hell with their paintings and has not been able to trust his own ears.

His love of classifying and collecting that serves Oscar so well in his profession also forms the backbone of his greatest, his only hobby. Oscar collects music on records, on tapes, and lately also on CDs. He brought a few for Ellen as a Christmas present. He thought a long time about the selection. He wanted to give her Mahler's *Kindertotenlieder* because that music had been his theme this past year and had helped him to express his sorrow over his young niece. He bought Mozart quintets. That's borderline. Motets by Monteverdi, they listen to them. Ellen is surprised by the stark, pure melodies that run so beautifully through each other. Every phrase is pulled together at the end like a knapsack with a tie. Silence. Control.

Now Oscar takes the most daring part of his present and puts it into the jaw of the machine.

"Sit, Ellen, and listen. Say nothing."

Bang. Oboe line. Bang. A horn starts to sing. Women's voices, smooth, stark. A chorus explodes: *exaudi, exaudi.* Ellen sits nailed to the couch, overwhelmed by the music which expresses exactly what she feels. Severe, with lifted heads they sing from a proud despair. The *Symphony of Psalms* by Stravinsky. Oscar places the information booklet on her lap, and Ellen reads along while the music peals at top volume through the room: *remitte mihi, remitte mihi prius quam abeam et ampleus non ero!*

Loud, the final chord stays hard, no elegant closing but a persisting scream.

Tears run over Ellen's cheeks. Leave me in peace, let me go so that I may still have a life before everything is gone, before I will be no more.

# Chapter six

# Empty Houses

Johan's studio was originally a tall garage, built out of nostalgia like a coach house at the left side of an expansive lawn that slopes up gradually from the gate at the street to the mound on which stands the villa to which all this belongs. The spacious, old-fashioned house supports a roof of blue glazed tiles and is therefore called "the blue house" by Peter and Paul. The owner lives in the villa together with his spouse. His car (a dark blue Rover) is stored in a garage that was later added on the right and which he can enter through the house. He is a sixty-year-old high-ranking official with the Postal Service, with a large personal fortune which is spent on his passion: ocean-sailing. In the giant, impractical garden pavilion where Johan does his painting, the sailor had a work place for many years. Helped by tanned men in corduroy pants, he built a ship that after completion was driven to the sea on a trailer. For this the façade of the garden pavilion had to be demolished, the street gate taken down; the neighbourhood turned out, cheering; the sailor thought: now life starts. The strangely empty boat temple was restored and rented to Johan, not out of financial necessity but from a need to have the garden pavilion remain an incubator for beautiful things. Mr Blue as the children call him, "Bob" to Johan, knew the artist from his position in the postal system that once gave Johan a commission for a painting in the boardroom. There was a modest reception during the afternoon of the delivery, commissioner and artist got into a conversation over a fairly good sherry, Ellen was charming, the children delightful, and Sally, Bob's American wife, invited them all to a barbecue on the lawn at their home. Johan hates chewing on almost raw or on the contrary bitter burned pieces of meat, dunked in greasy sauce and garnished with pickled salad; he detests the turmoil of primitive eating where all parts of the meal are never ready at the same time, but it turned out very differently at Sally and Bob's. There was a comfortable table, set with ceramic plates. A tablecloth. Everyone simultaneously received a steak grilled to perfection by Bob. The adults could sit and talk in a leisurely way while the children played on the lawn. That's how it went.

Sally, a small sturdy woman who always walks around in leggings with silk blouses, was a point of consideration in Johan's decision process about the rental. To be sure the face is old but it is always perfectly made-up. The instep and the ankles are frankly attractive. What does she do while Bob devotes himself to postal affairs? Replant rhododendrons in front of Johan's window, her ass in the air? Lie naked on the lawn, slip into the studio with freshly squeezed orange juice? What will he do if she invites him into her kitchen for morning coffee? This sort of thing is dangerous, before you know it, you're standing in a doorway that's too narrow, then it's kissing or beat an ignominious retreat, grace or disgrace. If he doesn't react when she places her hand on his when he gives her a light, if she is bent over him too long when she pours him his coffee, will she then lose interest out of disdain? Not nice. If he rebuffs her she will be hurt, angry, out for revenge. Even worse.

I shouldn't let it get that far, thinks Johan, that's the only way. We should agree from the beginning that we'd like nothing better than fooling around in her boudoir, but that such a thing is absolutely out of the question. She must continue to feel desired and I must have peace and quiet.

Sally looks at him with a friendly, ironic smile. She has a gardener who takes care of the rhododendrons and a maid who pours the coffee. None of that artistic stuff for her.

"What is left of the mail these days?"

Bob and Johan are sitting in wicker chairs on the grass in the shade of a chestnut tree. They're drinking beer. The warm summer day is coming to an end. The sound of slow but powerfully hit tennis balls would be suitable, but neither Bob nor Sally ever cared anything about tennis, all their passion is for the boat.

"It used to be an event when a telegram was sent. But who still sends telegrams? People have faxes, and car telephones. A special uniformed messenger came, on a bicycle. The telegram was in a leather bag; he rang the bell, the neighbours looked out of the window. There was something solemn about it. Often the delivery man would wait a moment while the addressee skimmed the message: good news, bad news? And who still writes letters, isn't that only for old men? Disappointing, that's what it is."

Johan only half-listens. He is thinking of the painting that is standing on the easel in the coach house and he's making a plan for tomorrow's work. Will he go and have another look later?

"We've sailed and broken her in nicely bit by bit; it's getting to be time for a big trip. No, I'm really thinking of retiring, I no longer take pleasure in it."

Johan pricks up his ears. While Bob continues musing aloud about the pernicious influence of the multitude of telephone models, Johan considers what will happen if Bob takes early retirement. Will he sell the villa? Will the studio be sold with it? He'll never again get such a magnificent studio! Ask for it? Wait and see? That seems the best strategy. Politely he contributes his part to the conversation about mail and telecommunication. But he's been warned.

This is why Johan is barely surprised when Bob storms, whooping, into the studio right after Christmas. He is standing in front of the materials cupboard and is organizing his Parisian purchases. From the whiskey bottle that Bob is waving, Johan sees that something spectacular is going to happen. Glasses. Ice. Cheers!

"In Cook's wake!"

Bob is almost shouting with excitement.

"We're going to cross the Atlantic Ocean, I'd actually like to round the cape at Tierra Del Fuego, if that isn't possible we'll take the canal. Easter Island. Tonga. Tahiti!"

Bob and Sally are going around the world in their hand-made boat. There will be a farewell reception at the highest official body of the Postal Service; furniture will be stored, nautical charts procured. Bob offers Johan the house.

"You don't have to buy it, I'd like to keep it in the family. Who knows, one of the children may want it later. I'd be glad if you'd come and live here, I'll have a rental contract drawn up so that you'll be certain. If we're in the country in the meantime, we can stay in the apartment or with one of the children. Just look around, you can do some rebuilding if you'd like that, the kitchen is perhaps a bit cramped for a family."

A few weeks later, Lawrence and Johan walk through the vacated house. Floor plans lie on a worktable and they fantasize about taking down walls, the placement of new windows, and building a new terrace.

"A cooking island," says Johan, "that you can walk around. And all the appliances in the wall. I want to pull this one part of the room into the entry hall, then the television can stand there, so that we don't have that racket in the room. Is that a load-bearing wall, can we knock it out?"

"What does Ellen think of it, does she want to move?"

Would you want to, leave the house where your dead child grew up? Lawrence has doubts. For Johan it's clearly no problem. Would it be different for a woman?

"Of course she wants to. It's beautiful: big, easy, nice area, no longer have to drag groceries upstairs. Nothing but advantages."

He showers the house with praises and in that way dispels the doubt sown by his friend. He hasn't even spoken with Ellen about the availability of the villa. When he returned from Paris, his head thick with drink, she was more dour than ever and filled his plate without saying anything. He had started out with flair, convinced of his mission, but at the family dining table he shrunk back under the bombardment of neutral looks that hit him. They acted as if nothing were the matter. Paul demonstrated the CD-player, and Peter let the plastic Christmas tree dance for him. When the boys were upstairs Johan wanted her to ask something, to call him to account, to call him names and reproach him—anything to break the strange tension.

She poured him coffee. She started to read the paper.

"How was Alma?"

"All right, I think."

"Didn't she ask where I was, didn't she think it was strange that I was away?"

"She said nothing about it, as far as know."

"And Oscar? Did he say anything?"

"No."

"And you, Ellen? Weren't we going to talk when I returned?"

Ellen looks up from her paper. She's already started three times on an article about mixing and stirring techniques.

"No. I have nothing to say. I'm not yet ready for it."

Three sentences! Hooray! Not ready for it, what does she mean? Johan harbours a kernel of anger. That's familiar terrain, that's action, it's safe and better than silence.

"What do you have to be ready for? What kind of nonsense is that? Can't you show some interest in me, can't you ask how my trip was?"

Johan has jumped up and walks back and forth through the room. On the table the Christmas tree has a surprise fit of dancing as he goes by.

"I couldn't care less how your trip was," Ellen says calmly.

Sighing, Johan sits down at the table next to Lawrence.

"Ellen isn't herself. She's changed so much after, after what happened. It's impossible to talk with her. I wish she were like before. Perhaps that will happen when she gets this beautiful new house,—it could, couldn't it? She's so withdrawn. I have no contact with her anymore. It's never nice anymore."

Lawrence looks pensive. He seldom gets to hear so many confidences from Johan.

"Actually I'm at a complete loss about it. What can you do to get things moving? I'm fed up, there's nothing cheerful in our house, we do nothing together anymore. The children are difficult, headstrong. She doesn't have any control over them, they go their own way. Where's the sense in it? She's got to be tougher with herself, dammit."

"Perhaps the meaning has gone out of her life," says Lawrence.

"The meaning of life? What are we on to now? We're like a couple of adolescents. Debate a bit to see if life has meaning! Of course life has meaning, you have to work full blast and become famous, that's the meaning of life. Or am I wrong; what do you live for?"

"To have a pleasant life, I believe. A nice bond with the people around you, the peace and quiet to erect a few beautiful and useful buildings. And the children, of course."

"Jesus, what drivel. Don't you have to improve the world? At least you aren't religious. Then you could go after your ethical ideals by orders from on high."

"Is it really that strange?"

"It's weak. It's feeble. Children, peace and quiet, usefulness, that's useless. You have to fight, you have to trample and crush all the good-for-nothings and bunglers. I live for my work. I want to make a mark on the world!"

This makes Lawrence fall silent. He thinks of Lisa who is of the opinion that you live because you have no choice. You simply must, you have no choice. Better leave it just now. How touchy Johan is, he worries about Ellen, for sure. Too bad he expresses it in

such a lousy manner, this way it'll only get worse. I do understand.
A depressed woman in your house is a disaster. And fucking, forget it.
You're powerless. But the fact that he messes around so openly with
another woman is certainly not going to be appreciated.

"Perhaps Ellen just wants to be consoled. Get attention. You
think that's crazy? That business in Paris, with that student of yours,
it's costing you a lot. That's stupid, isn't it? You hurt her with that,
don't you? Or do I see that wrong?"

"I think that Ellen doesn't care much what I'm up to. She thinks
only of herself, of her own feelings. I don't know her anymore. I want
her back, Lawrence, I want her back again!"

Rage flares up within him; he flexes his thighs and clenches his
fists. In this mood he gave Ellen a black eye during their Christmas
conversation. Provoked to the limit by her inaccessibility behind the
paper, he hit her in the face. He dragged her from the couch and
shook her back and forth while holding her arms, roared at her that
she had to say something to him, now, anything at all!

He let go of her so abruptly that she lost her balance and fell
against the wall. Crying, he crawled against her, took her in his arms,
whispering hush, hush. But Ellen had been silent the whole time, that
was more or less the problem. She had gone upstairs and he had slept
on the couch that night.

"Come with me to the studio. I want to show you what I'm working
on."

With big bouncing steps Johan precedes Lawrence through
the garden.

He's a child, he's a boy, thinks Lawrence. When he can move
again, start something again, tear something down or instead build it
up, it's all right. Put a stamp on the world, sure! Everyone's to know
that he's been there! That's how he seduces his women, too. He stamps
them: Steenkamer was here. It's not unnoticed by the competition.
Most likely Alma lets Oscar know daily that she's been stamped by
Johan. And Zina's young man, that poor soul, he knows all about it

too. Score points and win, in his work as well. With every painting Johan has to crush something, overpower something. Moreover he has to be cheered on, otherwise he has no existence.

Johan has entered the garden pavilion and has left the door open. Lawrence walks slowly behind him into the tall, light grey space. It is empty and orderly. To the right of the door in the short north-facing wall is a kitchen countertop on which washed glasses are draining. Brushes are soaking in jars on a shelf above it. In the corner is a door to the bathroom that Blue had constructed while he was building the sailboat. There are a few easy chairs and a bed which are separated from the actual work area by a bookcase with a stack of Playboys, a book of photos about the Pacific Ocean, travel books by Chatwin, and a thick book entitled *Research in Perception of Colors*. Along the long west side of the space, shelves and scaffolding have been installed where Johan keeps his materials in perfect order. In front of this cupboard stands a large worktable, half covered with sketches for the commissioned fresco. The east wall, across from the table, consists of windows. The original garage doors have been replaced by glass that looks out over the lawn. From floor to ceiling light comes into the room. Against the short south wall a two-level storage system with slats has been built for Johan's paintings. It looks like a storage space for giant long-playing records. Stickers on the side show the contents of each compartment. The storage area as well as the large windows can be closed off by long, light grey curtains.

From his position near the door, Lawrence sees the back of an easel which stands in the middle of the room. Johan flits around like a fish in its own water-barrel.

I don't do things right, thinks Lawrence. My workroom isn't even a quarter of this one, and when I enter it I'm not suddenly five inches taller as Johan is now. Weak, feeble, he said. He has no time for losers.

During his envious reflections Lawrence, his hands in his pockets, walks to the easel, around it, and back a few feet. Johan rummages in the kitchen.

A punch in the face. Jesus. Close eyes. Open again. The painting is four and a half feet wide and three feet high. Two women on a sofa. Lisa sits on the right. From the bloodless face her wide open eyes look straight ahead, at him. She sees nothing. She is wearing jeans with worn, bleached knees. Her upper body is naked. On her lap lies the head of Ellen who has fallen over from her sitting position to Lisa's left. The face is turned to the viewer, the eyes are closed, the mouth is pressed open against Lisa's knees.

Three small parallel streams (tears, snot, and drool) run down. Ellen has bare legs under a short black skirt; one leg hangs diagonally to the lower left corner of the painting, the other is pulled up slightly so that the knee extends forward. Ellen's right hand hangs down limply in between the knee and the oblique calf. Her left hand is held by Lisa, and—the tendons in the wrist are taut—squeezed tight in an uncomfortable and strange position. Lisa has placed her arm around Ellen's upper body. It looks powerless; with spread fingers the hand lies on the stomach. Ellen is wearing a sweater with a strawberry pattern that contrasts strangely with the despair on her face. Lisa's breasts are small, like those of a very young girl. The slightly swollen nipples give the impression that they were never suckled. There is no comfort to be found here. In the upper left corner of the painting, next to Lisa's horror-stricken face, there is a window. It's open. A soft breeze pushes the curtain aside slightly and pale sunlight enters. Through the window a solitary birch can be seen, a young tree with a straight trunk, vivid black spots on the white bark, and a light green haze of just sprouted foliage around the branches. Despite Lisa's wide open mouth, it is deathly quiet. She screams soundlessly. Despite Ellen's swollen face, she is not repulsive. She is at one with her sorrow.

Lawrence is bewildered. How is it possible that Johan feels so perfectly the mood of the woman who is a mystery to him in his everyday life? How can he give form so passionately and so exactly to a sorrow that he denies? If Johan has imagined this, why doesn't he understand Ellen? And who would go to Paris with his girlfriend if he knew that his wife were feeling like that? He clears his throat.

"How did you ever think of it?" he begins.

"I saw them sitting one time. They're not Lisa's real tits, but you can see that yourself. From Playboy. Their heads are from a vacation snapshot."

"But why—"

Johan interrupts him.

"A pietà, don't you think? It struck me immediately. I moved the cross beam, you see, tore the form of the cross out of its context. It also created a nice space for the window."

He's hopping from one foot to the other in front of the gruesome painting, a satisfied grin on his face.

"Nice, I like all that grey. The intensity of the lower part is much stronger than that of the upper half. I turned it around, you know, sort of a pale Jesus."

"But Johan, if you … I mean, has Ellen seen it?"

"No she never comes here actually, especially not now."

"But can't you talk to her?"

"No, there's no talking sense to her. And I certainly can't. That knee is good, don't you think? I'm also satisfied with the snot, that was difficult. You know, I've worked on it for half a year? All those hairs, boy, nasty work!"

No, Lawrence thinks, they're clearly not on the same wavelength. Johan pokes his friend in the side.

"Come, we're going back. I still want to look at that wall. And then we'll go and have a beer. Or do you have to go home?"

Inside, Lawrence recovers his equilibrium. They talk about moving the wall and the prices of marble, that's familiar territory. Johan is willing to be helped and advised, he's eager and very interested. Lawrence, who cannot get the blood-curdling image of the two screaming women out of his mind, keeps feeling that something isn't right, that he should offer his friend help in another way, but that he can't. Johan listens to him, will soon sit in the café with him for an hour, full of good fellowship and trust, but totally inaccessible.

I'm going about this in the wrong way, I can't do this, thinks Lawrence who feels increasingly uncomfortable. Or is Johan crazy?

He keeps putting me on the wrong track with his crap about use of colour and layout. I'm leaving, I've had it. He asks my advice about what he should do with Ellen and then he shows me something like this! I'm not letting myself be conned anymore. He'll have to figure it out himself.

Inner hyperbole that fades as soon as they sit in the car together. Friends. Men who remain together and, quite apart from words or understanding, stand together under the violence of the silent suffering of women to which Johan has given such splendid shape on canvas.

*   *   *

Unaware of the state in which Johan has portrayed her, Ellen climbs up the stairs with the shopping bags. She unloads on the kitchen table. If she sits down now, she'll never get up again, so she'll keep going. Coat off, briefcase in the room next to her own table, unpack the food, put things down for the time being, walk back and forth between table and refrigerator, table and toilet, table and bathroom.

It is close and stuffy in the house and she opens the windows. Sit for a moment on the wide windowsill of the kitchen, legs inside. It is cold, it's still cold but it's calm. Something in the air that Ellen inhales reluctantly betrays the coming of spring. What is it? A softness, a breath of water that has come above a certain temperature? Or the emanation of thawing earth? The maple which for months stood as a dead stockade in front of the window now shows swellings on its bare branches. Peering at the section of park at the end of the street, Ellen can't help but notice that the yellow-grey soil is starting to show a greenish colouring. The entire winter harvest of dog turds is defrosting there to the joy of the crocuses, which after a while will stick their silly heads through the soil. Everything warms up, starts swelling and growing, everything rejoices in light and warmth. Damn, what a filthy business. The world strives to flower, thinks Ellen. And me? I was glad that I didn't have to, that I could be busy surviving in the cold. That I didn't have to pay attention to how I looked. I think in the past, I'm already contaminated. For a year no one has looked at me except for Bijl, the dear. No one has whistled at me on the street or looked at me too long in the tram. And now? I don't want to defrost. That's what it comes down to. After this conclusion the window can be closed again. Where are the boys?

Ellen sticks her head into the hall. No booming from upstairs, no coats on the coat rack. Six-thirty. She puts on the Mozart quintets and has to laugh in spite of herself because in this music it's unmistakably spring.

On the table lies a note: Mum, we're eating at Max's and afterwards there's a school party. See you tomorrow! Ellen stretches, loosens her boots, and lies down on the couch with the evening paper.

Next week. Next week it will be a year ago and I live. I have a CD-player and a job and opinions about the seasons. Why do I do it? For the boys? They need me less and less.

Ellen sits up. Mozart's adagio starts. Never again. Never again so dependent on a man. Another one? Could I fall in love with another, sit across from a man in a rowboat, see the lush banks glide by and not think about the fact that I'm cold, look with all my attention at a man's face, and simply want to listen well? Not sleep again? I can do that only with spring in head and cunt, that's only possible in a completely defrosted condition.

Suddenly Johan stands in the room. The wild trio has masked his coming upstairs. He looks at her pleasantly. He looks good, satisfied.

"Are you sitting there comfortably, Ellen? Aren't the boys home?"

Ellen turns down the music and puts away the paper.

(This is my husband. He comes home. *Try* for once.)

"They're eating at a friend's, and after that they're doing something at school. Have you eaten?"

"Madam! Shall we dine together in the city, at the Carp for example?"

(He's doing his best. He's smiling at me. He wants to be nice. He *is* nice. Do it. You're hungry anyway.)

"I could make something here?"

(Stupid. I don't want to make anything at all. I don't want to be here with him. Stupid!)

"No, we're not going to do that. I have something nice to tell you and a festive meal goes with it. We're going out. You agree?"

"Yes I'll just put something on."

Johan pulls the telephone towards him to call the restaurant. The string quintet plays a rapid presto. Ellen goes upstairs.

In the "Lost Carp" all the tables are set with real linen. The ambiance is old-fashioned, with dark panelling, carpets, heavy table silver, but the kitchen is pleasantly up to date (much fish, little fat, reasonable portions). The Father, the old one, is a stocky man, light purple in the face, who putters about in the back between the wines and gasps for air with a permanently opened mouth, just like a carp. The Son runs the kitchen and receives the guests. Father is behind the heavy table silver, Son is behind the nicely legible menu.

He seems actually pleased when Johan and Ellen enter, and shakes both their hands.

"This is a pleasure. It's been a long time. I think that your own table is still available. Please come with me?"

Son is considerably taller than Father. His friendly brown eyes radiate something weak and limp. That's why Father still stands grumbling between the wine racks and follows Son's movements in the business with argus eyes. Father, in turn, is in full view of the guests who have just entered; Johan and Ellen's table is in the back, near the wines. Ellen sits on the seat against the wall and Johan sits at an angle next to her. They see Father brighten up somewhat and the mumbling increases in volume. With flailing arms the old one lumbers to Son, to whom he hisses something while shaking his head. Undoubtedly it's about placing guests and he would prefer to place a handsome couple enjoying their meal in front of the window. Son resists the attack and softly speaks in Father's ear (regulars, better like this, discuss it next time).

Johan orders wine and chats with Son about the dinner.

"I can recommend the fixed menu. Simple but very good. A

clear fish soup, and then skate wings in a saffron sauce. As dessert a chocolate creation.

"A sense of colour isn't your strongest suit," says Johan. That fish soup, I don't think much of it. Don't you have a nice paté to start?"

"Paté for the gentleman, most certainly. Do you agree with the skate? We have a red perch paté."

Johan nods. Ellen wants everything. Simply. And a bottle of water. Son is going to take good care of it for them and Father, gasping, watches him go through the kitchen door.

There are almost no guests. Piano music tinkles very faintly in the background, without rumbling drum, so it's probably classical. Ellen tries to listen but can't figure out whether Satie or Scarlatti is intended. All the conditions for a good conversation are present. The principal characters toast one another with the Chablis and prepare inwardly.

(Ellen: don't let everything go wrong right away, wait and see, he means well; the way he carried on to Son, I hate that; I've put make-up on and put on a skirt, I'll sit here and behave.

Johan: it's going well! I'll tell her *before* the skate. Saffron sauce, how did they think of it? The wine is nice. For the time being don't drink too much. That blouse looks beautiful on her. She has turned quite grey. And still too thin.)

Son comes to bring the soup and the paté. He asks their opinion about the wine which is frankly splendid. Johan lifts his hand in an appreciative gesture to Father who nods back, continually nodding his head.

"Don't you think it's strange," says Ellen, "that we sit here like this while it's a year ago when Sara, when Sara became ill. That she died. As if we're celebrating it."

God Almighty, thinks Johan. Exactly the right comment to spoil everything. That's what I mean. That's how she is. I try to cheer her up a little and she immediately puts her misery out in the open? He takes a gulp of wine, wipes his mouth with the large napkin, and waits before answering. She's right too, it's a year ago, I was working for the opera then. Now make the repartee tactful, follow her line.

"Yes. We've indeed gone through a whole year. And you're starting to look better, you're working again, and you're able to cope better."

Suddenly Johan can't control himself any longer, he brims with the urge to let everything be all right again, to start anew, to cross out all the misery once and for all.

"A great date to start completely anew. You get your own room where no one will bother you, if you want I'll build you a rack for your music paraphernalia. And the boys have a kind of apartment upstairs with their own shower and toilet, you'll see how wonderful that is. Actually I'll also be home all the time because I work in the garden so to speak. In the cellar there's plenty of room for a sauna, I've already looked at it."

"Johan, what are you talking about?"

He looks at her, somewhat bewildered.

"The house, Ellen, the house! We're going to move!"

The story of Bob and Sally, the round-the-world sailors, the inspection by Lawrence, and once again the qualities of the villa are now dished up more systematically for Ellen. Son waits for the opportunity to take away the plates of the first course and strikes when Johan has finished speaking and Ellen stares at him speechlessly. A well-chosen moment.

Thoughts race through her dazed brain. How did he get it into his head to rent that house without discussing it with me? Without asking if I even want it? Away from Sara, you can't do that. Such a sweet man, Bob, so nice of him to make Johan such an offer. Marble floors, a black bathroom. Start anew. *He* starts anew. *He* has started anew a long time ago and now at last he wants to pull me along behind him, to get me moving.

Son brushes the tablecloth and straightens the cutlery for the skate. He refills the glasses once more and moves away.

No matter how much Ellen tries to see herself as occupant of the villa, as someone with her own room, looking across the trees to the lights in the studio—it remains Johan's fantasy.

I simply don't want to. I no longer want to be with him in the same house, no matter how large and covered in black marble. Is it my period? Should I consider what I think of it in two weeks? Of course not, I haven't had a period at all this last year. My opinion has to be constant because everything stands still. Through the shock, through the weight loss. It will be nice to bleed again as before. I have to eat more. Less stress. Not move and take up residence in a palace with Johan. Which he designs, where he decides how it should look, where he is always present.

Actually I would like it, but not with him. How awful. He would like it so much.

The skate is being served. The wings lie powerlessly in a viscous yellow puddle. Son hopes that they will enjoy their meal.

"Well? Say something! Fantastic, isn't it? Such an opportunity for us!"

"Johan, I'm not doing it."

Excellent she thinks. Not "I have a feeling" or "I believe" but simply: no.

Now Johan is perplexed. He doesn't give in, he doesn't even think of defeat yet.

"Of course you have to get used to the idea, it comes unexpectedly for you. I've known it much longer. Start anew, Ellen, think of that. We leave behind all the horrible experiences in that old house. You can't continue living in such a dump, what do you say? Now that I'm doing so well.

"You know, I've thought about it carefully. When we live there, I'm going to do things differently. I want to do more things together with you, you don't have to worry anymore that I'll skip out as I have recently. That'll be finished when you're with me again, like we were before. We'll get a theatre subscription. We'll eat out. The boys are almost grown up, after all."

"I don't want to, Johan. I won't do it."

The skate is congealing. Without being asked Father brings out a new bottle. Without a word Son brings it to the table, Johan nods, Son pours, they drink.

Ellen takes a bite of fish. She feels calm. In her imagination, the villa becomes smaller and smaller until it lies like a speck in the green landscape.

"You don't understand, Ellen. I'm choosing you! No more messing around with other women! It's not too late yet, you're thirty-five, we can still have a child, think of *that*! That's really a new start!"

A baby. A child to to make things all right, thrashing about on the lawn. Well. Ellen is reminded of a theatrical production she saw once (*Macbeth*? A royal drama? In any case Shakespeare) in which all players bared their chests as soon as a loss was suffered. They cried, mourned, and almost suffocated in lamentations. After two minutes they all put their tight leather jackets and coats of mail back on again and started a new brawl. Full of enthusiasm and in good spirits, until there was another death. She clearly remembers the rhythmic flipping up of the theatre chairs and the audience sneaking out the side doors. The performance was given in old Catalan by a group of Australians who were living in Canada. It lasted four hours. There was no intermission.

"I won't think of it, Johan. Also it's not a question of getting used to the idea. I don't want a new child. I don't want to live in a new house with you. I can't start anew."

Father looks at them carefully from his trench in the wine racks. Regretfully, Son watches the untouched skate grow cold.

"Do you know what I'm giving up for you?"

Johan raises his voice now that it's finally dawning on him that he's not making an impression on Ellen.

"You don't have to give anything up for me, Johan. It's fine with me if you move. Perhaps Zina wants a child with you, or someone else. You can start anew yourself, can't you?"

"I'm offering you a magnificent house!"

Johan roars. All colour has drained away from his face.

"A magnificent house! I want you back, I'll be faithful to you, I want a child with you, and you say no?! What do you want, dammit?"

Peace, thinks Ellen. I'd like to be left in peace. But she doesn't have to answer.

"For a whole year I've tolerated these depressions of yours, it was unbearable. I was deprived. You never wanted to fuck anymore, you acted as if I were air. And I'm not leaving you in the lurch, I'm ready to put some energy into it; I work my fingers to the bone, and you say no! You're out of your mind. You are ungrateful, and uninterested. It's simply impossible to live with you, you're a refrigerator, a sack of potatoes, a rotten fish."

Ellen has risen. Slowly she puts on her scarf and her coat. The theatre chairs flip up.

"Yes, go ahead and leave, run away from your responsibilities. No wonder I have affairs, you're a worthless wife!"

Ellen looks at Son, at Father, and walks to the exit, watched closely by diners who are lingering at their tables in the front part of the restaurant.

Son, tactful as he is, has turned the music up somewhat during the discussion. Now he turns the volume back down. Johan drinks the Chablis in big gulps but he doesn't touch the food. It's clear that he isn't a man to sit at a table by himself. He can't eat without a public, but he is so shocked and paralysed that he also cannot leave. Drinking is best right now.

Son walks back and forth to guests who are paying and leaving and casts compassionate glances in Johan's direction, as if he would like to draw up a chair and feed Johan with lovingly prepared bites of saffron skate. When the restaurant is finally empty and the bottle almost, he comes to Johan's table.

"I suppose I'll take the skate away? I don't think it'll taste like much. Alas. Perhaps skip dessert this time? Yes, certainly."

Johan looks at him, with difficulty and somewhat drowsy from drinking so fast.

"Bill. In a minute. No rush."

Son starts clearing the table and fills the glass with the last of the wine. Some coughing and shuffling announce Father's approach. He lowers himself onto a chair facing Johan.

"Fucking bitch," says the latter.

With his slightly bulging carp's eyes Father carefully eyes his regular customer.

"May I offer you a cognac?" He holds up two fingers in Son's direction. "To mitigate this evening's disappointment somewhat. A lovely cognac."

Son comes with the large glasses and puts them down carefully.

"It's the wine, Mr Steenkamer," says Father. "A good Chablis releases things in people in my experience. Sometimes it's for the better, sometimes it's for the worse. With a Chablis the truth comes to the surface. That's how it is."

Father gets a coughing fit. Son rushes over to thump him on the back and take him along. Johan looks for his wallet.

*

The refusal has started something within Ellen. To be sure she was afraid that first night, and once Peter and Paul were home, she went down the long staircase to put the security chain on the door. But the fear did not affect her decision.

In her conversations with Johan she remains steadfast so that he has to resign himself to her refusal for the time being. Further he can't go. He absolutely refuses to consider a divorce. They're temporarily going to live at two addresses, that's all. In fact it was already like that because he was more in the studio than at home. At most the present situation is somewhat more comfortable.

He moves into the house for the time being and believes that Ellen will follow as soon as she's in her right mind again.

Ellen doesn't insist on a legal settlement. Once he's left, once it gets through to him, then the paperwork will follow, she thinks.

Her attempts to arrive at a sort of division of property founder. Johan doesn't want to take anything with him and above all to divide nothing. Whoever divides brings about a split; if you have half a set of dishes, you admit that you're divorced.

"I'm buying everything that we need new. I've wanted a new bed for a long time. You can dispose of the refrigerator and the washing-machine when you come. I'm ordering a refrigerator with self-closing doors, that's easier. I want beautiful things that go with the kitchen."

Finally Ellen convinces him to take at least the bookcases and the leather chair from his parents' home. She helps him to pack his books, at which time she secretly fills up the boxes with dishes and cutlery that originally belonged to Alma. The tablecloths. His clothes. A fishing rod. But she is not allowed to pack a watercolour that hangs above the conjugal bed (birds above the polder) nor sheets and towels.

"Those etchings from the hall, Johan, you're taking them, aren't you?"

"You never liked them much, I know that. Go ahead, put them with the rest."

The audio equipment and all the records remain behind, Johan can do without noise. Lawrence comes with a rented van into which they load everything. Doors stand open, wind blows though the stairwell, they shout through the windows and in the room which has become lighter. Aside from fear, Ellen feels unprecedented relief. She smells the spring wind; from the kitchen window she waves after the van.

The twins react in a remarkably matter-of-fact way to their father's departure. The boys, each separately, declined without hesitating Johan's offer to move with him "in the meantime" on the basis that the villa is too far from their school. The private bathroom and living area of their own cut no ice with them. Ellen tried speaking with them, Johan's move a year after the loss of their sister should mean something to them, but she has no handle on it.

"Let him go," says Peter. "He never comes on time for dinner. He's never here. It's better for him to leave."

"He has a vile temper," reflects Paul, "and you two are always fighting. We can drop by his place or something. He's still our father, he's not dead."

It makes Ellen unsure. Have they outgrown the family so much that they don't care? They're home very little; Peter keeps his drum set in a friend's garage, and that's where they spend whole weekends. They have a band, they make music. Paul writes the lyrics and sings. It's going well at school, they'll both easily get into the next grade.

There's something wrong with the house. Now that two family members are gone, it's too roomy, too large, too empty. It seems poorly filled by the reduced presence. When the boys are home, they sit on the couch with Ellen. The three of them eat in the small kitchen. Neither Peter nor Paul makes a claim to an emptied room. It has become a house with empty spaces where people no longer are.

When Bijl's bookkeeper asks Ellen if she knows anyone who would like to take over his apartment in the centre of town, she doesn't need to think for long. A small living room, two bedrooms, a large kitchen, and a sun deck on the roof, all together it's half the size of what they have now. Yet the boys are immediately enthusiastic, and Ellen feels at home in it. They do it. On the table lies a large piece of paper on which they've drawn the plan of the apartment, and on it they move back and forth pieces of cardboard that represent beds, tables, wardrobes. Johan, who sees this during one of his grumpy visits, flies into a rage. He considers it a slap in his face that they prefer such a cramped chicken coop to his spacious country house.

Ellen understands. She wants to move, but not with him; the children want her presence, not his. This makes him angry and aggrieved. Cardboard boxes are brought into the house to pack all the household goods. Whatever they won't need in the new house will be put in Lisa's immense attic, for later, for when Peter and Paul leave the house; to avoid the pain of throwing out.

Ellen dismantles Sara's small room. Toys. Clothes. The child's desk. The narrow bed. She is planning to take a few things (the doctor's box? the skirt with the flounces?) with her, but ultimately packs up everything together to ship to Lisa. A hard afternoon.

The boys choose their stuff themselves. When the moving van has left for the house on the river, they remain behind in an open space with small islands that are still habitable. The large dining table has gone to Johan, after all he also has the tablecloths; the conjugal bed goes to the twins' room, and the boys' beds go to the trash. For herself Ellen buys a full-size bed.

That it should go so easily. Pack what you want to take along and you leave for a new house. Just like that. You leave the place where you no longer want to be. In the half empty room the music sounds like in a church. Ellen is alone and listens to the *Symphony of Psalms*. Part two. In a calm walking tempo the oboe rambles over uneven terrain. Big steps. The flute follows, and another. And yet another oboe. When the low strings join the ramblers, the women's voices start to sing, solid and loud. The men follow, until the chorus is complete. A punctuating trombone leads them to a great outburst. They sing about solid ground underfoot, about a trek that leads away from the cesspool of vice and about new words that fill the mouth. Very softly, accompanied by stopped trumpets, the singers admit at the end that they are feeling manifestly hopeful. Ellen reads along with the text and disregards the references to the Supreme Being. A song is being sung that is meant for her. With this melody in her ears, she can go on her way to the new house.

The warehouseman of the lumber company has done the painting. The house receives them like a forest in the spring, with fresh smells and excessive light. The boys jump on their beds and let their loud rock music sound through the rooms. Ellen hangs the new curtains and sets the table in the kitchen. The three of them stand on the sun deck and look out over the roofs. On top of the houses a new, unfamiliar world has been built: plastic tents, plants and whole trees in pots and bathtubs, chairs, couches, awnings and gates.

"Wow," says Peter, "this is an awesome house, Mum."

Peter helps with arranging the bookshelves and Ellen does the dishes. Satisfied, they sit chuckling at each other over the lasagne from the take-out restaurant.

In her new bed Ellen has room. There is no empty space next to her. A narrow desk, actually a wide shelf, stands along the wall, put together by the warehouseman. Above it Ellen has hung photos of her children. They're all eight years old.

After a week, the house is lived-in, and as usual Peter and Paul go out in the evening. Suddenly Ellen hears the third part of her favourite symphony very differently. Sitting on the old sofa in her new living room, she listens to the triumphant hymn of praise. She is struck by the sinister rhythms of the "laudate", prepared by dull horn blasts at the beginning. Agitation. This is no mild ode of praise, this is close your eyes and act as though you're not afraid. In the middle, the sturdy steps from part two return, but now faltering, with dragging feet. Then roaring over resounding cymbals, strings, and trumpets. The chorus falls silent in an invocation and stumbles, breathing illogically, to the hushed final chord. Ellen turns off the CD-player and puts on her coat. Outside there is a cold wind that knocks the raindrops from the trees. She bicycles home.

Turn on the bare lightbulbs everywhere. Then to Sara's room. There sit on the wooden floor. Here my daughter slept. There she played and was read to. Here she lived, and starting next month other people, people who have never known her, will fill the room with other life. Place my hands on the floor. Be thankful that you've gone through it, that you didn't die? Certainly, at the kitchen table with the boys, *there,* without a doubt.

But not here. Not right now.

I left the child alone. I crept out of the bathroom, out of the row of children's graves. Out of this house. I didn't follow her, although I know how it can be done. Not across the wrist but lengthwise along the blood vessels. First the right one, then, quickly, left. Not standing at the edge of the roof, not looking down below but lying down; close your eyes and roll. I didn't do it. I turned aside and walked away.

The memory of Sara's living body surprises her with a fierceness for which she isn't prepared. Sara's shoulders between these intact wrists through which blood has continued to flow unobstructed. Sara's body between her thighs, between her knees which now bend and straighten when unpacking dishes and glasses in unfamiliar kitchen cupboards. Which are not crushed. Which have continued to carry her. Betrayal, betrayal.

Through her tears, Ellen starts talking to her daughter, telling her that she's still alive, that she's still there, that she's asking her forgiveness for her cowardly desire to live. She hears her own voice, she means what she says but thinks, as a gloomy counterpoint, that this is nonsense. That she doesn't speak to reach her child but to console herself. Screaming or whispering, she has to forgive herself.

For the last time she closes the door of the small room. She turns off the light.

The room downstairs has become an enormous ballroom. Using a cup that was left behind, Ellen drinks water from the tap. She dabs her eyes and washes her face. Now be in the room for a moment, walk along the walls, lie stretched out on the wooden floor.

The door!

Footsteps are coming up the stairs. Ellen bounds to her feet, she should be afraid but she isn't. Does she, even now, want to be stabbed by a confused burglar? She has good ears and an untrained but excellently working musical memory. At the moment the door of the room opens, she realizes that she recognized the rhythm of the footsteps.

"I saw light everywhere. I still have a key. I wanted to take a look."

Johan is wearing a windbreaker over his old fisherman's sweater. He's wearing jeans, like Ellen, and leather boots. Across the surface of worn wood they look at each other. Ellen raises her arms and turns up the palms of her hands.

"You've moved. You've done it. I was just there, to say hello to Peter and Paul and look at their room. It looks nice. Really. You three have done a good job."

Ellen melts under these unexpectedly generous words. She cries because she gets no vindictive comments. She's gone her own way, and she's not getting punished. Helplessly they stand facing one another in the empty space. Everything sounds different. Johan straightens his back and nods at her, bowing chivalrously: "Would milady the countess dance a minuet with me?"

Ellen smiles and forgets her tears. She shakes her crinoline and walks with small, elegant steps to the middle of the room.

"It's my pleasure, your lordship the count!"

While they hum together the worst minuet they know, over and again those thumping repeats, that ominous knocking motif on the weak beats, while they rhythmically beat their boots against the wood and their bodies conform to the music, they walk up to each other. They look at each other, they hold each other in this game, with their eyes, even when they touch each other, when her hand touches his shoulder, his hand finds her back.

Solemnly they dance together, slowly and seriously. "Permit me, madam," says Johan when he places both arms around her waist, "I wish to embrace you in this bare house."

"I don't mind, sir, I comply with your wish."

The movements become smaller, the feet stand almost still. The music has ceased but the bodies still dance and his eyes pierce her eyes, her look holds his look captive.

Until he puts his head in her neck, until he groans and starts to cry. Then they fall clumsily on the floor which suddenly is no longer a polished dance floor. Then Johan clasps his lost wife in his arms, then they both feel what parting is.

They cry without recrimination this time. It's not about persuasion or getting the other to see the light. It's about the fact that they lived on this floor, that they started their family in this space and that it escaped them. What they thought they had is transformed and vanished, what they built has become an empty room.

Wet cheek against wet cheek. Whispering in a warm ear, be still, be still; caresses in wet neck hair. Clinging like drowning people in a sea of wood.

Ellen lies with the back of her head on the hard floor and roars at the top of her voice, unreservedly. Johan has put his head on her chest and lies bent against her. With her arms she clasps his head, a bowl around a bowl containing memories of their joint life that will fade and disappear.

Her hair has come undone and is caught painfully tight under his elbow. She doesn't feel it.

This dance also comes to an end. The movement becomes gentler and less fierce. They still shake, they hiccup, they sniff up snot and tears while they remain lying close against each other, exhausted. Johan takes off his jacket and places it as a pillow under their heads. He pushes his arm under her neck. She settles her head against his shoulder. Snot gets on his sweater. He smells her sweat. Familiar. Nice.

His hand touches her breast and cups around it. She hears his breathing change and deepen. They don't utter a word. He sits up and bends over her, invades her open mouth with his tongue. Bitter. Salty. As a matter of course.

She kicks off her boots. He tears her blouse out of the jeans, folds it up over her face and rubs his head between her breasts, hard and fast.

Ellen sits up and twists the blouse over her arms. The grey silk flaps down like an evening bird. Johan has taken off his sweater and with fierce movements Ellen tears open his shirt. With quick clicks the buttons ricochet off the wooden floor. She pushes him over and hangs over him with her loose hair. She licks his nipples, his navel, with her hands she claws hard over his pants. Undone, off, boots off, everything, everything off. The naked man pulls her pants off her rear. What are we doing, what are we doing, thinks Ellen. Why do I feel this terrible pity, why do I want to do anything to make him stop crying? Do I want what is happening now, do I really want it?

Ellen's neck, thinks Johan. My wife. An icy fury rises within him about what he has lost, about what he is going to leave. He kneads her breasts so hard that she pants with pain, he caresses her body with long, pressing strokes, from top to toe. This is Ellen's body. This is the last time. With his mouth he follows the neckline to right under her ear and bites. His sucks his blood mark into her skin, crawls on his knees and bites and eats, breast, stomach, with his nose in the salty hair, eat, suck her up, have her. He pushes her thighs apart and bites her lips, folds his hot fleshy tongue against her cunt and licks her in her deepest folds. Furious, he feels that she's coming. Power. A button that he pushes. My wife whom I know like Papa his viola. Oh Ellen, you're leaving me.

"I'm leaving you. It's the last time."

Despair colours her voice. But despair will not prevent her from remembering. The unplanned meeting becomes a monument in her memory. She smells and savours all the familiar smells and tastes. Armpit. The inside of the elbow, an oasis of tenderness even in the crudest men. The prick, the world prick which filled her to bursting, which squirted her full, which was truly at home within her. Tenderly she bids farewell, her mouth whispers along the raised shaft, her palm closes around his balls, tenderly, tenderly. Until it's enough, until fury also flames in her about the loss. She lowers herself astride him, she sits down on that wonder rod and takes him up in her sex. Her head bends backwards, she is a rider in the wind and her breasts move beyond his reach. Her knees scrape over the floor. She doesn't feel it. He throws her off and turns her on her back.

Now. They look at each other while he enters her. Now. Now his knees thump against the wood and the splinters push into her buttocks. She sets her nails into his back and scrawls deep furrows. He pierces her shoulders with his teeth, they eat each others' lips and bite through because they place a stamp on each other for the last time.

With these scratches I let you go. With this bite I say farewell to you.

They taste blood in the kiss. Blood on the hands. Ellen stretches her arms and legs around him as they go into the air for the last time.

She bites into the hand which lies over her face, into the salty, strong hand that tastes of iron. She licks between the fingers and sucks the little finger, the small hairs tickle against her tongue. Over. Washed ashore on the beach. Lost. Loose. He takes her face between his hands, with his tongue he pushes her eyes closed and drinks her tears. Finished. Farewell.

Without a word Johan dresses. He leaves the torn shirt. Ellen hears the metal of the key jangle against the granite kitchen countertop, hears the boots drum down the stairs, the door creak and slam closed. Fading footsteps on the pavement. The silence of the night. The dizzy rustling heard by someone who lies alone on a wooden floor in an empty house.

# Part III
# Don Giovanni:
## *"più del pan che mangio, più dell'aria che spiro"*

*Chapter seven*

# The Woman with the Fish

Lisa sleeps miserably during the night from Saturday to Sunday. The bedroom window rattles in unpredictable wind gusts, it's too cold, she pulls an extra blanket over herself. It's too warm, she dreams. She awakens frightened from the dream, without any recollection. Only that it was terrible. She goes to drink a glass of water; the house is silent and the doors to the children's rooms stand open. There is greyish light on the floors, for the wind chases clouds past the moon and the curtains are open because the children aren't there.

Back in bed she lapses into the same fearful dream.

It has to happen. Towards morning the wind dies down and Lisa's sleep deepens, so that she awakens fairly late, with heavy bags under her grey eyes and a dissatisfied feeling. She pushes the pillow behind her back and sits with her knees pulled up. Through the window she sees crowns of trees full of almost ripe apples; behind it the restless river water. The sky is leaden.

The dream. She doesn't at all feel like recalling it but also, probably influenced by her profession, has great respect for the messages from the inner world. With her chin on her knees and her arms around her shins, she awaits. She had received a summons, an urgent invitation to be at a specified time in a parking lot from where her destruction would be organized. There was no escaping, she had to go. She pulled on a raincoat and did her best to be on time, there where she didn't want to be. Revolting, that slavish obedience. Why didn't she tear up the summons and drive the car in another direction?

Lisa shakes her shoulders. For what had she recently received a notice? For this afternoon, for the opening of the exhibition. Is that so bad? It's an intrusion on her day off, for sure. She has to put on make-up, wear a bra, be attentive and obliging as if it were a normal workday. She is also annoyed at the increasing tension and confusion in Johan's family and dreads the idea of the confrontation with all these excited people. However, she's also curious, and that balances things out. And what is threatening in this for her? Why is she supposed to be killed? There was another part, an unclear fragment of a warm orange dream that she can't reach now.

She throws off duvet and blanket and gets up. While making coffee, she thinks about the clothes for today. The warm summer weather has been blown away, and outside it looks bleak and rainy. That means stockings in any case because nothing is so awful as cold legs. She'll wear the calf-length black skirt with the straw-coloured jacket. And black heels; today she doesn't feel sufficiently sure or well-balanced for flats.

Yellow and black? Is that possible? Those are the secret colours of disaster: the wasp which stings inside your throat, the skull on the pirate's flag. The curse in fairy tales is pronounced by the evil step-mother in a black gown with gold embroidery. An ominous outfit.

She goes outside with her coffee. It is sheltered at the kitchen door, she sits down on the step and peers into the fish barrel, her bathrobe pulled tight around her. Legs like sticks again. Not enough hiking. Once she and Ellen hiked for a whole week over a path along the coast, high on the cliffs. At every creek, at every insignificant water course they had to go three hundred steep feet down and three hundred steep feet back up. They had calves like Greek columns when they came back home.

The water in the barrel is black. Near the bottom the big sluggish one glides back and forth. A snail is eating the algae from the side of the barrel.

The telephone. Without thinking, Lisa stands up quickly as if she were expecting a disturbance.

"Hannaston?"

It's the children, it's Lawrence, it's a message from overseas. She has to adjust instantly. The children chatter antiphonally about their adventures: "We went to Whitby yesterday. I won money! We bought a whole lot of candy on the street."

"Captain Cook was there. There was a museum in his house, but it was a regular house. He sailed there."

"We went up a very long staircase, then you saw everything. There was a church that'd fallen down. That's where we ate the candy. Daddy was angry but he thought the museum was nice."

"I got a sweater from Grandma, and we've played golf every day."

Now Lawrence comes in with his version of the excursion. His anger was directed at the architectural loss of his homeland, the preservation of the fussy pink painted Cook museum, the mobile home park at the cliff top next to the beautiful ruins of the abbey. He has made progress on the design for the hotel expansion, his father is satisfied and his mother is happy with the visit.

"And how are things with you? I called Johan this morning to wish him good luck, he sounded in good spirits. But everyone has gone crazy, he said."

Lisa tells him about Alma's confusion and the alleged coming of Charles.

"And Oscar is furious, he doesn't want to come to the dinner. Ellen is worried about him and about Alma. And she isn't very pleased about Zina being there either. Everyone is tense and confused, but Johan sits calmly in the middle of it all and prepares for his television appearance. It's too bad that you're not here."

"I agree. I wanted to come back earlier, but it hasn't worked out. Will you manage alone?"

"Yes, I'll just go and see what happens. Do you think he'll come?"

"Charles? That would surprise me. I don't think so; he never showed any interest in his children. And I don't know either whether Johan would really be that pleased, after all it's his day today. Attention is shifted if it's also the day on which you meet your father for the first time. Are you dressed yet?"

"No, I've been fiddling around, I just woke up. It was windy last night. The apples are plopping from the trees, I'll make a tour of the orchard shortly."

"Are the windows in the attic closed tightly? Did the roof hold?"

They're back to domesticity. Storm is something for which to be prepared, against which to take action—not a menace in which tricks and passion play a role. I lean on his reliability, thinks Lisa. He is concerned about the roof tiles, and that gives me the space to plunge into the wind.

Another quick cigarette next to the fish, with another coffee. From the plastic jar with fish food, Lisa lets colourful shreds fall on the water. It smells of fish. The fish eat ground and dried bits of their own kind. From the bottom they dart up and snatch away the feed while making a sharp turn as if it were a real chase. Their slapping tails make the water splash.

When the agitations have subsided and the first hunger is satisfied, Lisa suddenly sees a small black fish nibble carefully on a speck of food. And another.

Jesus, children. It worked. They haven't been eaten. They were able to hide between the jumble of water weeds until they were no longer considered as prey. Survivors. Conquerors!

Lisa considers calling back to England and to announce this news immediately but remains seated on the chilly step. The recollection of her dream takes possession of her once again. She is paralysed because she doesn't know why she dreads this afternoon so terribly.

A look into the barrel. Yes, they're still there. Both. I too have children, I've made two beautiful children who really exist.

Lisa blushes. She is ashamed when she realizes that she is jealous of Johan because of his paintings. He creates. And everyone comes to look, ooh and aah, and express opinions. Newspapers, radio, television, posters throughout the city. He thinks up something that wasn't there and takes it so seriously that he works on it for a year; he asks a lot of money for it if someone else wants to have it, and he gives it a name by which people will know it.

And what do I make? Children, jam, improved patients. Years of work, no public, no applause, nothing new. And I would like to, I would like to stand on a stage until it became quiet, until they listened breathlessly to something that was all mine. No lecture knowledge passed on, no attention for a higher purpose, no helpfulness—just glory.

She lacks something which Johan does have. The missing part is not a penis, not virility but something indefinably vague like creative power. Let's say: power. She has remained a slave to helpfulness, she would rather please than fight. Not because she's a woman but because she's cowardly.

She giggles. It relieves her. She can now find it comic that the jam stands sparkling on the counter. The purple mass moves slowly when she tilts a jar. Still lukewarm but already thick. It will be good.

Do I sit embittered at the kitchen table, do I grudgingly care for my children? Sometimes. Certainly. With fury because they consume me, drain me, exhaust me. The big sluggish one no longer knows that the plucky little fish are her fish; little does she care that they have food; she chases them away if they snatch the feed that she herself set her heart on. Children are uncontrolled growths of the cells that no longer obey the basic design but go their own way and become larger and larger; they're uncontrollable processes that take up space. Ultimately time carries out the operation and removes the swellings.

Weakened, the patient remains behind, liberation and loss dance on the same stage: there was something that belonged to me, I was one with it and was happy; it took possession of me and outgrew me. The surgeon cut it away and plopped it down in a student room, in a disco, in a meadow where a pop festival rages.

And I should be happy that it turned out so well. Pleased, I visit my tumours and am proud that they hold their own, that they can experience pleasure and sorrow. Yuck, how sick.

In her bath, Lisa continues mulling over the facts that in her dream she had to be punished so horribly for being jealous of Johan. Annoying. You should at least be able to be jealous, otherwise you have no life.

She stretches out in the hot water. There is a window in the bathroom with plants in front of it, easy. Nice plants that never flower but always produce leaves: piggyback plant, lemon geranium, and spider plant. Outside the window the clouds race past. She lets her head sink against the side of the bath and would like a fatherly arm around her shoulder—no, someone sits behind her, and she sits between his large heavy legs, she leans against his chest and feels how he embraces her. Gently and warm he bites in her neck, with Johan's mouth. He holds her, simultaneously tender and strong, she could melt at any moment. His black hair against her cheek, his warm breath in her ear.

Well, then. Well.

Before she puts on make-up and her party clothes, she traipses with a basket and a bucket between the scourged apple trees to pick up the fruits that fell last night when the storm shook the branches. She lets the apples stand outside; she eats one, it tastes fall-like.

When she is again reliably aware of the normal life that is draped over the world of dreams, she picks up the telephone.

"The jam turned out really well. How are you?"

"I'm going to pick up Alma now. She's already called three times, totally confused. I'm going a little earlier, to help her with dressing. Are you coming early, on time? Then we'll be able to talk a little."

"I'll be there at four o'clock at the latest."

"Ellen, is that you?"

Alma's voice sounds impatient. Ellen stands with the receiver clamped between shoulder and head, her hands entangled in panty hose, one bare foot on the couch.

If I want peace, I shouldn't pick up the phone, she thinks. My own fault. She drops the stockings and sits down.

"What's the matter, Alma?"

"Everything is fine, but a problem has come up. I put on my stockings, you know, the heavy ones that fit so smoothly, but now I want to fasten them and I noticed that a garter button is missing. On the right in the back. And with one it doesn't work, it isn't safe."

"Do you have another one?"

"No, it's dirty and also a bit too tight. Not comfortable for such a long day."

"What did you use to do when something like this happened? Use a safety pin?"

"No dear, then you'd prick a hole in the stocking. We took a coin which was the exact right size. But such coins no longer exist."

The button box! The boys used to play with it endlessly on the big table, dividing the buttons into colourful soccer teams, into big monsters and small victims, school classes, auto races, zoos. Look in the button box! Such a versatile object should also be able to function as stocking-holder.

"You should take one that is fabric-covered, slightly rough, then the stocking won't slide over it."

Ellen promises to come right away and sits for a moment with the telephone in her hand. She remembers a button rain, pattering buttons spattering in all directions.

She dials Oscar's number but no one answers. Then she pulls on the panty hose and steps into her shoes. Her clothing today will be the colour of used, deoxygenated blood: a deep red dress that shows her legs and her beautiful collar bones.

Oscar stands at the stove and stirs in an extremely dirty little pan. He's making hot cereal from flour, milk, and sugar. The counter is spotlessly clean, all the surfaces in the kitchen are wiped by him with a grubby, smelly dish rag. He wears a new, spotless shirt and his grey suit that just came back from the cleaner. His jacket hangs over the kitchen chair and he is wearing the waistcoat. His shoes, polished to a shine, stand next to the door, but his socks and underpants are already in their third day of use. Oscar is a man of hidden contrasts.

He does hear the telephone but is unable to pick it up. Last night's events have thrown him off balance, and he needs all his energy to re-establish his equilibrium. He can't have anything extra and must at all cost avoid a premature confrontation with Alma.

Pablum it used to be called. It glides down your throat and nestles sweetly in your stomach. It's food for sick and shaken children. At the thought of crusty, crumbly chunks of bread he nearly has to throw up. The applesauce and the custard are finished.

After the discovery in the museum attic, Oscar rebuffed Keetje Bellefroid's kind care because he knew that he wanted to be alone.

"Do come with me, Mr Steenkamer, I live close by; I'll make you a cup of tea, for the shock, you're trembling all over, you can't go out in the street like that!"

"No, no, I have to go home, I have to do some work."

"But I can't just let you go like this? Shall I come and bring you some food tomorrow? See how you're doing?"

"No, very kind of you. It's not necessary. I, eh, I usually don't receive, I'm not used to that, no, no."

Keetje looks disappointed and slightly piqued. They are standing in the rain, in front of the archway of the darkened museum. Oscar reaches into his trouser pocket and pulls out a sweaty invitation to the opening.

"You know, Mrs Bellefroid, if you'll come to the opening tomorrow, we'll see each other there. I'm truly very appreciative of your help. Now I really have to go. Au revoir. Goodbye. Really."

Oscar is already walking as he hands her the paper. In all haste he flees home. All lights on. Dry clothes. Sit in the familiar chair. Music. Eating with difficulty, he forces the soft-boiled egg and the banana down his narrowed throat. Sitting in the chair brings no calm, on the contrary, he becomes painfully aware of his agitated breathing. His legs itch. Rachmaninoff's Third Piano Concerto, which he put on because it went well with the wind and because it is expansive, increases his agitation. To his horror he starts sobbing at the very first theme.

Get up, turn off the music, go outside in his raincoat.

He walks through the city and looks, he does it often, evenings, nights on end; this way he feels like a person among people, without the misery of engagements and forced conversations. For the last few years, the only engagements that he can stand have been the subscription performances of the opera that he attends with his ex-sister-in-law. After her divorce, Ellen tried going with Oscar to a concert. That was not a successful evening, however much they both love music. Oscar tried frenetically not to touch anyone, winced at the rustling of his neighbours' programmes, and cursed the light in the hall. The next year they started their opera attendance. The darkness, the roomier seats, the drama that commands attention: all this caused him to feel clearly more at ease. Oscar chooses the subscription, Ellen places the order, they meet each other in the lobby and afterwards drink one glass of wine in a nearby café.

This Saturday evening he strides through the city, mumbling.

I've seen Charles' paintings. And so what? That doesn't mean he's there. He has done four paintings. And those still exist. Nothing for me to get excited about. Nothing's the matter.

But just as walking should not lead to conversations and contacts, so should having a father not lead to concrete evidence of his existence. The cake from Maison Davina was a rock through the window, the paintings in the museum attic an enemy invasion.

Oscar bumps into merry groups, he walks hurriedly because he wants to be filled with impressions. The tram, grinding over iron rails, loud conversations, and people in colourful clothes. Walking behind a group of blacks, Oscar ends up in a metro station. He doesn't care, as long as there's movement. He steps into the waiting carriage. A tall man wearing a cowboy hat is making a speech to travellers as they enter.

"The mail should be abolished if it can't have a better balance. Negative mail, look in your mailbox. Nothing but negative letters. Let's all demand more positive mail, on penalty of abolishment of the service!"

On a corner of a seat, in the back of the car, sits Oscar in his raincoat, with wet shoes and slightly fogged glasses. He appears to be totally lost in thought, yet he looks and listens with great intensity. At every stop a number of white passengers leave the train and some black ones come in. The time between stations becomes longer, and Oscar sees tall apartment buildings through the rain-sprayed windows. The black passengers also leave the train, except for three massive blacks who stand leaning against the poles in the aisle. All three look straight in Oscar's direction but over, past and through him. Two of them are wearing sandals. Their toenails are lighter than the skin. They are wearing jean jackets with rolled-up sleeves. They have incredibly large and thick lips which they move slowly while their jaws chew chewing-gum.

Oscar can't help imagining, whether he wants to or not, how these exuberant lips would touch his dull greyish skin, soft, warm pillows of skin against his hungry skin—flames shoot to his face, he pants, he has to get out, now!

When the train stops he dashes past the nonchalant blacks and runs outside as if they are chasing him. They don't even look up. Hissing, the car doors close; the train moves on, twisting like an illuminated snake.

The platform is windy and deserted. Exhausted, Oscar shuffles across the granite floor to a bench in an orange-painted shelter.

He leans back and closes his eyes. Slowly his breathing quiets down. He smells the odour of wet stone and places the palms of his hands against the wooden seat on the bench. When he opens his eyes, he sees a black man approaching on sneakers with fluorescent stripes.

Oscar sits as if paralysed, he can no longer become frightened, he can only look. The man stops right in front of Oscar. He is wearing strange cotton pants that flap about his legs. While looking intently at Oscar, he uses his left hand to pull down the elastic of the pants. The left hand pulls out a grey-black member that he presents to Oscar. Oscar sits on his hands. The man takes a step to the side and begins urinating against the wall. The urine runs along the front of his luminous shoes to Oscar's shoes. Oscar looks at how the warm liquid glides around his shoes; it steams slightly. He takes a breath and smells fresh piss.

*

Thank God daylight came. Oscar puts on his kitchen apron before he takes the pablum to the room. Don't make a mess, don't spill, finish the plate while Dvořák's Serenade murmurs on. When he came home last night, he washed his hands carefully under the kitchen tap for at least fifteen minutes. The wet shoes he simply placed under the coat hooks.

Now no thinking about nightlife or life in the open air. Soon to the competing museum, the brother's exhibition, to the colourful jumble of dresses and paintings. Nothing is the matter. There is a mother without a father, there is a brother and another brother, there are many women without men, everything is as usual. His fingers smell of strong soap with a trace of milk. Oscar cleans his glasses with a corner of the apron. He lets the telephone ring.

On the façade of the Municipal Museum a large white banner is hung which says 'AUTUMN EXHIBITION: STEENKAMER' in austere capitals. The glass entrance doors to the lobby are wide open to offer passage to all sorts of bustling people this early Sunday afternoon.

Two trucks from a catering business are parked in front of the steps. Platters and boxes are carried from the cargo space into the building by men in white overalls.

A television van is standing on the sidewalk, thick black cables run from its interior over the stairs into the museum.

Johan parks his car next to the director's red BMW in the private parking lot. He never wears seatbelts because he hates the feeling of being in a harness. Quickly he jumps out in his beautiful Italian shoes. The black suit is not too tight or too loose; under it he wears a light grey shirt of very thin cotton with a solid, bright red tie. Socks: light grey. Underpants: seagreen boxer shorts, a birthday present from Zina. Skin colour: healthy tan. Mood: slightly nervous good spirits.

In the draughty lobby, the director, wearing a grubby jacket with rolled-up sleeves, grasps Johan's hand with both hands and waits a fraction too long before letting go. Born before '50. I've got to have him, no matter what that fathead from the National dreams up, he thinks.

"Welcome, welcome. Are you ready for this? Kerstens is coming at two-thirty, he's looking forward to the interview. Last night he was here to look at the layout of the galleries. You know him? Always busy, busy!"

"I've met him on occasion, yes. And I've seen his programme a number of times."

Johan has mixed feelings about it. The corpulent art expert inspires him with the slight aversion which he harbours against all fat men and know-it-all critics. However, Kerstens' position as authoritative art pope with direct influence on Johan's status and finances also inspires a certain awe. Kerstens may be an arrogant arsehole who doesn't know what to do with a brush, but he is well-positioned and is heard by everyone.

"Do you mind if I leave you alone? It's very busy right now, I'd like to accompany the gentlemen from the TV and supervise the set-up of the food and drink department. Do go in enjoy your own work! We've really done our best."

Johan follows the black cables up the stairs. He tries to walk up with the loose, relaxed feeling with which one generally descends a staircase: the arms dangle with their own weight, the feet brush along the treads, and the head is held up proudly.

Panting slightly he reaches the upper floor and stops in front of the entrance to his galleries. On both sides two signs are set up: on the left the announcement of the exhibition, printed in bold type over an enormously magnified part of a painting—no image is recognizable, only spots of colour; to the right his own head in profile, looking away, with his name in red letters above it.

Johan enters the first gallery where water colours and drawings hang in identical dark blue frames. Different skies over the canal where he takes his morning run. On the back wall of this gallery are two openings that lead to the large gallery with the paintings. Tables are set up next to the passageways that go into the gallery. Two girls in black and white are busy covering the tables with cloths; a young man with a black apron is pushing in a cart with glasses. The three of them are discussing where they will set up what. All food will be provided in the first gallery so that people can then, with a glass in their hand, walk into the main gallery.

"You have to let these tablecloths hang down a lot more," says Johan to the girls, "otherwise you see all these bottles and boxes standing under the table. That's hideous."

The girls fix the tablecloths and look at Johan as he goes through the left passage. A man from the generation in power who gives a command that is short and to the point and then walks away, no catering girl can resist that.

The large gallery is taller than the front gallery. The ceiling is glass (air windows, the children used to say), with white cotton cloth stretched underneath, light like the inside of a refrigerator, like an open-air church, like pure space. In the middle of the gallery is a round bench with a view of all the different paintings. The pietà hangs on the wall in which the passageways have been cut; Johan now stands in front of it, nodding approvingly. From a side wall, *The Postman* looks penetratingly into the gallery. Johan turns around slowly, on his heels. No matter how absorbing the depictions all around, the attention is irresistibly drawn to the large back wall with the top piece, the masterpiece.

It is hung somewhat higher than the other works and is larger in size: five and a half feet wide and more than six feet high. Johan sits down on the round bench, facing it. He looks.

It is a dark painting in which the image is lighter. Against a velvet black background stands a woman with gold-tinted brown hair. A pale face with brown eyes that look straight at the viewer. Well-defined, naked shoulders. The skin has a winter hue. Against her right breast lies the head of a large adult male salmon, the fish eye and the pinkish brown nipple fight for attention. The woman has her right arm bent under the fish, she holds it like one holds a baby, encircling his silver back. The tail fans forward over the bent left arm which supports the right arm. The pale stomach of the fish lies against her naked torso, the silver scales with black flecks on his back are painted with infinite care. In front of the woman stands a rough wooden table, turned obliquely. On it lies a second fish, as large as the first one. His head points left, he lies with his back to the woman. The stomach is cut open. Intestines protrude. The tail lies limply on the table. The fish skin has been partially stripped off so that the unprotected meat is visible here and there. The salmon is indeed salmon-coloured. A sharp filleting knife lies on the table in front of the fish. Traces of blood can be seen on the blade.

Whoever looks at the painting from the bottom to the top sees: the knife on the wooden table, the intestines, the tortured fish, the stomach of the naked woman against the edge of the table, the cherished fish in pale arms pressed against the full breasts, the woman's neck, the face, the goldbrown hair.

An expensive painting, thinks Johan. Twice bought a whole salmon which was rotting away on the table at almost two hundred guilders a piece. Zina, who put her breasts and arms at his disposal, protested and, turning up her nose, stood pressing the fish against herself. After posing she lay in a bath for hours and washed her hair with fragrant balsam. As a reaction, they ate lamb chops and beefsteak for weeks on end. Zina's head and shoulders could not be used because of her excessive self-indulgence. For these parts Johan used another model, a woman who from a distance reminded him of Ellen and who, for substantial pay, sat facing him silently with bared shoulders.

People are coming into the gallery. The director walks up to Johan. In his wake walks a small man, bent under photo bags, a tripod, and a stand for lamps.

"From the *Avondblad,* a quick photo before the television crew begins, no problem, I hope?"

The small one unpacks his apparatus. Above the lamp he unfolds a white umbrella. He looks at Johan, at the painting, not to learn to understand it but to consider his own composition. A low platform has been erected in front of the woman with the fish. A table and two chairs stand on it for the interview that will start soon.

"If you'd take a seat there," says the photographer, "Then I'll take you from below." He dives behind his camera, mumbling to himself. Looking serious, Johan gazes straight ahead and holds his lips together.

"Look into the lens, please, yes like that, good, wonderful. Now please stand in front of the painting, shake the hands loose, not so stiff. And look into the lens."

Johan thinks it's not fair. He is to look at someone who doesn't visibly look back because the photographer's eyes are hidden behind his equipment. Through the photo he looks thousands of people straight in the eye, but who, and where, and what will they say?

Now that he's standing up he has a view of the whole gallery. A television camera is being rolled in, bright lamps are switched on and technicians are calling to one another. The director walks slowly past the paintings, in conversation with a fat man dressed in corduroy pants with red braces over a coarse cotton shirt. When they come closer, Johan sees that the bottom shirt button is undone. A bit of hairy stomach bulges over the low-hanging belt. The man's face has the same fleshiness and the small, light eyes lie sunk down in its folds. The man offers Johan his bulging hand.

"Kerstens!"

The voice is unexpectedly deep and resonant, the eyes look through Johan at the camera set-up.

"I've gone through the pieces with Kees, that's all recorded. With commentary. Now a quick conversation on the platform, it doesn't need to take long. Tonight I'll edit the discussion, Tuesday it will be in the programme. Fifteen minutes, the last part, probably."

Johan feels himself getting annoyed. He is being used for someone else's product, and that's not the intention. He doesn't want someone to look through him and not listen carefully because the position of the camera is more important than what he's saying. He doesn't want the director to comment on his work without his being present. The direction was taken out of his hands while he let himself be posed by the photographer. Now pay attention!

They sit down at the table on the platform. Kerstens puts down a notepad on which not much is written, a few words one under the other which Johan tries to read upside-down. Salmon? Is that about his masterpiece? Hungry radio, what does that say? Hungarian salami! It is a goddam shopping list! The meatball has written down his favorite foods as preparation for an interview with the master painter. Chocolate éclairs with a question mark. Sacher with a line through it. Fillet of sole with exclamation points.

Johan's stomach contracts with fury. Kerstens doesn't appear to be deterred by the dourness on Johan's face, but instead gets underway.

"Mr Steenkamer! The opening exhibition of the season in an important museum is devoted to you. How does that feel?"

As Johan opens his mouth and wants to proceed, the journalist interrupts him with an abrupt gesture. Questioning, he sticks his fat chin in the air, towards the camera man.

"All right like this?"

The video technician nods. Kerstens turns again to his interview partner.

"Mr Steenkamer, don't you think it's strange that the opening exhibition of this museum, of all places, is devoted to your work?"

"How do you mean?" grumbles Johan, immediately put on the defensive, "Isn't this an excellent museum? What do you actually mean?"

"Do you fit into this collection?"

"Why not?"

"Well, I'd like to get you talking. Do you understand why people might consider your figurative work as a regression?"

Jesus, Oscar's article. This man is really needling me, what's the meaning of this?

"I'm not concerned with others' opinions of my work, Mr Kerstens. I work. Formerly it was in a way that you could call abstract and now it is principally in the form of recognizable objects and representations. I don't consider one higher or better than the other."

"You have started to earn more since the change, isn't that so?"

This isn't going well. Johan who in daily life flies so easily into a temper and throws his opinion into someone else's face, feels inhibited and tied to his chair by the camera and by his awareness of being involved in the construction of a programme. His face flushes and he places his feet firmly on the floor.

"Let's talk about my work and not about my financial situation."

"Is that such a delicate subject? As you wish. Your work then. Personally, as an art critic, I would like to tell you that I think the change is a shame. I found your earlier work fascinating—the overlapping areas of colour, the continuation of the frame within the painting, the false diagonals—it revealed a searching attitude, it was daring. You let this style go rather suddenly in order to paint pretty pictures. You must have a reason for this?"

Pretty pictures! Johan is so furious that he can't utter a word. The camera looks him straight in the face.

When Johan finally breathes and opens his mouth, Kerstens' voice booms right through it: "Let's take something concrete then. The painting under which we are sitting is your most recent product. You yourself say that you regard it as your masterpiece."

Kerstens points with his meaty paw in the direction of the work and looks at the camera man who obediently starts exploring the woman with the fish with his visual vacuum-cleaner.

"Yes. I'm very satisfied with it. A beautiful painting. I think."

"But that is quite a pathetic comment. Beautiful. What does that mean? You are undoubtedly expressing something with this work, you are placing yourself within a tradition; do you have a message?"

"A woman with two fish," says Johan.

"Yes, undoubtedly. But why? A symbolic representation? Is it about debauchery? Is it a transcendent, possibly a religious theme?"

"It is a naked woman who is holding a fish."

"Mr Steenkamer, you must understand what I'm getting at: whoever paints a picture illustrates something. A story goes with it, you're telling something with this painting. Is it about the disappointing coldness of motherly love? Or perhaps about the lamentable rivalry between two children? Does it point to the ultimate fratricide? Do say it in your own words!"

Kerstens squints his narrow eyes even further shut as he smirks at Johan. The camera is whirring expectantly.

"Listen here, Mr Cursetense, I don't like this line of questioning. If I had wanted to tell a story in my own words, as you say so aptly, I would have become a writer, you understand? But I'm a painter, I think up an image and I place it on the canvas as well as possible. That's the whole story Mr Coarsetense, and if you know better, just say so in your own words! And now piss off, I've had it!"

Johan stands up and jumps off the platform. Meanwhile the director, alarmed by the raised voices, has rushed up to utter entreaties and smooth over problems. Kerstens, who has also got up, shrugs his round shoulders.

"Too bad, it was a nice set-up. I'll see if anything can be done with it. Sometimes it works, sometimes it doesn't. *Tant pis.*"

"You weren't terribly accommodating, I must say. And Steenkamer wasn't up to it, as it were. He can talk quite nicely about his work, usually."

"Well, Kees, those are the rules of the game. He's got to be able to debate with critics—if he chooses not to, I can't help it. Do you have something for me to drink? You're probably not offering any whiskey today?"

Johan has stalked off, and the director feels free to lead the art journalist to the board offices. There they'll find something under a cork or screw cap, there they'll be able to stretch their legs and outline art policy for the coming quarter century.

Meanwhile in the front gallery shiny refrigerator carts with wine and beer have been rolled behind the white tables. Johan takes a first glass of white wine and looks around, pleased. An intense feeling of well-being comes over him, as always after an outburst of rage.

The cables are being rolled up; the television crew disperses. It's close to four o'clock and the first guests are coming upstairs. What did that lump of meat mean by maternal love, fratricide? What an offensive way of thinking, trendy business with words and concepts. You've got to have good brushes. And you have to see before you, down to the smallest detail, what you want to do. That's where the obstacle is if you're stuck. Then you have to concentrate and think until you know how it is to look. When you know that exactly, then it works again. This sort of person hasn't a clue about that. They wrap everything in a cloud of words, and something isn't of value until it points to something else. If I get caught up in that, I'll never paint anything again, that's for sure. You shouldn't be stingy with your material. And you should have order in your work area. Clean up each evening. Technique, that's it. Just like an acrobat or a musician. Art gluttons they are, these journalists, yet afraid that they'll spoil their stomachs. Or that they might accidentally like an ordinary hot dog. Ugh.

A skinny boy lugs a cello up the stairs. Despite his youth he has a smooth, bald head. Behind him walk a long-haired girl with a viola and a sturdy curly head with a violin case in his backpack. In her hand the girl has music which she shows to the violinist. He nods, agrees with everything, but first unpacks.

They set up in the large galley to the side of the platform. The girl unfolds shiny music stands which look like flamingos in the space. Curly brings chairs, they form a triangle with the cellist in the centre. He jabs the sharp point of the cello into a small board that is tied with a rope to the leg of his chair. The black cello case stands against the wall next to a painting in which another trio is depicted: at an open window a mother and a son hold up a second child, a lifeless, fainted boy, felled by panic. Curtains are blowing in. On an empty chair lies a motionless fish.

The violinist takes the pitch from the tuning fork which he has taken out of his inside pocket and then passes it to the others. As soon as they have the tone, they all start tuning their strings at the same time. The cellist pushes the tuning pegs next to his ear to hear his instrument. From a distance Johan hears the open fifths and begins to feel unaccountably nervous. Who ordered a string trio? He doesn't want it, he doesn't want to be surprised by uncomprehended melancholy and meaningless tension. Moreover that noise distracts from looking at what counts.

"Is that your idea?" he asks the director, who meanwhile has reappeared to be present when his guests come.

"Nice, isn't it? They play quite well. And beautiful music. They won't bother you. Classical. Conservatory students who are earning a little extra. That girl is an acquaintance of mine, they play here often."

But I don't want it, Johan wants to say, I can't stand it, it makes me agitated, have them go away.

They have started with the slow opening of a Beethoven trio; the low cello notes vibrate into the front gallery with irrepressible intensity.

Bijl! Like a sailor towards a life raft, Johan flails towards the wood dealer. The tall figure radiates calm and deliberate curiosity. He extends his solid hand, the oar, the straw, to Johan.

"Well my boy, are you satisfied? You certainly should be, I think, never mind the critics. You're looking a little pale. Shall we drink a glass to a good start?"

Bijl throws his arm around Johan's shoulders and leads him to the refreshment bar. Ever since Ellen's entry into the wood business, Bijl has supported her then-husband. He continued to do so after the divorce, because he didn't do it out of friendship for Ellen but out of admiration for Johan's uncompromising skill. Bijl likes to have others share his wealth and he prefers to keep it personal. This artist has come his way, and Bijl stays faithful to him. Commissioned by him, Johan painted the cherry tree in Bijl's garden. It went without saying that Bijl would support this exhibition with a considerable sum.

"How is Ellen? Is she coming too, surely she must? And your children, the boys. Tell me, have they now decided on something? Love, ladies or men, alone or together, studies or a job, or perhaps nothing? They must be well into their twenties, right? Cheers, boy. I'm boring you with all my questions, but let's drink: to your skill!"

People are now coming up the stairs in twos and threes. They have left their coats in the cloakroom and float through the gallery like pretty spots of colour, looking at one another, casting glances at the works of art, calling to one another until they come to a stop in front of the table with glasses and let themselves be served drinks by the girls.

Behind Bijl's broad back, Johan sees Sally's firm legs. He excuses himself to one sponsor and pays his respects to the other.

"Wonderful that you could come! You must be right between two trips around the world?"

Bob has developed a tanned sailors' head and wears sailors' clothes: an unbleached wool sweater with wide cables, navy blue pants and boat shoes.

"He could have kept his captain's cap on," says Johan to Sally. "What do you think of it, almost everything was made on your own domain."

"Beautiful, Johan, you know that. I'm very happy that the Postal Services have continued to provide the means. You're still doing a few things for them if I'm not mistaken?"

"Are you happy in the house, Johan?"

Sally looks relaxed and content. Hard to believe if she has to sit in a boat day in day out. Stiff, bad-tempered, dissatisfied, that's what Johan had expected. And that she, because of these dissatisfactions, would yet go to him, with him? Difficult to take that she never took notice of any of his subtle advances. Now he wouldn't want her anymore, with that neck full of tendons and sinews, that face under a layer of paint. Leaving her legs out of consideration.

The director of the National Museum enters and looks annoyed at the table with drinks and the ashtrays placed here and there. Smoking in a museum, that would only be permitted by an innovator sucking up to everyone and who in addition hasn't a clue about preservation. There's nothing to do but to go and congratulate the windbag on his beautiful exhibition; it's a colleague's duty.

Serious-faced, stepping carefully around the string trio, the guardians of art stroll together past the paintings.

This has got to be in the National, that snotnose pulled it out from under my fingers with his scheming and his connections, thinks one.

If only that sourpuss would get a severe heart attack from pure envy, we could really move on, thinks the other.

They say very little to each other; a silence that could, of course, also be caused by viewing the paintings.

"My compliments, dear colleague. Beautifully hung and fine work. Please excuse me, I see someone whom I have to greet."

Leaving the young man alone and stunned is for the older man a small pleasure that he doesn't want to deny himself.

"Oh, Director, you're here also! Of course you would be. It's your job!"

Keetje Bellefroid has gone to great pains for the occasion. She is wearing a pleated skirt over her wide hips and a Scotch plaid cape around her shoulders. In her hands she clasps the crumpled invitation Oscar handed her in desperation the night before.

"Mr Steenkamer has invited me, our Mr Steenkamer I mean. Have you seen him yet?"

"Not yet, Keetje, but he'll certainly come. Can I get you something to drink, or would you like to walk with me?"

The director appreciates the straightforward friendliness of his gussied-up secretary. He's happy that someone from his own camp is present. He's actually happy that it's she who is there.

While they are waiting in front of the table, Zina makes her entrance. Red hair like a stiff halo around her face, the ample body pressed into a shiny green acrobat outfit, a green jacket edged with gold over it, leaving the giant ass free. She is wearing a wide gold necklace around her neck and throws her head back when she laughs out loud at a remark by the director. She slips her arm through his and leads him to Johan.

"My little competitor has arrived, Steenkamer, why not pour her a glass. Jesus, they'll have to wait with the hors d'oeuvres until after my speech! I've got to go after them, sorry, sorry."

Firmly he pushes the waiters back into the lobby with their platters of deep-fried shrimp.

Lisa raises her eyebrows. At the gallery entrance the men perch on a narrow table, dangling their legs. They wait and from time to time discreetly pick a shrimp from the spurned platters. She goes inside, looks around for a minute, but doesn't see Ellen and Alma, instead very many other people. Where is Johan? Then she enters the large gallery and comes face to face with the masterpiece. Dear God. Lisa is stunned. How terrible! It chills her. Neglect. Mistreatment. She shivers involuntarily.

From behind, a warm body snuggles against her. Johan throws his arms around her straw-coloured jacket and kisses her on the neck. Whiskey? Alcohol at any rate. Lisa leans against him slightly too long, too briefly however to distinguish all parts of the body precisely, but too long, too long.

Blushing, she extricates herself.

"Johan. How beautiful. How *can* you."

The director has climbed on the platform, the trio put away their instruments and, against the current, slink to the wine buffet. It becomes quiet in the gallery, fragments of the speech can be heard clearly: overcoming the supposed schism, figurative and non-figurative, hope for a productive solution to the long drawn-out question, the collection, pride, a thorough and inspired talent, thanks to the sponsors, join hands, shoulders to the wheel, opening of a productive season!

Johan is toasted. People burst out in applause. Now the waiters come dancing in: cheese croquettes, salmon rolls, asparagus spears. People grab handfuls, emptying the platters, before pushing back into the drink gallery.

Slowly Johan walks with Lisa through both galleries, through the entryway, to the staircase. At the bottom of the white marble waterfall stand three figures. The grey man with the glasses has the blue woman with the cane at his right side and at his left the woman in the blood-red dress. Solemnly they begin to ascend the stairs. Are they wearing masks? No, they are not wearing masks.

"Now it's going to start," Lisa whispers in Johan's ear.

\*   \*   \*

Johan kisses his mother. The knuckles of the hand that is holding the cane are white. She trembles with exertion.

"Couldn't you have come earlier? The speech is already over. Why can't you adjust to someone else's tempo, is that asking too much?"

"There was quite a lot to organize," intervenes Ellen, "it took a while before we could leave, that's my fault, Alma was ready, but I was too late."

"You don't have to stand there and apologize," says Lisa to her friend. "All those concerned should be happy that you're here. What a gorgeous dress you're wearing!"

Oscar has turned pale in his brother's presence. Johan shook his hand nonchalantly, as if nothing had happened. Alma, who hung heavily on his arm on the way upstairs, has now forgotten his existence. He grabs his stomach and writhes.

"I think I'd better go downstairs again, please excuse me, I'll see you soon," says Oscar to no one. They don't hear it. He walks downstairs quickly. With a sigh he lowers himself onto the toilet, the last stall of the row which he bolts firmly and where no one can bother him.

Johan has taken Alma by the arm and starts walking past the walls with her.

"You look good with that new hairdo. And this blue looks nice on you. You're so tense, I feel you trembling. Are you in pain?"

Alma doesn't want to have pain. She barely looks at what is on display but intensely examines the people walking around. The director comes up to them. He places his hand on Alma's blue sleeve.

"The artist's mother! A proud mother, I assume. And rightly so, rightly so."

They stroll past the buffet into the large gallery where *The Postman* is hanging. It's the only painting in front of which Alma stops. People see what they recognize and what they wish to see, thinks Ellen, who has followed them at a short distance.

"Can't I sit down somewhere so that I can see everyone? There, on that seat!"

With her cane Alma points to a row of chairs near the platform. Obediently, Johan leads her there. Cane under the chair, handbag at her feet.

"You haven't seen all of the paintings hanging here, do you realize that?"

"Everything in its time, Johan. Let me recover a bit from the trip. And first look around. Was that the director? He certainly disappeared quickly, are you important enough? Do go on, you don't have to stand around here. I'm sitting just fine. Do get a cup of tea for me if they have it."

Ellen has looked at the woman with the fish. Her eyes go back and forth between Alma and the painting. A deep burst of laughter makes her look around, at Zina, as it happens.

Her husband's girlfriend stands chatting loudly with Kerstens and the director. When Johan walks past, she puts her hand on his neck. He smiles and goes on.

Goddamn it, thinks Ellen. That's how it is. She has the right to touch his body. Of course. Why not? He does it with her. I see it. I pay for my freedom. But it's not exactly my idea of fun.

Suddenly Johan stands next to her. "Will you give this to Alma?"

He pushes a glass of orange juice into her hands.

"Go and sit with her for a while, she's alone. I can't manage, anyway I have to see an awful lot of people."

I, too, Johan. So take care of your mother yourself, don't make me get stuck with her, I no longer have anything to do with it. Why don't I say that? Why don't I come here for nice conversations and exciting new acquaintances, for my own pleasure?

Because I cringe with pity for the mistreated fish in the arms of the cold woman, with compassion for the fish woman herself who is stiff with fear, because it has remained my family, somehow, because I'm not here for my pleasure but rather for them, for her.

"Yes, give it to me, I'll go to her. Do you see how she's peering around the gallery? I think that, against her better judgement, she's still hoping that your father is coming. Have you heard anything?"

"No, he's not really coming. I didn't think that he would for a moment. It was rather that I wanted to have done it, send that invitation. I didn't expect an answer."

"Incidentally, that cake was a dirty trick! How could you do such a thing? Of course you were angry, you weren't thinking."

"For just a moment."

They smile at one another. Then Johan pulls Zina away from her gentlemen and Ellen sits down next to Alma. Because there are ashtrays on legs everywhere, Ellen lights a cigarette and leans back. The string trio plays an opera arrangement, a stately minuet with an innocent melody but a menacing rhythm. Zina pushes her hip against Johan, he puts his arm around her. They sway through the sea of people, together. (Madam, thinks Ellen, this minuet? Will you do me the honour? Stop it, cut it out, act normal. Be glad you're through with it.)

"Charles was a tall figure," Alma says suddenly.

"I don't think that he's coming, Alma. You should try and enjoy yourself a bit."

"Enjoy myself? Among this riff-raff? With this pain? What do you think I am? I don't want to have anything to do with these people. They're rude. I'd rather be at home. All that racket. Where is Oscar? And why doesn't that girlfriend of Johan come and introduce herself, I've even invited her to the dinner!"

Distraction, another subject. Good.

"Shall I get her?"

Ellen jumps up and goes up to Zina. She's had to do worse things than this. Amiably she shakes hands with her successor, points to Alma, takes Zina along.

Alma lets her eyes skim over the green figure: the gold necklace, the plunging neckline, the wide hips and then again the unlined face under the wreath of hair.

"What lovely jewellery you're wearing," she says.

Zina sits down next to Alma and tells her about Mats, about forging, and about the sale of consumer art. Ellen stands watching the uninhibited chatting and thinks that Zina understands nothing because she's occupied with her own world, with the dog-collar around her neck, and with Johan's moods. Zina takes things as they are and doesn't dream. She cannot imagine anything that isn't there, and therefore she can now enjoy herself with Alma. This woman doesn't get wounded, though; at most, she has bad luck.

Ellen walks to the front gallery to get a glass of wine and from afar sees her sons coming up the stairs. Even though they haven't lived at home for years, seeing her children still gives Ellen a feeling of completeness and peace, as if they should be there. Now all is well. Their faces reflect her sentiment.

"Mum! How nice!"

"What a beautiful dress!"

"You should have red wine with it! Shall I get it?"

Paul runs away. This is my contribution to the family, thinks

Ellen. This is evidence of what I have with Johan, and no one comes between that. Suddenly she feels less of a slavey, less a slave and more as though she belongs here. Peter is wearing a beautiful dark blue suit and looks very much like his father, especially when he looks at her sidelong from under his dark hair.

"It's off again," he says, referring to the girlfriend whom he introduced rather solemnly to Ellen not too long ago.

"Oh, darling, how did that happen?"

"I simply can't get along with any one as well as with Paul. When I'm in love everything is all right, but when we simply have to live afterwards, then I'm drawn to Paul. It made her angry, she felt excluded. That was actually true. And I didn't feel like going to an angry girlfriend anymore, for fear that she would break it off. I really preferred going fishing with Paul. Terrible, that's how it always goes."

Paul shows up with a tray: wine, beer, and a plate with different kinds of fish. They can't have relationships and they can't learn a normal trade, thinks Ellen. Still, I don't worry about them, not really. Will they still live together when they're sixty? And be involved in their half-baked projects? What began as an amusement typical of students (organizing trips on Dutch sailing vessels and fishing boats for class weekends) has over the years expanded to a complete ichthyological travel bureau with an office and a division of labour. Paul gives fishing advice and delivers the equipment. His part of the store is filled with rods, waders, and series of strange hooks, arranged on velvet like jewels. Peter is the travel expert, he provides custom fishing expeditions: trap flatfish on beaches uncovered by the tide, a children's party (swimming certificate required) with bass catching, brook-trout hunt in the mountains, pull up codfish on ninety-foot ropes from a furiously rocking fishing boat, and salmon vacations in Sweden.

They are registered with the Chamber of Commerce. They are businessmen, entrepreneurs—but they look like playful students. Paul is wearing a reddish cotton sweater

*Peter and Paul*
*Creative Fishing*

it says on his back. Their newest project concerns catching fish on the sea of Galilee, for the true enthusiast.

Johan regards them as failures and never wonders where their money comes from. They keep their success hidden from him, without difficulty, because he doesn't want to look.

Observing is surviving. Lisa walks around and looks. She holds brief conversations with people she knows or gets to know, and meanwhile looks over their shoulders at the players in today's drama. Healthy goldfish search out one another's company, she remembers from the *Goldfish Handbook*. It's true. Alma sits grim-faced on a chair and finds an excuse for getting rid of anyone who comes to be with her. A cheerful circle of people has formed around Peter and Paul. And Johan? She sees him gesticulating next to a fat man in front of the woman with the fish; a moment later he walks over to the director. Price negotiations, no doubt. When they land in Alma's territory, the director is pricked in his back.

"Could you come and sit with me for a moment?"

Lisa manoeuvres to be within hearing distance.

"As an expert, what is your opinion of my son's work, can you tell me?"

The director is slightly under the influence and in addition he's annoyed by the premature business negotiations during his reception.

"Madam! The most neglected aspect of art is the placement aspect. As a museum man I know that quite well. Your son is an excellent painter. If he hangs across the street, in the National Museum, he remains just that, nothing more. *But...*" He stands up, bends his knees, and breathes into Alma's ear: "If he remains here in my stable, with his whole oeuvre, then, madam, your son will be a *great* painter."

Because of his abstinence these last days, the wine has a strong effect on Johan. His face is flushed and the time span between thinking and doing has become very short. He finds himself facing Lisa. Both have a glass in their hands, they toast each other.

"Why did he leave, your father?"

"Because I had won," Johan says without hesitation. "I had more talent and Alma loved me more. He was defeated, that's that."

He looks around and sees his work on all the walls. Daylight has gone and the lamps have been lit, and still people stroll admiringly past paintings that he has made. On the large bench in the middle of the gallery Kerstens sits talking with Zina. He has placed his fat arm around her shoulder and looks up annoyed when Johan approaches.

"Now listen carefully, Mr Curbtense:

> He who writes must bend the knee,
> But he who paints is always free!"

He has grabbed the dumbfounded journalist at the collar and recites the verses slowly and clearly right in his face.

"Freedom, Curbtense. Freedom!"

Johan turns around and walks away like a victor. He moves his shoulders loosely under his jacket. Right, right.

For more than an hour Oscar has taken cover in his small cell. Fortunately it's a real cell, with walls that go up to the ceiling and a door that locks—not a stall enclosed by particle board with large open spaces above and below, through which someone could, for instance, stick his head. In that kind of toilet Oscar feels so threatened and spied on that his sphincter becomes permanently cramped. This stall is a real little room, unfortunately without a private fountain from which he would be able to drink water, but with a thick roll of toilet paper and another one squeezed between the water pipe and the wall. He can stick it out here for a while. He has taken off his jacket and has hung it on the door hook, thereby covering "I've had it, man!" written down with a felt pen. It must be a recent message for the toilet has been well cleaned.

During Oscar's stay in the stall, people have come into the toilets from time to time. He heard muffled noises. Sometimes two or three men stood peeing at the same time, and Oscar hoped that they would talk about the paintings in the exhibition. ("A touch of the gypsy girls, don't you think?") That didn't happen. People spoke, insofar as he could understand, about the disadvantages of a Sunday afternoon for such a reception ("What can you do afterwards, I always say, you no longer feel like eating, and have already had too much to drink"), and about the bad weather. Once someone jiggled his doorknob; frightened, Oscar saw the sudden movement and wanted to shout: "Occupied, occupied!" But his throat was too dry.

After inspecting the floor, he lets his pants drop down to the ground; the underpants are around his knees. Oscar has a stomach ache, but it's only after sitting for fifteen minutes that he feels safe enough to shit. He doesn't enjoy the defecation; all his life he has experienced it as a defeat. He knows that he is defenceless at the moment of his bowel movement and always realizes that he cannot run away or strike back. Going to the toilet for him implies obedience, finally doing what is required of him, after much nagging and resistance. His triumph is in the refusal. Him they won't see on the toilet, he squeezes his buttocks together and keeps going with his pellets until, hard and black like beans, they bounce against the porcelain. If he wants that.

Now he has diarrhoea. From what? The applesauce, the banana, the egg? When he knows for sure that he's alone, he lets out loud farts. A sour, rotten smell rises. Oscar feels scared. He can't wash his bottom here, and his hands only after he opens the door. With his elbows on his knees he supports his head and sighs. He inhales the foul air. Defeat.

Sitting, he flushes and feels the water spatter against his buttocks. What is there to be afraid of? Soon he'll go upstairs and look at the exhibition. There will be people who know him; after all, he is a respected professional. His old mother will be there, walking with difficulty. He had a slight quarrel with her, it hardly needs to be discussed or settled, who knows, everything will automatically be as it was before. His brother Johan, his little brother, will be there. He has become famous, and perhaps is angry because of the article. Of course not, he doesn't even think about it anymore, Johan thinks it's utterly unimportant, Oscar can write what he wants to, he can pound his fists to bits on the small boy's head, type his fingers to pulp without Johan caring. He is fighting air.

Now the body again demands attention. Carefully Oscar wipes himself clean and straightens out his clothes. When the coast is clear, he steps out in order to wash his hands at length with the strong soap that comes out of the plastic container. He leaves his jacket hanging on the door for the time being. In the mirror an old man in shirtsleeves, bent shoulders and a worried look, is busying himself. Oscar doesn't look at him. With a corner of his shirt he wipes his glasses clean.

At the top of the stairs he encounters Lisa, whom he has always considered somewhat creepy. A psychiatrist, what does she know, what is she thinking, does she look through him with those grey eyes? And does she then see things that he doesn't know? Furtively he brings his fingers to his nose: a hint of shit can still be smelled, he has been marked by the capitulation. He extends the same hand to Lisa.

"Oscar, we were wondering where you were!"

He mumbles something—a question, a curse, a general excuse?

"Why did your father leave when you were small?"

Oscar is so surprised by this question that he starts thinking unsuspectingly about the answer. He looks at the scary woman and sees sincerely curious eyes. She simply wants to know. She considers it important!

"He left, I think, because he no longer found it interesting. Actually I fear that he was disappointed in me. Perhaps I wasn't a very attractive child, not an older son of whom such a man can be proud. It was something like that, it must have been, I've always thought, yes."

Behind Lisa appears a familiar figure: plump, sturdy, waddling, and covered in Scotch plaid.

"Oh, Mr Steenkamer, finally! I've been looking for you!"

"Keetje, you're here too! Do you know Dr Hannaston?"

He introduces the women to each other. Lisa doesn't have much to say, she is confused by Oscar's answer to her prying question. Keetje slips her arm through his.

"We'll get something to drink, that will do you good."

A glass of water. Acidic wine wouldn't sit well right now. Keetje does everything for him. In the front gallery, while she is getting the glasses, he recognizes the watercolours and the etchings. Nicely hung, well done, fine work. They drink.

"You know, the television was here! The paintings all hang there, in the large gallery. Shall we go and look? Perhaps you know all of them already, there won't be anything new for you? For me it was a bit of a surprise, if I may say so. Rather creepy sometimes, and so real that it gives you shivers. But I'm just chattering, you know about it, I simply look at what I see."

Not answering, not having to answer, and still continuing to hear the familiar chatty voice next to him. Moving into the large gallery, what a lot of people, music! oh, the Mozart Divertimento, they dare, beautiful. That dreadful pietà, Ellen was so heart-broken, how *could* he have painted it like that? *The Postman,* God, there's Alma sitting alone on a chair, she stares so intently. Where is her cane? Oh, on the floor, next to the platform. Empty chairs on it, how messy. Look up. See the knife lying there. And what the knife has brought about. Look into the eyes of the woman who presses one of the two fish against her breast. Know that this is the masterpiece on which his brother worked for more than a year, which he considers the final proof of his artistic skill.

Unable to move the feet anymore. Have totally forgotten the

scene on the toilet. Again stand next to Keetje Bellefroid, hear the rain and see the woman.

Oscar turns around and runs down the stairs.

*Chapter eight*

# Grim Minuet

There is a nagging pain in Alma's hip joint. Time after time, the head of the thighbone rubs against the worn-out hip socket from which the cartilage has disappeared long ago and from which raw nerve-endings ceaselessly send their desperate messages to the brain.

"Get on a waiting list," Ellen said. "So many people walk around with a new hip, it can be done these days, you get a painless synthetic joint with which you can walk for fifteen years, really walk, walk by yourself—do it, Alma, treat yourself to it!"

For a moment Alma lets herself go in this fantasy: wake up, put the legs next to the bed and not, and never, feel the pain shoot through the bone. Walk to the toilet without the cane. Perhaps let the hips sway. How that feels. Perhaps dance! The surgeon saws off the head of the femur, holds it up between thumb and index finger, the assistants laugh, the discarded bone fragment falls into the stainless steel bowl that's held out for it, plonk; the nurse's assistant goes outside with it, the bone disappears into the bucket for human scraps, is carbonized in the incinerator, settles as greasy smoke on the parked cars of hospital visitors. All flesh.

How does she look lying there? Unconscious, with a tube through her throat and a Pakistani anaesthesiologist behind her head. Naked and shaven under green sheets, the muscles pulled open with hooks, her insides visible for the curious looks directed at the lower part of her body.

Alma shifts and arranges her leg in a position that causes the least pain possible.

Never, she thinks, never will I let myself be so ill-treated that I have to be motionless and dependent for weeks on end. Perhaps even too weak to eat, perhaps I couldn't, I wouldn't be allowed to sit up and they'd give me cereal through a straw. Drool on the pillowcase, not swallow in time, let the cereal run out of the corner of the mouth. See disdain in their eyes.

How would such a young nurse walk out of the room carrying a bedpan filled with my piss? And how would I ever be able to pee lying down?

Wait for someone to visit me. And the awkwardness if they come. You can't defend yourself, can't just leave, but also can't get angry because then they won't come back.

The stream of her thoughts preoccupies her to such an extent that her face looks even more closed than usual. Guests walking by cast a look at the old lady sitting erect in the shiny blue dress; the painfully pinched mouth, a stretched minus-sign, makes them look away quickly.

Alma looks at the cane that lies on the floor, her weapon, her key to mobility. Sometimes she has such severe pain that she can't even manage with the cane. And going shopping is difficult, she refuses to wear a backpack.

A walker is the next step. And then the wheelchair. Pushed by whom? My own house will also become a prison where wardens will come from time to time to give me an airing.

For a moment Alma sees before her a motorized invalid's vehicle in which she goes tearing over the pavement, sparing no one. Children, indoors, because Alma is coming! She is imprisoned between the daily threatening encroachment on her independence and the fear of total surrender to anaesthesia. Between these two obstacles she would like to race away in her magic chair.

Zina comes swaying towards her on green shoes with very high heels.

"Would you like a cheese croquette? They're really quite delicious!"

Alma shakes no and looks at the way the ample, straight, unwrinkled woman curves her mouth around the croquette, and bites, and swallows.

"Shall I get you something to drink? Or would you like to speak to someone? Has Johan sat with you yet?"

"I don't need to see anyone, my child, and I'll talk with Johan later. Have you met his children yet?"

Unashamedly stirring up trouble and manipulating is a hidden pleasure of old age which Alma likes and does a lot. It would be a lesson for Johan if his girlfriend were to fall in love with his son, it would make him aware of his age.

Of course not, it would only make me aware of his age. It would make him furious and rude. He would get furious at Zina, kick her out. Yes, have her leave with that silver platter full of croquettes, piss off. Out of my sight! I don't want to see these thighs and those healthy legs.

"There they are, at the passageway, you see? They both look like their father. You should go and meet them."

Being alone is also a pleasure of old age. No longer to be bothered by nonsense. But that is nothing compared to the bitter loss of unrestrained possession of the body, nothing. Nothing helps to shorten the long nights, nothing softens the dreadful question: when? and how?

Now that the gallery is emptying, and it's almost five-thirty, Alma gets a view of the musicians who have put Mozart on the music stands. The wrist movements in stroking and massaging the strings with the bow. The fingers of the left hand that are placed on the string, shaking. The heads tenderly bent towards the instrument. Ugh! Concentrated music making seems affected and repugnant to Alma. She hadn't expected anything else from the long-haired girl, but in those boys it's disgusting. Charles with his viola. It was as if he lost all virility, a sentimental visiting nurse who was caressing too large a baby, the picture of weakness and dullness. He loved it, he did it with pleasure and too often. When he played, his eyes were turned inward and he no longer saw her. He didn't hear her speak through the racket they made. Bramelaar sat next to him, Leo with the curls, with an identical viola. If you didn't hear the music along with it, you'd think that they were a pair of washed-out chronic patients in a locked psychiatric hospital with their tilted heads and vibrating hands. Their private parts lay defenceless on the kitchen chairs, tucked away behind the buttoned charcoal-grey flies. Legs spread. Sometimes Charles and Bramelaar would look at each other when they played a melodious passage together. Then they smiled like sweet girls.

Stomping, Alma would go upstairs and turn off the light in the boys' room, unreasonably strict.

Then I could still stomp. Walk out of the house, into the city. Not calculate how far I could go without pain but trust my legs.

What is keeping Oscar, did he get stuck in the front gallery? What a dope, he's never there when you need him. Not that she needs him now, actually. Perhaps she would even be embarrassed if he sat hunched up next to her on the bench for the disabled. But she would like to see how he took in Johan's paintings, staggering from magnificent painting to masterpiece, slowly but surely becoming ashamed of his malicious article, not knowing what to do, embarrassed. And then the confrontation with the brother, screaming, a quarrel, until she would raise her cane to call them to order. After that a meal bulging with smoothed-over rage. That's living.

Suddenly journalist and art connoisseur Kerstens, no longer sober, plops down next to her.

"Your other son, madam, the art historian, will we have the pleasure of seeing him today?"

"I believe that we haven't met yet?"

"Well, I do hope that you know your sons," roars Kerstens. "Please excuse me, a joke, Kerstens, from broadcasting, at least today."

He gives her a warm hand.

"A very penetrating article, I'd like to speak to him about it, perhaps an interview? Well, I'll just call him then."

He gets up with difficulty, bows, and walks straight to the drinks table.

There he is. Finally. Now I can walk with him and the cane past the paintings. That he lets me wait this long! What woman is that next to him? What a bag! Scotch plaid and a pleated skirt, that's too impossible. Would Oscar, with her? Such an old woman, dolled up almost like a Belgian, not really?

Her eyes popping out of her head, Alma looks at her first-born son. She sees how his companion smiles at him amiably and that he returns the smile. They walk slowly past the paintings, Oscar points out something, the woman nods and listens. They stand still for a moment at *The Postman*. Then Oscar turns around, his eyes slide over her to the showpiece. He takes a few steps to the middle of the gallery, to get a better view. It seems as if he doesn't breathe, he's made of wax, a statue. Surprised, the mother sees how the bent back of her son straightens, how he pushes the plump woman away with an abrupt gesture and quickly, resolutely, takes to his heels. What now?

He sails down the stairs and feels for the big bunch of keys in his trouser pocket. You shouldn't carry them all because it makes your suit sag, says Alma, but now he's glad he always does it anyway. Get the coat? No, waiting in the cloakroom, fiddling with a number, money, one of these women who expresses opinions. Prefer just getting out of the building, it's not far.

At the end of the boulevard he sees the National Museum, a massive, dark lump of stone, barely outlined against the rapidly darkening sky. Evening is falling but the wind doesn't lie down, even seems to increase when Oscar steps out of the shelter of the Municipal Museum. The old trees stand creaking, the storm drags their branches back and forth and brushes out the dry leaves. There are hardly any people on the street, people are eating at home and have closed the curtains. No one sees the thin man with glasses who hurriedly steps though the fallen leaves and sometimes skips, once even kicks up a rain of leaves with his foot, and who starts talking to himself.

Don't kick the leaves, Oscar! Your clothes will get dirty, and your shoes. There are dog turds on the street and you'll step in them. Do think! Yes, yes, I'm thinking, Mama, and how! I may not have a face that makes a good impression, but I do have brains and a memory!

Wind at the back. The feeling of flying, of being carried. Oscar spreads his arms and flails as if with windmill arms through the gusts of wind coming from behind.

Admiration! Never enough admiration for the little dear, for that talented little boy with his original drawings. Ooh, and aah, and beautiful they all shout, without thinking and without doing research. Such an original artist! Such a new and daring choice of subject! It's fashionable drivel. He certainly can paint. And I also like to see a painting that depicts something. I sometimes used to think that what he made was very beautiful. I kept a drawing of a steamboat in my secret drawer. He wasn't supposed to know. Alma found it. Hunting for mice, supposedly. Then I got mad. You have to stay out of my drawer, I screamed, you have no business in there, that's mine. I think I pissed in my pants, out of fear, out of confusion. She didn't see that. It ran into the back of my shoes. At night I hung the pants out of the window. I was afraid that she would find my songs and laugh at me. She did find them, but she didn't know what they were, she couldn't read notes. Johan's drawing, that attracted her attention, she was moved by that. To think that you kept it, Oscar, how sweet! I tore it up in front of her eyes, a mistake, oh is it still there? From years ago. I don't give a damn about it. Rip, rip, gone. She smacked me, I had to go upstairs. Smell of piss. But he *can* draw. I can think. My article won't remain unnoticed. Silence the admiration, that's what

I want. Give the ladies and gentlemen of the slime circuit a kick in the teeth. Make my brother change his tune. He can't even sing! He can't, he can't, he can't!

Running through the rustling leaves, float in the storm, towards the dark building. The night guard rummages in his kitchen, he is making coffee when Oscar enters and sticks his head around the door, mumbling a greeting.

"Well, Mr Steenkamer, you're not having much of a weekend! Couldn't it wait until tomorrow?"

"No, I'm going to look up a couple of things that won't wait. You should turn off the alarm for a moment because I'm going to the attic."

Oscar is surprised at the casualness with which he carries on. Now no clumsy and misplaced excuses, no superfluous explanations, no hesitation. Wings of audacity! Suddenly he's standing in the lift. The top button. Shaking, the service lift begins to move, it is a square steel tomb with dents in the walls. You would be able to live in it, it's large enough.

What am I doing? What am I doing? I'm going up. In my own museum. Good, you see. Lights on, all lights on. Now walk like Keetje walked, back there, in the corner, it should be there.

Like a sleepwalker Oscar walks between the racks. He has squeezed his eyes half shut and sees the plump figure of the secretary in front of him like a shadow. She leads him to the place where he has to be. He may not be able to paint, but there's nothing wrong with his spatial visualization. Tilting his head, he reads the stickers on the sides of the racks: Schröder, Silbermann, Steenkamer. He pulls on the rack which doesn't give. With both hands he lifts the rack over the dead point, and then the paintings come rolling to him. Oscar doesn't think. He carefully loosens Alma's portrait from the lattice and puts it down in the aisle. He pushes the rack back and lifts the portrait, with outstretched arms. He breathes straight into the face of his young mother.

Johan is squatting down in front of the old woman. She smells the alcohol on his breath and feels the weak stream of air against her cheeks.

"Come with me, shall I help you? You should go around to look at least once. You've been sitting here the whole time!"

Small, red veins in the whites of his eyes. Greasy skin on his forehead. Drops of sweat.

"He's not coming, is he? He never received your letter. The cake was a mistake. He's not coming."

"Jesus, you're on the look-out! It's about me here, remember? This is not an institute for reuniting families but a museum where I hang. I don't give a damn whether he comes or not, or where that letter is. That's not the point. For all I care he's dead, disappeared, crashed, who knows. It's about me here, and about no one else!"

Over his shoulder Alma sees how the musicians pack up their instruments. The violist polishes her viola clean with a dust cloth. The cellist pushes in his instrument's endpin. They loosen their bows and snap shut their cases. It's six o'clock.

Johan gets up to thank them. He looks around, looking for the director who undoubtedly has in his inside pocket an envelope with money to hand to the music students in a fatherly way. In the large, square galley he sees four women, four colours. Blue sits frozen on her chair, yellow and red leave together for the front gallery, green chats with the director. Therefore go over there.

"To the Ladies' for a moment?" asks Ellen.

Lisa nods. Together they walk down the stairs.

"Let's go and sit in the back of the hall, out of the way."

Lisa has taken off her shoes, pulls up her legs and clasps her arms around her knees.

"The way Johan can do it," she says, "we don't do it like that. I don't fight. Yes, fight for your children, or possibly for your marriage, for peace in your home, that certainly. But for yourself? I manipulate the situation so that I get my way. If it really can't be helped, I let others fight for me. Daniel managed to get the new consulting rooms at the clinic, I stayed quietly in a rebuilt cupboard. But you did it, with your divorce.

"They don't think that a strong woman is sweet. And evidently we're ready to give up and hand over everything on condition that they find us sweet. Fathers, mothers, husbands, all. Difficult to swallow. Your dearest wish? That they think you're nice. Yuck!

"A woman like Alma who always really went her own way, she isn't sweet. I don't know anyone who thinks she's nice, do you?"

"No, but I am fond of her. That has nothing to do with being sweet. Was her strength not real, Lisa? How can she suddenly let her life be determined by the thought of a man? You should see how she sits there, upstairs, in anticipation, afraid to wrinkle her dress, ashamed of her cane!"

"Fathers," says Lisa, "it's about fathers. The father's approval. You think you've conquered it, but as soon as you're not vigilant, it pops up again, the desire to be father's favourite. Right? I had no father, but I became the favourite student of all the professors. I thought I had succeeded in conquering that desire, but that's not so. A girl cannot surpass her father. In the end we want to be on our father's laps, once and for all, forever. Not mother. Father."

Silently, the two women sit facing each other and blow smoke at the window.

How do you hold a painting that is more than three feet wide and six feet high, therefore as large as an over-sized kitchen door, as a small double bed? If you clasp it widthwise with spread arms you're rubbing against your mother's body, if it's a painting of your mother. You can turn it around, or not, you can do that only with great difficulty and much bumping and stumbling, perhaps the piece in question or you will even topple over; it is better to walk around it carefully, holding it with one hand until you stand facing the linen back. If you walk on the street like that, they'll see your mother's head. And how do you actually move in that position? Turn your head, place an ear against the canvas and slide through the aisle, walking like an Egyptian. After thirty feet your underarms start stinging. The frame of your glasses keeps pushing up, and your glasses are now askew on your nose and threaten to tumble off, impossible to find between the dark racks. Stretch the neck sideways to avoid contact with the canvas. After sixty feet, lower the painting and lower the arms for a moment.

She will be damaged if I place her against the iron rails like this, thinks Oscar. Before you know it, there'll be a dent in her face or a paint fragment scraped off. I have to turn her around.

He crawls into the space between painting and wall, he again takes hold of the velvet woman but now pushes the canvas forward without lifting it. That goes a lot faster, but every time his feet graze against the frame, a shock goes through his tensed arms and the painting threatens to escape from his grip.

Oscar is sweating. He loosens his tie and opens his shirt when he reaches the door, Overconfidently he tilts the painting, and it slams against the floor with a bang. Turn off the light, open the lift. A cart like at the airport is what he needs. However, he's had to let a filled shopping cart in the supermarket bump into the shelves many a time out of pure inability to guide it. He pushes the thing into the lift, with his bare hands, with his feet. Sit on the floor in this little room and decide how to proceed. For Aeneas it wasn't easy either way back when, with that paralysed father on his shoulders. And yet he managed to get a long way. Or did he throw Anchises off along the way?

He stands up and starts the lift. The sweet swaying stops with a shock when the lift comes to a halt. Oscar opens both doors and starts dragging the painting outside. Curious, the guard comes closer.

"Come and help me, Bolkestein!"

Oscar's voice has an unexpected authority to which the guard yields. Together they carry the work of art down the steps to the front door. Once at the guard's cubby-hole, Bolkestein remembers his duty and throws a monkey wrench into the plans.

"The pieces are not allowed out of the museum without permission. There has to be a delivery receipt. Signed."

Oscar opens the doors and secures them into the floor with

iron pins, as if it's Sunday afternoon and the public is about to stream in.

"And who has to issue this certificate, Bolkestein?"

"Head of restoration and preservation, sir."

Propped against Oscar's legs, the painting stands with its long side on the ground. It comes to above his waist. He stands up as straight as possible and tries to hold his head slightly back.

"And who is that?!"

"Mr Steenkamer, sir. Yourself, in fact."

"Well, give me such a form. Then I'll sign."

"I don't have it here, that's not my responsibility, it's upstairs, you know."

"So, what are you going on about? Good evening!"

Through the opened doors an enormous draft starts up that makes Oscar's pants flap. Heavy clouds hang above the plane trees on the boulevard. In the distance the illuminated windows of the Municipal Museum glow. With all his might Oscar pulls up the painting and starts dragging it outside.

"You lock up, Bolkestein!"

The guard has no words and looks dumbfounded at the wiry man with the unusual load. He pulls the pins out of the floor and closes the door.

At the top of the white marble staircase stands Johan. Like a general, he looks at his withdrawing troops. The party is over, people are going home. They look for their coats, their car keys, and in their thoughts are already out of the door. Johan has shaken their hands, has listened to their words of thanks and their compliments and now listens to his own thoughts. Something is wrong: despite the words of praise, the perfect installation of his work, the presence of fervently desired foreign agents and the increased market value of his paintings, there is no triumph. Johan records and crosses off the wishes on his wish list: everything received, the loot is in. Why does there remain a last bit of restlessness, why is there a feeling of unquenched desire when all wishes have been fulfilled and all expectations have been met? He is waylaid by the Scottish cow whom he saw all afternoon navigating through the crowd.

"Please excuse me, Mr Steenkamer, for accosting you like this, I'm from across the street, from the National, The secretary of Mr Steenkamer, your brother, that's his name too, that's so strange, but I did want to ask you, he keeps on disappearing, keeps on leaving—where he is, or, do you know?"

Keetje's lips tremble. She actually has a sweet face, thinks Johan. Pretty light skin, well-placed eyes. But then butterfly glasses on it. So it's she who types the secret memos that everyone would like to read. She looks incorruptible. Johan shakes her hand.

"Nice to meet you. My brother is rather unpredictable. If he's gone now, he most likely won't come back. It's almost over, as you can see."

"Yes, I'm a bit worried. He acted so strangely. He suddenly disappeared."

"Very nice of you, but you do work for him? Then you must know that he sometimes behaves peculiarly! Do go and get your coat, it will all turn out all right."

Shaking her head, Keetje goes down the stairs.

*

Too much but not enough. All the success in the world, but no father to overwhelm. Or to show it to, so that he's proud of his son.

Drunk too much, that's it. But not enough! Johan turns around, on his way to more drink. Tonight they keep pouring as long as he wants.

"Well, my boy, satisfied?"

Nicolaas Bijl places his hand on Johan's upper arm and squeezes it amiably. Johan looks up at the oval face.

I only have to think of a father and one appears. I want to paint him, standing, naked. Not made of flesh but of wood. Unfinished, polished wood in which you can see the grain. Living but protected from decay. The prick made of root wood, shining. He'll never approve. Or perhaps he would. He isn't bothered by anything. Don't ask now. Too much.

"You know Johan, it's too bad you let that dear woman go. I was always so fond of her. But I shouldn't talk about that now, this is your day. You're going to sell a lot. Do pay attention, don't make any stupid promises."

Fond of her. Yes yes. She should never have set foot in that crazy wood office, then she would still be in my bed. In the background, out of his field of vision, I'll place a saw and an axe. And in the sky a thunderbolt, or is that too much? Instead a bright blue summer sky, that's beautiful with that colour of wood. An old-fashioned lumber-jack's saw with shiny teeth.

"I'll seek expert advice, of that you can be assured. Now I'm going to see if Kees has a whiskey for me."

"Go ahead, my boy, you should drink on an evening like this."

Bijl sees a strand of hair over a face with closed eyes, a skirt that slides to the floor. Long ago. Ellen knows what she's doing. It's none of my business. I'm leaving, I'll have a nice walk in the wind.

The wind catches the painting as soon as Oscar is outside. It is torn out of his hands and sails down the steps by itself. Alarmed, Oscar goes after it and tries to lift it. Headwind. Raindrops. Now it's a matter of crossing the street, that has priority. After that on the boulevard, under the trees, it is quiet and reasonably dark.

Here people walk and cars whoosh by. Upright is an unsuitable position for the crossing because the storm then has better hold on the tall canvas. Oscar loses his balance and staggers right in front of a honking car. In the middle of the road he takes the painting alongside with the risk that onrushing traffic will knock off half.

A bicyclist points his finger to his head.

A taxi, thinks Oscar, but that won't work, the thing is too big. If only the wind would die down. I have to think about sailing technique. Tack. With the wind dead against you you can only sail back, that's useless for me. Up again, like in the attic, that worked best. I can't keep it up for long, pain in my arms. Stupid, such large paintings. Makes no sense at all. In God's name not meet any people now. A painted lady with men's feet moving underneath, dogs will start jumping up against it, police will come straight for it, there will be screaming.

He shuffles among the autumn leaves, his glasses are fogged-up by moisture from both sides; he sees almost nothing. The wind shakes the canvas. It ripples, there is barely any tension on it anymore. Torn branches are lying on the street. Take the painting frontally, width-wise, in front of the stomach? With bent arms he clasps the painting and holds it up. With every gust of wind there is frightful creaking sounding on the sides. Danger of cracking. Not good. Can't move legs like this. What have I started? It's much farther away than just a while ago. African women carry whole barrels of water on their heads! He sets the painting upright in front of himself and places his head against the middle of the canvas. Then he rises up, with raised arms bearing the painting above him. Like an enormous bat he walks along the street.

The wind makes the painting topple over, it hits the back of Oscar's knees so hard that he almost falls. With a grating sound it sails over the pavement, is lifted up and slams down in the grass along the road. Oscar sits down next to it. A ping-pong table. It's raining.

There is no help. Up again, perhaps it will work better through the grass. Drag, if necessary through dog turds. It snags in the branches and in the junk lying between the trees. Lift again after all? I can't, my arms don't work any more. No bullshit, just up. Not too fast, hold on tight. Jesus, that wind!

Knocked over by a storm blast, Oscar steps straight through the canvas. During his fall he feels a stabbing pain in his lower leg. He lands on top of the painting, pulls back his leg and loses his shoe. The trouser leg is torn from knee to ankle, blood wells up from the pale leg. He no longer feels anything. He looks for the shoe under the canvas and pulls it back on. He trembles. Tears run along his nose. There is a big hole in the canvas next to Alma's head. It's too high to be able to look through it while walking.

There are black and greenish smears on the painting. Leaves are sticking to it. An autumn piece.

"Shall I help you?"

A laughing man walks towards Oscar. Away, keep on walking, but how? Oscar tries a trot and crashes against a plane tree. His glasses are knocked off his face, he hears them clatter against the pavement. Crawling on all fours, he looks for them; Alma is parked against the tree, would that creep come after him, knock him down? Better to go on, without glasses. He drags the painting after him like a pushcart, bumping over the paving bricks. He drives his head into the wind and breathes in howling gasps. He cries but doesn't know it.

He can set down his load against the side of the Municipal Museum in order to remove the clinging foliage. Alma's face swims vaguely in his defective field of vision. He uses his coat sleeve to wipe it.

"I'm doing it for you. I have to. Do you think that I like dragging evidence from that so-called father of ours in front of your eyes? Well? That for the good of my health I run the risk that you'll only look at him? Well, I'd rather dump the whole mess into a canal, you hear. But I have to."

He sits on his knees in front of the painting and speaks increasingly loudly.

"I'm doing it for you! I've never opened my mouth, it's Johan this and Johan that. And where was Oscar? In the back of the gallery, left behind, forgotten. You should see that he can't do everything, that he isn't the most original artist since Michelangelo, that darling of yours. I'm there too!"

Sobbing, he addresses his mother. The rain runs simultaneously down his neck and over the bumpy finish behind which she is locked up.

When sociability among adults is slow in starting or gets stuck in a stiff silence, it's children or dogs that bring relief. They knock glasses from the table and in this way unite the women around washrag and basin, they make noises that cause men to look smiling at one another.

Such small ice-breakers are no longer available in Alma's family, but her grandsons are trained in this function and know their duty. They push together the available chairs in the large gallery and urge those who have stayed to sit down. Paul arranges the left-over hors-d'oeuvres on a serving tray and goes around offering them. Peter has tackled the drink supply with the director and is pouring whiskey, gin or wine as desired.

It's over, it's time to take a deep breath and sit down and stretch your legs out in front of you. Time to look around calmly to see who is still there, who is not.

Zina has not sat down in the circle but stands leaning against the wall and talks with Kerstens. She is trying to interest him in the objects displayed in her gallery and shows him her necklace. His glance drifts down to the green-edged bosom below. He suppresses a burp and with his whiskey glass makes a requesting gesture to Paul.

"Aren't you on the editorial staff of that art programme?" asks Zina. "Those things standing in my gallery are really very good. Wouldn't you like to come and take a look some time?"

"Come and look at your goodies, yes, would you like that?"

"Yes, fine. And if you like it, then you can maybe get it in, right?"

"Yes, yes, that's what that woman said last night!" the art connoisseur splutters through a small cloud of whiskey drops.

"Sorry, girl, it was too much for me!"

Zina, who had let herself be swept along by her desire for publicity, changes direction.

"You know what, you give me your card and I'll call you next week, is that all right?"

"May I tattoo you?"

Kerstens takes a felt pen out of his trouser pocket and starts writing a number in her décolleté. It tickles. Zina giggles, she feels her victim is solidly hooked. Success.

If the woman with the fish could look, she would see the company sit in horseshoe formation at her feet. On one side is Johan who can't relax and with a residue of alertness remains sitting on the edge of his chair, as if it isn't over yet, as if he's still waiting for something. The director sits next to him and has placed the bottle under his chair. He is satisfied and contented.

In the middle sits Lisa, flanked by Peter and Paul. She pushes her chair back a little, her inward-looking mood has lingered and she gives herself over to silent observation. She sees how Ellen's eyes continually stray to the corner of the table where Zina stands laughing with the journalist. To the right of her friend sits Alma who hasn't moved from her place all afternoon. She too looks over the circle at the gallery entrance, she is waiting but sees nothing coming.

"We should have a campfire," says Paul.

"My boy, consider my insurance premium!"

The director pulls out the bottle and fills Johan's glass.

"Tell stories! Everyone should in turn tell a part of the story, I always thought that was so exciting when we used to do it. Grandma has to start!"

Ellen smiles at her son. Behind him she seems to see a girl of about twenty, a young woman with a slender neck and a perfect face. Her long filly's legs still move in a childlike way beneath the short skirt, as if she's walking on high heels for the first time. There is no chair for her, and she vanishes.

"Dear people, do stay here for a while, all night long as far as I'm concerned, the guard can let you out at any time. I wish you a pleasant and delicious meal!"

"Come with us," Johan mumbles, "why do you on earth have to leave?"

"Boring meeting tomorrow, need to check some things and so forth; no, I'm delighted with the invitation but unfortunately I can't accept. Madam, it was a pleasure!"

Alma gets a handshake, the younger ladies a kiss, the boys a slap on the back. Johan walks with him to the passageway. The director hugs him and formally hands him the half-empty whiskey bottle. His rapid steps fade away in the front gallery.

"Come and sit with us," Johan says half-heartedly as he passes Zina. "We'll have one more before we go. Coarsetense, may I refuel you?"

Bonk, bónk, bonk, bónk, hears Lisa. She looks around the circle. Johan has sat down again. No one seems to hear anything. Bónk, bónk, bónk, bónk. Is it her own heartbeat? She tries to let her shoulders relax. Sit slouched. Quiet now, relax, there's nothing wrong. The dull strokes are followed by a dragging, grating sound. She turns around halfway in her chair and sees Oscar enter the gallery, almost completely hidden by a greyish fence.

Alma inhales quickly, she wants to say something but nothing comes out. The company is numbly looking at what is happening now.

It's something serious, thinks Ellen, he's lost his glasses and his trousers are torn. He's bleeding.

Oscar looks at no one. His eyes are fixed on the woman with the fish, and he goes in her direction, using two hands to drag along his man-sized load. He climbs up the platform. A deep, bloody scratch can be seen in his calf. He pulls up the flat object. Leaves fall off. He turns it around with difficulty and places it against the wall, next to Johan's masterpiece. With both arms he presses it against the wall. It's a painting. There is a big hole in the upper left corner. The canvas undulates when Oscar steps back. Now two paintings stand next to each other on the platform.

Zina feels wetness. She senses unerringly that she, and certainly her conversation partner as well, have got to get away. She presses her hip softly against the journalist's thigh: "I know of a nice spot where we can continue our conversation. Come with Zina, you'll really see something!"

She stands in front of him and bends down to fix something on her shoe. For a moment her breasts hang loose in their green frame. Kerstens is sold. He is too tipsy to realize that he's going to miss out on the sweetest art scoop of the year, but still sufficiently with it to like the fact that he's going off with the hero's girlfriend. He turns around and lets himself be led away by Zina. Over her shoulder she looks at Johan: I'm doing it for you, and for art!

A taxi, jokes, bantering foreplay. With his head in her lap the exhausted reporter falls asleep in the back seat; that will cause few problems, she'll have to be up early tomorrow morning.

\* \* \*

An icy silence hangs in the large gallery. The hard white light comes from everywhere. Two paintings stand on the platform. There are seven people in the gallery who are looking at it. The woman with the fish now has a sister with blond hair and a black velvet jacket. She has ice-blue eyes and a beautifully shaped mouth with narrow lips. In her arms the woman carries an enormous steamed mackerel. Its head rests on her elbow. From under the black velvet comes a long skirt with brightened golden pleats.

The small bare feet are standing on a wooden floor. Letters and numbers are carved in the planks: Steenkamer 1945; Alma with mackerel.

Almost half a century, thinks Alma. God, how I hated that fish. I absolutely had to hold it in that way and I knew I was irreparably ruining my most beautiful jacket. It will never come out, that stench. You can't wash velvet. I tried absolutely everything. Soap. Stain remover. Eau de cologne. The sleeves had indelible circles.

Alma had thrown away the jacket. You *kept* smelling that awful fish odour. And hunger! Charles came home on the bicycle with a big package wrapped in newspaper. On the table he untied the strings: A fish larger than you had ever seen, with grey and gold ripples on its skin and shiny round eyes. There were grease stains on the newspaper, she was salivating. Alma had to put on her evening gown and pose. Inwardly crying with hunger, she stood with the fish at her breast for hours on end.

He had made an exchange with a fishmonger whose wretched boat, wife or dog he had painted. Art for fish.

When Alma was allowed to put it down for a moment, she tried to pick out the fat tissue with a fork. He became furious, she was harming the line of the back, she was out of her mind, she was destroying his work. "The fish goes first," she screamed, "paint its back as fast as you can, after that we'll see." Red-hot with anger, they stood still in the cold room. After two days the fish was on the canvas. A fat, round back. Filled. Then Alma gutted the fish and filled plate after plate, finally. She stuffed the skin with hay from the hay box and stood for weeks with the rotting fish skin in her arms. At night it went on the balcony, with the wash tub over it.

To think that the neighbours never complained about the stench! thinks Alma. Never again have I seen such a large mackerel. That's me, there, with that perfect pale face and the straight posture. Me.

The silence still shimmers in the gallery. Oscar stands as if nailed to the floor in front of the platform. Now Johan stands up. He flings the whiskey glass to the floor. A hail of splinters, a reliable signal of disaster.

"Well, goddammit, Oscar."

His voice sounds strange, pinched. Slowly Oscar turns his head and looks in Johan's direction.

"Wasn't it enough, you jealous runt, haven't you said it clearly enough in the paper. Did you have to come at this ungodly hour to sabotage me? You're a jerk, a jealous arsehole!"

The more Johan talks and screams, the tighter his muscles get. The pace is increased, the volley of his own invectives sweeps him into action. He comes towards the motionless Oscar, first threatening, then fast, then blazing. He grabs his brother at the throat and, roaring, gives him a good shaking.

Oscar becomes anxious; his thrashing movements are not

intentional but seem to come from his spinal cord. Johan's reactions are affected by the alcohol, and his grip weakens for a moment when he is surprised by a sudden change in Oscar's position.

Oscar begins flailing his arms indiscriminately like a drowning person in the throes of death. He hits Johan's nose accidentally. It hurts, Johan covers his face with his arm and winces with pain. Now Oscar scampers off, a blind mole's run. At the same moment Alma stands up.

A quarrel. The boys are fighting. Walking away is not allowed, it's not yet over. Alma walks to Oscar and tries to pull his sleeve. He pushes her away and storms to the passageway, down the stairs. Alma falls. The cane is still lying under her chair.

Nice pose, thinks Johan. Beautiful, that grey and silvery blue with the pale blue face. The position of the legs reveals there can be no question of walking, a double halt, beautiful. Jesus, blood on my suit. If my nose is broken, I'll beat him to pulp, I'll kill him, that sneaky bastard.

Covertly he feels his nose under the bloody handkerchief nothing seems to be loose. Everything hurts.

Broken bone. I have to go into action. I'm a doctor, Lisa thinks. She pushes aside some bits of glass and kneels down by Alma. Respiration, size of pupil, pulse, position of the limbs. Listen, feel, smell, look. The loss of consciousness isn't very deep, she is already coming to. The right leg is twisted out in an unnatural manner. Don't touch, don't move. Terrible what must be taking place inside: bone fragments piercing though the periosteum, torn-apart veins emptying out into an unsuitable space, nerves becoming overloaded like telephone cables in rush hour, chaos and upheaval. Would she be wearing a corset, should I try to loosen it? Lisa carefully feels Alma's stomach and then moves her hand down. Moisture. The blue silk becomes dark from wetness and a sharp smell of urine rises up. Now she sees how the urine slowly spreads between the old lady's legs.

"I can't stop it," whispers Alma, "it just comes."

Didn't urinate all afternoon, of course. Full bladder. No control due to pain, due to loss of consciousness, due to nerve damage? What a stench! How humiliating. How hopeless.

Immediately after his grandma's fall, Peter ran outside, he was already calling out to the guard as he was racing down the stairs: an ambulance, the emergency number, a doctor has to come!

When he gets downstairs, the guard is already holding the telephone. Tersely he speaks into the receiver.

"They'll be here in five minutes! I'll open the doors in the meantime."

Paul sits on the floor by Alma. He's holding her hand and is speaking into her ear.

"It doesn't matter, Grandma. Everything will be all right. We're going to the hospital. I'm coming with you, I will. You've broken something. It will be all right."

Lisa has brought a towel which she hands to Paul. He places it between Alma's legs and dabs the pee from the floor.

Ellen still sits nailed to her chair and looks at the paintings. Alma's fall is just too much. She registers the event but detaches herself from it as soon as she sees the relief forces rush forward.

Your own fault, she thinks in spite of herself. If you mistreat and use your children like that, you shouldn't be surprised if you're punished. What a mean, nasty thought. Fortunately Peter and Paul are nicer than I am. Johan is also doing nothing. She monopolizes all the attention with her fracture, but the person who is really broken is Johan. Plagiarism. Without being aware of it.

*On father's lap,* Lisa said. He too, so he too! Ellen looks at Johan. He's busy with his nose, with the stains on his shirt, he kicks away glass fragments near his feet.

It isn't sinking in. He can't stand pain, his nose occupies all his attention. Any left-over energy he uses to curse Oscar. He doesn't know yet that he's standing by an abyss.

"Someone has to cancel that Carp," says Johan.

Lisa will do it. She walks downstairs, glad to be able to move again. Family circumstances, unfortunately. The old lady. No, not dead. Speedy recovery then. Strange word. A cigarette. Would like a drink. Better not, right now. I'm part of the situation but not of the family. I can be away for a while.

The ambulance has arrived and stands on the pavement with the back opened and lights flashing. Two husky men pull out the stretcher. They are wearing white overalls. The older one has a big moustache, a fat stomach, and a bald spot on his round head. He is in charge. The younger one has driven.

"An old lady. Fallen," says the guard.

"Must be a hip? Take the air mattress along now, Jon, otherwise you'll have to go back."

Jon takes a bright orange plastic package from inside the car and places it on the stretcher. The guard precedes the men to the service lift.

The man with the moustache whistles appreciatively on entering the front gallery that is still filled with glasses and bottles.

"Will they still serve us a beer, Jon? It must be back in there, come on, she shouldn't have been playing soccer!"

Rapidly they push the stretcher into the gallery where Johan and Ellen still sit facing each other. Between them lies the fallen woman with a grandchild on either side.

"And here is the ice-cream man," Jon keeps trying, cheerfully. The joke fades into the silence.

"Grandma," says Paul, "the male nurses from the hospital are here to pick us up. We're going now."

"But I can't walk, my child, they'll just have to lift me. You will stay, won't you?"

"You're going on the bed that they've brought with them."

"Lying down?"

Alma opens her eyes wide. Above her hovers a kindly round

face with a reddish-brown moustache. The whiskers hang down stiffly, like a kitchen brush.

"Do you hear me, little lady? We think that all is not hunky-dory inside you. We'll fasten you nicely because you're not supposed to move."

Jon shows Alma the orange package and unfolds it.

"A kind of air mattress. Like camping. Push it underneath. Around the leg. Blow it up."

"You have to explain, Jon. You scare a person out of her wits with that blowing up. See, you're lying on the pad."

Very carefully he pushes the plastic underneath Alma, barely lifting her wounded leg from the floor. Jon sits with his knees on the pad and holds Alma's leg in the original position. The two men don't seem to notice the smell of piss.

"And now I'm folding it upward, then it goes around the leg. In a moment I'll pull out the stopper and then it'll swell up as if you had pumped up your bed, yes? Completely around your leg, nice and solid. A leg cast of air, as it were.

Hunky-dory, camping, an explosion. Alma has given up. She squeezes Paul's hand tightly. Eyes closed.

The orange pad grows into a veritable lifeboat in which the leg lies solidly anchored. They carefully push the whole affair onto the stretcher. Paul pulls her arms on board. She is lifted up and is placed on the undercarriage.

"Mum, we're going along to the hospital. Are you coming later? Or shall I call you?"

"Yes," says Ellen, "or no. I don't know. I'll call over there in an hour or so. If you stay. Her bag. Take her bag along."

"And the cane? What shall we do with that?"

"I'll take it with me, sweetheart."

Jon in front, Moustache in the back, Peter and Paul on either side. Pale, with eyes closed, Alma lies on the stretcher, fastened with sil-ver-grey straps. The light is so bright, it seems like a summer day. In the rowboat with Charles, rocking among the reeds. Where are the fish, had he caught fish for me? Everything is gone, cannot be found. Why does he say nothing, why has he been so quiet all afternoon? No talking, then they won't bite, you chase them away, quiet! He looks at the float. He wants to go away. I want out of the boat, I have to lie in the grass where the ground is solid and doesn't move under me. I have to clean the fish, otherwise they spoil. The knife, I'm going to cut them open and take out the guts, watch out for the gallbladder, if you leave it in, the fish is inedible.

I open them from top to bottom, in one motion. The knife tumbles away into the depths.

*Chapter nine*

# A Guest of Air

I've *done* it, I've *done* it, I've *done* it, I've *done* it!

To the rhythm of these thoughts, Oscar walks in a brisk tempo through the streets. Because the accent sometimes falls on the right and then again on the left, his gait is bouncy, a fast dance forward. His half-blind eyes register the light from the shop windows as yellow-white stripes, the passers-by as black intervals. He has done it.

What have I *done*? Accidentally broken my brother's nose, in passing knocked over my mother, not on purpose. It happened. I did it. They hadn't thought that, oh no, Oscar would be good and behave, that's what they thought, but he won't.

Now I can also get an aquarium. No animals in the house, she declared. Good, agreed, if she had dogs and cats in mind. A dog who puts his mouth with strands of slobber on your trousers. Who growls when you enter your own room. A cat whom everyone looks at admiringly so that you feel ashamed when you'd like to throw him out of the window. A cat who jumps on your lap unexpectedly; through the cloth you feel his nails penetrate the skin of your legs, the filthy claws with which he was scratching around just a moment before in the stinking cat box under the sink. Faint from disgust, swallow the wave of vomit, brace yourself to put your hand under the cat's stomach, lift him, release him too high so that he falls and people look at you reproachfully. Your fingers smell of cat's hair, you wipe them furtively on the sofa seat. No, not such animals. But a simple fishbowl with clear water and white rocks? A goldfish is the cleanest animal, it does nothing but wash, his swimming is bathing. I'd feed him every day at the exact same time, he would know me and would start coming when I came closer. The fishbowl must stand on my desk, under my lamp.

"Then you won't study anymore," says Alma. "It's distracting, such an animal in front of you. Absolutely out of the question, better think of something else for your wish list."

Yes, I would look at the fish for hours on end. How he washed himself in the water. His smooth, inviolate body with its harness of scales. When he eats, the digested food comes out again like a strand of black thread that drops down and disappears between the rocks. Maybe I'd buy another one after a while, a small one, to see how the fish with the oldest rights pushes the newcomer aside and makes him wait until he himself has eaten enough. Maybe the old one would bite the new one, they are predators. They eat everything.

"An aquarium, that has to be cleaned. And who would do that?" asks Alma, already accusing. "Moreover it will start leaking, the glass will develop a crack, and fifteen gallons of water will stream onto the floor. Fifteen gallons! The room will be flooded, the floor will start rotting, the house will collapse!"

Johan wanted a dog. To boss around of course. But he didn't get it, fortunately. Not my fault. Alma. She was the boss. No argument possible. Until today. I held the remnants of her husband right in front of her. So that she *had* to look. The remains. So that he's really gone. An empty spot. The head of the family, the man of the house. Me.

Now they'll finally take me seriously. After what I have done.

He was bleeding. She fell. They'll kill me. They won't listen to me at all because I will no longer be allowed in!

Oscar feels a tingling in his stomach. He stands still and shivers.

Alone in the world. Outcast, banned. No longer a mother and no brother. Would Ellen still want to see me? No, ultimately she would still choose Johan. I have committed a capital offence. I didn't think. If I had been able to think, I would never have dared. I no longer have anyone. If Bolkestein says what I did, I'll also lose my job.

A curator who kicks through a painting! Who drags the museum's possessions through the rain, without thinking!

Calm now, calm! Think. Keetje, would she still, could I still, or is she also…? Disappointed of course, I left her standing just like that. She helped me and I left her alone. When she hears what I've done, how I misused her help… She'll slam the door in my face. Where does she live anyway? I don't even know. Be calm. Try to think slowly. I have to flee. They're waiting for me at my front door, hidden in the doorway. No, I'm not going there! Where to instead? I can go and live in cafés, from one to the next. At night in the coffeehouses near the harbour. If they say anything to me, I'll pretend I'm deaf. Deaf and dumb, that's best. Everywhere I'll sit on a wooden chair and look. But I have no glasses. And no money. To the harbour, the water. Then I can think. There are no cars and bright lights there.

Oscar quickens his pace. The torn trouser flaps around his wounded leg and the keys jangle in his pocket.

Perhaps I can sleep in the attic of the museum! People almost never go there, and when anyone came, you'd hear it. You could hide really well there. How would I get in? They'll arrest me! I have to get rid of the keys, if they find them on me it will be evidence, they'll pick me up. I have to get rid of them! I have to get away from here. Keep walking. It's so blurry. Are they looking at me? They're sitting at the windows, I'm quite aware of it. The women sit in front of the windows in their most beautiful dresses, they call me, they tap against the pane—if I remain standing here, their man will appear and hit me in the neck with the side of his hand. That's how it goes. I won't fall for that! I don't look, I keep on walking. Even if they act nice, even if they say: come to me, darling! It's a plot and I have to flee.

When I'm safe, I'll bandage my leg. I'll make a bandage from my shirt. It's white. It won't be easy to catch me, oh no. I'll grow a beard because I'm done with shaving. When they lead me to the lineup, Alma's eyes will slide over me. No, that's not my son. My son doesn't wear a suit without a shirt. Let that homeless person go free, it's not him. My son wears glasses, you know.

There are very few inhabited houses in the area where Oscar is now walking. The distance between streetlights has become greater and dim light shines on shipping companies, offices and transit warehouses. A bridge leads across the water to a dark island with deserted shipyards: broken gates and sagging buildings. The end of the city. Here begins the domain of minimal people. Oscar slows his walking pace. His leg is stinging and causes him to limp. As it becomes darker and quieter around him, he starts breathing deeper and slower.

Here they're not looking for him. Here it's safe. He walks over neglected rails along a wharf. The water shimmers. The rain has stopped. At his left is a row of wooden sheds with overhanging roofs. Dark lumps lie beneath them here and there: sleeping homeless. No one calls after him, he can simply go his own way. In the distance he sees the light of a fire. He's going there. Get dry. Sit. In safety.

The brick building has three floors. It is a warehouse with doors instead of windows. In front of every door is a wide loading platform and every platform is a drifter's home, furnished with cardboard boxes folded flat and plastic bags. A narrow fire ladder has been set against the wall to take the homeless up. However, only one place is inhabited on the top floor. It is windier there than downstairs, and the ridge beam gives only partial protection against the weather. A husky man in a Norwegian sweater has taken up residence there. On the wharf a few people are sitting by a fire. A man with iron teeth bites the crown caps from the bottles and spits them, clattering, on the bricks. A woman wrapped in a blanket pushes loosened slats of an orange crate into the fire and looks intently at how the printed letters carbonize. A salutary silence reigns, people can hear the water lap against the wharf, hear the fire crackle, hear the drinker burp. People can hear dragging, irregular steps come closer. They are not afraid. People see the tattered trouser leg around a bloody leg, the dishevelled head on a sinewy neck, and they make room. Oscar drinks and feels his thirst. He sits down next to the fire woman and breathes again. Freedom. Rest.

The woman starts tearing a cardboard box into pieces to feed the fire. Iron dentures places his hand on her arm and with his head nods in Oscar's direction: "Don't do it, the professor can sleep on it! Right, no? A nice mattress for the gentleman, to be sure."

Oscar is touched. They look after me, he belongs.

"Have a blanket, perfesser? No, sure? Take some plastic with papers under it, that's warmer. There's some with the supplies, no?"

The fire woman nods. She puts the cardboard aside and starts putting a stack of wet branches on the fire, one by one. It smokes. The smell of campfire, adventure. From upstairs comes an unintelligible shout.

"Scando wants a swig," says iron dentures. "Who's the waiter?"

A small thin man, still a boy, thinks Oscar, run-away from home perhaps, climbs up swiftly with an opened bottle in his left hand. Oscar looks. The giant in the Norwegian sweater slowly raises his hand, in thanks, blessing, in peace. He lifts the bottle, toasting the newcomer. Oscar blushes before holding up his half-empty beer bottle in answer.

The flames have gone out. The woman has fallen asleep with her head against the kindling wood. The only light now comes from a lamp-post twenty yards away; it makes the teeth of the iron dentures gleam.

"Hops," says the man. "Beer's made of hops. We'll take another, professor. Here's hops to you, beer is healthy and I should know. Here, take it, for you."

Oscar half stands in order to accept the bottle across the

sleeping firewoman. The keys jangle in his pocket. Jesus. The keys. Have to get rid of them. Forgotten. Stupid. Better right away.

Staggering, Oscar walks in the direction of the water, he hears the small waves hit the wharf wall. It smells of oil.

He pulls the heavy key chain out of his trouser pocket. A passkey gets caught in the seam. Oscar tugs at it forcefully, it has to be done now. The key comes loose, Oscar loses his equilibrium and stands balancing at the water's edge. Slowly he topples forward, the key chain clasped in his hand.

In the water he feels the cold immediately. He lets go of the keys. His waterlogged jacket hampers arm movements. His legs are ungovernable because of their weight. They want to sink. Small waves hit his face as soon as he gasps for air. Water, water. With your clothes on into the water in the public swimming-pool. How the cold climbed into your pants, how the water pulled at your shoes. I was so frightened that I forgot to move and sunk away into the green chlorine water. The borders between the tiles were wavy lines that I looked at in a daze. The hook! Iron at the back of my neck, a ring of steel that dragged me to the surface where Miss Ada was standing, on the high edge of the swimming pool. Legs like pillars, above which began a giant body, wrapped in white, ending up in a face that was linked to only one word: power.

"You over there. What did I say. Draw up-spread-close. Fingers above the water. Pay attention."

The shame. They hear it. Alma with Johan on the bleachers. Miss Ada can kill you by looking, you have to avoid her eyes because you'll be paralysed. Angrily she hits the water with the hook, smack, smack, smack.

The knife. I killed the cake. Which came from Papa. I bashed it in with my sword. Until nothing was left of it. We have no Papa, I said to the boys at school. We don't need a father at all, my mother has me!

Boast about their fathers, they did, how strong they were and what they all could do: ride motorcycles, buy as many French fries as you could eat, catch thieves. Nonsense, I didn't want to hear any of it. I always paid attention to Alma, to see if she was pleased. Most of the time she was angry, then she got the mouth like a line and I knew that something wasn't good. But what? I couldn't do it, make that mouth disappear. Johan made her laugh. I kicked her in the face. If it can't be done willingly, then unwillingly. Accidentally on purpose.

Ever stronger, the water sings in my ears.

Sound. The first and the last. The favourite. They are making music for me, I have to listen, a melody that goes up and down like surface of the sea, a choir is singing, *Sanctus, sanctus*—French? Modern but yet with dark romanticism—Duruflé?—Let it be, just listen.

It is sea music, we're on the beach, at the edge of the water where the sand is hard, with large grains, brown, black, white. There comes Johan, he has just learned to walk on his fat little legs. He runs. I open my arms wide and bend my knees. He holds up his chubby baby arms and clasps treasures in his small hands: a shell, a fist full of sand. His eyes sparkle, foam splashes over our feet. He screams with pleasure while running to me: Osser, come, look here, look here, Osser!

Smiling, Oscar floats downward.

*   *   *

After the commotion with the ambulance, the guard turns down the lights.

Facing each other, Johan and Ellen lie almost stretched out in the museum chairs. From the wall the two fish women, the naked one and the one dressed in black, stare into the gallery. In the dim light the floor looks like a beach at low tide, the pieces of glass shine like mother-of-pearl shells, and in the shallow water lie objects that were washed ashore: a shawl, a dirty plate, a forgotten cane.

"I didn't lift a finger for her," says Ellen. "Nor did you. She was lying there, and I thought: no."

A fresh cigarette from the pack that lies next to her on the floor. Doesn't feel like looking for an ashtray, just let the ash fall on the floor. Look at the smoke while leaning the head back on the comfortable pillows. Questioning, lift the package to Johan who shakes his head no.

"For days I've sympathized with her, answered her telephone calls, helped her with her clothes and her hairdo. Strange that you suddenly know that it's enough. Our boys are a marvel of humanity. When she comes home, she'll get under our skin with her demands and her orders. She'll monopolize us and make us worry. With or without a hip. What did she fantasize, Johan? That Charles would press her to his heart again?"

"Hah! That she'd use her cane to throw a monkey wrench into his plans, you mean! Even more people to rattle and play off against each other. Do you know that I never lost to Oscar from the time when I was four? From that time on I was stronger. Always won. Until now. The bastard.

"Gave me a bloody nose with his weak little hand. And then walked off, the chicken."

"He saw nothing, his glasses were gone. He was terribly upset. Did you love him when you were small?"

"Love him? That worm? That creep? I *hate* him, dammit, that sneak. What's that supposed to mean, dragging paintings around? Why does he do that behind my back? He tries to destroy me, and then I'm supposed to love him? Writes nasty pieces about me and screws up my opening—come now, I won't put up with that.

"Zina left just in time with that journalist. Otherwise that would have caused an uproar. Then I would really have lost face, and he would have had his way, Oscar. She immediately caught on that things were all wrong. I saw how she flirted with him. He was sloshed, he followed her blindly, the lecher. Too stupid and too plastered to notice anything. Fortunately."

Johan rubs his eyes and sinks deeper into the chair.

"That dress is very nice, you know that?"

Ellen nods. Clotted blood. Full-bodied wine. Very good. An exhausted dress, a battlefield gown. Goes well with his nose.

"He always sat whispering with Alma. He did what she wanted, he was always there. If you looked at her, you saw him. Always sucking up, always afraid. In fact now, for the first time, he's done something himself, something that makes everyone furious, a *deed*. And that they looked at him, that's also a first. Everyone always looked at me. And then he beats it. The coward. What could he want? Don't care either. God, I'm so angry. Angry, angry, angry!"

"They're all crazy in that family of yours. Impossible to live with. Dangerous fools. Without exception. A cage filled with wild animals. When I sit next to Oscar at the opera, I feel the tension radiate from him. He's barely holding together. He jumps out of his chair with fright when I ask him if he wants a peppermint."

"Ellen?"

"Yes?"

"Do you often think of Sara?"

Ellen sighs. A question to which there is no answer. Yes, always. No, never. I don't need to think about her, I always have her with me. The loss is an undershirt that I can never take off, I can't stop being a mother of a dead daughter. I've been affected deep within. A condition. A state. It is as I am. I, I am this with her, with my lack of her.

Johan has continued talking in, for him, an unusually self-accusing tone.

"I wasn't much use to you then, I know that. I just couldn't handle it, I wanted to leave it behind me. I wanted to safeguard my work. You dragged me along with your sorrow!"

Is the self-reproach turning into an accusation? Wearily Ellen listens, not knowing if she wants to go into the subject.

"I let you down then. And you left me because of that. Things were wrong between us long before Sara."

Ellen has risen to her feet. Whence this rush of energy? With small steps she walks back and forth between the chairs. The glass breaks under the soles of her shoes, and her red dress is a dark stain which obscures Johan's paintings.

"Come back to me, Ellen."

What are we getting now? What's he talking about?

"The way you're living, that's so miserable—such a rotten small place in the city, slaving at such a shitty job. It was a mistake. Why don't we start over? What do you want to prove with that independence?"

With all your might hold back time, force it back. Sometimes something happens that makes you think: this can no longer be denied, from now on everything will be different, this can never again not have happened. An insult, an abandonment, a wound. The morning after, you wake up, too early, surprised you look at your alarm clock and you don't understand its hands.

Ellen sighs. Why do we speak about our drowned marriage and not about what's really the matter? Why doesn't he realize what song those women sing on the wall at which he isn't looking?

After her telephone call in the guard's cubicle, Lisa goes to the Ladies'. With dashing skating steps she walks into the dimly lit lobby. In every gentle turn she feels her hips and directs her feet with utmost precision. If it all weren't so sad, she'd sing a song, a waltz melody. The straw-coloured jacket sweeps over her buttocks. The more intensely she thinks of dancing and skating, the further recedes the image of a broken woman, of movement painfully halted.

She turns on the light in the tiled space and stands, still swaying, in front of the mirror. Let water run over your hands and your wrists. Notice that you have to pee. Later bring your face close to the mirror. A private conversation.

What do you want now, Hannaston? Go home? Have nothing more to do with this? Tomorrow the alarm will go off early. In the evening I'm driving to the airport to pick up my family. After that, no sleeping for hours. A long day. You need to get rest.

Or do you perhaps want to remain in this strange palace? I'm an important extra in this fairy tale. I had to kneel by the poisoned evil stepmother, I had to keep the princess company, and who knows, I may yet have to console the prince. Stay, then.

Lisa smiles at herself in the mirror. If you're not a knight but only a page, then you should see the advantages of that position. How she would have liked to have Johan's razor-sharp conviction, how she would have liked to stand in the limelight as the heroine. But it's not like that, it's never like that. She is different. That she can't fall off the hero's horse if she has never sat on it, is the least of her consolations; the endless opportunity for peeping and speculating gives much more satisfaction.

Parents and children. The child has to murder the father and strike down the mother. But how is it with child murder? What does the child feel who is intended as food for its parents? When knife and fork are placed on the table? When the parents have sat down full of anticipation? Then the child lies down obediently between knife and fork, arched like a trout. Then the child waits patiently until the flesh is pulled off its bones, piece by piece.

Lisa looks at and listens to the stories of others' lives with insatiable curiosity and silent surprise. How do people do it, live? And especially: how do they ward off the blow, how do they scramble to their feet after the final blow, how do they find the escape route out of a locked house?

Upstairs a story is taking place with an unknown outcome, a story that screams to be looked at and listened to.

Screaming is not what Johan and Ellen are doing when Lisa comes up the stairs. They speak with raised voices, they make remarks in which violent emotions lie on the surface and even rise beyond the spoken language, and can already be heard in the dark front gallery so that Lisa hesitates to keep on walking. She doesn't want to go so far that she understands what her friends are saying to each other. She doesn't want to interrupt the conversation. She doesn't want to leave. What now? *S'asconde sotto la tavola,* Da Ponte wrote. Lisa obeys a centuries' old law when she quickly crawls under the wine buffet and hides behind the overhanging tablecloths. In this tent she has momentarily been placed outside time and space and can calmly deliberate her possible action. The conversation comes to her like unintelligible muttering; she'll certainly notice the speakers' walking away since they will have to go through the front gallery to go to the staircase, and when it is that far, she can go after one or the other. Or both. Or not.

Johan has also risen and together with Ellen looks at the paintings.

"Damn, they're exactly the same, do you see? The same position, the same facial expression, the same placement and function of the fish! The same size! Unbelievable, inconceivable!"

He squats down to study the signature on his father's work. Surprised, Ellen watched his untroubled reaction. Why isn't he furious, desperate, or totally shattered?

"Start anew! Then you will have to get rid of that gluttonous singing wonder. That's not for you, a relationship out of an operetta. I'll break off with Zina. I want only you."

Johan comes towards her, throws his arms around her. Wordlessly her body nestles against his, she places her arms around his waist and adjusts her step to his. Slowly they stroll together along the walls. The children are out of the house. Now we have only each other.

"What does it mean to you, that painting?"

"Canvas, paint, salmon. Mackerel."

"No, seriously. It can't—"

His tongue paralyses hers. His whole warm body besieges and enthralls her. Hands on her buttocks, in her neck, on the secret place at the base of the skull. She can't withstand this attack. Eyes closed. Go along. Hands under his jacket, under his undershirt. Skin. The hairy spot above his buttocks. Oh Jesus, this song is in the bones.

His tongue in her ear. His hot whispering voice: "Be still, still. I only want to make love to you. Has nothing to do with it. No harping. It's only a painting. Nothing's the matter."

Wrong, wrong, everything is the matter. It's a painting that emasculates everything, that makes a little boy of you, that erases you.

Pity. I feel compassion for him.

Immediately all fire is extinguished. Both dancers hear their own music and this can soon be seen from their movements. The conqueror now embraces a consoler instead of his prey.

"You must have seen it as a little boy."

"Don't babble like that. We can go to Siena together, to Florence, if you give up that stupid job. Starting next week!"

Ellen throws her arms around him protectively. Across his dark hair she sees the paintings. Her eyes are moist and her voice sounds moved.

"Johan!"

The head buried at her breast doesn't let itself be consoled. Johan has torn open the buttons of the red dress and has pushed down the bra. He bites the nipples, with his tongue he draws a possessive track around each breast, blows across the delicate skin at the armpit, recaptures the body of his lost wife.

But she doesn't glow. His wounded nose registers no excitement in the hairs of her armpit. His lips don't detect increased temperature in the manipulated skin, and the nipples remain soft in his mouth.

He breaks away, straightens up, takes her shoulders and shakes her.

Ellen buttons her dress, turns around, and walks to the staircase. Finished. Relieved? Not yet. Later perhaps. Visit Alma in the hospital. Call Oscar. Live in my own house. Lisa, talk with Lisa. Walk. Walk away from Johan. Because it is like that. Lisa, under the table, sees Ellen's feet walk slowly past the wine buffet. Now. Decision. Into the gallery to bring the stricken hero back to himself? Or to go after the girlfriend to leave together, arm in arm, and leave behind this nerve-wracking drama?

In any case, push aside the tablecloth and begin to move.

\* \* \*

Finally alone. Finally got rid of the reproving, demanding and interfering women one after the other. How am I doing? In my head drones the start of a headache, the legs are heavy from the alcohol and from standing. There is a nagging tension in my balls. With the hand push the still slightly swollen member into its place in the crotch of the silk shorts. Stretch, yawn, stand on my toes; turn around.

Yes, a mackerel and two salmon. The similarity of shape is nice. I imagined and created the same thing he did. Awful?

No, it doesn't feel like that. Oddly enough I'm actually proud of it, I did it well. Just like him. I have a father!

Undeniably I now have a father. He demonstrated, and I copied him as well as possible. It's beautiful. He'll be satisfied when he sees it.

"Very beautifully done, my boy, it looks exactly like mine. Now to bed, it's already dark. Can you put on your pajamas by yourself? Take off your little shoes right here, then I can help you with the laces. When you're both in bed I'll come and say goodnight."

His hand through my hair. A kiss. In the kitchen Alma rattles the pots. Oscar walks up the stairs behind me. Is he going to grab my legs? No. He walks slowly and scowls.

"Are you angry, Osser?"

The big brother shakes his head. He's not angry but worried. He even helps Johan to look for his sleeper and to pull off his sweater. Lucky, because sometimes that's difficult and then your head is stuck in the knitting, you tug at it but your arms are stuck straight up in the inside-out sleeves, you can't move, and if you scream you get wool in your mouth. Oscar pulls the arms out of the sleeves and carefully pulls the sweater over my face. Then we sit listening on our beds. Now Papa is also in the kitchen. When I'm big, I want real pajamas like Oscar, and Papa. A cloth suit, with buttons. Is Papa helping with the dishes? They are talking, you can hear it.

"You can choose; either you give up that slut or I leave."

"She's not a slut, she's a very talented artist. She sings like an angel."

"I don't care. I simply don't accept it. I stand here boiling your turpentine rags and keeping your house while you're getting off with that singing tramp. Count me out. You can choose."

"It's your own fault. You reject me, you snap at me, you don't leave me free. I can no longer stand it, Alma, I no longer want it."

Clattering, a plate hits the ground.

"He no longer wants it! He can no longer stand it and goes crying his heart out on the bosom of such an operatic hippo!"

"Yes, yes, yes, because you're always needling me. Nothing is ever good, you always create fights and tension around you, and when I play the viola you go stomping up the stairs. You're a sourpuss, you. If I want to have dinner with you, you're sick to your stomach, and if I want to go to bed with you, you have a headache. I'm banging my head against a stone wall with you."

Bang; a bowl crashes down on the kitchen floor. The screaming moves to the hall from where it's much easier to hear. It sounds as if Alma and Charles are fighting, you hear frenetic shuffling and tugging. They are panting as well.

"Let me go! I'm leaving!"

"No, we have to discuss it! In the room!"

"Give back my coat, I want to go! Now!"

"But Alma, the children! You can't leave just like that?"

"Oh no? You don't take much interest in that either, do you? A nice father who lies in the bed of a whore half the time. I don't want to argue anymore. Enough."

The door slams. A little later there is faint clinking of broken dishes. Charles is sweeping the floor. A plopping sound: he is pouring himself a glass.

Upstairs the boys have put on their night clothes. Without brushing their teeth they've silently got into bed. Johan is still wearing his socks. He doesn't dare to ask Oscar what is wrong, if Alma is coming back, why Papa isn't coming upstairs. Both children lie in bed without moving, on their backs, their eyes wide open.

What is a slut? wonders Johan. And does Papa really know a hippopotamus? Did he go away with the circus? Did Mama get angry about that? Are many dishes broken? And where did Mama go? Is she wearing her coat?

When a car drives through the street, light splotches come up through the curtain and move across the whole room like a toy train. Oscar's eyes are open as well. They wait. It's quiet for a very long time. Then they hear a jingling sound, followed by loud rattling. Charles is calling someone.

"Leo? The time has come. You would do me a big favour if you'd come and help me."

"Yes. On the back of the bicycle, one riding and the other holding them. That way it'll work. There's no wind tonight.

"Yes. I'll leave them with you too.

"See you soon."

Slow steps up the stairs. The door creaks open and Charles enters. The light from the hall radiates around him and makes him into a large, dark statue with a gold edge.

"Get out of bed, boys, come with me to my room. I want to show you something."

Oscar, in his striped pajamas, on bare feet, steps fearlessly on the linoleum. Johan comes behind him, in his sleep-suit. In Charles' room the floor lamp is on, the light is yellow. He is wearing the black sweater with yellow stripes, the painting sweater, and over it the nice jacket that smells of tobacco and father.

When the children are inside, Charles turns on the big light. Oscar remains standing at the door, he leans against the door post and with a frightened face looks fixedly at his father.

"You have to remember this well. I want you to look carefully and never forget, so that you'll still remember it when I… when I'm no longer here."

Oscar's cheeks become as white as a sheet. He doesn't dare to ask anything ("Are you going away, Papa, When are you coming back? Are you coming back? Who with? Where?"). Johan looks at his brother; if something were really the matter Oscar would open his mouth, now it's just something that's happening, being allowed out of bed at a strange time. Sleepless in their room, the boys talked so often about staying up all night so that they could be there, see what the grown-ups did. They wouldn't go to sleep until it was dark, until it had become quiet outside, until everyone else had gone to bed. Now the time has come. Charles doesn't talk about sleeping and children's bedtime. They are allowed to see grown-up things. Why isn't it nice then? It *has* to be exciting, after all isn't it night and they're not sleeping?

Johan slips his little hand into Charles' hand and lets himself be led. Charles has placed a painting against each of the four walls of his workroom. Mr Bramelaar stands against the right side. He is planing the neck of an unfinished violin. With infinite precision Charles has painted the wood curls that lie on the worktable. Kindly, the violin-maker looks up from his work. The large hands lie protectively around the instrument.

"He is my best friend," says Charles. "What if I didn't have him? He has taught me how you can sing with a viola. I wanted to paint him while he was working. He has respect for the material. And he persists, he keeps at it until it's absolutely right. You have to learn that also: think of everything in advance, how it should be, and then keep at it until it's exactly right." Oscar throws a quick glance at the painting, he understands it because he's crazy about Bramelaar and the beautiful sound that comes from the violas. Papa's best friend, of course. When Charles starts his speech, Oscar's anxiety flares up again and he can only look at the father, wonder how long he'll still be father, if Alma will return, if children without parents are allowed to go to school, if he'll be able to take care of Johan all by himself? Oscar really feels like crying, but he doesn't dare to.

Facing Oscar, a very large painting stands against the wall. It is Alma with a fish in her arms.

"Is he dead?" asks Johan.

"It's a smoked fish. He's been dead for a very long time. I expect you both to be sweet to your mother."

Oscar is rigid with fear. It's true, he's leaving! When Alma comes back (but when?), I'll do everything she says, everything, so that she'll never have to get angry. Get coals from the coal-shed, I can do that fine. And take Johan to school, watch out when crossing the road. Drying dishes, I know how to do that too. When she comes back. Johan doesn't get it yet, he's still too small. Maybe none of it is true. But why is Papa acting so strangely? He talks as if we're grown-ups. I want to dream this and later just wake up.

Breathless, Johan stands in front of the work of art. Finally he sighs and lifts his hand to feel the back of the mackerel and the beautiful golden folds of Alma's skirt. With big eyes he drinks in the colours, follows the lines of the figures, and instinctively imitates Alma's pose with his fat toddler's arms.

They step to the left wall where there hangs a wide painting with an enormous black steamship on it. Yellow portholes, people saying farewell on the wharf.

"Are you going with the boat, Papa?"

Charles has taken Johan's hand again.

"You have to keep drawing diligently, my boy. Every day. And always a little better. First think of what you want to do, and how, and then draw. You can do it, I'm sure of it."

Now they walk towards Oscar. Next to him stands a fourth canvas, an apple tree with a tattered grey trunk. It's a very old tree which looks tired, it's ages old, much older than Papa or Aunt Janna, maybe as old as St Nicholas, immensely old. It is surely starting to be autumn in the painting because lots of yellow leaves are lying on the grass under the tree.

The tree lifts up its branches, but they're so heavy that it's almost impossible. On every branch grow at least a hundred apples, small yellow apples that shine like stars, cheerful, carefree apples on a sad tree that is almost exhausted.

"That's how it is," says Charles. "I can't say anything else about it. That's how you should live. This is how it is."

Suddenly reeling with sleep, Johan walks ahead through the hall. He is drunk with the art of painting, the golden mackerel continues to shimmer before his eyes.

Oscar looks at his father's face. Questions boil inside him like lava in a volcano: why, what next, what's the matter, explain it, tell me about it, say something, Papa, Papa! Charles presses the boy with already spindly legs and clumsy movements against him. Oscar smells the paint of the yellow-black sweater, the comforting smell of the jacket. The tears are right behind his eyes but he is big, he doesn't cry.

"Take good care of her, will you? You know how."

But where is she? Will she come back? Where can I find her?

"Aunt Janna's telephone number is on piece of paper next to the telephone. You know how to call?"

Oscar nods. He knows how it should be done, you hear the tone and then you dial the number with the zero before it. If you do it right, you hear another tone, and then you can dial the next number. He reads numbers like the best of them. After that you hear the telephone ring on the other side. When someone picks it up (Mama!) you say your name. You can also say hello, that word is part of telephoning. If you can't talk, like now, if your throat is totally blocked, what then? Charles has tucked Johan in and has given him a kiss.

"Bye my sweet boy. Go and paint nice mackerels. You'll need gold paint, then it will work."

Now it's Oscar's turn. He is so stiff that he can't get comfortable. He is as cold as the chilly sheets. With big scared eyed he sees how Charles pulls up his sheets a little, looks at him briefly, twists his mouth strangely, and walks to the door.

Papa's door continually opens and closes. He is pushing things, across the hall, down the stairs. He carries something down slowly and then quickly comes running back up the stairs. You think: he'll come in and say that it was a joke, everything is all right again, Mama has also come back home, and no one is going away, never. But he opens the other door and again starts dragging something big. He swears under his breath, and you hear something bang against the wall. "Dammit, it doesn't work like this. Turn it around, then. What an impossible size. I need rope. And the blankets."

It sounds as if wooden slats are being pushed down the stairs: clunk, clunk—too heavy to lift.

Then the bell rings. Oscar immediately sits up. He whispers: "Are you awake?"

Yes, Johan was awakened by the bell.

"Is that Mama?"

No, thinks Oscar. Mama doesn't ring the bell, she can come in by herself, she has a key. "We're going to look. Through the window."

The window between their beds is ajar. Oscar carefully opens both sides. On the last hole. The boys take up position at either side of the mullion. They hang over the windowsill, the curtain like a veil behind their heads.

There is nothing to see on the street... It is a windless night, the street-lights are burning like candles, and the shadows of the trees don't move. The door opens. They see Mr Bramelaar's curls. His head stands like a black circle on his plump body. Papa also comes outside. Together they carry something big, a table without legs or an enormous blackboard. It's the paintings. Papa has tied them together with rope and packed them in the grey blanket that is always in his room.

It's heavy. Mr Bramelaar sighs and moans. He rubs his hands when he can let go of the package for a moment.

Papa gets his bike. Very carefully they place the package across the seat rack. On the back wheel are the footholds for little boys who are allowed to sit on the back. They are still folded out. Papa has the viola on his back. It's also going with him. Mr Bramelaar takes Papa's shoulder and says something which they can't hear. Papa shakes his head and takes the handlebars of the bike. He starts to walk with it. Mr Bramelaar walks on the other side and holds on to the big package with paintings. You see them walking slowly to the corner of the street where the street-lamp stands. Carefully they make the turn and then you see Papa's face in the lamplight for a moment until the men disappear behind the houses.

It is very quiet in the house. Oscar sets the windows ajar again. They go back to bed, that is how it should be when it's night. Maybe it's so quiet because the grown-ups are already asleep. Maybe Alma would call upstairs if Johan walked through the hall to go and pee. Maybe you'd be able to go down to get a sandwich, then they'd say, not now, out of the question, tomorrow you can eat again. Maybe.

When it is this quiet you don't notice that everyone is gone.

"Osser?"

"Yes?"

"Can I come into your bed?"

Oscar breathes again. Luckily he isn't *asking* anything. No difficult questions to which you have to invent an answer because you don't know it, no questions that make you cry so that you can't think up anything at all.

"Bring your pillow, come on."

Oscar throws back the blankets and lies against the wall. That way there is room for his little brother who is standing next to his bed with pillow and bear.

Johan's legs come to Oscar's knees. Johan is still small, but he already knows how to console a little.

"We're together, right Os?"

"Yes Johan, we're together."

Johan takes his brother's hand and pushes close against him. Oscar feels cold, he has to get warm again.

"We're now going to sleep, right Os?"

"Yes, and tomorrow we're going downstairs. Then we'll call Aunt Janna. I can read the number. We'll do that."

"And I'll help you, I will."

"Yes, good."

When Johan closes his eyes, he sees the painting before him, exactly as beautiful as it was. Alma looks a little stern, but that's how she is. The fish shines as if it's a magic fish, as if he gives light from inside his body. The fish lies contented in Alma's arms. The father has left, he walked around the corner and was gone. Really.

Johan shivers. I should leave, what am I still doing here. Stand up, coat on, home.

He remains seated in the wide armchair directly opposite the two paintings. Sit and wait. Wait? For what is happening. Yes. Wait. I let my feet stand next to each other on the floor. They stand fine there. My hands on the arm rests. I don't have to hold anything. I don't move anymore. I wait. The host can't leave before all the guests have come.

Downstairs in the museum a door bangs shut. Is it Ellen who's leaving? Did she cry in the toilets, did she stay there to wash her face and to figure out what she was going to do? Or Lisa, who finally decided to leave?

Johan sits like a statue, eyes closed. Is a gust of moist air blowing up the stairs? Did someone come in, is there the sound of slow footsteps on the stairs? Who knows, a man may be entering the gallery, of course he has aged but under his ordinary coat you see the yellow and black painter's sweater. He pants slightly from the climb and coughs politely to announce his arrival.

"Well, my boy. You've done it. Very beautiful. Your masterpiece."

The women slide over each other until there is an Alma who looks like Ellen. The golden mackerel gets a silver shine. Very faintly in the foreground the ghost of a salmon can be seen and the blade of a fillet knife shines through the yellowish folds of the skirt. Johan sighs. How beautiful. Now he's less cold and feels his body again. He sees that his hands rest on two heavy arms. The chair has become higher and warm, a pleasant glow radiates against his buttocks and thighs. He smells an odour of turpentine and tobacco. Now let your head rest against the wool sweater, the strong arms surround you like a hedge. All is well.

# About the author

*Anna Enquist*

**A**nna Enquist, a psychoanalyst and classically trained musician, was born in 1945. She began to write poetry a few years ago, as she said, "from one day to the next". Today, she is one of the Netherlands' best-selling poets, with a large readership in Germany, Austria, Switzerland and Sweden. *The Masterpiece* is Anna Enquist's first novel. It has proved a runaway bestseller in the Netherlands, having already sold more than 200,000 copies there, and has been translated into several European languages.

*The fonts used in this book are from the Garamond family*

Other works by Anna Enquist
are published by *The* Toby Press


*The Secret*
*The Injury*
*The Ice Carriers*